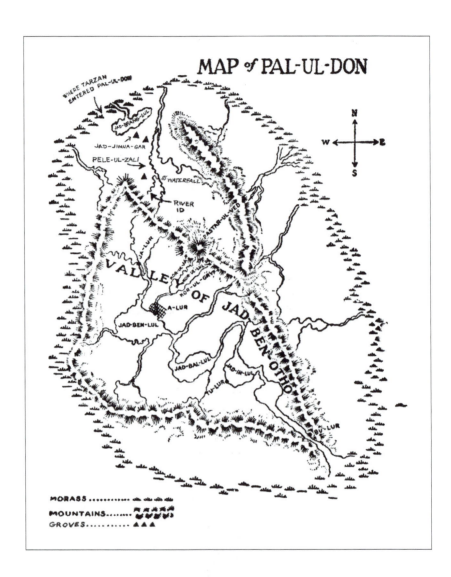

MAP of PAL-UL-DON

WHERE TARZAN ENTERED PAL-UL-DON

JAD-BANG-LUL

JAD-JINNA-GAR

PELE-UL-ZALI

WATERFALL

RIVER ID

ASTAR-UL-VO

VALLEY OF JAD BEN OTHO

JA-LUR

KOR-UL-JA

A-LUR

JAD-BEN-LUL

JAD-BAL-LUL

KOR-IN-LUL

UL-LUR

BU-LUR

N
W — E
S

MORASS............
MOUNTAINS........
GROVES...........▲▲▲

TARZAN® Return to Pal-ul-don

By

WILL MURRAY

Illustrated by

Joe DeVito

Altus Press • 2015

THANKS TO

*Jim Beard, Gary A. Buckingham, Lynn, Allen and Gary Buckingham,
Edgar Rice Burroughs, Inc., John R. Burroughs, Dave McDonnell,
Dafydd Neal Dyar, Jeff Deischer, Ray Riethmeier,
Jim Sullos and Tyler Wilbanks.*

COVER ILLUSTRATION COMMISSIONED BY
Gary A. Buckingham

First Edition — June 2015

DESIGNED BY
Matthew Moring/Altus Press

Like us on Facebook: "The Wild Adventures of Tarzan"

www.adventuresinbronze.com

Printed in the United States of America

Set in Caslon.

For a True Original—

The Immortal Edgar Rice Burroughs

TARZAN: RETURN TO PAL-UL-DON

Chapter One

SECRET MISSION

A SLOWLY rotating ceiling fan stirred the superheated air in Flight Commander Colin Armstrong's Cairo office as he addressed the towering man standing before him.

Those who had known John Clayton, Lord Greystoke, in the less civilized phases of his remarkable life would not recognize him as he stood now, stiffly at attention. His powerfully-knit body was encased in a crisp military uniform whose insignia proclaimed him to be a flying officer in the Royal Air Force of Great Britain. He looked every inch an English officer, and no less a gentleman. Chiseled features reflected a thoroughly civilized intelligence.

Only a slight burning of the ancient battle scar on his high bronzed forehead earned during his jungle youth gave any hint of past savagery. There were other scars, of course, but the close-fitting khaki jacket concealed these from even the most observant eyes.

Clayton had not gone by the name by which the uncivilized world knew him for many months now. He was entirely dedicated to defending the British Empire against the Axis forces which had engulfed the globe.

Yet for all that, there was something in his clear grey eyes that bespoke of wilder days. A glint of something akin to tempered steel. A flash of fire as elemental as a Neanderthal banging flint together to produce a warming spark. For beneath the impeccable uniform, with its pilot's wings stitched over the left breast, stood poised the individual who was once renowned as Tarzan of the Apes.

As the flight commander continued to address him, the scar on Flying Officer Clayton's forehead reddened.

"I will confess that I was skeptical as to your qualifications to undertake flight training," Armstrong was saying as the hot desert winds blew in through the open window. "But according to all reports, you have adapted admirably to military discipline and as an aviator acquitted yourself with consummate skill, if not a rare ingenuity. You have shown yourself to be proficient in all tasks and maneuvers demanded of you—air-to-ground firing, shadow firing, et cetera." He glanced at the open folder on his desk. "Particularly are you ferocious in aerial acrobatics and dog fighting." He cleared his throat. "Given your rather—er—unorthodox background, I imagine these last qualifications should prove no surprise to anyone familiar with your history."

The scar was now fully inflamed. The clear grey eyes remained resolute.

Clayton replied stiffly, "I offered my services to the King in order to defend my African homeland, as well as England, the natal land of my parents."

"I am not questioning your patriotism, Flying Officer Clayton. But you must admit that it is rather unorthodox to insert a man with your—ah—shall we say unusual heritage into the R.A.F. during wartime."

"There are no civilians in a World War," returned the flying officer simply, his voice edged with the barest trace of steel, like a knife blade felt through its scabbard.

"Yes, yes. Perhaps I fail to make myself clear. By all accounts, you are rather above the customary age for a combat fighter pilot. Only your reputation and hereditary title, Lord Greystoke, cut through the red tape that would normally have barred a man of your maturity from participating in the Operational Training Unit. Not to put too fine a point on it, but had Prime

Minister Churchill not insisted, you would not today be standing before me."

"I have the good fortune to have retained the skills and reflexes of my youth," said Clayton simply.

"So your record affirms," allowed the flight commander dryly. "I am merely expressing my reservations. Now, to the matter at hand." His frowning eyes went to a manila folder on his desk. "I have here orders for you to report to the Personnel Transit Centre at Almaza pending a formal determination of the most suitable role for you in this war. We have been considering assigning you to the A.D.U. No. 1."

"I am anxious to test my new skills against the enemy," said Flying Officer Clayton, bristling slightly.

"Of course you are. No doubt about it," replied Armstrong. "But we are short-handed at our Aircraft Delivery Units. No matter. For something has come up, something on the order of a confidential mission, as it were. We were wondering if you might be the right man for the job."

"What job is that?" asked Clayton, the inflamed scar on his forehead cooling.

"Intelligence has lost track of an operative known by the code name of Ilex. This person has disappeared in a trackless area southwest of your plantation. In the Colony of Kenya, isn't it?"

"Kenya is what used to be known as British East Africa," admitted the other.

"This person has come into possession of certain knowledge that may prove useful in the weeks and months ahead. But we have lost all contact with Ilex. You know the terrain. Therefore, I am assigning you the important task of undertaking a thorough search for Ilex, and returning the operative to our custody. Failing that, you are charged with obtaining the information this operative was carrying from whomever may possess it. Do you understand?"

"Perfectly," said Clayton, scar burning again. The ape-man was not accustomed to being spoken to as if his intelligence was in question. But such was the way of ranking officers the world over. "How do I recognize Ilex?"

"I personally do not know," admitted Armstrong diffidently. "But my superiors inform me that if I set you on the trail, you will undoubtedly locate and identify the agent. Rather like a sleuth hound, I imagine."

A puzzled expression overtook Clayton's sun-bronzed face.

"I do not understand," he allowed.

The flight commander sighed. "Nor do I. But such are my instructions for you. A transport plane will ferry you to Landing Ground 44. From there, you will be provided a suitable aircraft and cut loose, so to speak, to play fox and hounds."

The frowning puzzlement did not relax its grip on Clayton's chiseled features. "That does not seem very much to go on," he commented.

"I agree. You have a reputation as an expert tracker, Flying Officer Clayton. My superiors seem to have supreme confidence in you. How can I doubt them? For that matter, how can *you*, old fellow?"

John Clayton searched the officer's face for any sign that the unexpected familiarity carried a dig, but perceived none.

"I may add that, in order to verify the identity of Ilex, there is a sign of recognition and countersign. The sign is simply this remark, 'The sun is boiling.'"

"And the countersign?"

An expression of distaste flattened the officer's craggy countenance. " 'And the moon is in the soup.'"

"And the moon is in the soup," repeated Clayton, committing the phrase to memory.

Lifting his gaze from the folder, Flight Commander Armstrong remarked, "I see that you have trained on Hurricanes and Harvards. I can have either type placed at your disposal. Which would you prefer?"

Clayton answered without hesitation. "Neither. I prefer the P-40B Tomahawk."

One silver-shot eyebrow quirked. "Oh. Why is that?"

"It suits my nature."

"Very well. I will see to it. Good luck, Flying Officer Clayton. You are dismissed."

Sharp salutes were exchanged and Clayton turned smartly on his heel, exiting the flight commander's office.

As he left the headquarters building, and reentered the dusty heat of the Egyptian afternoon, the feel of the sand-colored uniform on Flying Officer Clayton's skin became like a prison of cotton weave. He ached to throw it off, to allow his bare limbs to rejoice in the warm kiss of Kudu, the Sun. But in the Royal Air Force, being caught out of uniform was a crime punishable by reprimand, with the probable loss of flight privileges.

Having subjected himself to the rigors of R.A.F. pilot training, the newly minted flying officer was not about to cast to the desert winds his opportunity to engage the enemy without sound reason.

Striding confidently to his quarters, the ageless man who had been the indisputable Lord of the Jungle chafed under the restrictions his military rank had placed upon him. But this was the price John Clayton had elected to pay in order to safeguard all that he held dear from Axis aggression.

There would be time enough to return to the jungle after the war was concluded. Provided he survived.

Chapter Two

AERIAL MAP

FLYING OFFICER CLAYTON reported to the flight line at dusk.

Waiting for him there was a Bristol Bombay bomber-transport plane. The pilot was already in the cockpit, starting the big radial engines.

An R.A.F. wing commander whom he had never before met greeted him and handed off a manila envelope, saying, "Everything you need is in this folder, Clayton. Good luck."

Flying Officer Clayton accepted the envelope, feeling that it was very thin. But the entire mission felt thin. Thin and insubstantial. Not for the first time, he wondered if this mission wasn't simply a ruse to get him out of combat duty, in favor of younger officers. His few short months in the R.A.F. had revealed to him the cunning and duplicity that pervaded military establishments in wartime.

There had been official resistance to his joining the Royal Air Force from the first. Clayton had overcome all objections with a single-minded firmness that no officer could brook. Young men possessed reflexes suitable for the acrobatic rigors of aerial combat, they explained. This keen sharpness of mind and body eventually dulled the older a man got. A fighter pilot was often washed up by the age of thirty. It was nothing personal; it was merely a law of nature.

John Clayton had pointed out that British citizens from Australia, New Zealand, and elsewhere in the Commonwealth were being trained for Article XV squadrons under the Empire Air Training Scheme. This was countered by the argument that he did not belong to any Commonwealth air force.

There was also his reputation. It was so formidable, having carried to all four corners of the globe that, even attired in khaki, his tremendous muscular physique and the sheer vitality that belonged wholly to Tarzan of the Apes, somehow communicated itself. Thus, he had overcome all opposition.

Shaking off his concerns, Clayton approached the vibrating aircraft. The cabin door was open and he climbed aboard.

A young pilot officer greeted him with a snappy salute, saying, "Welcome aboard, Flying Officer Clayton. We are ready to take off."

"Thank you," returned Clayton, returning the salute crisply.

The pilot officer pointed to the rear. "This is a transport run, not a bombing mission, so we don't have a tail-gunner. That's where you will squat."

Frowning, Flying Officer Clayton went to the tail of the transport and climbed into the turret housing the Vickers K machine gun. Donning the leather helmet with its radio headset, he keyed his throat microphone.

"Flying Officer Clayton, on station," he reported.

"Glad to have you with us, Clayton," came a cheery voice Clayton took to be the pilot. "Please make yourself as comfortable as you can."

The Bristol Bombay was vibrating from Plexiglas nose to twin-boom tail as the starboard Pegasus III radial engine coughed into life. The clapping of the hatch door being shut and secured signaled the imminence of take-off.

Rather swiftly, the Bombay began trundling down the runway, bumping along as it hit cracks in the tarmac created by the baking Egyptian sun. Soon, the tail lifted, then the bumping ceased altogether as the bomber leapt into the sky.

It rose upward several thousand feet, then banked sharply on a southwesterly heading.

There were only three others in the crew, the pilot in his cockpit, the radioman in the cubbyhole behind him, and the navigator in the nose. It had been the radioman who had welcomed him on board.

After the plane leveled off, Flying Officer Clayton untied the tiny cord that sealed the manila envelope.

INSIDE, there were two photographs. Both were aerial shots taken from a high-altitude plane, showing a mountainous terrain in which the wreckage of what appeared to be a high-winged de Havilland D.H.95 Flamingo transport lay broken in brushy lowlands.

Flying Officer Clayton studied both photographs, attempting to place the locality. Until recent years, he had rarely seen Africa from the air, so the perspective from which these photographs were taken was not especially helpful.

There was a great gorge in the middle of the scattering of mountains, and around this were lowlands that might have been grassland or even swamp. Due to the high altitude at which these pictures were taken, there was no telling.

The broken Flamingo lay in the northwest quadrant of both photographs. Nothing more could be discerned about it, or any further clue as to the terrain or its locality.

Turning the pictures over, Clayton discovered that the reverse was blank. There was no map, nor any instructions. Yet Flight Commander Armstrong had assured him that the envelope would contain everything he would require to reach the objective. He carried the photographs forward to the cockpit and made the acquaintance of the pilot.

"Flight Lieutenant Stanhope here," the pilot called over the motor drone. "Happy to have you aboard, Clayton. Have heard many good things about you."

"Thank you," said Flying Officer Clayton. Brushing aside the pleasantries, he remarked, "These photographs I have been provided evidently show the target to which we will be flying."

"Precisely," returned the flight lieutenant.

"Where is this place?"

"Regrettably, I cannot divulge the longitude and latitude," stated the pilot.

Clayton frowned slightly. "Map coordinates would be of little use to me. Have you a chart of the area?"

"Yes, of course. But I cannot show it to you."

"Why not?"

"It would not do. This mission is confidential. In the event of a downing or a crash landing, I have instructions to destroy the map and the photographs you carry."

Understanding dawned on Clayton's bronze face. "That is wise, if unhelpful."

"Well, we seem to have an understanding. I cannot tell you anything, and you must return the favor."

"Then how am I to reach the objective, not knowing where it lies?"

"Did no one inform you of the mission procedures?"

"No. No one has."

"Typical, I suppose. When we reach Landing Ground 44, you will transfer to your personal plane. We will then lead you to the objective."

Clayton frowned. "I should be able to manage a landing in the terrain indicated on this map. What about you?"

"We will not be landing. The last aircraft to overfly the target zone was fortunate to return intact."

"How I am to return after I have accomplished my mission successfully?" asked Flying Officer Clayton. "The warplane I requested seats one person."

"The brass must have a lot of confidence in you," laughed Stanhope. "They are leaving that entirely up to you."

"I am beginning to believe that this is what the R.A.F. sometimes calls a suicide mission."

"Whether it's suicide or not, that, too, is your affair. This is do or die, I will grant you that."

Clayton said in a low growl, "I intend to do. To die does not appeal to me at the present time."

The pilot laughed heartily. "That's the spirit, old man!"

With that, he turned his head and concentrated on his flying.

Flying Officer Clayton returned to his position, focusing his attention on the view from his tail gun turret.

LONG hours passed in which the Bristol Bombay droned south. As he watched the undulating desert below turn to savannah, and then jungle, the morning passed interminably, shaded into blazing afternoon, which stretched on into an eternity or two.

Dark thoughts lashed Clayton's brain. He had not rid himself of the concerns that he was being shunted off to a corner of the war where he would be no bother to the officers in charge, who seemed to have very definite, if indirect, notions about how to prosecute the war.

On the other hand, the photographs clearly depicted a downed British aircraft, implying that there was a crew in need of rescue. The roughness of the terrain, its inhospitality, as well as its apparent remoteness, definitely made this a fit task for the former Tarzan of the Apes.

Whatever the truth might be, Flying Officer Clayton was determined to carry out his mission to the ultimate degree.

Chapter Three

THE BLACK TOMAHAWK

THE ROYAL AIR FORCE Bristol Bombay transport reached Landing Ground 44 just after dawn, having flown long through the impenetrable night of the Dark Continent with only one further stop for necessary refueling at a Free French Forces aerodrome in Bangui.

Flying Officer Clayton had chafed in the close confines of the rear gun turret. This was not how he had envisioned his first mission for the R.A.F. He looked forward to climbing into the cockpit of a P-40B Tomahawk. It was no roomier than this, but at least he could take the control stick in his hands, and feel the response of a powerful Allison V-1710-19 engine and nimble control surfaces to his physical commands.

He soon began wishing for a German Messerschmitt fighter to pop up in his sights, but the Bombay encountered no aerial challenge. The flight was uneventful.

Landing Ground 44 was little more than a dirt airstrip carved out of the jungle. Quonset huts served as makeshift aircraft hangars. The operations shack was a mere framework of timber held together by hammered tin siding. It was little more than a rude refueling depot, serviced by men manning hand pumps.

The landing was very smooth—far smoother than the take-off had been. The close-packed dirt made a better landing surface than heat-blistered macadam.

Swinging about on one engine at the far end of the runway, the Bombay jerked to a stop. The port power plant fell silent, propeller blades snapping into clear view.

Throwing open the hatch, the navigator called out, "Every man out!"

Flying Officer Clayton unfolded his cramped limbs and made his way forward.

Stepping out into sunlight, he was met by a squadron leader, a young chap of about twenty-eight.

"Stiff, eh?" asked the pilot.

"Where is my aircraft?" returned Clayton.

"They will bring it out for you after breakfast."

"I am not hungry," countered Clayton. "I would like to check over my plane."

"Suit yourself." Lifting an arm, the squadron leader summoned a mechanic from his duty and called out, "Show Flying Officer Clayton to his aircraft."

"This way, sir."

While the crew of the Bombay went in search of breakfast, Clayton followed the mechanic into the Quonset hut hangar and got his first look at the warplane.

The Tomahawk had seen action. That much was certain. Perforations riddled both wings, along the fuselage, but none in critical spots. It was a tough warbird, the American combat plane the R.A.F designated as the Mk IIA. It could take a great deal of punishment and remain airworthy.

Clayton walked around the aircraft. The three-bladed propeller felt sound to the touch. When he took them in hand, control surfaces appeared sturdy.

Remarkably, the Tomahawk was not painted in the customary desert hues of the R.A.F. in Africa, but was coated in a flat, unreflective black. Nor did it sport any squadron insignia. The prop spinner was as dark as the rest of the sleek aircraft.

The famous eyeballs and fanged shark mouth were painted on the stylized snout, after the fashion of the famous American Volunteer Group known as the Flying Tigers. The craft's air intake scoop created the impression of a yawning mouth forward.

"Special plane," explained the mechanic. "Used for night missions, for the most part."

Flying Officer Clayton nodded silently. He finished walking around the ebony aircraft and asked, "Tell me the condition of the engine?"

"Tip-top. I keep her running all right."

Climbing into the cockpit, the flying officer examined the controls, saw all were in working order.

"She's a very sound bird, sir," remarked the mechanic. "This is the same model the Flying Tigers used to tear apart the Japanese over China. If you wish, I can paint you a name on her nose."

Clayton climbed into the cockpit. "Kala."

"Sir?"

"My mother's name."

"Right away, sir." The mechanic ran off to fetch some paint.

Flicking the ignition on, Flying Officer Clayton listened as the powerful engine banged into snorting life, sending the propeller spinning. Soon, it was a whirling disc that verged on invisibility.

The smoke coming out of the supercharger exhaust pipes was a good color. Releasing the brake, he steered the snarling ship, which went trundling out into the morning air.

Lining up on the runway, Clayton advanced the throttle, sending the Tomahawk scooting ahead. In a flash, it was airborne, and climbing fast.

Down on the ground, the Bombay crew came spilling out of the mess hut, waving their arms and yelling at the top of their lungs. But Clayton paid them no heed.

Leveling off, he pushed the nimble fighter through her paces, tested the wing-mounted machine guns and, after closing the cockpit, flew upside down for a bit, enjoying the acrobatic release of flight, which was to his mind second only to the unbounded freedom of the jungle.

For twenty minutes, Flying Officer Clayton roamed the skies, sensing the feel of the fighter, listening to its engine thrum, satisfying himself that it was a worthy steed.

Cracking the flaps, he came around and set the black ship on the ground as smartly as riding a high-spirited stallion back to its stable.

Flight Lieutenant Stanhope came charging up, complaining, "That was unnecessarily risky, Flying Officer Clayton."

"More risky to fly an untested aircraft into rugged terrain," said Clayton as he clambered from the cockpit and dropped to the dusty ground.

"Well, then. Satisfied?"

Clayton nodded firmly. "Entirely."

"Stand ready. We take off in less than thirty minutes."

"I will ask the mechanic to top off the fuel tanks," said Clayton.

This was done and the name *Kala* was hastily painted on the nose, above the ferocious shark mouth design that made the P-40 look so fearsome in combat.

Precisely thirty minutes later, the crew of the Bombay assembled and climbed into their high-winged aircraft, which had been refueled by a crew who pumped petrol out of great jerry cans with single-minded fury.

The pilot gave final instructions to Clayton. "Simply follow us to the objective. Then you are on your own."

"I understand."

Reclaiming his own cockpit, Flying Officer Clayton waited for the transport to get aloft, then he followed in its dusty wake, climbing fast and leveling off to the starboard wing of the big Bombay bomber.

"Radio check," came the voice of the flight lieutenant over the bulky headphones zipped into Flying Officer Clayton's leather flight helmet.

"Loud and clear," returned Clayton.

"Very good. Maintain radio silence unless I say otherwise."

That made the journey south more to Clayton's liking. He preferred the solace of his own thoughts to idle radio chatter. That had been one of the vexing things about being in the R.A.F.: Military men often talked without purpose, much the way idle women did. He preferred to hold his tongue unless it could be wielded to purposeful effect.

Three hours passed in which Clayton studied the terrain below. He had but the vaguest sense of which portion of the Africa continent he traversed. No ocean could be discerned, so he knew he traveled through central Africa.

He studied the mountains to the east, but did not recognize them. During a long and adventurous life, the ape-man had travelled far, but by no means had he tramped every corner of the so-called Dark Continent.

FOUR hours along, radio silence was broken by the voice of Flight Lieutenant Stanhope crackling through Flying Officer Clayton's helmet headphones.

"Approaching objective."

"Roger."

"Signing off. Good luck, old chap."

With that, the Bristol Bombay peeled off to port and began the long journey back to Landing Ground 44, leaving Clayton's buzzing black Tomahawk alone in the sky.

Flying Officer Clayton nosed the P-40 lower, endeavoring to discover the downed de Havilland Flamingo where it had crash landed. He had the two photographs out of the manila envelope and on his lap.

Keen grey eyes flicked between the black-and-white images and the colorful ground below, searching for natural landmarks.

He began recognizing the terrain. Dropping lower, he sought the downed transport plane.

Sunlight glinting off its piebald khaki-and-sand wings helped him pick up the crash site. Banking sharply, Clayton began circling the wreckage, at the same time studying the ground, seeking a safe landing zone.

None immediately presented itself.

The Flamingo, he soon discovered, had come down below a dense thicket that was part of a greater expanse of thick, impenetrable brush. From the air, this thicket began to assume a strange familiarity. There was no time for him to dissect the foggy memory, for he needed to locate a suitable landing spot in order to conserve fuel.

As he circled, Flying Officer Clayton saw that beyond the thicket lay a swampy morass. This, too, seemed to tickle old memories. He shoved them aside while he concentrated on the task at hand.

Swooping lower, Clayton sought the ground and beheld an unusual sight.

At the juncture where the thicket devolved into the swamp, stood a great bull elephant, bespattered with mud, but otherwise the reddish-brown of raw chocolate. This hulk of a pachyderm was engaged in a desperate tug-of-war with an immense creature Clayton perceived to be nothing less than a crocodile, but of a size approximately five times that of the average Nile River specimen.

The monster crocodile had evidently lunged out of the swamp and clamped its long, narrow jaws on the pendulous right ear of the elephant. Tantor—for that is the name Tarzan gave to all elephants—raised his trunk and trumpeted his objection, while simultaneously endeavoring to pull free of the crocodile's massive jaws.

The saurian was attempting to drag the elephant into the morass, but Tantor would have none of that. Digging in his broad tree-trunk feet, he strove to hold his ground while the equally determined reptile struggled to pull him into a position to finish him off by brute-force drowning.

The ferocious crocodile was stubborn. It did not want to release its next meal. The elephant was equally obdurate. He preferred to keep his ear, as well as his life.

In the hurtling seconds during which he buzzed by, Flying Officer Clayton recognized that a battle of heroic proportions was shaping up. The bull pachyderm possessed great curving tusks, but was unable to bring them to bear, owing to the reptile's low, spraddle-legged stance and acute angle of attack.

Seeing this unequal struggle, Clayton decided to intervene.

Circling back, keeping low, he put the steel ring of his gun sight on the knobby protrusions that armored the crocodile's long, sinuous back. He tapped his gun trips. The wing-mounted machine guns stuttered, expelling searing lead.

As the smoking slugs ripped through its primitive armor, the crocodile reared and twisted, almost doubling up on itself. This convulsive action naturally caused the lean jaws to fly open, releasing the struggling elephant. But not before Tantor lost a large patch of the afflicted ear to pinching rows of conical teeth.

Mortally wounded, Gimla—as crocodiles were named in the language of the great apes—sank into the mud, which rapidly turned crimson.

Flinging back the canopy of his cockpit, John Clayton thrust out his head and for the first time in many months gave vent to the victory cry of the bull ape. The carrying sound reverberated in the African air and, hearing it, Tantor lifted his trunk in joyful salute.

As the Tomahawk hurtled by, the victory cry of Tarzan still ringing out, Tantor trumpeted back loudly and gratefully.

Regaining altitude, Flying Officer Clayton flew on. Again, keen grey eyes scanned the complex terrain below. He was now approaching a low range of mountains and he could spy a great valley beyond them.

In that instant, the perspective from which he perceived the land below brought a light of awakening to Clayton's searching gaze. There was no mistaking one stupendous peak, nor confusing the surrounding mountains with any other mountain range with which he was familiar.

The peak was known to him as Pastar-ul-ved, Father of Mountains. He knew where he was now.

As this knowledge sank into his brain, Clayton reversed course, once again seeking an appropriate landing spot.

TO LAND too far away from the broken transport plane would defeat the purpose for which Clayton had come. He could not alight on the grasslands above the morass, for he would have to struggle back on foot through the thorny brush, nor could land below it, then ford the swamp to reach the stricken Flamingo, not without leaving his Tomahawk to the mercy of wild animals—and even more dangerous men.

For Clayton knew what manner of beings dwelt below in this place that was known to its inhabitants as the Land of Man.

Pointing the howling nose of the Tomahawk north again, he resumed his search for a safe place to put down. The P-40 banked smartly, like an extension of his own sinewy limbs.

Strange are the ways of fate. In the beginning of this mission, Flying Officer Clayton had selected the Tomahawk because of all fighter planes in which he had trained, it was the one that felt most comfortable, and most responsive to the power of his steely muscles. Other Allied fighters were considered superior, of course. But Clayton was well aware that in the correct hands, the American-made P-40B could be made to achieve miracles. The Flying Tigers had proven that over Free China. They had accomplished a kill ratio no fighter group in recent history had ever matched, much less exceeded. And that against the swifter and more nimble Japanese Zero.

Such was the confidence of John Clayton, Lord Greystoke, that he firmly believed that what the Flying Tigers had accomplished over China he could more than equal in the battle skies above North Africa's desert sands.

The fact that the P-40 was painted with the eyes of the shark and the great toothy mouth of the sleek predator of the deep was simply an aesthetic consideration. Clayton appreciated the psychological advantage the design conferred upon Tomahawk pilots. But otherwise it had little to do with his selection of fighter plane. That it had a certain appeal to Clayton's more savage nature was beside the point. He had chosen the Tomahawk because he understood that a superior pilot can wring from the vaunted fighter plane superior performance. All through his R.A.F. training, he had possessed the confidence that he would become such a superior pilot.

It had not crossed his mind then, nor did it cross it now as he winged his way south, that the psychological advantage conferred by the shark's snout against enemy pilots might be detrimental under other combat conditions. In his wildest imagination, Clayton never considered flying an aircraft that looked from a distance like a winged predator of the skies could in fact draw peril in his direction.

But that is what happened, logical or not.

As he swooped over rugged ground, skimming again past Tantor, who was charging determinedly through the thorny thicket wall, seeking a way out onto safe savannah, Tarzan could not resist again giving vent to his thrilling victory cry.

Once more, Tantor heard, and replied in kind.

Tarzan drove off. For even though he wore the flight jacket of the Royal Air Force, and his usually wild mane of hair was cut short and encased in a leather flying helmet, he was in that moment once more Tarzan of the Apes.

Unfortunately for Tarzan, the sound of their mingled cry was heard by other ears.

Somewhere among the jagged cliffs behind them, creatures stirred in a high rookery. Cold black orbs snapped open, and vast leathery wings unfolded. Out of a disorderly, litter-strewn nest marched on frightful talons a trio of angular creatures that took to the sky.

Up from the cliffs these great wings unfurled, found support in the humid air, and rose in search of the author of that unique cry.

With his steady eyes sweeping the skies ahead, the ape-man failed to perceive these weird leathery wings lifting off from the hidden rookery. Lizard-like eyes as beady as the pair painted on his fuselage caught sight of the metallic bird with the inflexible black wings.

Not recognizing this intruder upon their domain, three sets of flapping wings redoubled their efforts and attempted to overtake the Tomahawk. With the instincts of hunters, the determined trio beat madly in the wake of the alien black bird they had never seen.

His eyes fixed on the skies ahead, Tarzan saw them not.

Chapter Four

MAD WINGS

FLYING OFFICER JOHN CLAYTON searched in vain for a suitable landing spot near the crippled de Havilland Flamingo.

Now that he had recognized the territory over which he flew, Clayton began to doubt a suitable landing spot would present itself. For this was a remote place of towering mountains, dizzying precipices, and deep, rock-bound gorges. During the period many years ago when he first explored the place, he had noticed nothing on its outskirts that would have permitted landing in the vicinity of the Flamingo.

It would accomplish little to alight so far from the crash zone that tracking back to it would leave the Tomahawk exposed to assorted dangers.

But Clayton had little time to ponder this conundrum. For, banking once more in search of just the right patch of flat earth, he discovered that he was flying into a chevron of madly beating wings.

There were three of the things. From a distance they resembled nothing so much as a cross between mammoth bats and Ska, the narrow-skulled vulture. But neither bats nor vultures grew so large that they had thirty-foot wingspans, nor were vultures birds of the higher altitudes, being circling scavengers whose eyes were always fixed upon the ground.

Pulling back on the stick, Clayton sought altitude and an aerial vantage from which to observe the oncoming creatures.

Their color was not definite. Here they were grey, at other points they verged upon the verdant. The membranous bat wings were maroon. Black orbs no less sinister tracked him with malign interest.

As the Tomahawk climbed, the three pursuers convulsed their bony wings to follow, whiplike barbed tails trailing behind.

Rolling away, Clayton got his first good look at them as they sought higher altitude. These were pteranodons—prehistoric reptiles the like of which he had never before encountered in the Land of Man. They seemed intent on challenging him for mastery of the skies over the jagged escarpments below.

At first, they came on in the same slinking manner a hyena pack would stalk prey. Clayton marveled at the way in which they flew in formation, so much like military air forces the world over. But even as this thought crossed his mind, the group broke apart, arrowing in different directions as they separated for the kill.

Twisting the Tomahawk over onto one wing, Flying Officer Clayton zoomed after one of the oncoming pterosaurs. The thing, which by all rights should have recoiled from the counterattack, opened its wide, toothless beak and gave vent to an ungodly screech that could be heard even through his helmet earphones.

Hitting the trips of his machine guns, he sent a burst in the pteranodon's general direction. The winged thing did not flinch. Probably it did not understand flying lead. Switching about in the air, it plunged onto an intercept path with the Tomahawk.

Realizing that a collision was imminent, Clayton centered the bat-winged enemy in his steel sight-ring and tapped his trips again.

A second burst of machine-gun lead shredded the wings of the angry pteranodon, which gave forth with a bloodcurdling outcry. This sound trailed off as it collapsed in on itself and plummeted out of the sky, a suddenly frail fragment of life.

Righting his warplane, Clayton looked about, seeking the other attackers. He half expected them to flee in terror. For what creature that walks on two legs or four legs or flies through the air does not quail when faced with the unknown?

Not so these two circling kites of flesh and lean bones. Seeing their nest brother go down in ignominious defeat, they redoubled their efforts to challenge the howling Tomahawk, devil-wings and satanic tails churning angrily.

In order to conserve ammunition, Clayton attempted to outrun them. But the pteranodons proved very nimble in the air. And as ungainly as those stretched-skin wings seemed as they flexed and gathered, these thin-boned creatures were also exceedingly fleet.

One pounced upon his tail assembly with a ferociousness that was unexpected as a dog seizing an ankle.

Fighting the control stick, Clayton attempted to barrel roll in the hope of shaking off this scrawny leech with wings. But the controls were stuck. Seizing the horizontal stabilizer in its terrible talons, the thing clamped its long, scissors-like jaws on the vertical fin and was worrying it the way a canine worries a bone.

His head swiveling around, Clayton saw that the pteranodon had attached itself to the tail in such a way that it refused to be shaken off. Its enormous skin wings, whose hollow bones served as the framework for its devilish design but were also elongated finger bones, were wrapping around the vertical stabilizer as if to smother the rudder and elevators.

Testing the flight controls, Clayton found the latter unresponsive.

Hastily, he slid the greenhouse canopy back. Slipstream filled the cockpit. He wore a sidearm—a .38 caliber Enfield No. 2 revolver. Yanking this out of its holster, Clayton kept one hand wrapped firmly about the stick and, turning, lined up on the bony skull of the pteranodon.

Once, twice, three times, the pistol bucked. The pteranodon's skull split. That did for it. Angry eyes flared wide and then the light of animation went out of them.

Unfortunately, even in death the great quadruple-taloned creature refused to release its stubborn hold.

Barrel rolling, Clayton attempted to throw the hideous monster off his tail assembly and regain control of his aircraft.

But it was not to be. While his attention was riveted on the ugly thing clamped upon the Tomahawk's tail, the third pteranodon suddenly leapt up into his path.

The creature knew nothing of airplanes, of course. It saw only the strange flat wings of the black challenger. The speed with which the nose propeller spun naturally made it all but invisible in the bright African sunlight.

So when the third screaming pterosaur swept in to tackle the Tomahawk head on, it had no inkling that it was blundering into a vicious buzzsaw.

His attention focused in the opposite direction, Flying Officer Clayton saw too late that the Tomahawk and the pteranodon were on a collision course.

Suddenly, the air before him filled with a storm of blood and bone fragments, and other animal matter. Jerking his head back, Clayton beheld the pteranodon disintegrate upon contact with the three-bladed propeller. The canopy windshield became smeared with blood. Visibility became impossible.

Visibility was the least of his worries now. The propeller had torn itself to pieces against the prehistoric phantasm. The power plant began to smoke and sound strange, then the aircraft stalled into an agonizing tailspin.

There was no hope for the Tomahawk now. Flinging back the canopy, Clayton stepped up onto his seat, and flung himself out and away from the spiraling P-40.

He fell the regulation ten seconds, grasping the aluminum ring of his ripcord and yanked once, very hard.

The parachute pack fell open, vomiting a bell of white silk that greedily devoured air, and rudely yanked Clayton out of his free fall.

Dangling by the canvas shroud lines, he looked upward, found the stricken Tomahawk with his level grey eyes. The pteranodon was still affixed to the tail, the way a dead spider sits in an old cobweb.

The blundering pterosaur that had run afoul of the propeller was falling in fragments and fleshy shreds of which the only recognizable shape was the decapitated head, which resembled a bizarre double-headed axe with stricken eyes.

Calmly, John Clayton watched this arresting sight as his hurtling Tomahawk and the bodies of the two pteranodons smashed into the thicket below. The Tomahawk hit with a splintery crash, and very soon gave up the last of its chemical life when the fuel tanks began uncoiling brown smoke, followed by puffs of saffron flame.

When his boots struck the ground, they broke stiff underbrush with an ugly crackling. Clayton tried to roll upon impact, but only managed to entangle himself in the thorny thicket. After the collapsing canopy of his parachute settled over him, there was a period of silence in which nothing moved.

Then a sharp steel fang of a knife pierced the silken shroud, sliced downward, and withdrew. Bronzed hands expanded the tear with undeniable strength. Flying Officer Clayton extricated himself from the limp parachute bell and looked around to ascertain where he had landed.

His eyes went to the near mountains, and their savage familiarity caused him to speak aloud the name of the land to which he had, at long last, returned.

"Pal-ul-don."

Chapter Five

WRECKAGE

TARZAN OF THE APES had landed some distance from the downed de Havilland Flamingo, he soon realized.

The leather scabbard on his belt sheathed a non-regulation steel hunting knife that he had carried since youth. Producing this blade again, he made short work of the parachute shrouds entangling him.

Stepping free, the ape-lord cast his mind back long years to the time during the First World War when he had returned to his plantation only to discover that it had been burned to the ground by German soldiers, and his wife, Jane, had apparently been slain.[*]

Setting out in quest of her slayers, Tarzan had eventually come to the Land of Man, which was the meaning of the syllables Pal-ul-don. The difficulties he had encountered in this isolated enclave were great, but his ordeal ended in the unsurpassed reward of the discovery that Jane had not perished after all, but had been spirited away to this wild place.[**]

And now, after so many years, fate had seen fit to plant his feet once more on the outskirts of the Land of Man.

Taking a deep breath through his flaring nostrils, Tarzan again inhaled the myriad scents that were specific to Pal-ul-don. There was no mistaking them. Nor was there any doubt in the

---

[*] *Tarzan the Untamed*

[**] *Tarzan the Terrible*

26

ape-man's mind that this was the Land of Man, to which he had not returned in the long, intervening years.

After taking stock of himself, and satisfying himself that he was uninjured, Tarzan struck out in the direction of the downed bomber, using the sun as a directional marker.

The way was difficult, thorny, and unpleasant to traverse. The ape-man employed his long blade to hack and slash some of the barbed vines, many of which were flexible and grew in profusion, while others were as dry as kindling but no less difficult to breach.

Momentarily, Tarzan longed for the freedom of tall trees through which to climb and swing his way over this encircling natural fence of nettles. But no trees grew in this thorny expanse. He was grateful for his boots which, while they confined his feet in unaccustomed manner, protected them from the lacerations and abrasions of the profusion of tiny fangs.

Working his way painstakingly forward, the ape-man at last came to the shell of the de Havilland Flamingo. The camouflage-colored transport aircraft had come down hard, its nose crumpled, one wing entirely sheared off, and the starboard-side hatch had sprung open.

Tarzan approached cautiously, employing his nostrils to seek the scent of man, or any other inhabitants the breached fuselage might have attracted after coming down.

Searching grey eyes told him that the aircraft had plummeted earthward without extending its landing wheels. This could have meant a mechanical problem, but it could also bespeak of the crew bailing out of their stricken bird, leaving it to finish its sickening plunge unmanned.

Creeping closer, Tarzan saw the tail had been riddled by machine-gun lead. Strings of perforations crawled along the fuselage, and cockpit windows had been shattered, whether by violent impact or ripping lead was difficult to determine at a distance. Enemy fire had done this.

As Tarzan drew near, his nostrils quivered. He did not smell the familiar odor of human perspiration, nor for that matter of spilled blood. Altogether another, less pleasant, smell wafted its way to his sensitive nostrils.

"Histah," murmured Tarzan.

Stealing up and around, the ape-man came to the surviving wing and leapt atop it. Moving rapidly, he ran its length atop the fuselage.

Employing the horn hilt of his hunting knife, he crouched down and began banging the top of the plane. Before long, a rustling sound preceded the emergence from the open hatch of a serpent, the like of which he had never before encountered in all of Africa.

In its ophidian muscular length, it suggested a ball python. But its coloration was nothing like any python known to mankind. Violet at the blunt head, it shaded from there to a purplish-blue tail—an elongated bruise that crawled.

It crept out, tongue flicking, resembling an animated segment of bowel, and began wending its serpentine way through the thorny underbrush.

Having no quarrel with the great constrictor serpent, the ape-man allowed it to pass freely into the brush.

Nimbly, he crouched above the open hatch, dipped his head downward, and searched the interior with his eyes. Other than the odor of a snake's den, there appeared to be nothing troublesome within the aircraft cabin.

Grasping the hatch edges with his strong bronze fingers, Tarzan flipped his body lightly and swung into the plane's interior.

A quick search of the cockpit showed that there were no bodies present. Of blood there were scattered dapplings, and a dry but rusty-looking trail led from the pilot's compartment to the open hatch.

As easily as he read jungle sign, Tarzan saw that the crew had bailed out before the craft plummeted from the sky, stricken by machine-gun lead.

There was a radio, which was operated by battery power. He warmed this up, and discovered the set to be in sound working order. Inasmuch as his instructions were to maintain strict radio silence until he had achieved his objective, and since he had nothing substantive to report, he switched off the set, which would no doubt prove valuable once he found the missing aircrew.

A hasty search turned up nothing else of interest, so Tarzan stepped out into the afternoon sunlight, and turned his frank gaze in the direction of the ramparts of Pal-ul-don.

All around this foreign thorn thicket encircling him, the ground lay as flat as savannah. Had the pilot or any of the crew parachuted to safety on this side of the marsh, their ivory-hued parachutes would stand out in the treeless greensward. As it was, no sign of the silken bells blowing in the wind had been visible from the air. Not among the thorns, nor in the grassland beyond.

This led to only one conclusion—the crew of the Flamingo had bailed out over the Land of Man. This conclusion was all but inescapable. The surrounding zone was barren, untrammeled by humankind. Had the parachutes been buried upon landing, disturbances in the earth would likely have shown that fact.

Climbing back atop the fuselage of the plane, Tarzan cast his gaze in the direction of the Land of Man, seeking any sign of billowing silken fabric amid the towering crags or the lowland trees within range of his powerful vision.

Tarzan saw no such signs. But some unerring instinct told him that if he penetrated deep into the shunned area, he would discover spoor. This would no doubt lead him to his quarry.

Climbing down the aircraft, the jungle lord began making his way toward the marsh, which constituted a natural moat about Pal-ul-don, and which was protected from intrusion by the great natural thorn boma which surrounded its still, turbid waters.

Tarzan had not gone far along when he detected a disturbance among the thorn bushes to the east. Unhesitatingly, he veered in that direction, impelled by a mixture of curiosity and understanding that it is better to confront something in the wilderness than have it steal up on you unawares.

Chapter Six

THE PACHYDERM

A TRUMPETING sounded in the air behind him.

Tarzan turned. Not terribly far away stood the mud-splattered brown elephant whom the ape-man had succored from a grisly fate. The pachyderm lifted his trunk anew, and bellowed out a boisterous greeting. Possibly, its sharp eyes recognized the erstwhile Lord of the Jungle.

Tarzan knew all the calls of the African jungle, and immediately understood that this elephant was signaling that it was friendly. He began to approach on his plodding tree-trunk legs.

Cupping his mouth with his hands, the ape-lord called back in simulation of the elephant's cry.

This caused Tantor to approach more rapidly, his great left ear waving like a palm leaf. Tarzan could see the other ear had been all but torn off. It dripped crimson at its ragged edges.

Examining the beast from a safe distance, he found thorns sticking out from its rugged, wrinkled hide at various points on its massive legs. It was obvious that the creature had blundered into the forest of thorns from the grazing lands beyond and, not wishing to brave the nettles again, had wandered toward the only source of water available to it—in the inner moat of foul water.

There was a first-aid kit in the wrecked aircraft, and the ape-man had excavated it, removing several items for later use.

Stepping rapidly, Tantor approached. Tarzan lifted a hand, and made a noise that caused the big brute to slow his majestic gait.

The elephant halted, hesitating. Its small eyes were quizzical.

Carrying the medicine openly in his hands, Tarzan approached the big creature, who promptly knelt down.

Approaching carefully from his uninjured side—for the ape-man understood that elephants can become easily enraged, especially by pain—he gave the broad skull a reassuring pat, and allowed the pachyderm to explore his uniform with his flexible trunk.

To call the elephant tame would be to employ the term too broadly. But the animal employed his olfactory organs to sniff and investigate the ape-man's personal scent in a manner that was not threatening.

The creature must have approved of what he inhaled, for the elephant allowed Tarzan to move carefully to the other side, where his massive right ear hung in forlorn, bloody rags.

Carefully, the ape-man washed that aural appendage with water from his canteen, and then proceeded to apply red Mercurochrome to the ripped edges.

This evoked a grunt of elephantine displeasure, and a frantic flexing of his trunk. Hesitantly, the brute backed away several paces.

Tarzan left off his ministrations, and spoke reassuringly to the patient creature. When the pachyderm had calmed down again, he began plucking out the vicious thorns which bedeviled the great legs, adding to the brute's feeling of relief. Then the ape-man turned his attention back to the injured ear.

In time, the damaged ear was thoroughly disinfected. Finally, Tarzan stepped back, saying, "Now you will heal, Tantor."

The elephant sat passively, small eyes regarding him, the questing trunk returning to explore Tarzan's powerfully-muscled person.

This merciful task accomplished, the ape-man looked around again. His warplane had crash-landed on the far side of the great marsh, which he knew from past experience to be difficult to ford. Not only did enormous saurians lurk beneath the noisome morass, but the same muddy waters were deep and no doubt troubled by other creatures.

To cross these turbid waters on foot would be difficult to impossible. Beyond the broad marsh that encircled Pal-ul-don lay the mountainous heart of the Land of Man. Although he had no means by which to return to his base, Tarzan gave no thought to that problem now. His mission was to locate the missing intelligence operative code-named Ilex. His present intention was to investigate his surroundings, and determine if any of the crew had survived.

Standing in the wilderness of thorns, recalling memories of his past defiance of them, Tarzan felt a mighty urge to divest himself of his regulation uniform and once again stand half-naked and unashamed as Tarzan of the Apes. But he was a military man on an official mission, and so resisted the primal urge to feel Kudu the sun and the raw elements caressing his unadorned bronze skin.

It was not that the months of flight training had entirely civilized the Lord of the Jungle. Far from it. Tarzan had been raised by apes, and felt more kinship to that tribe than he did to his fellow humans. Deep in his heart he was still a feral creature of the jungle. But the iron discipline that had given the ape-man the fortitude to survive his wild upbringing was now channeled into service to the land of his forebears.

Standing before the pachyderm, Tarzan made motions with both outstretched hands for the elephant to rise to his feet.

The creature was slow comprehending these gestures. Holding his palms upward, Tarzan lifted them in unison, then let them fall. He spoke words of encouragement.

Tantor watched these gestures with curious interest in his tiny eyes. But the brown brute failed to respond in any way.

Seeing that this specimen was slow to comprehend his meaning, Tarzan swung around to the elephant's left side, and carefully but nimbly climbed aboard his ponderous bulk.

Seating himself directly behind the padded brown skull, Tarzan spoke again.

"Up, Tantor! Up!"

With lumbering grace, the elephant climbed to his feet, his leathery skin wrinkling at every knobby joint. The bull was young yet, but his hide suggested age and experience.

Murmuring words of encouragement, Tarzan kept his balance with no more than the scissoring action of his powerful leg muscles. Very quickly, Tantor rose to his full height.

Giving the pachyderm a reassuring pat on the back of his hairless skull, the ape-man used his knees and ankles to encourage the creature to lurch forward.

This was easily comprehended by the great beast, who promptly began stepping forward. Pleased, Tarzan encouraged the elephant to advance upon the sullen edge of the marsh.

To that very edge, the amiable hulk proved willing to go, but there he stopped.

It had been Tarzan's plan to employ the elephant to convey him across the morass, but Tantor was having none of it. He still smarted from his earlier encounter with the great Gimla. Having escaped death by a narrow margin, the injured brute had no desire to tempt fate anew.

Still, Tarzan endeavored to impel the hesitant creature to enter the unsavory-looking water.

Stubbornly, the pachyderm refused all entreaties. He lifted his trunk in distress, torn between a newfound loyalty for this human creature who made sounds he understood, and his mortal fear of the unknown terrors that lurked submerged in the swampy moat.

Tarzan spoke soothing words, and the questing trunk groped its way back to touch his shoulder. The ape-man gave the flexible appendage a reassuring pat. The nostrils in the fleshy tip quivered spasmodically as the ape-man detected a tremor of fear running the entire length of the creature.

Although the pachyderm was doggedly stubborn, Tarzan of the Apes was manfully determined to achieve his objectives. Again, he used his steel-strong legs to compel the beast forward.

With a reluctant lurch, the elephant whipped his trunk forward, and placed one stumpy foreleg into the water. The creature held it there. It was at once evident that Tantor was testing the waters for a response.

None came.

Tarzan murmured words of encouragement, and the creature took another tentative step forward. The edge of the marsh was naturally spongy and unstable, and this forward action produced an unexpected consequence.

The muddy bank gave way, and the elephant found himself sliding forward against his will. Tarzan clung with arms and legs to his back, and Tantor lifted his trunk, trumpeting fresh alarm.

However, there was no going back for the leathery brute. Slipping and sliding, he blundered into the water. In order to keep from toppling over, Tantor was forced to churn the mucky marsh bottom with his powerful legs.

This changed the color of the marsh in this area from simply dirty to virtually black hue.

Having been forced to commit to the crossing, the elephant transformed into a charging mass of muscle, as he battled desperately to reach the opposite side as rapidly as his churning legs could propel him. Tantor had no eyes for anything other than dry land. Hence, he failed to spy danger when it reared itself up from the primordial muck.

A pair of filmy, yellowish eyes, cold and watchful, emerged from the brackish water some rods distant. These orbs seized upon the human figure astride the lumbering colossus, and their half-submerged owner began advancing with paddling motions of its massive talons, augmented by a swimming action of its broad, muscular tail.

The creature was utterly silent in its approach. Silent—but not invisible.

The sharp eyes of the ape-man had been sweeping the water swirling all around, and they soon spied the unblinking orbs. Half-concealed by the muddy marsh, the long scaly body behind those staring orbs floated like the trunk of a rough tree that had toppled in death.

Tarzan of the Apes gave no sign or outcry that he saw danger approaching. He reached for his Enfield revolver, but had second thoughts, realizing that he carried few shells, and still faced certain dangers ahead in Pal-ul-don proper.

On the other side of his belt was strapped the long steel fang of a knife, which had been the hunting blade of his long-dead human father. Tarzan withdrew this from the sheath without making the gesture seem hostile.

Pretending not to notice the advancing reptile, the ape-man carefully moved one leg, and then the other, until he was kneeling on the ridged back of the swimming elephant.

When the yellow eyes had drawn as near as he dared permit them to, Tarzan gathered himself up and executed an astonishing leap.

In reaction, the elephant reared back, and threw his great hairless head around, giving forth a frightening bellow. Confusion augmented the noise of this alarm.

For in his springy leap, the ape-man cleared the expanse of water to land upon the nodular back of the saurian, which wallowed half submerged.

Landing skillfully, Tarzan went to one knee, and drove the blade once, twice, three times into the spine back of the skull. Here, the crocodile's anatomy was not as heavily armored as elsewhere. With three swift blows, the ape-man managed to sever the spinal column, with the result that the great crocodile lifted its upper jaw, and gave forth a ghastly sound that was partly a honk but also akin to a confused croaking.

The paddling taloned feet and thrashing tail combined in their determined animation to carry the reptile along as it sought escape from its terrible tormentor.

It bumped its fanged mouth into the elephant's flank. Tantor began to flail about with his trunk, simultaneously attempting to veer away from the horrible marauder.

Tarzan stepped forward, placing his feet, one after the other, along the long snout of the crocodile, his weight causing its terrible jaws to click shut. He might have been walking across an inert log for all the crocodile objected.

A nimble leap cleared a crimson patch of water, and Tarzan of the Apes reclaimed his nervous mount. Back upon the elephant, the ape-man smacked it with one hand, impelling the brute forward again, while with a free foot, he pushed the crocodile back.

The creature wallowed for a bit, and then as water began to fill its open mouth, it began to lurch drunkenly. Rolling like a shark, it entirely upended itself until its smooth ochre belly had revealed itself.

The crocodile floated as lifelessly as the log it so resembled, no longer a threat. Blood oozed from it in a spreading cloud that stained the water.

Tantor had no eyes for that sight, for he was churning forward madly, finally reaching the opposite bank, where he struggled up onto dry land.

Once safely on solid ground, Tarzan slipped off his mountainous steed and took stock of his uniform. Despite everything, it was virtually dry—except where his boots had trod the saurian's back. The leather would soon bake dry in the sun.

Tarzan frowned slightly, for had the uniform been ruined, he might have been justified in shedding it. But as yet the ape-man had no such excuse. He turned to face Tantor, but the pachyderm's eyes were not upon him, for they were watching the marsh and pensively observing the corpse of the great crocodile float helplessly along.

Something of dull comprehension seemed to flicker in those morose eyes and, without prompting, the brown beast sank to his knees, awaiting the bidding of the powerful jungle lord who had vanquished a creature much larger and more powerful than he.

Tantor knelt in silent recognition of the prowess of Tarzan of the Apes.

Chapter Seven

THE TANGLED MAN

D USK found Tarzan of the Apes riding the dusty jungle
lanes penetrating the northernmost reaches of Pal-ul-don.
The ape-lord swayed serenely on his customary perch just in
back of the pachyderm's wrinkled old skull. Tantor flapped one
ear lazily, while his maimed mate hung like a soiled rag. He
seemed untroubled by the loss of the appendage, which showed
no outward signs of infection.

Tarzan's eyes were busy scanning the leafy canopy on either
side of the jungle trail. He was seeking any signs of parachute
silk or, just as probably, dangling bodies. For Clayton understood
that, for the crew to have bailed out of the de Havilland Flamingo over this section of the Land of Man, chances were great
that they came down in thick jungle and, as likely as not, would
have become snagged in the treetops.

From time to time, the ape-man cast his clear gaze upon the
trail ahead. It apparently had not rained in some time, and the
way was dry; and with each ponderous footfall, Tantor raised
brownish dust that clung to his wrinkled sides, mingling with
their dun hue.

Tarzan knew that the central valley of Pal-ul-don was inhabited by tremendous survivals of prehistoric triceratops, which
were known to the inhabitants as *gryfs*. These were not merely
the triceratops of the British Museum or the books studied by
paleontologists around the world. These specimens were much
more massive and, worse yet, entirely carnivorous.

The ape-man fully expected to encounter one specimen sooner than later, although during his previous explorations of Pal-ul-don, he had come to conclude that other prehistoric beasts also foraged this isolated land. He never before encountered anything other than *gryfs* and the marsh saurians, yet the ape-man remained convinced that varied prehistoric survivals held sway in different parts of this savage land. The pterosaurs that had attacked his warplane were but one example.

His keen nostrils took in every passing scent and found many that were unfamiliar. Tarzan gazed skyward at intervals, alert for the possibility of wheeling pteranodons of the kind he had earlier battled. These flying reptiles had not been among the creatures he had previously encountered, and this knowledge made him wary of unexpected dangers.

Curiously, it was Tantor who first scented something unusual. The elephant slowed to a plodding half halt, and lifted his trunk, inquisitive nostrils opening and closing spasmodically.

"What is it, Tantor?" Tarzan whispered. "What do you smell?"

The elephant slowed perceptibly, but did not halt his advance. He ceased to sway as before, and his trunk seemed to probe the way ahead, tasting the air on either side of the jungle trail.

Raising himself, the Lord of the Jungle came to his full height and balanced atop his slowly swaying mount. He searched the darkening way ahead, seeking signs of movement, sniffing the air for scent spoor, or approaching predators.

Tantor continued to slow and then scented something that brought him to a rigid halt. An eerie sound emerged from his mouth—a mournful, trailing call.

Tarzan had by now picked up the scent which had caused the pachyderm to hesitate. It was an odor the ape-man recognized. No less than the smell of death. A sultry afternoon breeze was filtering through the dense forest, and a stray tendril of this breeze carried the faintest odor of putrefaction.

Now Tarzan had been raised in the jungle, and knew its ways well. The scent of death comes in many flavors. The rotting carcass of Bara the deer smells different than that of Numa the lion. So, too, does the stench of a dead man.

Slipping off his massive mount, Tarzan dropped to the ground, feeling encumbered by the heavy boots that cushioned his fall. Carefully, he padded forward, following the vaguest scent spoor, until it drew him into the forest itself.

Here, Tantor could not follow.

Tarzan worked his way between looming trees, until the denseness of the forest began to defeat easy reconnoitering. Removing his boots and socks, the ape-man tied the boot-laces together and draped them over his neck, so they dangled upon his khaki jacket. His socks went into one boot.

Thus unencumbered, Tarzan climbed up the handiest tree bole, found the lowermost branches and worked his way up, higher, ever higher, until he thrust his magnificent head out of the forest canopy.

Turning in a careful circle, the ape-man scanned the horizon in all directions, seeking signs or spoor. He discovered nothing of the sort.

The lack of the visible trail meant nothing to Tarzan of the Apes. For the scent was stronger now, here where he could move about freely.

The horrible odor was coming from due southwest. Dropping back into the branches, the ape-man commenced making his way in that direction.

So dense was the forest here that it was unnecessary for Tarzan to swing from tree limb to tree limb in order to navigate his way south. Indeed, it would have been reckless to do so, for the woody terraces formed a virtual web in which it was far simpler—although infinitely more cumbersome—to simply climb from branch to branch, making fair time—and certainly far less risky than attempting to walk where myriad predators prowled. Monkeys traveled through trees in exactly this fashion and, while it did not suit Tarzan's impatient nature, it was a way of going that he knew well.

The death reek drew him unerringly to his quarry. For ahead, in the dying light, he began to discern a fluttering white blob that seemed to pulse as if alive.

A popping sound similar to that of a sail troubled by the wind reached the ape-man's alert ears.

Tarzan forged ahead, and his nostrils filled with the overwhelming stench of corruption. Thus he was not surprised to find the British pilot snared in the trees, like a fly caught in a spider's web.

Something like a chill touched the back of the ape-man's neck. For the way in which the man was tangled in the shrouds of his collapsed parachute canopy—which was the thing that flapped and chattered—made it appear as if he had been deliberately ensnared by his own parachute, almost as if the silken bell had somehow stirred to life and turned upon him.

Hackles raised, Tarzan approached with the caution of an alert jungle hunter who knows that at any moment his prey could turn the tables, with the result that he might become *their* prey.

The dead aviator was dressed in an R.A.F. uniform whose insignia revealed him to be a flight lieutenant, and it became evident that he had dropped from the sky at this precise spot. Higher up in the tree hung broken branches, whose raw ends told that tale.

But the manner in which the unfortunate man had apparently landed told another.

The ape-man circled the tree in which the pilot swayed in death. He was, Tarzan quickly realized, hanging downward—something highly unlikely had he parachuted feet-first into the tree.

The arms and legs of the man were so entangled in the shroud lines that they kept him from falling all the way to the ground. Above and slightly to one side, the ripped billows of his parachute bell fluttered like a shroud that had become separated from its corpse.

Everything about the way the unfortunate pilot hung in this silken skein was unnatural. There was no doubting this.

As he approached more closely, Tarzan noticed something else. The twisted body was quilled by long thin reeds of some sort. These ended in red-feathered tufts. The needle-like tips had been dipped in a brownish dye. A few of these feathery tufts were a ghostly white.

Creeping closer, Tarzan reached the aviator. He clung to a supporting branch as he examined the inert corpse. The pilot's face was black with death. He had been dead many days. Curiously, no flies buzzed about him, nor had any animals made of his dead flesh a meal.

This, too, was unnatural.

Reaching down, the ape-man found one of the tufted reeds, and extracted it. He sniffed the tip, and while he did not recognize the faint odor, Tarzan instinctually understood it.

"Poison."

Harvesting the white-tufted reed, the ape-man also sniffed it carefully. A different odor clung to the tip, mingled with the stale tang of human blood.

Studying the awkward angle at which the man had been snared—for the evidence of the ape-man's senses told him this was so—Tarzan drew a mental picture of what must have happened to the downed pilot.

Evidently, he had landed in this very same tree, breaking several branches, whose loose ends were scattered below in the dirt. The way his right leg cocked askew, trouser cuff soaked in dry blood, suggested that the airman had broken his leg upon impact.

With his knife, Tarzan sliced open the uniform trouser leg, exposing the damaged leg. A three-inch jagged section of femur jutted out from the dead flesh, confirming his supposition.

Such a severe break would have incapacitated the man, and prevented him from cutting himself free of his parachute. Tarzan observed the empty scabbard of his knife dangling from his belt. There was no sign of the missing weapon among the trees, or below on the jungle floor.

Injured, the aviator may have simply hung entangled in his shroud lines, awaiting rescue—or, more probably, his inevitable fate. While so ensnared, he had been discovered by natives and apparently his discoverers had taken advantage of his helplessness and employed his own shroud lines to tie him fast to the tree, rendering him even more helpless and pathetic.

Tarzan surmised that the unfortunate one's tormentors had employed these poison quills to further render him helpless, or possibly to torture him after they had ensnared him unbreakably.

In any event, the pilot's death had been a type of mercy, for timely rescue was out of the question. As likely as not, he would have bled to death in due course.

This realization did not diminish John Clayton's anger over the fate of the poor flight lieutenant, for the pale scar slashing his forehead began to redden.

The R.A.F. pilot, whose name Tarzan did not know and did not need to know, was a countryman and fellow comrade-in-arms. Silently, the ape-man vowed to inflict punishment in full measure and exact vengeance upon those who had done this.

Employing his blade, Tarzan carefully cut the unfortunate free, and lowered his body to the jungle floor using the shroud lines.

Once again he was reminded of a poor fly caught in a spider's web. In this case, the sight of the man's body deposited on the ground was reminiscent of the dried house fly after he had been evicted by the satiated spider.

Tarzan had no tool suitable to bury the man, but the ground hereabouts was soft, and so he employed his hands. One of the broken branches, once he hacked off the excess, made a serviceable entrenching tool.

DARKNESS had fully fallen by the time Tarzan finished smoothing dark loam over the pilot's body. From the deceased man's throat, the ape-man had removed his identity discs. These he placed in one of his own pockets without bothering to look at them. There was too little light by which to read the medallions anyway.

Returning to the trees, Tarzan began to make his way back to where Tantor awaited him. He traveled monkey-like through the treetops. By now it was too dark to properly reconnoiter the area, but the ape-man knew that where one crewman had landed, others might not be far off. His jungle-wise eyes scanned his surroundings relentlessly, as would one who knew that death might rear up from any direction at any time.

As he worked his way along, Tarzan noticed a curious phenomenon.

In the webwork of interlacing branches moved luminous spots, suggestive of fireflies, although not as bright. They did not float like fireflies flitting amid the branches. Rather, they moved stealthily, shifting around, neither winking nor approaching.

Something compelled the ape-man to remove his service revolver and load it with the spare rounds he had found on the dead pilot.

Pausing in the crotch of a lofty tree, Tarzan raised his pistol and fired twice, straight up. Two saffron flashes made the surroundings stand out in stark relief. In that instant, Tarzan saw more than one presence skittering along the branches in retreat. There was no time to discern more than that sudden movement before darkness returned, blacker than before.

Tarzan's ears easily detected scuttling sounds mixed in with the creak and groan of laden branches being used for escape.

Whatever the arboreal things might be, they were retreating.

Wasting no time, the ape-man worked his way back to where Tantor grazed patiently. The pachyderm had not moved from his station. He was a sturdy, resolute hillock in the fathomless night of Pal-ul-don, broad ear flapping, his thin whiplike tail slapping at insects who were bedeviling him.

Evidently, the brute had discovered a deposit of reddish soil, for his great hide was caked with it. It was an ingrained habit of the species to coat themselves with loam, which they scooped up with their prehensile trunks, in order to ward off heat and insects.

"I have returned, Tantor," Tarzan called softly.

The elephant gave a tremulous trumpet of a sound, and instantly the ape-man froze. He knew elephants well, had grown up among them, spoke their language, and could all but read their thoughts.

Tantor was frightened.

Approaching, Tarzan reached out to touch his shoulder, and the leathery flesh trembled slightly.

"What is wrong, friend of Tarzan?"

Exploring the beast with his hands, the ape-man quickly discovered the truth.

Along one dusty flank of the pachyderm sprouted a half-dozen quills of the type which had feathered the deceased R.A.F. pilot!

Chapter Eight

The Turtle Folk

MOVING swiftly, Tarzan of the Apes removed each of the long reed darts that had struck Tantor in his massive reddish-brown side.

The pachyderm made no sound as these barbs were extracted. In the darkness, the ape-lord wasted no time examining the quills. Instead, he felt the elephant's wrinkled flank, eventually encountered moisture.

Bringing his fingers to his nostrils, Tarzan inhaled the odor, and recognized it as similar to the scent of the white-tufted reeds. No salty odor was mixed in, which told the ape-man that the quills had not pierced the leathery epidermis.

Ascertaining by scent alone that no blood had been drawn, Tarzan thus determined that the elephant's thick hide had protected it from the poison.

To test his theory, Tarzan stepped around, found Tantor's trunk, and used it to lead the elephant forward. The reddish-brown brute wrapped his wrinkled appendage around the ape-man's great bronzed wrist, and came willingly. He was steady and resolute, but even in the darkness Tarzan could see the deep concern in the creature's small eyes.

They plodded along until stealthy sounds in the branches brought the ape-man to a sudden stop. Tarzan listened, raising his head, sniffing the air.

Somewhere in the rustling forest, tiny greenish-white spots showed, disappearing and reappearing like fireflies, but not like fireflies.

Tarzan tracked this phenomenon with his eyes, a chill sense of danger lifting hackles at the back of his neck. At that moment, he wished he had taken time to fashion for himself a bow and arrow set, but he was a flying officer now, and it was expected that he depend upon his regulation sidearm and his military training, not primitive tools.

A soft sound from not far away caused Tarzan to drop to one knee. Just in time. Over his head whisked something that cut the air. It made the tiniest of breezes, ruffling his exposed hair.

With an animal celerity, the ape-man dodged behind Tantor, and drew his revolver. Almost as soon as he'd done so, Tarzan realized that to discharge the weapon this close to his elephantine ally would have unfortunate consequences. He did not wish to stampede Tantor.

Reluctantly holstering the weapon, Tarzan waited and listened.

The whisking sounds came in volleys, and resulted in soft ticking noises as weird darts struck dry dirt or stones or, on the far side of him, looming tree trunks.

There was no doubt but that many were making their mark on Tantor's other flank. Soft grumbles of concern emerged from the nervous beast.

The ape-man dared not expose himself, lest he be feathered by the potent missiles. Nor could he simply wait for his unseen foes to exhaust their store of deadly darts.

Cupping his hands over his mouth, Tarzan unleashed the chilling victory cry of the bull ape, which caused startled Tantor to suddenly rear up, unfurl his coiled trunk, and trumpet a thunderous bellow of defiance. The two sounds blended, amplifying one another, and in the trees, skittering figures scrambled madly.

The soft hail of darts ceased altogether. Silence returned.

Stepping around to the elephant's other side, Tarzan carefully harvested many darts and using his hand wiped down Tantor's flank, simultaneously satisfying himself that once again blood had not been drawn.

Tantor had by this time dropped back twenty feet, and his head was swaying back and forth as his tiny eyes sought any evidence of further danger. His one good ear flapped listlessly.

Nothing came to light, so Tarzan grasped his ally by his flexible trunk, and led him forward.

This time, they were neither challenged nor molested.

Before long, a three-quarters moon rose, producing strong silver light that began painting cool shadows on either side of the jungle aisle.

The scent of fresh water, drinkable water, was the next thing they encountered. As they made their way along, Tarzan and Tantor kept vigilant eyes open for the source of the welcome scent.

Before long, they rounded a bend, and the night wind brought a stronger smell, and soon enough, sparkling moonglade revealed a sizable lake impounded by low hills.

They abandoned the trail, Tantor blundering down toward its rippling surface in his eagerness for drink. Tarzan leapt atop the elephant and piloted him down to the water's inviting edge.

Stopping there, Tantor dipped his thirsty trunk into the water, and began inhaling great draughts of the cool refreshment, which he first used to spray over the flank that had been peppered by many darts. Then, he conveyed the rest to his parched mouth, squirting volumes within. Thus did he drink.

Tarzan was on the ground by this time, and knelt among the reeds and rushes at the water's edge. He replenished his canteen, after first drinking his fill.

Beside him, Tantor greedily imbibed until his great belly swelled.

They stood there some moments, satiated, and watched the play of moonlight on the calm surface of the lake. It was hypnotic, and held their attention.

At first inspection, the lake did not appear to be very large, but as his eyes searched it, Tarzan perceived that they were merely looking at one arm of the glistening body of water. Through jungle trees, they could perceive dancing moon gleams that told of a greater expanse of water further along.

As if to prove this supposition, something came around a little headland that could not be clearly made out.

Tarzan's attention that moment was fixated elsewhere, so Tantor was the first to spy the approaching mass. Lifting his trunk, he tootled a warning trumpet.

"What is it?" Tarzan asked.

As if by way of answer, the flexible trunk stretched out, and made a grotesque pointing finger.

Tarzan's steel-grey eyes focused on the shape rounding the headland. At first, he thought it was a ship of some sort, perhaps a long dugout canoe. No canoe would be constructed to that scale, however. For the thing exhibited the proportions of a small barge.

Squat shapes suggesting men stood atop the floating object. Tarzan could not discern these individuals clearly, but they were broadly built, and many of them held up what appeared to be poles or possibly blunt spears.

As they approached, sailing in the stately manner that might have been matched by the barges of the ancient pharaohs, one individual on top of the object stabbed out with a blunt finger, and directed the attention of the others on Tarzan and his elephant.

This brought a definite alteration in the behavior of the standing group. Some strode forward, halted in unison, and brought their poles stamping up and down, while others went to the rear, and did the same.

Slowly, ponderously, the barge-like object diverted from its course and headed in the direction of Tarzan and Tantor, its method of propulsion obscure.

The ape-man stood his ground. At his side, the nervous elephant lifted his trunk and began sniffing the humid air. He emitted sounds of concern, if not confusion.

"Steady," Tarzan told him, patting Tantor on the flank reassuringly.

As the floating assemblage of men hove into clearer view, Tarzan beheld what at first glance appeared to be a monstrous figurehead at the blunt bow of the barge. It was flat, squat, and very broad. It possessed a saurian configuration, as if the carver had modeled the great figurehead on some species of reptile.

The ape-man had only a few moments to absorb this, when the dark, sleepy-looking eyes of the figurehead closed and then reopened again!

Then, and only then, did Tarzan realize that this was not a ship bearing passengers, but a creature of some sort—controlled by men.

From behind, something lifted skyward—an appendage that resembled a thick tail but with a knobby end. This reared up and slapped down, creating a significant splash, apparently slowing the oncoming creature.

Tantor began backing away from the water's edge; Tarzan remonstrated him not. The ape-man's eyes were studying the approaching creature as the barge of a thing slowed in the water, trailing a broad wake. All the while, the men perched atop it were pacing, striding about the broad back as if they were the absolute masters of the monster gliding along the tranquil lake surface.

These navigators did not look like ordinary men. Nor did they resemble any of the races of Pal-ul-don to which Tarzan had become acquainted during his earlier visitation. The people of the Land of Man could be classified into several types, most of which boasted prehensile tails and others of whom were wholly tailless.

Among the races were short, brutish individuals similar to cavemen. These new arrivals smacked of that species, but they were different in other ways. Instead of animal skins, they wore armor of some type. This armor was not metallic, but appeared to be of some bony or horny substance. Helmets encased their broad heads, and greaves sheathed their otherwise bare arms and legs. They did not wear footgear, curiously enough.

On either side of the ponderous swimming creature, Tarzan could observe monstrous flippers at work. These reared up, and began to splash and play, creating a braking action.

It became evident that the creature was going to beach itself on the very spot where Tarzan stood. Prudently, the ape-man withdrew from the water's edge and guided Tantor back, giving the new arrivals wide berth.

As the silent creature approached, it opened its great beak of a jaw and began clambering onto dry land, beaching itself. The armored men jumped off, landed heavily, and approached, using their long poles like walking sticks.

By that time, Tarzan had an excellent view of the moon-washed creature. It was nothing less than a giant sea tortoise, whose horny shell served as the deck on which the new arrivals sailed. Evidently, these men were mariners of a sort.

The men who approached might have been sprung from the same loins as the massive aquatic reptile, for they were armored the way a turtle is encased in its shell. They strode up, boldly and unafraid, as if their armor was proof against any threat or menace. They walked slowly and heavily, like upright human turtles.

Their faces were human enough, although broader and more brutish than the other races with whom the ape-man was acquainted.

Raising one hand in the universal gesture of greeting, Tarzan attempted to speak to them in the language of the southern races of Pal-ul-don.

These turtle-men responded with a series of grunts and clucks that were wholly incomprehensible to Tarzan. A concerned notch appeared between the ape-man's intelligent eyebrows. He fully expected these new arrivals to know the language of the southern tribes who dwelled in the vicinity of the Valley of Jad-ben-Otho, which cut a diagonal swath across the rift-riven breadth of the Land of Man. The jungle lord next tried Swahili, even English, but these dull-faced fellows were equally baffled by his speech.

Stepping up, they took positions of frank challenge. The turtle-men seemed as equally perplexed by Tarzan as they were by the ape-man's lumbering companion. It was evident that they had never beheld a European man, much less an equatorial pachyderm.

A deep-chested individual stepped forward, one who had the bearing of authority and the resolute expression of command. Presumably, this was the leader of the turtle-men, or at least the captain of the massive reptile that served as a living barge.

This worthy took his staff, and drew a circle within another circle. Along the edges of the outer circle, he drew crosshatch marks, and then he brought the staff down in the uppermost part of the inner circle.

He grunted a single word, *"Pal,"* which meant "land."

Observing this, Tarzan immediately took the inner circle for a rough approximation of the Land of Man, the outer circle for the surrounding marshy moat, and the crosshatch marks for the thorny barrier beyond.

The turtle captain lifted his staff and pointed at Tarzan as if to ask, "Where are you from?"

Tarzan made a mark far to the northeast of the outermost thorn indications. Pointing to the rising three-quarters moon, he lifted ten fingers and attempted to express that he had traveled ten moons in order to reach Pal-ul-don.

The eyes of the turtle captain narrowed, as if attempting to squeeze down his astonishment. A ten-month march was a

greater distance than he could ever have traveled to any destination. That much was evident.

While this was being absorbed, one of the other turtle-men
had moved around and was eyeing Tantor waiting nervously
nearby.

Suddenly, this worthy fellow began jabbering excitedly. He
summoned the others. One man stepped up to Tantor and from
his lower leg pulled one of the quilled darts—one Tarzan had
overlooked in the early evening darkness.

This item was passed from hand to hand and examined
carefully. Finally, it ended up in the hands of the turtle captain,
who looked at it, and then stepped on it with a look of disgust,
snapping the reed in twain.

It was obvious to the ape-man that whatever creatures wielded
the poisonous darts, they were the mortal enemies of the turtle
people. It also suggested rather strongly the main reason that
the turtle-men went about armored with the shells of tortoises of various sizes.

Tarzan made quick gestures, intended to convey his curiosity over the origins of the darts.

The captain of the turtle-men walked his staff over to a
smooth patch of dirt, and began working furiously. Before long,
he had made the image of an eight-legged spider, squatting in
the center of a crude orb web.

The man spoke a single word: *"Jinna."*

As if suddenly remembering that they had not been properly introduced, the captain brought his fist hard against the
turtle shell that protected his barrel chest and said, "Grom."
Evidently that was his name.

Tarzan indicated his own person and said, "Tarzan-jad-
guru."

In the tongue of the races of central Pal-ul-don, this translated to Tarzan the Terrible. It was a sobriquet the ape-man
had earned during his previous sojourn.

The tortoise-man possessed some rudimentary understanding of the language, for he grunted, "Tarzan?"

"Tarzan," the ape-man replied affirmatively. "It means White Skin—Ho-Sat," he hastily corrected, remembering the proper words in the local language.

The captain of the tortoise folk narrowed his eyes in careful thought. What passed through his brain remained forever unknown to the ape-man. But at length, he lifted his staff and pointed it at the waiting tortoise and seemed to invite Tarzan for a moonlight cruise.

"Brang," he grunted.

Here was a word Tarzan understood. In the common tongue of Pal-ul-don, brang meant turtle. He searched his mind for the word for lake, for south of these northern reaches lay several lakes with which he was acquainted, and whose names were burned into his memory. Among them were Jad-bal-lul and Jad-in-lul, the golden and dark lake respectively.

This impoundment tucked into the northwest corner of the Land of Man was unknown to him. Pointing to the dark waters, Tarzan attempted to frame a question. "Jad-lul?"

"Jad-*brang*-lul," corrected Grom, nodding ponderously.

Thus did Tarzan learn that this body of water was known as the turtle lake. The ape-man did not hesitate further, but pointed to his elephant and spread out his hands as if to ask, "What shall I do with my friend? I cannot leave him behind."

This inquiry appeared to register perfectly with the armored man, for he pointed his staff at the pachyderm and then swept it down to the water as if to say, "He may follow."

Tarzan allowed a smile to answer for him. It was the ape-man's thinking that since he was in an unfamiliar part of the Land of Man, if he were to discover the remainder of the missing plane's crew, he would be unlikely to do so before dawn. Here were inhabitants no doubt intelligent, and who in all probability witnessed the parachutes come down. If he could learn to communicate with them, the jungle lord reasoned, a great deal

of unnecessary expenditure of effort could be avoided by inter-
rogating these tortoise people.

At least, that was Tarzan's rationale for accepting a ride on
the giant sea tortoise that served as a barge.

Glancing over to Tantor, the ape-man motioned for the
elephant to follow. Without waiting for any response, thus
signaling that he expected no opposition, Tarzan followed the
turtle mariners down to the waterline.

Behind him, Tantor followed faithfully, but made uncertain
burbling sounds indicating his distrust.

Chapter Nine

LAKE FORTRESS

A S HE approached the great tortoise ship, Tarzan studied the head of the creature, which by itself was as large as an automobile.

The sea turtle, resting its head on the ground, kept both eyes closed. It was evidently resting. There was no question in the ape-man's mind that the reptile was fully trained. Which was fortunate, for the jaws of the thing were so formidable that they could have bitten a sizable tree trunk in half. A mere man would not have stood up to it.

The creature lay supine and unmoving as the turtle crew clambered aboard the flange of its great shell.

Tarzan climbed aboard as well. Soon, he was standing on the sturdy armored deck, and saw that, unlike the tortoises with which he was acquainted, this one possessed spikes arrayed around the peripheral edge of the shell. When submerged, these defensive barbs projected down into the water, but on dry land they were quite visible. No doubt they were designed by nature to repel aquatic predators.

The turtle-men gave Tarzan sufficient room to explore. The ape-man strode to the stern of the living vessel, and examined its tail. He had seen it in action before, and now was curious as to its configuration.

The tail was longer than those of land or sea turtles, and ended in a bulbous knob that was remindful of an ankylosaur, an armored dinosaur that possessed some qualities of a turtle while not resembling that reptile in its general form. The club tail could be a formidable weapon if brought into play, the ape-man realized.

Heading to the center of the tortoise's shell, Tarzan folded his arms and waited, his posture resolute. Tantor blundered down to the lakeside weeds, and carefully slid into the water.

Without preamble, the captain of the turtle-men stepped forward, and brought the blunt end of his staff banging down atop the tortoise's skull. The creature roused, its heavy head lifting, and on either side the great flippers commenced to dig into the mud, reversing themselves.

Like a ship—or more properly a submersible—being launched, the immense tortoise slid backward into the water, and was soon floating free. Its flippers stirred to life and, churning water mightily, it began to turn as if on a pivot until the massive head was pointing out into the lake's placid center. Once oriented, the creature commenced swimming in a direct line, impelled by wooden staves which tapped and pounded different places about its durable shell.

These were the signals by which the captain and his crew commanded the living barge.

Behind them, Tantor slid into deeper water, and soon became sufficiently buoyant to swim. With a cheery trumpeting of victory, the elephant signaled that he was following behind.

TARZAN took in all the sights of the tortoise crew and the surrounding land. He kept his eyes sharp, seeking any signs of movement or life in the surrounding trees.

The majestic tortoise swam for over twenty minutes, rounding the headland, and going deeper into the heart of Jad-brang-lul, the turtle lake.

The ape-man assumed that the incredible vessel and its armored complement were seeking the opposite shore of the lake. But he soon learned the error of his assumption. For in the center of the lake bulked up a high hump of an island, one that was surrounded by earthen works which served as protection, much the way the tortoise shell armor protected the bodies of the turtle-men.

The tortoise paddled toward this fortress, and from Captain Grom's thick throat issued a lowering cry, not unlike that of a cow or ox giving voice.

An answering call came from the ramparts. Blunt heads popped up. Staves were lifted in answer.

The obedient tortoise drew closer to land. It turned south, under the prodding of the pounding poles.

Unexpectedly, a sturdy log drawbridge fell, lowered by thick ropes made of woven vines, and thus a ramp was created for the benefit of the arriving barge.

Seeing this, the tortoise seemed to need no further prompting, for it redoubled its paddling, and arrowed straight for the round-railed ramp.

Up this rampart he clambered, much like an anxious terrapin returning to its spawning ground. During this phase of the operation, it was necessary to drop to one knee and take hold of the horny protuberances of the outer shell, lest they be thrown off as the plodding monster climbed up the ramp. Observing this procedure, Tarzan followed suit.

It was a difficult climb, but the thing was soon accomplished. Finally, the struggling tortoise stood on level ground in a kind of a holding pen that had some of the qualities of a great mud wallow.

Standing up, Tarzan looked back and saw Tantor attempting to climb the same ramp. This was not an easy task, for the elephant's blunt forefeet had difficulty finding purchase.

Stepping off the tortoise shell, Tarzan raced for a coil of vine that was not in use, quickly fashioned a lariat from it, and went to the lashed-log ramp, carrying this.

Casting it once, the ape-man made the loop settle atop the elephant's massive head. It would not be possible, of course, to bodily haul the creature up by this means. Nor was it necessary.

For Tantor reached up for the loop with his flexible trunk, and took firm hold. Using this to steady himself, the mighty pachyderm managed to find footing, and with this purchase, painfully and not without stumbling, he dragged his moist brown bulk onto dry land.

Tarzan pulled with all of his might, providing encouragement for the laborious operation.

All around, the turtle-men watched in something like awe, as the gigantic creature lumbered his way into the mud wallow, giving the giant tortoise a wide berth before coming to a dead halt. Tantor's creased flanks heaved with the strain of his exertion, and he lay down with ponderous difficulty, evidently tempted by the cool mud.

Staves began stamping the ground in a kind of rude applause.

Once Tantor was established on firm ground, Tarzan was invited into the city proper.

It was more of a walled city, but it had the qualities of a castle or fortress. Everything was of a piece—ramparts, homes, other structures. They were built of mud that had dried and been faced with something that brought to mind stucco, but was entirely different.

Tarzan thought of a nest built by mud dauber wasps, but much more blocky and crude in construction. Spectral moonlight washed everything, giving it a weird glamour that belied its mud foundations.

Tarzan walked fearlessly, confident in his power to face whatever might come. He sensed no threat from the turtle-men, but was prepared in his mind for any alteration in his circumstances. They did not treat him like a captive—although that could change at a moment's notice.

The procession came at last to a structure in the center of the fortress, which was built after the fashion of a tin of rations. It was round, flat on the roof, and had a solitary entrance. Adornment was modest, and consisted of a facing that was modeled after the pebbled surface of a tortoise shell.

The captain of the tortoise ship entered first, waving Tarzan to follow. The ape-man half expected to be brought into the inner chamber or throne room of whoever ruled this island fortress.

Instead, the ape-lord was mildly surprised upon entering to discover that Grom himself walked to a kind of throne that consisted of a great tortoise shell that was encrusted with semi-precious stones, and took his rightful seat, where he proceeded to hold court. Evidently, he was the *gund,* or king, of these tortoise folk.

Tarzan stood before the throne, which was elevated on an earthen mound that served as a rude dais, while all about him assembled the other members of the tortoise-barge crew. There began a halting exchange in which the ape-man and the turtle ruler attempted to find a common speech.

The jungle lord had mastered many languages in the course of his adventures, and was adept at picking up new tongues. But the language spoken by the turtle folk, although it had words in common with the speech of lower Pal-ul-don, was difficult to decipher.

There was much pantomiming, and abrupt speech, as they struggled to comprehend one another.

Tarzan pointed to his uniform jacket, wordlessly indicating he was seeking others who wore such attire.

This much the tortoise ruler seemed to comprehend, and it was at this point that the other turtle-men stepped up and began touching and fingering Tarzan at different points of his magnificent physique.

The ape-man permitted this. They did not seem threatening. Excited words were exchanged, and the murmuring group seemed to marvel at the fabric in some way.

One of the turtle-men produced a specimen of the dart that had been used to pierce Tantor earlier in the evening. Plucking up a section of Tarzan's khaki sleeve fabric, he inserted this through a fold, and discovered to his astonishment that the dart penetrated easily.

There followed another excited exchange, which Tarzan immediately comprehended to be surprise at the ease in which his uniform was breached.

Apparently, these turtle folk were so accustomed to going about heavily armored that the sight of Tarzan wearing such flimsy garments filled them with an emotion akin to horror.

The ape-man made an attempt to steer the conversational exchange back to his original point. Dropping to the floor, he traced out a circle indicating the island fortress, roughing out a shape representing the lake, and again pointed at his uniform jacket and made gestures suggestive of a search.

This seemed to engender some understanding. From his pocket, Tarzan produced a military-issue handkerchief, which he folded in an approximation of a parachute, and pantomimed such a thing falling from the sky.

This brought more satisfactory results. Grom, chief of the turtle-men, raised three fingers to indicate that three parachutes had been witnessed.

With eager gestures, Tarzan inquired as to which directions the other parachutes had fallen.

The turtle chief pointed first south and to the west, grunting excitedly.

At that juncture, food was brought in, was spread out upon the floor for casual consumption.

They promptly sat down, forming an egalitarian circle, and fell upon the plates, which appeared to be of polished shell. The food was tasty, and consisted largely of fish, with some greens which might have been plantlings thrown in. It tasted nourishing, at least.

Over this rough repast, conversation shook off the rust of unfamiliarity and Tarzan discovered certain words that the others could grasp.

From these broken exchanges, the ape-man determined that the turtle people had dwelt on this island fortress for many generations, and that they lived in fear of another race, whom they symbolized by tracing out a common spider.

Tarzan made gestures at this symbol, inviting more information.

Grom attempted to communicate as best he could. He drew an oblong and called it "Jad-brang-lul" and, shifting his pointer, made a jagged line southeast of the turtle lake, drawing what looked like tall trees, dubbing the area, "Jad-jinna-gar."

The ape-man knew from their previous conversation that jinna stood for either spider or spider web. Therefore, Grom was saying the spider or spider web something. But what did gar mean? Not lake, obviously. The terrain of Pal-ul-don was a rugged expanse of mountains, gorges, cliffs and caves, interspersed with jungled forests and wild, rumbling rivers. The word might mean any of these things—or none of them.

Tarzan attempted to elicit more information, but the paucity of common words among their languages defeated all efforts.

One of the turtle-men—it could be noticed that they did not remove their armor even in the safety of the throne room—rose up and fetched something.

He set the thing in the center of the circle. This was a hairy spider, of a hue so brown it was nearly black. And of good size, although apparently not venomous because no one shrank from it as the thing scurried about in a desperate attempt to flee.

Tarzan observed the spider, and saw nothing unusual about it. Africa was full of arachnids of this type. This appeared to be a baboon spider, which greatly resembled the tarantula of South America.

As he watched, the turtle ruler stood up and lifted his staff once, bringing it down on the scuttling creature. He destroyed it with a single smash that burst its bloated body, releasing bodily fluids.

Everyone who had a staff lifted it and began pounding it in a boisterous approximation of applause. It was clear that the unknown people represented by the hapless spider were mortal enemies of the turtle folk.

More food was brought in. This appeared to be lizard. Tarzan tasted it and realized that it was a species of skink. He ate some to be polite, but soon pushed his shallow plate aside.

Tarzan passed the evening eating and questioning, and the conversation did not progress much beyond a rudimentary understanding of the nature of the spider foes.

At one point, every morsel of food was consumed and they stepped out into the open air to take in fresh oxygen. The chief of the turtle-men led them back to the mud wallow where Tantor had lain down in the corner where he felt comfortable. The patient pachyderm showed no signs of discomfort or serious illness from having been punctured by so many quills.

Carefully, Tarzan went over his side to make certain of this. Moonlight happened to strike the leathery skin perfectly so that Tarzan could be certain of the elephant's condition.

Not far away, the great tortoise slumbered, its sleepy but wise eyes closed, offering no threat whatsoever.

THERE commenced to Tarzan's surprise an animated exchange. Turtle-men began bringing various gifts, which included food, but also other trinkets. Most of these were beaten metal ornaments, not having any great value by themselves, but evidently prized as the work of artisans.

Tarzan attempted to follow the excited entreaties of the group. Eagerly, they pointed to the offerings, then went to the elephant's side, smacking at its great corrugated hide, and apparently marveling at it.

"I do not understand your speech," Tarzan told them.

They continued jabbering, to no great result. Grom began to look frustrated in a dull-faced way.

Then, the turtle-men began slapping at their tortoise armor and indicating the elephant's thick skin.

Only then did understanding dawn on the ape-man's high, intelligent brow. It became undeniable that the turtle-men were attempting to barter bushels of trinkets in return for Tantor, whose hide they prized for its flexibility as well as its ability to resist poison darts.

Tarzan shook his head firmly, saying, "No. This is not an acceptable trade."

The turtle-men appeared to have something in common with the old-time Yankee traders. Four bushels of trinkets were fetched and laid at the ape-man's feet.

Again, Tarzan shook his head firmly and repeated the stern word, "No."

The mood of the turtle-men darkened, but Tarzan of the Apes stood firm.

"No," he said again.

Finally, his words sank in. At a curt gesture from Grom, the offerings were carried away, and Tarzan was shown to a block of earthen works that reminded him of a mud hut. Heavy curtains of split bamboo were pulled aside and he was shown in.

Apparently, this modest structure was to be where he would pass the night.

Tarzan accepted this with a gracious smile and waved his hosts good night. The turtle-men lumbered off, and sought their own homes and beds.

Carefully, the ape-man removed and folded his R.A.F. uniform until he stood attired only in his undershorts, revealing a powerful physique remarkable for its symmetrical proportions. On his bronzed chest glittered the diamond-encrusted gold locket that had once belonged to his human mother. Along with the knife of his father, the locket was the only keepsake John Clayton possessed to remind him that a human couple had brought him into this world. For his only clear memories were of the great apes who reared him to splendid manhood.

Two hours passed by rough reckoning. After an absence of sounds indicating the island fortress had quieted down for the evening, Tarzan slipped out, and made his way to the mud wallow, his panther-like muscles gleaming under Luna's cool smile, a bronze-skinned Apollo who made no more sound than a scudding cloud.

Tarzan carried with him a bundle of dry grass which was apparently his bedding, and lay down next to Tantor. There, he promptly went to sleep. It was not that the ape-man did not trust the hospitality of the turtle folk, but that he did not know them well enough to trust them fully.

Better to guard his one true ally in Pal-ul-don than to risk the loss of the loyal elephant to a misunderstanding.

For all that, Tarzan of the Apes slept well and soundly.

Chapter Ten

THE PALE ONES

WHILE the inhabitants of the island fortress slumbered, deep in the jungles of upper Pal-ul-don, pale, furtive forms moved among the trees.

Here, under the forest canopy, little moonlight fell. What lunar splinters did penetrate picked out lean, leaf-disturbing fingers as they grasped and released branches, making their silent way along. Few leaves trembled for long, for the tree-dwellers were exceedingly stealthy.

They crept along, their bald white heads foremost, in the manner of spiders negotiating their woven webs. But it was not upon webs of spun spider silk that these unnatural entities progressed, but rather upon the natural web-work of interlacing branches.

Stray shafts of moonlight picked out details here and there. The hairless skulls. The equally hairless hides that were as smooth and white as alabaster. The elongated fingers and toes which numbered six, possessing not one, but two opposable thumbs on each pale hand.

With these, they formed sure, unbreakable grips so that none of these creeping creatures faltered, or fell from their perches, no matter how rapidly they scuttled.

All the while, the pale pygmies spoke not, but signaled to one another with cabalistic signs formed by combinations of their remarkably dexterous fingers and thumbs.

At no time was more than one hand needed to communicate, so at all times, at least one fist gripped a supporting branch.

Once, the ghostly individual in the lead of the hunting party—for indeed this was what the group was—paused and lifted a foot, as if in warning.

The bony toes began to flex, each digit separately forming discernible shapes in the half-light, and making crackling sounds as knuckles and cartilage were flexed.

By this means, too, did the puny tree-crawlers communicate.

Below, and to the west, something was moving through the underbrush. A rank odor filled this part of the foliage.

Had Tarzan of the Apes been present, he doubtless would have recognized the scent. It was a *jato*, the peculiar species of saber-tooth tiger which hunted in the primeval forests of Pal-ul-don, and which also possessed attributes of the mighty lion, being the product of untold centuries of interbreeding among those different species of feline.

The white ones climbing in their boughs froze into immobility and allowed the tiger-striped hunter to pass. A great interval of time passed before animation seized the sharp-eyed leader.

Once again, he employed his long toes to talk.

After completing his semaphore-like foot manipulations, the ghostly leader advanced. Behind him, his squad spread out and advanced as well.

They moved with great cunning, and soon surrounded a gauzy patch that hung high in a great tree, the bole of which was stuffed with short sharp thorns reminiscent of the sandbox tree of North America. But this towering trunk was greater than any sandbox tree that ever lived.

Avoiding the sharp thorns, the white ones surrounded the tree and carefully stepped upon the sturdiest branches, working their way further like pale monkeys, using both hands and feet, inching forward so as not to disturb the diaphanous cloud that hung suspended therein.

When at last they ringed it, the leader lifted a single hand, and closed his four fingers, leaving both thumbs cocked outward. All eyes were upon this gesture.

When the thumbs curled inward, the pygmies leaped as one, and began tearing off great patches of gauze from the clouds.

Writhing in this cottony substance, tiny white creatures awoke to their peril....

Chapter Eleven

CLOUDS OF DANGER

IT LACKED less than an hour before dawn when Tarzan awoke with the clarity that comes from one who dwells habitually in nature.

Although having been immersed in the military life for several months, that interval had not dulled the keen edge which permitted the ape-lord to survive in savage environments, which was a heritage of having been raised among a tribe of great apes when a mere foundling.

Grey eyes snapping open, Tarzan sought the source of the disturbance that had roused him from deepest slumber. The nearly naked bronzed giant soon discovered it.

Close by, Tantor had insinuated his trunk into the dry bedding that cushioned the slumbering ape-man from the hard ground. Gathering up a bunch in a loose loop of his nasal appendage, he brought this to his mouth and began masticating it. Methodically, massive molars chewed the matter into a suitable mash for swallowing.

Sitting up, Tarzan smiled.

"Hungry?"

In answer, the groping trunk sought more grass. Tarzan willingly offered up a clump. This was accepted, conveyed to the eager mouth, and the chewing process resumed.

"Tantor is very hungry," grunted Tarzan.

It was true, for the more grassy matter was offered, the more the elephant gratefully consumed. It was not long before Tarzan's bedding was reduced to shreds of no use to anyone—certainly not suitable to cushion his magnificent form as he slept.

But the Lord of the Jungle had no intention now of returning to slumber. He was up, and having awoken, Tarzan began studying his surroundings.

There was very little light; the tortoise folk probably did not believe in illuminating their little redoubt after they had retired for the evening. Nor apparently did they believe in sentries or guards. For their earthen ramparts with their stony foundation, which sloped down into the tranquil lake, were entirely unmanned.

Padding toward one bulwark, Tarzan bolted to the top, and found a flat surface suitable for defenders, should the need arise. There was nothing like a tower—or even a pillbox—from which a sentry might safely observe the expanse of peaceful lake, alert for interlopers.

Beyond the calm waters of turtle lake, the jungle bulked up, dark and ominous. Predawn breezes stirred the leafy crowns, and here and there came sounds commensurate of prowling beasts.

Tarzan scanned the skies with level eyes, half expecting to see pteranodons or some other devil-winged pterosaur wheeling about. There were none. Other than the stray cloud scudding along in the moonlit air, the skies overhead were cobalt shading into a clearer blue. Here and there, a stray star twinkled, but soon they, too, would vanish in the rays of the rising sun.

The giant of the jungle was enjoying the morning air and the peaceful calm that preceded the waking up of the lake fortress and its stolid inhabitants. He stood waiting for the sun to rise, and when the first smoldering rays crept over the horizon, he turned to face the sun, which was known to him and his ape kin as Kudu.

Tarzan stood in his regulation white cotton drawers, letting the solar warmth kiss his brown hide. He never felt more free than when he had shucked the garments of civilization. To once again don the tight summer uniform of the R.A.F. was not something he looked forward to. But it was his duty to do so and, when the time came, he would.

But for now John Clayton, Lord Greystoke, was enjoying the untrammeled freedom that went with being the Tarmangani—white man to you—who had come to be called Tarzan of the Apes.

A freshening breeze began to blow, stirring his black mane of hair, which was shorn far shorter than his usual custom. Something caught Tarzan's attention. Something in the wind, perceived out of the corner of one watchful eye.

Turning, the ape-man directed his full attention to the thing. He soon saw that there was more than one such apparition blowing in the wind.

For a fraction of a moment, Tarzan thought they might have been pieces of parachute fabric being blown about. His attention quickened.

Very soon, however, the alert ape-man saw that these were not parachute shards. What they were could not be immediately determined. There were several of them, each floating separately and each one coming his way.

They were nothing like he had ever seen before, except that they were fluffy and cloud-like, resembling freshly picked cotton. So far as Tarzan knew, cotton did not grow in the Land of Man. Inasmuch as he had not fully explored Pal-ul-don, the ape-man was forced to reserve hasty judgment.

As he watched, a downdraft seized one of the gauzy clouds, and precipitated it onto the lake's rippling surface. It floated, but soon filled with water just as cotton would absorb moisture. Eventually, it sank.

Tiny specks of white were left behind, like loose cotton batting, but as Tarzan stared, these tiny specks appeared to move in a manner that was not consistent with the wavelets of the tranquil lake.

So intrigued was the ape-man by these wiggling specks that he failed to notice that one of the diaphanous apparitions was blowing his way. It sailed over his head, and drifted into the center of town.

Leaping from the parapet, Tarzan dropped to the ground and raced to investigate. Some instinct caused him to run. His bare feet were virtually noiseless as he coursed through the hard-packed dirt roads of the fortress town.

Climbing to his feet, Tantor the elephant decided to follow. Curiosity is a trait most often associated with monkeys, but elephants also possess it in good measure.

Tarzan had tracked the descending cloud as it wafted its way downward. He negotiated the narrow and crooked trails that passed for streets, and only made one false turn, from which he swiftly recovered by leaping atop a modest residence whose roof was as flat as a kiln.

Spying the cloud, Tarzan saw that it had descended nearest a low adobe structure that he took to be a well dug deep and ringed in stone for drinking water.

The cloud lay there, quivering as if breezes plucked at it. But Tarzan could tell from the way the humid air was moving over his naked skin that the intermittent trembling was not the result of playful breezes off the lake. The gossamer apparition was quivering from *within*.

Leaping off his perch, Tarzan approached carefully, and came to a halt six feet from the shuddering white mass.

The ape-man studied the phenomenon. As he did, he gained the impression of tiny things moving and scuttling within the gauze, but at first he could not make them out. It seemed to his eyes that the entire cottony substance was somehow living, for its animation seemed a quivering of its white heart as much as its fuzzy surface.

Then, something seemed to fall or scuttle out over the edge, followed by another, similar white speck. Others followed suit, and the cloud began disgorging its unpleasant contents.

The crawling things, Tarzan swiftly realized, were fat white spiders, decorated by myriad ebony eyes. They had an unreal quality about them, for they resembled artifacts carved out of pure ivory, except that these creatures moved on eight nervous legs.

With a caution bred from a lifetime of facing unknown danger, the jungle lord stepped back from the advancing arachnids. It registered now that these were spider webs which had been woven high in the jungle, had somehow become torn loose from their leafy anchorage. Tarzan had heard of spiders that spun webs upon which they would ride like magic carpets through the air. But those spiders were tiny, while these things were as large as the first joint of a man's thumb.

There was no reason to assume that they were venomous. But neither could the ape-man exclude the possibility.

Tantor arrived at that moment, and lumbered up to join Tarzan.

At sight of the scuttling spiders, the pachyderm's small eyes grew sharp. He lifted his trunk in warning. The trumpeting Tantor made roused the inhabitants of the fortress town.

Turtle-men came charging and stumbling out of their rudimentary homes, buckling on their tortoise shell armor. Converging on the spot, the first arrivals took note of the gauzy mass and the escaping spiders, and in unison raised their deep-chested voices while simultaneously stamping their staves on the ground.

All over the city, similar staves began stamping, telegraph fashion. Evidently, this was their version of talking drums, or Comanche smoke signals.

Two turtle-men rushed up to the ape-man, and with alarmed gestures of their staves, attempted to compel him to retreat.

They spoke a single word over and over again, *"Burbus."*

Tarzan did not understand the word, but he deduced it was not the term for spider, inasmuch as the nature of the spreading creatures was self-evident to anyone.

Swiftly, a group of turtle-men formed a ring around Tarzan of the Apes, their attitude that of stalwart protectors. Only then did it become abundantly clear that these ivory spiders must be poisonous, and that this might be the meaning of the unclear word.

Tarzan of the Apes was not one to allow other men to protect him, even if their intentions were pure and honorable. It was not the way of Tarzan, who was wise in the ways of self-preservation, to shirk his responsibility to himself, nor to shrink from a mortal threat to his life.

Firmly, but without anger, the ape-man separated two of the thick-bodied turtle-men, and freed himself from their confines. Lifting their heavy voices in warning, they shouted at him, gesticulating for him to keep back.

Advancing, the vanguard lifted staffs and began using them like pistons to pound the spiders into jelly. The skittering things made noisome chittering sounds until they were pulped and pulverized.

At this juncture, Grom, captain of the turtle-men, arrived. In his thick hands waved an ironwood club whose bulbous knob resembled that of the tail of the great tortoise that served as a swimming barge. This was his rod of rulership, it seemed.

Seeing the commotion, Grom rushed in, and began laying about the spiders with his club. The weapon appeared as if it was designed for this purpose, because he needed to strike only once to destroy any spider he targeted.

The panicky arachnids dispersed, seeking cracks and crannies through which to escape the methodical but relentless onslaught.

Watching, Tarzan began to discern the craft behind the techniques of the turtle-men. Two stout fellows had fetched a pot of boiling water, then flung the contents into the gauzy fallen cloud. It quickly began to flatten, then an odor burst from it that was indescribable. It was the wretched stink of scalded spiders.

The turtle-man who had been busy smashing a trio of spiders saw that the spiders were making for the rock-rimmed well, which was not far away.

On heavy feet, he strode over to intercept them. His hardwood staff stamped once, twice, thrice—with the result that all three spiders became blobs of pus from which a radius of broken legs quivered in mindless death.

The fellow lifted his staff, and turned to shout his triumph.

Only Tarzan perceived the fourth white spider creep up on the unsuspecting man's exposed ankle. Sweeping in, the ape-man bent, scooped up a handful of hard earth, and flung it forward.

The clod of dry earth struck the spider, knocking it off balance, and causing it to spin frantically in place in an effort to shrug off the clinging dirt.

Roaring, the turtle-man pivoted, saw the moving clump of dirt, and brought down his staff once, decisively. The dirt became moist and moved no more.

The squat-bodied fellow directed his staff in the direction of Tarzan of the Apes, as if in solemn salute.

However, shrieking came from another quarter. Another turtle-man had found himself surrounded; alabaster spiders were advancing on him from three directions.

This individual was using his club and both feet in a frantic dance designed to evade and crush the approaching arachnids. He was successful to a point, destroying two, but a third suddenly leaped from the ground to a shocking height and landed on his bare wrist.

The man howled horribly, and began shaking that wrist wildly and furiously.

Stubbornly, the spider clung on, and even Tarzan, who was unfamiliar with this particular species of bush spider, realized that the arachnid was not clinging to its victim with its eight legs, but by its *fangs*.

Abruptly, the frantic fellow gave a last wild shriek and toppled forward, fracturing the turtle shell that protected his chest. His entire body began shaking and shivering, as if a tremendous chill was creeping into his nervous system.

The spider that had emptied its venom reservoir into his bloodstream was pinned down by the folding wrist, but was struggling to extricate itself.

Tarzan stepped up, and brought a bare foot down upon the wrist, with the result that the spider burst like an egg breaking open. The yolk was not yellow, but a viscous green....

The ape-man needed no further evidence that the spider was a poisonous thing. Nature often bequeathed such vivid hues to creatures who were deadly.

The sound of Tantor's trumpeting yanked the ape-man's attention around again. For the pachyderm had entered the fray, employing its thick, blunt-nailed pads to press down upon any spider coming his way.

Elephants are not known for their agility, but the dance of Tantor was a thing to behold. Any arachnid that came blundering in his direction met a crushing final fate.

All around the dirt intersection, it was the same. Turtle-men ranged about with single-minded determination, finding and squashing every spider still at large. The ghostly colors of the arachnids made that task relatively simple.

Finally, it appeared that every arachnid had been extinguished.

There was a strenuous effort to ferret out any others which had escaped. But nothing came of this operation.

Presently, the chief of the turtle-men strode up to Tarzan of the Apes and there was a strange look in his eyes.

Tarzan realized that Grom stood stunned by the ape-man's naked brown skin. It was evident the night before that the turtle folk did not remove their armor except to sleep and, no doubt, bathe. They had eaten their feast in their armor, and before they stepped out of their homes, they had donned their personal tortoise shells before investigating.

It became clear to Tarzan that the threat of the clouds of spider webs was not a new one. This manner of ambush had happened before.

Walking to the steaming mass of collapsed spider web, Tarzan made gestures indicating inquiry.

The captain of the turtle-men lifted one broad palm of his right hand, and overlaid it on the other hand in a hand signal that appeared to be fraught with meaning. Grom wiggled forefingers and two thumbs so that Tarzan could see them clearly.

This sign appeared to have great significance to the turtle-men, for others copied the cabalistic gesture. But to Tarzan, it carried no meaning.

While the ape-man was pondering the meaning of these hand gestures, he remembered that this cloud was not the only one to be borne in this direction. Pointing to the steaming web, Tarzan lifted four fingers, then pointed toward the ramparts over which the first floating web had drifted.

The turtle-men seemed to grasp his meaning at once. Lifting his heavy club, Grom barked out swift orders, and the turtle-men charged toward the ramparts.

Others of their kind were pouring out of family homes, wielding staffs, clubs and other implements of war.

Tarzan attempted to follow. Two turtle-men, noticing this, reversed course and tried to block him. They pointed to their shell armor and then indicated his naked chest, as if to say that the ape-man had no place in this form of combat.

Breaking free, Tarzan raced to follow the converging force. The Lord of the Jungle was not afraid of man or beast—and certainly not any mere arachnid that crawled upon the earth.

Chapter Twelve

TARZAN-JAD-OJO

WHEN the force of turtle-men, followed by Tarzan of the Apes and his loyal elephant Tantor, arrived at the ramparts, they discovered that only one other of the gossamer clouds had managed to breach the earthworks barrier.

It had landed in a peculiar spot. The webbing plopped down on the broad horny back of the monstrous sea tortoise that served as a community barge. Already, the first scuttling spiders were emerging, tiny black eyes gleaming.

The titanic turtle slept on, oblivious to this incursion. That the spiders were venomous was not an immediate issue, for no arachnid fangs could hope to penetrate the horny carapace that protected the body of the reptile.

Once the spiders had fully dispersed, however, it would be another matter. The skin of the tortoise was very thick, but no doubt possessed soft spots, and crevices, too, which might be vulnerable to spider fangs.

The great tortoise slept on until the captain of the turtle-men plunged into the mud wallow, leading his men in attack.

What transpired next had its comical side. In snapping awake, the enormous terrapin assumed that he was about to be taken out onto the lake, as was customary.

So while the turtle-men charged for his shell, the great creature began digging in with its flippers to orient itself so that its broad beaked head pointed at the upraised ramp that would be lowered to allow it to slide into the lake.

79

This convulsive movement made it all the more difficult to climb upon the massive shell, since it was now moving. The captain of the turtle-men leapt, missed his step, and plunged backward. Grom made a great splash in the mud, and struggled to rise to his feet as he was nudged by a ponderous tortoise shell spike both fore and aft of his bulky body.

Others had to step in to assist him to his feet.

During this confusion, the scurrying spiders continued to spread over the great tortoise ponderously circling in place, its claws gouging and pushing aside the heavy, encumbering mud.

Arriving behind them, Tarzan took all this in. To leap aboard the shell now would be difficult, if not dangerous. But the ape-man spied another opportunity. Charging in, he scooped up clumps of heavy mud in both hands, and began pelting the white spiders as they crept into view.

The thick matter was as dense as stone, and the first clods dashed two arachnids into ruin.

Seeing this, Grom saw the wisdom of Tarzan's line of attack. Shouting orders, he directed his men to initiate a barrage of mud-slinging. Shouting low-voiced imprecations, they commenced pummeling the tortoise, whose head swung back-and-forth in confusion, for the great reptile did not understand what was happening. This was new behavior on the part of its masters.

But there was no time to be concerned about the creature's dull comprehension, or lack thereof. Working their way around, the turtle-men surrounded their living barge, and continued pelting the spiders who were dribbling off the shell with manic celerity.

More orders were shouted, and before long pots of scalding water were fetched. These were flung atop the tortoise, whose shell still supported the great spider-disgorging web.

In very short order, the back of the tortoise became a heap of steaming mud in which half-seen things wriggled and struggled in their death agonies.

By this time the turtle-ruler had stamped to the head of his armored barge, employing his staff, banging on either side of the turtle's leathery cheeks, then tapping its beak of a nose, causing the confused monster to cease moving.

Orders were given, the great log ramp was lowered by vines.

Then and only then was the tortoise prodded back into life. Scrambling in the mud, which had been depleted, the great reptile slid down to the lake water, splashed vigorously and commenced swimming about.

In this ingenious fashion did it clear himself of the mud and the wriggling things that struggled within the soaked web.

Meanwhile, the turtle warriors stamped carefully around the mud remaining in the pit wallow, pounded it with their poles, seeking any surviving spiders.

Only one specimen was discovered. It was quickly dispatched with a well-timed downward stroke.

Satisfied that the threat had been dealt with, Grom strode up to Tarzan of the Apes and again eyed him in dull wonder. It was clear from his confounded gestures that he thought the ape-man very foolhardy—if not stark raving mad—for entering the fray with no more protection than his cotton drawers and his gleaming brown skin.

Tarzan shrugged his shoulder and said simply, "Tarzan-jad-guru."

To which the turtle captain replied, half under his breath, "Tarzan-jad-ojo."

The ape-man did not understand that last word, but the way it was expectorated from the turtle-man's mouth, he wondered if it might not translate as "crazy."

With that wry thought, the ape-man smiled. For what was he to do? The customs of the tortoise folk were as strange to him as his ways no doubt were to them.

The search of the fortress environs showed clearly that no other airborne web had landed within the confines of the city. This intelligence was relayed throughout the town by telegraphic stampings of staves. It appeared to be a good system, somewhat akin to the smoke signals of the American Indian in its simple effectiveness.

But Tarzan could not read it. He could only surmise what it all meant.

Chapter Thirteen

THE MUMMIFIED CLAW

THE ASSEMBLED group waited stolidly for the great swimming tortoise to rid itself of the muddy burden. The creature submerged several times, obviously fully amphibious, and when it finally surfaced, water running off its horny carapace, the captain of the turtle-men raised his staff and gave out a hoarse bellow three times.

The circling tortoise appeared slow to respond, but that was only because of its great size. It began maneuvering, and finally oriented its beaky snout toward the open ramp.

Swimming directly up to it, the ungainly creature started clambering. The half-log ridges provided certain purchase. On the previous night the tortoise had difficulty in climbing the ramp, but evidently that was due to the added weight of its crew. Having no passengers to be concerned about falling off, the tortoise crawled up the ramp with noticeable agility, finally easing its bulk into the disturbed trough of the mud wallow.

Once back in its lair, it lowered its heavy head, slowly closed wise-looking eyes, and went back to sleep, basking in the early morning sunlight.

Up until this point in his sojourn on the island fortress of the turtle-men, Tarzan had not seen a female of the species. He would have inquired about the missing women, but his still-rudimentary command of their language lacked the female pronoun. Tarzan was stymied at how to address the question.

Once the inner fortress was scoured for signs of any more floating webs, the first children appeared. Both were boys, and Tarzan was amused to discover that they, too, carried tortoise shells on their backs, chests, and as helmets. They lacked only the arm and leg coverings of the adult turtle-men.

The boys approached the ape-man, their eyes round and curious. Tarzan smiled to show that he was friendly.

The boys grinned back, but their smiles lacked warmth, and immediately Tarzan's noble heart went out to them. It seemed that the children of the turtle people were virtual prisoners of their island fortress, at least until they came of age.

The warriors repaired to the great building in which they previously feasted. Still no women appeared, nor were any children allowed within.

Breakfast consisted of eggs, and tough meat that the ape-man quickly realized was terrapin. He was not greatly surprised, for every man and child wore turtle shell, and obviously the meat that once supported those untenanted carapaces had to have gone somewhere.

The food was good. And Tarzan ate slowly. A leisurely hour passed in this fashion. Speech was scarce; the turtle-men seemed preoccupied with the events of the morning.

Tarzan understood that this was not the first time that they had been subjected to a barrage of spider-laden webs. Again, he wondered about that. Less and less, the ape-man considered the possibility that winds had torn the webs from the trees and borne them in the direction of Jad-brang-lul. More and more it seemed as if this was a deliberate act perpetrated by some unknown foe of the turtle-men.

Tarzan searched his memory for those races he had previously met in the Land of Man. This seemed not to be the work of the white-skinned, hairless Ho-don, nor the ebony-skinned hairy Waz-don. Perhaps the brutish Tor-o-don he once encountered were the enemies of the tortoise people. They were similarly built, although very different in their civilization. These turtle-men appeared to be far more advanced than those crude cave-dwelling pithecanthropi who so resembled the so-called "missing link" of evolutionary speculation.

Time perhaps would answer that question, Tarzan thought.

Once breakfast was consumed and the leavings disposed of, a discussion rose up among the tortoise folk. It was quite animated, and Tarzan attempted to follow it with no discernible comprehension. Their speech was too rapid and convoluted for him to do more than make out the occasional word.

One word or phrase that repeated was *"Schara."*

The turtle-men appeared to be discussing the Schara, whatever that was. Something like an argument appeared to rage, and Tarzan pointedly stayed out of it, having nothing intelligible to contribute.

Finally, the chief of the turtle-men stood up, stamped his stout staff once. It appeared to settle the matter. Stalking off, Grom invited Tarzan to follow. The ape-man arose, and padded barefoot after him.

He was escorted to his own hut, and pointedly invited in. Gestures were made that he cover his nakedness in clothing.

Tarzan entered, and methodically donned his R.A.F. uniform, emerging into the full sunlight, once more a British officer—even if the look in his fierce eyes was that of the undisputed Lord of the Jungle.

From the grunting of the waiting turtle-men, this transformation seemed to satisfy them. Grom bid Tarzan to follow again.

Starting off, the procession went to the far southern end of the fortress city. Here an earthen wall bisected the length of the isle's compass. There was a wooden door set in it, and this was methodically and ceremoniously unbolted.

Once the door opened, they were escorted inside and Tarzan saw a section of town that seemed very different from the rude clay dwellings of the menfolk.

The habitations here were more elaborately faced, and Tarzan touched one surface to discover what appeared to be broken shards of dyed turtle eggs used as facing. The designs were pleasing to the eye, and distinctly feminine.

Thus, the ape-man was not astonished when the first females emerged from these ornate dwellings.

"*Schara*," said Grom proudly, and the meaning of the word was at once plain.

Tarzan appraised these females. The women of the turtle folk did not go about armored, although they wore ornaments as women do the world over. These were fashioned of polished tortoise shell. They were beautiful in their way, again as women are wont to be all over the world. Their beauty was not perhaps the beauty of London or Paris, for these women were not delicate flowers. Quite the contrary in that they were sturdy and full-figured, but in a pleasing manner.

They wore their hair upswept and piled on their heads. Makeup was at a minimum, and what could be discerned was artful and understated. Every single woman possessed lustrous dark eyes that reminded Tarzan of the now-closed orbs of the great tortoise.

With his expanded chest betraying his pride, Grom began making introductions, and only then did the womenfolk approach. There were children, little boys and girls, mixed in among the females. They were initially very silent, as if awestruck by the new arrival.

Swiftly, Tarzan was surrounded, and blunt fingers plucked at his uniform sleeves, blouse—even his belt.

These women had obviously never seen a European before, and Tarzan began to suspect they might not have encountered any of the Ho-don or Waz-don of the south either. Their curiosity compelled tapered fingers to explore the fabric of his uniform, and little ripples of laughter emerged from their pale lips.

Firmly, Tarzan placed one hand over the walnut butt of his service weapon. But he neglected to do the same with the hunting knife sheathed on the opposite side of his belt.

One surreptitious hand slipped out the horn hilt. A young woman held it up, staring in wonder at the exposed fang of steel.

Tarzan explained patiently, "It is only a knife."

The women heard his words and feminine heads cocked curiously at the unfamiliar syllables.

Gingerly, Tarzan recovered the blade, which had belonged to the father he never knew, was therefore of great personal and sentimental value. Then the chief of the turtle-men stepped in and stretched out a hand as if demanding to see the weapon.

No harm in it. Tarzan complied.

Grom took the knife by the haft, examined the blade with dark eyes that nearly crossed in curiosity. He grunted several times, and displayed the sharp tooth to the others, who examined it closely and also grunted out their interest. There was a quality to their grunting that made Tarzan think they had never before seen edged weapons.

This seemed highly unlikely, for the turtle-men obviously had employed some type of sharpened tool to make their armor and cut their staves. At the same time Tarzan realized he had not seen a blade or knife or even a spear during his brief time with the turtle folk.

Grom handed the weapon back to Tarzan blade-first, again showing a blatant ignorance of such weapons.

Carefully, Tarzan took it in hand so as not to cut himself, flipped the blade so he was holding it properly, and then tossed the knife swiftly overhand.

The blade of his father flashed through the air, embedding itself in the side of a shell-covered house.

This brought great interest and consternation from his audience.

A turtle-man lumbered over, extracted the knife and attempted to fling it. He did a very poor job of it. The knife tumbled end over end, and dropped into the dirt, hilt first.

Striding over, Tarzan picked up the weapon, repeated his feat of accuracy. The horn handle quivered, its long blade buried its full length in a wall.

This time the turtle-men began pumping their staffs in a way that suggested enthusiastic applause.

Having demonstrated the weapon, Tarzan returned it to its scabbard and attempted to engage the captain of the turtle-men in conversation. He pantomimed the idea of clouds floating overhead and dropping into the fortress, and used his hands to mimic the scuttling of escaping spiders. Then he pointed in all directions as if to ask, "From where did these things come?"

This pantomime soaked in immediately, and Grom directed a command to one of his men. The other left hastily.

The fellow was not gone long, and when he returned he bore something wrapped in rough cloth. This was unwrapped, and Grom held out a grisly object for inspection.

Tarzan saw that it was the bony forearm of a human being. It seemed to belong to a child, but the more he examined it, the more he began to suspect that it belonged to a very small man. Pygmies in Africa do not grow very large, even when fully developed. This reminded him of a pygmy's arm.

It was rather old, obviously mummified, the skin black in a way that even dried dead skin does not darken. Tarzan arrived at the idea that the forearm had been preserved by baking or roasting it.

The fingers of the thing were exceedingly long, but they were also curled up. This prevented the ape-man from immediately noticing the most unusual and distinctive aspect of the talisman.

For while the fingers were half-clenched, they appeared to possess an extra joint. But that was not the most arresting thing about them. One thumb protruded, calling attention to itself. Thus the ape-man was slow to recognize that on the other side of the black palm was a matching jointed bone—an opposite thumb.

Whatever human-like creature that once sprouted this appendage, Tarzan of the Apes realized that the creature possessed six digits!

Chapter Fourteen

THE GIFT

TARZAN OF THE APES returned the mummified forearm, after noting that it appeared to have been hacked off by something insufficiently sharp to do a clean job.

The ape-man pantomimed his curiosity as the captain of the turtle-men rewrapped the relic. With his staff, Grom traced a circle in the dirt, and pitched out four legs on either side of the circle. The meaning of this was abundantly clear. The symbol signified a spider.

"Jad-jinna," he stated firmly.

This confirmed the impression Tarzan had gotten that the cloudy spider webs had been sent by the mortal enemies of the turtle-men. These enemies appeared to be miniature humans, of a species hitherto unknown to the ape-lord. For in all his roaming of the Dark Continent, the Lord of the Jungle had never before encountered any tribe possessing two thumbs. Was the grisly relic a freak of nature, or did these pygmy people all possess an extra digit?

Tarzan's mind flashed back to the unfortunate R.A.F. pilot who had been tangled upon his own shroud lines like a hapless fly in a makeshift spider web. Had the creatures who had sent the spider-silk webs in the direction of the turtle fortress been responsible for that? Were the pale shadows that he had discerned among the trees the previous night specimens of these unknown beings? If so, these were the wielders of the blowguns that had launched the flitting darts that Tantor had shrugged off his rugged, elephantine skin.

It was something to ponder. For there remained two members of the downed transport plane yet to be accounted for. If they had fallen into the hands of the six-fingered pygmies, their survival was very much in doubt.

Tarzan began to make gestures indicative of his desire to leave the lake-bound fortress and return to the forest in search of the missing air crew. Again, he took out his handkerchief and pantomimed a falling parachute.

The captain of the turtle-men listened intently, raised his staff, and commenced another procession. The menfolk followed them out, but the women were obliged to remain behind. Tarzan of the Apes came to the understanding that the unprotected women were not allowed in the main city, but were permanent prisoners of their walled enclave. This did not appear to be an example of any cruelty on the part of the turtle-men; on the contrary, this was their way of protecting their precious females and children, the future of their race.

Tarzan had his own opinion on this matter, of course. The ways of the turtle-men were not the way of Tarzan of the Apes. Besides, he did not command sufficient speech to raise any objection, had he any inclination to do so.

The procession wended its way back to the mud wallow where Tantor waited, flicking flies from his leathery hide with jerking sweeps of his trunk and tail.

Grom brought them at last to the great aquatic tortoise, slumbering in the sun. He turned and indicated certain individuals with his staff of command. When he was done, Grom began climbing back aboard the great shell, signaling for Tarzan to follow.

Slowly, the heavy, wrinkled lids of the sea tortoise began lifting, revealing eyes that somehow suggested ancient wisdom in their deep, dark depths.

The ape-man clambered aboard, taking a position in the center, as the picked crewmen arranged themselves around, and began working their staffs in a strident rhythm, which brought the great turtle turning about once more and clambering for the ramp which was only now beginning to be lowered by two gangs working matched vine ropes.

Where before the sea tortoise had plunged down the ramp with great abandon, now he was more cautious and wary, mindful of his human cargo.

It was not an easy thing to remain balanced atop the tilting shell as the great creature tipped forward and worked its way downward. Tarzan was again forced to kneel and hold on with his steely hands.

The crewmen, built in such a way that they appeared to be almost as broad of width as they were high, had a better time of it. They also possessed staves with which they could balance themselves, by jamming a notched end into the interstices of the horny carapace.

Craning his head around, Tarzan looked back and called on Tantor to follow. The elephant seemed only happy to do so, although he took his time lumbering to the edge of the ramp and then moving carefully downward, swaying as he struggled to keep his majestic body in balance.

The general resemblance of the tortoise to the great crocodile that had previously maimed him no doubt contributed to Tantor's understandable caution.

Soon, both lumbering brutes were in the water and swimming their way toward dry land.

The solar disc by this time was fully up, and the splendor of the day had begun to reveal itself. Night-roosting birds were now aloft, about their daily business.

Tarzan scanned the horizon, once again seeking any sign of parachute silk in the treetops. Now, he also sought any glimmer of silky spider webs clinging to branches. He saw no sign of either.

The turtle-men soon began to cast nets into the water, and hauling back, lifted wriggling silver lake fish aboard. These were permitted to perish in the nets, which were not opened. New ones were cast instead. Soon, they had quite a catch. Fishing appeared to be one purpose of the unique terrapin vessel.

Not surprisingly, the sea tortoise reached the lake shore before Tantor, although the elephant had been churning its thick legs mightily. No doubt it feared lurking crocodiles. But there appeared to be none. This lake, unlike the marsh, seemed not to hold saurians of any size.

This was not surprising to the ape-man, for he reasoned that had any Gimla dwelled in these waters, the tortoise would not have such free rein.

Lumbering like an armored tank, the great reptile pulled himself up onto high ground, and lurched to a stop. It lowered its flat, paddle-like claws, splaying them out to either side, and rested, apparently accustomed to the routine in which it was expected to progress no further than dry shore.

The turtle-men began climbing down, Tarzan following.

There ensued a minor ceremony, although Tarzan did not become cognizant of this immediately. One of the turtle-men removed his shell from his back, and presented it to his captain. Grom, in turn, offered it to Tarzan with a few solemn words.

The ape-man accepted the gift, examining it closely. He saw straps of some kind of leather, to which were attached buckles of bone, and with these he could don the carapace; although it was sufficient to cover his broad back, it would not fit him comfortably.

Evidently, Grom realized this as well. Taking back the shell, he manipulated the straps until they were tied together, then inserted his armored forearm into the webbing. Raising this, he demonstrated that the carapace could double as a shield.

Handing it back, Grom inclined his head. Tarzan accepted it with a nod and a friendly smile. It was not the way of the Lord of the Jungle to rely upon a shield of any type, but to decline a friendly gift might be construed as an insult. So Tarzan accepted the cumbersome contrivance, knowing that he could always dispose of it later.

That appeared to conclude the ceremony.

They waited patiently for Tantor to arrive and when the wading elephant began feeling mushy ground under his legs, he climbed out, stumbling only slightly in the muddy bank.

Once free of the lapping lake, Tantor lifted his unfurling trunk and blew clean water from it. Then he turned his broad head in the direction of Tarzan of the Apes. Their gazes met. No words passed between them, nor were any necessary.

Striding purposefully with the fluid grace of a stalking lion, Tarzan set out upon his quest, mighty Tantor swaying amiably in his wake.

Looking back over his shoulder, the ape-man watched to see if the turtle-men were prepared to join him in the hunt. It was evident upon their broad faces that they were not. Indeed, as soon as Tarzan commenced his ascent, they retreated to their waiting barge. It was clear to the ape-man that they disdained the jungle, and probably rarely ventured from their aquatic existence upon Jad-brang-lul.

Lifting a hand, Tarzan bade them farewell and they called out to him, "Tarzan-jad-ojo."

Once again, Tarzan wondered what that meant in the language of the tortoise folk, and once again the only thing that came to mind was the thought that he might be viewed as mad.

Chapter Fifteen

THE TRICERATOPS

TARZAN struck out for higher ground. It was the ape-lord's firm intention to range the surrounding forest verging the lake of the tortoise folk in search of the missing British transport crewmen for so long as daylight lasted.

The ape-man had gotten an early start, and would not waste it. For Pal-ul-don was a mountainous, gorge-gouged land, cut off from the rest of Africa by a sweeping range of encircling swamp and impenetrable thorn forest. With luck, the other crewmen would have landed not terribly distant from the spot where Tarzan had discovered the dead pilot.

If not, he would have to strike south, and possibly enlist the assistance of the Ho-don or the Waz-don, with whom he had been allies in the past. But the preserves of those tribes lay very far from here, and to seek out assistance would consume precious time. There was no telling what manner of menaces prowled the jungles of these northern reaches. Hours expended in seeking help would be precious time taken away from the urgent duty of rescue.

Tarzan remembered the military identity discs he had taken from the dead aviator, and for the first time took them out and examined the stamped medallions, one red and the other green. The name of the man was Alec Colby. He did not think Colby was the military intelligence agent who was known as Ilex. This man had worn the uniform of a flight lieutenant. Ilex was not attached to the Royal Air Force, which had carried the operative as a passenger.

This meant that the co-pilot, and the mysterious Ilex, were still to be discovered. Tarzan pushed off into the jungle trail, Tantor following majestically behind.

When the elephant had at last reached the dusty lane, Tarzan paused to permit him to catch up.

Giving Tantor a reassuring pat, Tarzan immediately climbed aboard the great brown beast, tucking his knees behind the waving palm-leaf ears. The pachyderm emitted grunting noises of appreciation, indicating that he enjoyed having the weight of his master perched behind his knobby skull.

The ape-man gave no word, merely urged Tantor ahead with but a simple squeeze of both knees. Majestically, the pachyderm lurched forward, and began swaying along the lazy trail. Tarzan's eyes were on the leafy crowns of the trees, the looping lianas, and the brush with their riotous orchids and other tropical blooms. Insects buzzed in the drowsy air.

From his swaying perch, the Lord of the Jungle was seeking signs of parachute silk. He also kept his eyes sharp for the webby clouds that he knew to lie in foamy patches high up in certain great trees.

Tarzan, however, saw neither.

At times, the ape-man stood up whenever he spied something that might be interesting. Things moving in the trees caught his eye, but Tarzan descried nothing remarkable. Sudden movements among the branches invariably turned out to be colorful birds of different types. He recognized some, but not others.

Pal-ul-don, Tarzan knew from past experience, was a place where evolution had produced strange branches and offshoots of mankind. There were the white-skinned Ho-don, who resembled modern man except that they sported long, prehensile tails and possessed hands and feet that suggested the monkey. Their counterparts and occasional rivals, the Waz-don, were hairy and as black-skinned as any African native. They, too, sported long flexible tails.

An intermediate race, called the Waz-ho-don, who were apparently produced by the mating of Ho-don and Waz-don, also could be found in the Land of Man. But Tarzan had not encountered any of that tribe, having only heard accounts of them from the other peoples of Pal-ul-don he had met.

Then there were the tail-less Tor-o-don, who were beast-like humans of a lower order. The turtle-men rather resembled the beast-men, but were more civilized and of a higher and more evolved type.

That other branches of the human race also inhabited Pal-ul-don, Tarzan did not doubt. The evidence of the severed pygmy forearm, which possessed exceedingly long fingers and matching opposable thumbs, remained in the ape-man's mind. He had never encountered beings so strangely equipped. He wondered if they were arboreal in nature.

Tarzan stood balanced against the measured strides of Tantor, turning around, seeking with eyes and ears and distended nostrils any spoor that would impel them to enter the jungle.

It seemed unwise to go among the jungle aisles where Tantor could not follow until a definite trail was detected. If one did not materialize, then Tarzan would be forced to penetrate as deeply as necessary and trust that the loyal elephant would encounter no misadventures during his absence.

That necessity did not immediately arise, however. Instead, a heavy odor made itself known.

Tarzan scented it first, and dropped back into a seated position, slapping Tantor lightly on the great brown dome of his skull saying, "Slowly, slowly."

Obligingly, the great pachyderm slowed to a measured, plodding gait. Tantor lifted his trunk, and his sensitive nostrils began feeling the air like an inquisitive serpentine antenna. Waves of trembling rolled along the muscular elephant's back and rugged flanks. For Tantor did not recognize this heavy scent.

But Tarzan did, which explained his admonition to proceed cautiously.

Casting a glance behind him, the ape-man assured himself that he was not being followed. The jungled lane was not very straight, but its curvatures varied. This was a straight path, but ahead the trail curved to the left.

The sound of footfalls, heavy and dull, next reached their ears. They were coming from around the bend, and with that realization Tarzan commanded his mount to halt. Tantor lurched to a dead stop, tail and trunk alone moving nervously.

They waited. Up ahead, strange animal sounds, mingling impatient grunts along with other beastly vocalizations, told of the approach of something formidable. The earth beneath them did not shake, but the trees trembled.

Detecting this, Tarzan quickly urged Tantor to commence backing up. The elephant was unaccustomed to this command. He did not seem to know what to do.

He turned his great, lowering head, preparatory to pivoting about. But Tarzan gave the broad head a remonstrative smack, indicating that this was not wise.

Confused, Tantor froze in place.

The reason for Tarzan's admonition immediately became clear. For around the bend in the jungle trail crashed a colorful creature, fully as large as the elephant, and perhaps larger in some of its heroic proportions.

The slate-blue thing moved on stubby legs, and its massive crested head was a riot of ochre and crimson. Three long horns protruded from a bony carapace that grew back from its elongated skull like a broad, upcurving shield. Blue rings encircled the glowering eyes that fixed them belligerently above blowing nostrils. The beaked face was yellow, as was the brute's belly. Altogether, the monster stood over a dozen feet high, and over half again as wide.

Tarzan barked out one terse word, *"Gryf!"*

For this was a member of the peculiar species of triceratops that inhabited Pal-ul-don. Built like some prehistoric engine of destruction, it was no mere herbivore, as were the triceratops of the Mesozoic era. This lumbering monster also fed upon raw flesh. Nor was it discriminate in its appetites. A man was as succulent as any animal to a hungry *gryf*.

Eyeing the unfamiliar elephant walking its accustomed path, the triceratops lowered its belligerent head, snorted loudly, and began to charge.

Lifting his trunk, Tantor trumpeted out an alarm. If the strident sound could be translated into human words, it might be understood to demand of Tarzan, "What do we do now?"

Chapter Sixteen

DUEL OF IVORY

DURING his previous exploration of the land called Pal-ul-don, Tarzan of the Apes had encountered many of the three-horned triceratopses. Although wild, some of these prehistoric beasts had been trained by the cavemen of the south as beasts of burden. As such, they responded to a peculiar call voiced by the Tor-o-don.

Long ago, Tarzan learned this call, had in the past employed it to good effect.

As the triceratops lurched forward on its ungainly legs, the ape-lord cupped bronzed hands over his mouth and gave vent to the peculiar cry.

"*Whee-oo!*"

If Tarzan expected the *gryf* to alter its charge, he was greatly disappointed.

The lumbering creature seemed to recognize the sound, for it shook its great bone-frilled head, tossing its long horns and parrot beak. But it did not slow its purposeful advance.

Seeing that a collision was imminent, Tarzan took up the great tortoise shell shield given to him by the turtle-men, and flung it ahead like a discus.

The heavy object sailed true, and dropped between the two jutting horns about the creature's eyes, confusing it. Like Buto, the rhinoceros, which it vaguely resembled, the *gryf* jerked its head about, causing the shield to rattle between its matched long horns, until finally the shell went clattering away.

Resuming its charge, the *gryf* lowered its head, and again in a gesture remindful of a charging rhinoceros, presented its blunt nose horn for what promised to be a savage upward swipe.

This gesture struck Tantor as familiar, for no doubt in his past the brown elephant had tussled with the occasional territorial rhinoceros. For once it recognized this gesture of imminent attack, Tantor flung himself forward, lowering his head, and prepared to meet his squat attacker head on.

Tarzan braced himself for a stupendous collision. It had been his hope to steer Tantor around, and encourage him to make a flanking attack with his great four-foot tusks. For the side of the excited triceratops was relatively unprotected.

But it was too late for such a maneuver now, for animal instinct had seized both behemoths. Primal rage had inflamed them; they were determined to force the issue, to see which would prevail in mortal combat.

The anticipated collision did not come in the way the ape-man expected it. Seconds before the strangely similar triceratops horns and elephant tusks would clash, both animals slowed their stumbling forward gait.

What happened next was less a collision than it was a stubborn, primeval duel. Standing several hands taller than his opponent, Tantor lifted his trunk, and dropped it to one side of the *gryf's* beak-like jaws. Employing this powerful proboscis, he guided the awkward stabbing horns aside, deflecting their attack. Although powerful, this thrust was less an awkward stab than it was an attempt to probe the elephant's jaws and throat for a weak spot.

Determinedly, Tantor thrust the triple-horned head aside, while the triceratops struggled to hook its fore horn into living meat.

Time and again, Tantor deflected it with his heavy trunk, sometimes by the simple expedient of slapping at his foe's tiny, blue-rimmed bloodshot eyes, until the frustrated triceratops broke off this futile form of attack.

From his perch atop the elephant's back, Tarzan sensed what was coming next.

Both animals lowered their heads, and ivory tusks and bony horns crossed, scraped, withdrew and clashed again. The sound was as if hardwood batons the size of trees crashed in contention.

Both behemoths attempted to stab and strike, but the bony skull of the triceratops jerked around to defeat the incoming tusks, catching the curved ivory spears. Conversely, every time the triceratops attempted to drive its twin longhorns into the forepart of the elephant, the pachyderm grasped one or the other of them and, digging in his blunt feet, wrested it aside with a contemptuous gesture.

Animal sounds of frustration began to be heard. Stymied, the triceratops grunted and bellowed in a manner once again reminiscent of a bull rhinoceros. While it possessed tremendous ripping talons, the configuration of its splayed limbs inhibited their use in close combat. For his part, Tantor emitted a strident trumpeting, as if to overmaster the lower grunting of his antagonist.

Tarzan knew elephants well. He had seen them use their broad heads to butt down trees, and then strip the tasty bark with their prehensile trunks. It quickly became clear that Tantor wanted nothing better than to butt heads with the challenging *gryf*. But the prehistoric creature's longhorns made this a dubious goal.

A grunting, clashing stalemate followed. Neither combatant could lunge or stab past the other successfully. The barrier presented by the bony frill which crested up behind the *gryf's* twin horns defeated every effort by Tantor to breach its horny defenses.

Nor could the *gryf* lift its powerful beak, to take a bite out of the elephant's active, serpentine trunk. Every time it attempted to do so, Tantor brought the heavy appendage slapping down, knocking the great armored jaw into the dirt.

Neither monster did any appreciable damage on the other, although the *gryf* at one point nearly lost an eye to one of Tantor's sharp ivory tusks.

Realizing that they were accomplishing little, the two brutes backed away from one another and began regarding his opposite with malign, suppressed fury.

Tarzan sensed that they were girding their mighty muscles for a final charge. It was just a question of which animal would break into mobility, and initiate the first lunging thrust.

Tarzan had held onto Tantor by the viselike muscles of his thighs. The animal's fierce intent communicated itself through his wrinkled hide to Tarzan's powerful leg muscles. Moments before the elephant charged, he would sense it.

Tantor refrained from charging. He stood calm and strangely serene, as if in anticipation of the *gryf's* next action. Only his great ears, one a mere rag of its former majesty, flapped impatiently.

It soon came.

Lowering its formidable tricorn skull, the *gryf* began its charge. The earth shook, dust was kicked up in brownish clouds, yet still Tantor stood his ground.

Tarzan waited with equal patience. If necessary, he would fling himself off to one side, should the elephant fall in battle.

Something wholly unexpected transpired instead. The *gryf*, blue-banded eyes red with rage, pounded on, and as the three horns dipped in anticipation of a powerful upward rip, Tantor suddenly wheeled, lurching to one side, displaying enormous agility for such a stupendous beast.

The triceratops, considerably less agile, blundered on, missing the pachyderm entirely.

Tantor, however, did not miss. As the *gryf* stumbled on past, he reared back, simultaneously swiping at the triceratops while thrusting in with both tusks.

The long ivory spears sank into the splintering ribs of the *gryf* nearly their full length. Lifting its massive head, the enraged pachyderm hoisted the triceratops off its taloned feet, then slammed it down again, driving the air from its laboring lungs and stunning the astonished monster most forcefully.

Backing up, Tantor withdrew, displaying ivory tusks that were a wet, gleaming crimson for half their prodigious length.

The *gryf* let out a howl of pain and confusion that contained an element of bafflement. Plainly, it had never encountered such a foe as an elephant, nor had it ever been ambushed in such a clever way.

Stumbling, the exhausted beast lurched about, its short taloned feet collapsing under him. Folding to earth, it lifted its heavy head in agony and moaned out, but the triceratops, unwilling to accept defeat, attempted to regain his footing.

Tantor would not permit that. First, he lowered his enormous head, and used it to butt the *gryf* further off-balance. The dripping red tusks came in again, sank into the heaving flank, goring it thoroughly, producing unpleasantly moist sucking sounds as blood and flesh were tormented.

Extracting his twin tusks from the fresh wounds, Tantor next brought his ponderous feet up and then down and began to press this enormous weight against the side of the mortally wounded *gryf*.

The heavy triceratops shook its entire body, attempting to organize its stubby legs with their vicious talons and bring them into play, but in that it was thoroughly outclassed. Tantor outweighed it by too much.

Pressing his inexorable weight atop his fallen foe, the elephant employed his coiling trunk to grasp the now-useless nose horn, and by this method he shook the creature's head vigorously.

The *gryf* made a final effort to snap at the trunk with its powerful jaws, but to no avail. It was rapidly weakening from loss of blood, which was now oozing from its blowing nostrils.

As its life fluid flowed from the heaving, gory flank, the *gryf* commenced closing its eyes, and a great shudder shook the thick hide.

Sensing victory, Tantor stepped off his victim, and backed away to observe the *gryf's* remaining will to fight.

No such resolve showed itself. No longer encumbered, the prehistoric monster had lost all strength.

Finally, the dulling eyes closed completely, and a last series of snorting breaths emerged from bloodied nose and mouth. The parrot-like jaw gaped wider, then the creature shuddered and was still.

Seeing this, Tarzan spoke to his long-snouted steed.

"I have in my time encountered many elephants, but none as brave and resourceful as you, Tantor. For this I must call you by a name that recognizes this distinction. From now on, I will address you as Torn Ear."

Thus did Tarzan of the Apes raise this great elephant above the common herd of pachyderms whose individuals he invariably called Tantor. No more would that simple term suit the mighty Torn Ear.

The encounter over, Tarzan urged Torn Ear to continue on his journey. The morning was still new, and their search was only beginning.

Chapter Seventeen

GROVE OF GIANTS

B ALANCING easily atop Torn Ear the elephant, Tarzan of the Apes resumed his quest, his tortoise shell shield lashed behind him.

The jungled lane through which they traversed the thick forest wound its sinuous way in the manner of a lazy snake. Overhead, branches on either side of the way reached out with woody fingers, forming an intermittent canopy interlaced by heavy creepers. In time, the trail began to widen, and widen again, while the awning of greenery ceased to offer significant shelter, and soon petered out.

The open lane devolved into a clearing, in which a sparse cluster of baobab trees reared upward. The ape-lord was naturally familiar with the unusual tree, which was known variously as the bottle tree, the upside-down tree, and the monkey bread tree. Still, the sight that greeted his eyes was remarkable.

In the approximate center of the clearing towered the largest baobab Tarzan had ever beheld in all of his varied travels. One hundred feet high, it reared. Its fat, grotesque trunk shot upward, smooth and brown, until very close to the top twisted branches sprouted, festooned with oval green leaves.

It looked rather as if the tree possessed roots that were growing downward from the sky, plunging its towering trunk into the luxuriant earth like a gigantic wooden stake. Among some of the neighboring natives of Africa it was truly believed that the bottle tree in fact grew upside down. But Tarzan knew better.

The central trunk was stupendous in size, and the satellite trees—of which there were four—were merely gigantic. These lesser giants were formed differently than the great pillar of the central tree. Although great in girth, they were not so tall, and tended to sprawl outward, as if deformed. The branches, too, were closer to the earth, but were no less formidable for all that.

Tarzan knew that these trees were often hollow, and could be tapped for drinking water. Hence, the common name, bottle tree. Too, their smooth bark was of the type that Torn Ear would enjoy munching.

Patting the elephant on his rounded skull, Tarzan remarked, "We will pause here and refresh ourselves."

Torn Ear emitted an inarticulate mumbling, but it could have been the rumbling of his stomach mimicking vocalization.

Majestically, the pachyderm plodded toward the central tree, which Tarzan studied with interested eyes. As they approached, the ape-man noticed something that struck him as unusual. Stretched between several of the crowns, and connected to the central bole, were jungle creepers. Vines were not the product of the baobab tree. Nor were there any nearby growths that might have produced them.

To all appearances, the vines might have been strung there after the fashion of simple rope bridges. Studying this unnatural network, the ape-man noticed a flash of white that appeared to be moving high up in the central shaft. Steering Torn Ear's head around, Tarzan circumnavigated the sparse grove of giants to get a better look at the furtive white object.

It was while doing so that a freshening wind caused the white object to fluff and flutter, and Tarzan's face grew very interested in expression. For there was no question as they rounded the circle of trees that the ape-man had discovered another parachute canopy.

Calling upon Torn Ear to halt, Tarzan leapt off his sturdy perch, strode into the meager shade of the great tree. Shielding his eyes with one hand, he looked upward, and saw the wind-troubled silken mass. No question of what it was now. One of the missing crewmen had had the misfortune to land in the monster crown, far, far above safe ground.

Working his way around, Tarzan attempted to see if the parachutist, or his body, was hung up in the high branches. But he saw no sign of any such unfortunate.

This was a worrisome discovery, for it was nearly impossible for an ordinary man to clamber down that smooth and virtually branchless trunk from such a supreme height.

This strongly suggested that a body hung somewhere above. For Tarzan perceived no sign of footprints in the sandy soil of the weird grove, nor any disturbance that might have been made by a falling body.

Torn Ear approached the tree trunk and, employing his elongated proboscis, began stripping off the soft, delicious bark. Tarzan circumnavigated the baobab, and came to a spot where he discovered a line of pegs which had been hammered into one face of the mighty bole.

The ape-man knew that, in other parts of Africa, honeybees made nests high in the bottle tree, and natives had learned to hammer wooden pegs into its length, in order to form a crude ladder to reach them. No doubt this was the case here.

The pegs were quite small, and did not make for the most convenient hand or footholds, but the ape-man judged that they would support his weight, provided he distributed it among two or more pegs.

Casting a glance in the direction of Torn Ear, and seeing that he was contentedly munching harvested bark, Tarzan commenced his climb. He soon discovered that climbing the line of pegs was more difficult than he had first imagined.

Dropping down, he tried again. Leaving his boots and socks behind, and removing his other clothing, the ape-man resumed scaling carefully. The manner of his ascent was to keep one hand and one foot always upon a peg, reaching upward, pulling with his free hand and simultaneously pushing with a moving foot, thus gaining height in steady increments.

Here and there a peg broke off under his weight, forcing him to hold on or scramble higher. Tarzan began to appreciate the fact that the people who had built this crude ladder of dowels were certainly not large individuals.

A third of the way up, the ape-man was forced to halt his progress, for more and more of the pegs proved to be unstable.

Once, after two pegs dropped out beneath his bare feet, the ape-man was nearly precipitated thirty feet to the hard ground below, saving himself only by dint of his steel-thewed grip, which held tight to one peg while, with his free hand, he took out his knife and embedded it into the trunk, creating a more reliable hand hold. It would not be practical to continue climbing, even using the blade in this manner. Reluctantly, the ape-man gave up his ascent.

Removing the knife, he dug it in again further below, repeating the process until solid pegs again supported his bare toes.

Transferring down backward, Tarzan found his feet back on Mother Earth, and stared upward, seeking to measure with his eyes if another try was worth the peril entailed. He could not see anything more than the fluttering white silk, but the sparseness of the upper branches more and more looked to him as if they could not possibly conceal a full-grown man.

Yet no matter how far he ranged in the clearing of trees, the Lord of the Jungle could find no sign of footprints or other spoor indicating that a missing parachutist had escaped.

Could it be that the unfortunate aviator had managed to work his way along one of the vines to another tree, and then to the jungle floor and safety?

Studying these taut lines, Tarzan decided that was unlikely. The vines might or might not be sufficiently sturdy enough to support a fully grown man, but to reach them would require a downward climb of at least twenty feet.

The more he investigated the clearing, the more the ape-man felt confronted by an impenetrable mystery. As he continued his investigation, Tarzan noticed other strange things. For one, no birds roosted in the high, twisted branches of any of these massive trees. Beyond the clearing, they twittered and circled other, lesser, trees. For some unfathomable reason, the local avian population appeared to shun the great, isolated bottle trees.

Sniffing the air, the ape-man could discover no reason for this. While large and impressive, this collection of trees did not appear to harbor anything inimical to the winged creatures. He wondered if this weird grove was what Grom, captain of the turtle folk, had sketched in the dirt and called Jad-jinna-gar. The jungle lord thought it likely.

Finally, Tarzan decided to take another approach. Stepping into the thick jungle, he rooted around until he found a suitable vine from which to make a rope. Hacking a healthy specimen at both ends, he fashioned a lariat at both ends and, draping this around one brawny shoulder, the ape-man padded back to the tremendous central tree and began mounting the fragile ladder of pegs once again.

Having ascended a third of the way before, Tarzan was able to move more rapidly, for he knew which dowels were weak and which were strong. When he reached the gap that had earlier defeated him, the ape-man rested, and then attempted to cast his lariat higher.

It was a very awkward thing to do, inasmuch as Tarzan needed to rest both feet and one hand on pegs, but after three tries, he snared one considerably higher up. Drawing the line down, he closed the loop of the lariat, tested its pull, and found that it would hold.

Now Tarzan let go of the pegs, and climbed hand over hand until he reached the supporting noose. Testing different pegs with his dangling feet, he found two that would support him, and transferred his one-handed grip to another strong dowel above his head.

Releasing the fiber rope with one hand, he reached up and found the noose, then released it by severing it with his knife. It dropped free, whereupon Tarzan caught it before the line could fall to the ground.

The loop he had earlier fashioned at the other end had remained intact.

Once again, the ape-man cast his lariat upward, finally snaring a stubby branch that had been maimed by a wind storm, leaving only a short stump. Releasing his grip once more, he climbed the rope hand over hand, employing the powerful muscles of his upper body.

Like an agile monkey, Tarzan made his way up to the lowermost branches, and there crawled onto a perch. From this lofty vantage point, the ape-man could survey the twisted branches that grew all around him.

There was no one up here. No one and no thing. Not even any specimen of the coconut-sized bottle tree fruit, which tasted like grapefruit and vanilla. Only the parachute fabric which had become tangled in such a way that it was reduced to a fluttering blob of white.

The parachute harness dangled from this and appeared to be intact. To the ape-man's surprise, the man who had come down in this particular parachute had apparently extricated himself.

But the mystery remained. Where could he have gone? If he had worked his way down the wooden pegs—which would seem to be a remarkable feat for anyone other than Tarzan of the Apes—surely he would have created or left spoor on the ground below. Yet there was no spoor.

Nor was there any sign of breakage among the branches, as would be expected if a man had landed among them. It was very puzzling, and led to a nearly inescapable conclusion—that the owner of the parachute had landed elsewhere and his rig conveyed to this high crown for some obscure reason.

Crawling out along the branches, Tarzan came to the billowing parachute fabric, and pulled it free. To his surprise, he discovered it was entirely intact. This gave Tarzan an idea.

Donning the harness rig, the ape-man stood up, and walked out to the furthest extent of the thickest branch that would support him. It was quite thick.

Holding the parachute silk bundled under one arm, Tarzan considered the drop. One hundred feet was not very high for a parachute drop.

As R.A.F. Flying Officer John Clayton, he had extensive parachute training. Twelve thousand feet was considered a safe height from which to bail out of an airplane. This, to create a margin of safety in the regrettable but not entirely unavoidable event that the main parachute should malfunction and it became necessary to deploy the reserve canopy.

Tarzan was considering whether to jump, relying only upon the reserve chute, which was still packed in its pouch, when a freshening wind sprang up.

It was a strong blow, no doubt created by wind currents colliding with the vast mountain ranges that separate the deeply-riven lowlands of Pal-ul-don. But it gave the ape-man a better idea than the risky one he had, out of sheer necessity, been contemplating.

Retreating to the leafy, tangled crown, Tarzan arranged the great expanse of silk in such a way that it began to fill with blowing wind. This took careful manipulations, but gradually the silk expanded and expanded until it became difficult to control the billowing, wind-rippled bell.

Paying out the shroud lines, he let the canopy lift like a great silken kite. Soon, the lines were tugging at Tarzan's strong hands, pulling him along.

Simultaneously racing along a gnarled branch, the ape-man, clutching fistfuls of line, stepped off into space.

Down he fell, with the parachute silk billowing overhead like a great mushroom wheeling in the sky.

The expanding canopy of a deployed parachute will make a sound like a thunderclap when it finally filled with air. No such sound came, although Tarzan listened for it from sheer habit. For the bell was already yawning wide. The sound the ape-man half expected to hear was the crack of the silk splitting open under the sudden strain of his weight. But what he truly feared was the possibility that the unstable bell would spill air from one pale lip and collapse.

Below, Torn Ear stared upward with small eyes growing round. Lifting his trunk, he blared out a scream of surprise and alarm.

It appeared to the frightened elephant as if his master were falling to his death!

Chapter Eighteen

CONUNDRUM

TARZAN OF THE APES fell to the sandy ground smack onto the soles of his bare feet, jarring his entire body from ankles to the crown of his magnificent head. He rolled with the impact, until he came to a stop, arrested by canopy lines which soon tangled his lean limbs. The silken parachute canopy fluttered down to cover him like a settling white shroud.

With his knife, the ape-lord cut loose of the entangling lines and silken mass, and found with grim satisfaction that he had no broken bones. He had collected some fresh scrapes and abrasions along his splendid physique, but what were a few more scars to the mighty Lord of the Jungle who had cheated death so many times?

The parachute had retained its fully open shape long enough to break his fall—although it had been a near thing. For, during the downward plunge, air had begun spilling from the skirted edges, precipitating the beginnings of a collapse of the unstable, deflating bell. Ironically, the abbreviated fall had prevented a total collapse. A longer plunge might well have resulted in disaster.

Shrugging off such now-trivial considerations, Tarzan struggled out of the harness, tossing the heavy canvas rig aside.

The desperate maneuver was not as foolhardy as it might have seemed. Even if the canopy had not filled to its maximum, the ape-man had reasoned that he could pilot even a partially buoyed bell into the branches of a lesser bottle tree, thus snagging one, and permitting him to climb down from a safer height.

Provided, of course, that the frighteningly short drop permitted him the luxury of such a risky move. Deploying the reserve chute was out of the question if not done immediately upon jumping.

Torn Ear came lumbering up to investigate. His corrugated trunk quested about Tarzan's lithe form, as if in sympathy.

"Tarzan is intact, Torn Ear," the ape-man informed the elephant.

He cast a wary glance about him, and more than ever his sun-bronzed face wore an expression of puzzlement. For in his investigations Tarzan had discovered no honeycomb or bee nest among the high branches. It might be that the pegs had been placed there very long ago, and the bees removed entirely. He also knew that some baobab trees were hollow, but nowhere in his climb did he spy any sign of a cavity or other entry that would permit a man to enter into any hollow space the bole might harbor.

This further suggested that the missing parachutist had not landed among the leafy branches of the treetop. But the ape-man had to be certain.

It would be all but impossible to explore the entire circumference of the trunk, and its daunting hundred-foot height, so Tarzan cupped his hands before his mouth and gave voice to a loud roar, calculated to rouse into wakefulness anyone who might be so concealed.

The outcry went unanswered. Tarzan did not repeat it, for it was not necessary.

Abandoning the mystery, Tarzan and Torn Ear pressed on. The day was already half expended and, while the ape-man had discovered one clue as to the fate of a surviving crew member, that clue regrettably led him in no specific direction.

It would be up to Tarzan of the Apes to pick up the spoor, if any such existed. So he pressed on, the loyal elephant lumbering behind him.

Many miles they ranged, and many hours passed in the heat of the day as they proceeded along the jungle lane into which pressed the common trees of Africa, the breadfruit and the thornwood, among others, growing in unchecked profusion in Pal-ul-don.

Once, Torn Ear paused to abide by a small pool of water, and Tarzan halted so they did not become separated. It was then that he noticed a slim thorn dart that had embedded itself in the elephant's rolling rump. It was tipped in white—evidently with a tail feather plucked from a tropical bird.

Going to it, the ape-man removed the barb carefully, sniffed the tip, and broke it in twain. Scowling, he drove the poisoned end deep into the earth, so that no animal or person would come to harm by it.

Tarzan looked about cautiously. Somewhere in the last few hours, that dart had been sent in the pachyderm's direction, but accomplished nothing. So swiftly and silently had it been unleashed, even the keen senses of the ape-man had not picked up on the cowardly act.

Frowning, Tarzan reached up and removed the tortoise shell-shield which had been balanced on Tantor's corrugated back. Knowing that he had no other defense against a sneak attack, the ape-man pressed on, keeping the sturdy carapace at the ready, thankful that he had not discarded it, as was his earlier intention.

The monotony of the day was broken when an antelope flashed into view, crossing the trail, and darting back into a woody glen on the opposite side.

Now Tarzan of the Apes had not eaten since breakfast and that repast had not been entirely satisfactory, owing to the fact that it had consisted of turtle meat and the associated eggs.

Descrying the tawny flanks of the nimble antelope reminded the Lord of the Jungle of how long it had been since he had consumed fresh meat. Months, as reckoned by the calendar. During the period of his military training, a great deal of what he had eaten had come out of tin cans. Nourishing fare, perhaps, but wholly unappealing to uncivilized tongue and palate.

Without warning, the ape-man sprang from his surprised steed and padded after the unwary creature, the hunting knife of his father flashing in the sun.

In a matter of minutes, his intelligent eyes alighted on the tawny coat, whereupon they grew narrow and feral. Creeping toward his intended prey, Tarzan leaped at the last, falling upon the gentle creature's throat.

One steel-thewed arm seized the struggling neck. The blade plunged downward once—but once was sufficient. With a short bleat of astonishment, the antelope was conquered.

Kneeling beside the kill, Tarzan of the Apes cut out a section of haunch and devoured it raw, enjoying the warmth of the flesh and allowing the red juices to run down his chin and throat.

Once the last pangs of hunger were satisfied, the ape-man cleansed himself at a still pool of water and returned to the patient Torn Ear, mounting him once more.

Feeling more alive than he had in a good long while, Tarzan resumed his search, fortified in body and soul.

DUSK began falling and twilight made its initial appearance. A quiet commenced as the birds of the day came to roost and fell silent in their tree boughs. Insects grew scarce.

Tarzan and Torn Ear pressed on, but the trail had gone cold. Before long, the noises of rushing water invited their interest.

Working toward it, the pair soon came to a dark cleft in the earth, on the opposite side of which rushed a mighty waterfall.

The ape-man was familiar with the great gorges that cut through the central and lower portions of the Land of Man.

This was another such declivity, one he had not explored during his previous visit. It was narrow and jagged, forbidding in a way the wide Kor-ul-gryf—the Gorge of the Gryf—to the south was not. It appeared to be a rift in the earth, a fissure such as might have been created by a cataclysmic convulsion of antiquity, for it was exceedingly narrow except where it widened at the point where the torrent of rushing water formed a turbulent pool on the otherwise-barren ravine floor.

Dropping to his stomach, the ape-man thrust his head over the cliff, and peered downward. It was quite sheer, and to climb down would have been no easy task. Tarzan might have braved it, but it would have meant abandoning Torn Ear, and since the dirt trail down in the ravine held no particular promise, he decided to abandon this track.

Climbing back to his feet, Tarzan signaled Torn Ear to follow him, for he decided to retrace his footsteps, having reached an apparent dead end.

Twilight brought out a jeweled sprinkling of stars overhead as the cobalt sky of evening turned into the velvety black welkin of the African night.

They worked their way back, trudging for over two hours, during which Tarzan decided to make camp in the clearing of the baobab trees, there being no other suitable spot by his reckoning.

The moon was up by the time they reached that clearing, and Tarzan entered first. It had been his thought to salvage the parachute canopy and rig a makeshift shelter from it, should the night be plagued by tropical rains. But when he located the spot where he had left the parachute pack, it was no longer there.

Something stirred in the sandy soil, however. Kneeling, the ape-man laid interested eyes upon a disturbed spot. Picking up a pebble, he dropped it onto the patch of sand experimentally.

Instantly, a sand-colored spider emerged. Wriggling its eight legs frantically, it swiftly and expertly reburied itself, and was soon invisible to the naked eye.

It was a six-eyed sand spider—a species Tarzan knew to be mildly poisonous and which laid in ambush for passing prey, obscured by its natural hue and propensity for concealing itself with cunning camouflage.

Rising to his feet, the jungle lord resumed his investigation and soon discovered the missing bundle of silk wedged into the hollow of a breadfruit tree beyond the grove of giants. Pulling it free, he discovered that the canopy had been severed from the parachute pack, which was missing. The shroud lines were also gone.

By moonlight, Tarzan examined the sandy ground around the grove, but other than the padded prints of Tantor and his own bare feet turning into boot prints, there were no signs of who might have made off with the canvas pack.

"Another conundrum," murmured the ape-man.

His grey eyes lifted and swept the grotesque and dizzyingly high branches of the tremendous baobab tree, which looked like a clenched fist of roots thrust high in the sky.

If there was an answer to the riddle in those stunted upper boughs, Tarzan of the Apes failed to discern it.

Chapter Nineteen

WHISPERING DEATH

GORO the moon was peeping through the leafy foliage and the wind murmured intermittently as Tarzan of the Apes prepared to make camp for the evening.

The ape-lord employed his long-dead father's hunting knife to fashion from the section of parachute canopy a suitable hammock. With this, he cut out a great bolt of silk with the intention of stringing it between the upper branches of one of the lesser trees to form the sling.

It was during this work that Tarzan discovered the solitary footprint impressed upon the soft earth beneath the parachute fabric.

At first, the ape-man took it for a monkey's paw. For it was strangely formed. Insufficient moonlight helped to trick his otherwise keen eye.

Kneeling there, Tarzan studied the print and, in spite of himself, felt the hackles at the nape of his neck begin to rise. This was not fear, but the instinctual reaction to a phenomenon unknown to the Lord of the Jungle.

While the footprint was small like that of Manu the monkey, and the toes splayed in simian fashion, Tarzan soon realized the print was human. And yet, at the same time it was not completely human. For the splayed outer toe was matched on the other side by an identical crooked member.

Tarzan's memory flashed back to the mummified hand which had possessed two thumbs. This small foot was like that. Removing the parachute, Tarzan studied the ground more closely, but that solitary footprint was all he discovered.

The ape-man looked upward, and saw only one of the lianas which stretched between the great baobab tree and one of the lesser specimens.

Frowning, Tarzan tried to imagine how a solitary footprint could impress itself upon the earth, without there being any other spoor. But no explanation came to mind. It was a profound mystery.

Gathering up his makeshift silk hammock, Tarzan went to the lesser tree that seemed most suitable in which to pass the night. It, too, boasted a ladder of pegs, ones sufficiently sturdy to climb safely. Torn Ear followed him a short distance and, as Tarzan ascended the trunk, the hammock slung over his shoulder, the elephant ponderously rolled over and lay down to sleep, all four legs stretched out.

At the base of the great trunk, Tarzan had once again divested himself of his khaki uniform, and folded it so that it could be stored in a makeshift bag of parachute fabric. He tied this tight.

Climbing the tree was difficult, but Tarzan managed it. Once he reached the top, he strung the parachute fabric hammock between two stout limbs. The top of the tree was somewhat rounded, but it permitted him to do his work.

Hanging the bag of clothes on one branch, Tarzan crawled into the hammock, there to pass the evening.

The ape-man was not one to lie awake for long. Once he had settled in, the sounds of the jungle disturbed him not. Yet as he lay upon his back, staring up at the rising moon, sleep did not come.

Tarzan was not the nervous type of city dweller, who tosses and turns before slumber reluctantly embraces him. Once his mind told him that he was safe, sleep almost always came rapidly.

On this night, high in a strange tree in an even stranger grove, Tarzan of the Apes failed to fall asleep. Some instinct, possibly a primordial sixth sense, prevented Morpheus from visiting him.

Tarzan lay quietly, his eyes closed, listening intently. He tasted the air with his sensitive nostrils, but nothing untoward or unusual wafted his way.

Below, Torn Ear was quiet. Slumber had already come to the loyal pachyderm.

As Tarzan listened, he detected a stirring. This new sound was hollow and muffled. As he focused upon it, the ape-man heard curious noises that he could not place.

Sitting up abruptly, his grey eyes snapping open, Tarzan looked about his immediate environment. Nothing unusual seemed at hand.

Balancing carefully in his hammock, he peered downward. Below, in the moonlit dark, nothing seemed to move. Even the tree shadows were still.

More subtle noises came, reminiscent of insects at work, and these brought the sharp attention of the ape-man skyward.

Grey orbs searching, Tarzan soon discovered their source. The sounds were coming from the great bottle tree which he had previously climbed. High up in the mighty tree, amid the root-like branches. Tarzan watched them closely, but they were not restive. So it was not the night wind making the odd commotion.

Knowing that the baobab tree was naturally hollow, the ape-man began to wonder if some voracious species of termite or other tree-dwelling creature was stirring within the great and mighty trunk.

Studying the weird branches, Tarzan saw something vague and pale in the moonlight: a long reedy arm, ending in unnaturally long fingers. Something about those fingers smacked of the uncanny. In a moment Tarzan realized what it was. The tiny hand boasted not five, but six fingers!

A round head popped up and it was as bald and pale as a cave mushroom. Dark eyes gazed about, studying his sleeping elephant one hundred feet below. Then they came to rest on the pale sling of white silk in which the ape-man sat balanced.

The dark eyes went wide, and narrowed again. A long, jointed tube resembling bamboo suddenly appeared, clutched by two six-fingered hands. The barrel pointed his way.

Tarzan had had the foresight to carry his tortoise shell shield up into the bottle tree, strapped tightly across his broad back. He had used it as a lid to cover and protect his bundle of clothing in case of jungle rain.

Now with the air full of sharp whispers, Tarzan sprang from his hammock and lurched for that protective shell. Naked as he was, the ape-man knew he had no protection against poison darts. Only the knobby shield could afford him that.

Tarzan reached the top of the trunk in one springy leap, seized the clumsy shield by its straps, and swung it up before him.

The sinister whispers slipping through the moist night air continued apace. A new sound was heard—an intermittent ticking, as something struck the shell time and again.

Similar soft sounds followed, persistent as striking hail. Soon, Tarzan was sheltering beneath a veritable rain of hunting darts. They arrived so rapidly he knew more than one blowpipe and more than one six-fingered attacker sought to bring him down.

Stealing a glance around one edge of the shell, Tarzan spied numerous bulbous white heads bristling atop the mighty baobab tree like sinister fruit. Equally alarming, some of these creatures were slipping along the strong lianas, like spiders upon their own silken webs, toward his own tree.

It was clear that the top of the central tree had opened up in some fashion to disgorge these creatures. Having spied Tarzan of the Apes, they were determined to lay him low. Some pointed fat bamboo blowpipes, others wielded thin reed blowguns, which necessarily had a shorter range. The former weapon fired reed quills, while the latter spat thorny darts. All were tipped in white.

Tarzan had no weapon at hand suitable for fighting back. His service revolver hung in the bag of clothing. If he could extract it, he could account for several of these man-things. But the relentless rain of missiles prevented him from availing himself of that resource.

As he hunkered down, not daring to move lest he expose bare flesh to the swift-flying poison-tipped missiles, the ape-man observed with quick glances pale pygmy people dispersing themselves among all the trees via the web-like lianas and vines obviously strung there for that very purpose.

Soon, Tarzan grimly realized, he would be surrounded. It was perhaps one of the most difficult positions in which the ape-man had ever discovered himself. This sheer tree trunk did not permit easy descent. Nor were the surrounding branches sufficient to allow him to swing to an adjacent tree.

Even if those feats had been possible, Tarzan could not perform any of those actions while he was under the relentless assault of poison darts. Soft sounds they made cutting through the night air. The way they struck nearby branches, their feathery tails bright in the moonlight, told the ape-man that he could not move one jot without being brought down.

Keeping the sturdy turtle shell before him, Tarzan saw out of the corner of one eye two of the spidery white pygmies performing a flanking action by slipping down to one of the lesser trees.

They reached the twisted limbs there, found perches to which they clung monkey-like with their six-digit paws, then brought to bear the long, barrel-like bamboo blowpipes.

Tarzan shifted his shield, and intercepted the first of the arriving quills. A second barrage struck with tiny tick-tick-tick sounds. The night air became busy with whispers of sudden death, sounding as if some subtle and sinister forest demon were calling his name—summoning him to his death.

Switching his shield back and forth, the ape-man was successful in intercepting every hissing missile that came his way.

But he knew he could not long keep this up. What was more, one of the white pygmies had managed to slip down another tree, and now he was surrounded on all sides.

Seeing the way of it caused Tarzan to make a decision. He had coiled his lasso beside his bag of clothing and now he reached down to grasp the loop with one brown hand.

Standing up, Tarzan left the shield atop the bundle and lifted both strong arms, saying in the language of Pal-ul-don, "Tarzan-jad-guru surrenders to you."

Whether the creatures understood him or not, there came a cessation of white-tipped darts.

Chittering sounds could be heard—sounds that might have been a language, or the clacking of mandibles created by great insects. Whatever the noises were, they were not understandable to the ape-man.

Under the burnished moonlight, many pairs of black button eyes steadily regarded Tarzan of the Apes, whose frank grey gaze was returned in full measure. No one moved.

The liquid orbs of the spider people reflected an alien curiosity. Then, peeping out from the top of the great hollow central tree, emerged one of the ghostly creatures, whose dark eyes were matched by luminous spots on his shaven forehead, giving him the aspect of a deformed spider with eight blank eyes.

This alien being studied Tarzan of the Apes for a long interval. Then, pointing in his direction, he screeched out a single syllable.

Blowguns lifted to tiny mouths, and lungs resumed working with breathless speed, but the ape-man was faster still.

Employing his lariat, Tarzan snagged a nearby branch, and leaped into space, clutching the vine in a double-handed grip.

A dozen pale cheeks puffed in and out. Then the air again became filled with the soft whispers of searching death.

Chapter Twenty

HOLLOW TRAP

TARZAN OF THE APES opened his steely-grey eyes in an utter and irredeemable darkness.

The ape-lord sensed that he was confined. No breeze touched his bare skin, and the air entering his nostrils was not fresh. Rather, it was filled with odors that reminded him of old wood and decaying vegetable matter. The stifling air entering his nostrils was moist and cloying.

Searching his memory, Tarzan recalled leaping into space on the vine rope that he had trusted to take him to safety.

Tarzan's plan had been a simple one. To swing downward as rapidly as possible, avoiding the blowgun darts of the white pygmies, until he reached the end of his rope, then to drop the rest of the way through empty space to the cushioning back of Torn Ear the elephant.

His plan had worked well enough. The ape-man's feet smacked the broad back of the Tantor, after which Tarzan had momentarily lost his footing and rolled off, landing harmlessly on the ground.

Leaping to his feet, the ape-man had positioned himself behind the rousing pachyderm, whose thick, corrugated hide stood immune against all barbed missiles thus far launched against him.

As proof of the soundness of his plan, Tarzan saw in the moonlight tiny quills sprouting magically from Tantor's wrinkled brown back.

The elephant was moved to climb to his feet, but at a whispered admonition, he settled down.

The air soon filled with the weird whisperings of seeking darts.

Hunkered down, Tarzan searched the treetops all around. Purely by accident, he had seen, out of the tail of his eye, the white fletching of a tiny dart protruding from his left shoulder.

The ape-man had only time to pluck it free when his senses swam, and a cold darkness soon crawled across his brain. After that, Tarzan knew no more until awakening in this strange Stygian blackness.

As his eyes adjusted to the dark, the ape-man slowly perceived luminous white patches here and there. His eyes shifted from one to the other and soon saw that they were all about him. They appeared to be very near. Looking up, he began to spy other leprous patches, which were remindful of the spots of Sheeta, the leopard. Except that they were white, not black.

Tarzan began to conceive the idea that he was held in a pit of some kind. From the way the ghostly patches receded above him, the pit was exceedingly deep. Evidently, it was capped at the top, inasmuch as no shred of moonlight showed directly above him.

Attempting to move, the ape-man discovered that he was bound in some fashion. Wrists were held tightly together, and there was a noose about his ankles that appeared to be affixed to the hard surface against which he had been propped. The floor under his feet was rough and uneven. Against his naked skin, it had an unpleasantly granular feel.

Tarzan set his mighty thews to break free of his bindings. But to no avail. Whatever material comprised the lashings, they stretched only so far and no more.

Again, the ape-man sniffed the air, attempting to determine his whereabouts. He did not appear to be standing on soil, but on some other form of matter. The more he sniffed the air, the more he had an impression of moist moss or lichen. No doubt the white patches were some form of luminous plant growth.

It seemed possible, by bracing his spine against the hard surface and straightening his knees, to work himself up into a standing position. Tarzan proceeded to do so.

Turning to face this wall, he rubbed his bare chest against pale patches until it was smeared in luminous white. The illumination thus shed was feeble, but it was better than nothing.

Slowly, Tarzan turned around again, making a circuit of the confined space in which he had been cast by creeping along on his bound bare feet, for the noose that confined them was long enough to permit some lateral movement.

The wall curved around until he reached the spot where he originally stood. The warmth left by his bare feet on the floor told him this.

Mentally calculating the number of paces he walked, the ape-man came to a different conclusion than what he had originally conceived. He was now certain that he had not been cast into some foul pit, but consigned to the hollow of one of the baobab trees—apparently the largest of the group.

It was now clear to him that the spidery white pygmies had emerged from this very space in the dead of night by means of some sort of lid that had been cut into the top of the hollow trunk. This suggested that there was a way up, if only he could free his hands and feet and avail himself of it.

Tarzan lifted lashed wrists to his face. The luminous matter on his chest helped illuminate the situation. He saw that the bindings consisted of multitudinous strands, which in combination gave the bonds great strength. They were not rope, nor vine, but some other organic material with which he was not familiar.

Because the lashings were woven from smaller threads, the ape-man took a segment of this experimentally between his strong white teeth. He began to chew. This substance tasted strange, rank. The stuff was exceedingly tough, but by methodical jaw action, Tarzan parted first one strand, then another, and soon a third.

It was difficult and unpleasant work, but over time his teeth prevailed against the binding strands. When he had parted sufficient numbers of them, Tarzan was able to separate his wrists, flexing his muscles, finally snapping free of his wrist lashings.

Sitting down, he went to work on the noose that wrapped around his ankles. These he attempted to pick apart, but the going was even slower.

Feeling around the dark, the ape-man found something hard and rocky. Taking it in hand, he smashed it against the floor under his feet until it broke, producing crude but sharp shards.

Thereby Tarzan sawed his way through the bindings, eventually freeing one ankle, and then the other.

At last, he stood up. His eyes had by now fully adjusted to the absence of natural light, and he began feeling his way around the base of his confinement.

Tarzan soon discovered a small notch cut into the interior wood of the hollow tree. Feeling about, he found several other notches both above and below it. They seemed to constitute finger- and toe-holds and, while they were meant for a much smaller individual than the strapping ape-man, his great strength enabled him to begin a careful ascent.

The notches were perfectly and closely spaced, so that even in the absence of light it was a simple matter to find reliable purchase and climb up effortlessly.

Tarzan knew that he had reached the top when his hair came into contact with something hard like a ceiling. Balancing on two feet and one hand, he reached overhead with his free fingers and attempted to push upward.

Nothing happened at first, and the ape-man moved his hard palm about, seeking leverage.

Abruptly, the roof lifted and Tarzan continued his climb, pushing upward with the back of his neck and shoulders until he found himself crawling out on a stout, root-like limb.

Behind him, the cunningly contrived lid of the hollow tree dropped back into place, showing no sign or seam of its existence.

Tarzan had stood on this very spot several hours before and failed to detect the cunning artifice. For here, in truth, he stood atop the giant among the great bottle trees, one hundred dizzying feet above the jungle floor.

How the spider pygmies had conveyed him to their lofty aerie defied reason, but Tarzan, in examining his tremendous physique, discovered rope burns beneath both bronze arms, and that mystery was partially resolved—but only partially.

Looking down, the ape-man discerned Torn Ear walking about in an agitated manner, swinging both tail and trunk aimlessly. The need to preserve silence constrained Tarzan from calling down to the faithful animal.

There was only one certain way down: via the wooden pegs that had barely supported the ape-man on the way up. And now he had no rope by which to aid his descent.

You or I might have known terror at that sobering realization, but you and I are creatures of comfortable civilization, whereas Tarzan of the Apes is the Lord of the Jungle. Where you or I might quail at the daunting task before us, and consider throwing ourselves to our doom rather than face the prospect of being marooned to starve to death one hundred feet above the ground, the ape-man reasoned that if men had carried his panther-muscled frame upward, then there must be a safe way downward. And if he were to discover it, he must do so at once before his great strength ebbed due to lack of sustenance.

Moving quickly, Tarzan found the topmost wooden pegs by which he had originally ascended, and made his painstaking way down to the ground. For, as the ape-man had surmised, the deficient dowels had been replaced during his period of senselessness. Ere he got more than three quarters of the way down, Tantor lifted his trunk, and began sniffing the air noisily.

Tarzan continued downward, occasionally encountering short gaps in the peg ladder, and began to wish he had another path to the ground. But his knife had remained firmly ensconced in its tight leather scabbard, and the ape-man used it more than once to drive its sharp blade home, turning the weapon into a temporary handle strong enough to support him.

The fact that he was lowering himself downward, and not ascending against the force of gravity, made the ordeal less onerous than otherwise.

Once, Tarzan came to a wider gap, and was forced to reconsider his descent. Hanging high off the ground, it seemed as if the ape-man had been stymied. But Tarzan of the Apes is rarely thwarted for long.

Reversing course, he returned to some of the looser pegs and harvested them. These he took into his mouth and, one by one, captured between the first and second toes of his feet, which possessed nearly prehensile grip acquired during his boyhood among the great apes.

Holding two of these dowels firmly, he resumed his difficult descent. When he again reached the long vertical gap, the ape-man paused and carefully inserted one peg into an open hole midway along the gap. Using this for a temporary foothold, he rested, then resumed his course by climbing down, employing only his steely grip.

Tarzan's dangling feet toed the smooth bark, finding a lower hole by feel, and into this the ape-man inserted the remaining peg. This was sufficient to enable him to bridge the gap.

Twelve feet off the ground, Tarzan dropped the last distance, and raced to the elephant's side, whispering an admonition for silence.

Torn Ear restrained his trumpeting welcome and the two friends looked into one another's eyes with concern and appreciation mingled inextricably.

Searching about, Tarzan saw no sign of the chalk-white pygmies who so resembled human spiders, but did discover that his tortoise shell shield and his tied bundle of clothing were still hanging from the lesser bottle tree. He fetched them down without difficulty.

Returning to Torn Ear, the ape-man bid the animal to kneel. Then Tarzan extracted a handful of deadly quills from along the elephantine spine, pulled himself atop Torn Ear's rough back, and urged the pachyderm to lift his great bulk to a standing position.

Once this was accomplished to the jungle lord's satisfaction, Tarzan of the Apes directed his swaying steed to depart the area, his personal possessions tied securely behind him.

This was not cowardice on the part of the ape-man. No, far from it. But he had no wish to be present when the ghostly pygmies returned with their lethal blowguns, for even his tortoise shell shield offered no reliable protection against their poison-tipped darts.

Moreover, as R.A.F. Flying Officer Clayton, the ape-man was still acting under official orders. He had to find the British operative designated as Ilex. A full night's rest would have been preferable before undertaking the next phase of that quest, but Tarzan remained anxious to get on with the mission.

Chapter Twenty-One

The Tailed One

DEEP in the darkness moved a figure as different from Tarzan of the Apes as the ape-man was to the turtle folk of the lake isle of upper Pal-ul-don.

This individual crept with the stealthy gait of a born hunter. He wore little more than a loincloth of spotted tawny *jato* hide, for his pale skin was covered in coarse black hair. Around his muscular throat was a gorget of gold. Silhouetted against the tropical moon, he cut a striking figure, for in addition to these accoutrements, he trailed a prehensile tail, which flicked silently as he stalked.

Mu-bu-tan was far from his home preserves in the southern reaches of Pal-ul-don. Bu-lur was the name of his natal city, which was situated in the lowermost tip of the Valley of Jad-ben-Otho. In the common language of the Land of Man, the name translated as Moon City. Silently, he stalked, for not only saber-toothed *jato*, but *ja* the man-eater hunted here. Mu-bu-tan had no wish to encounter either tiger or lion this night. He had been sent north into the wild zone where his people seldom ventured, for people lived here of races unknown and unallied to the Waz-ho-don. Moreover, some lacked tails.

Possessing a tail was a hallmark of distinction among the Waz-ho-don. It had once been gospel among his people that the Great God Himself, Jad-ben-Otho, boasted a tail, and a mighty one, at that. From the tip of this awesome appendage had sprung the Waz-ho-don tribe, in ancient times. And so

Moon City was established at the root of the Valley of the Great God, representing the length of that eternal member. For, after creating his chosen ones out of the tip of his only tail, the Great God had cut off the rest of that holy appendage and laid it in the earth, where, by some sorcery, it had carved out the deep valley named after Him. The Waz-ho-don therefore were the chosen of the Great God. Not having a proper tail classed an individual as pitifully maimed, or belonging to an inferior tribe.

Mu-bu-tan was neither. His name meant Strong Moon Warrior. In his hairy right hand he toted a long spear whose sharp point was hammered copper and around which was coiled the severed tail of the spotted Pal-ul-don lion called a *ja*. From time to time, this weapon changed hands, and on occasion was carried upright by the warrior's sleek tail alone.

Mu-bu-tan had been dispatched north to investigate the landing of the great bird of metal, and the white things that fell from it, which resembled giant mushrooms. Metal birds rarely crossed the skies over the Land of Man, but in recent times, such visions were becoming more common. Never had one landed, however, nor had any disgorged large mushrooms until this recent advent.

It was said by the ones who witnessed these things that tailless men had been seen hanging from the white mushrooms. It remained to be seen whether this was true, or a figment of the imagination of those who reported the singular event.

Mu-bu-tan pressed on, mindful of the dangers of the unknown north, even if he was ignorant of precisely what those dangers were....

Chapter Twenty-Two

SNARL OF A TIGER

THROUGH the Pal-ul-don night also eased a figure unlike either Mu-bu-tan or Tarzan of the Apes.

This individual was attired in the flight uniform of the R.A.F., which bore the insignia of a warrant officer. Moonlight picked out worried features and, as the figure stumbled through rank jungle growth, worried brown eyes ranged over the melting moon shadows, alert for danger.

In one white-knuckled fist was gripped a .38 caliber pistol— an Enfield No. 2 service revolver ready to be brought into play at the first inkling of danger.

Danger seemed to be all around, for although it was well past the midnight hour and the birds of day had sheltered for sleep in high branches, wild animals roamed the forest, seeking their evening meal.

Once, a snarling roar, evocative of a tiger, ripped through the humid night air. But it could not be a tiger. Tigers did not dwell on the African continent.

Yet, the outcry was exceedingly tiger-like, for the listening ears had once served in India, where tigers were common....

Picking his way forward, the aviator kept his weapon at the ready, lest he encounter the prowling creature who could imitate a tiger's throaty growl with uncanny fidelity.

For five days, he had trudged through this mad place, evading and avoiding creatures out of a nightmare of inebriated pale-ontologists. It had been a near thing, a time or two.

On another occasion, nothing less fearsome than a triceratops had come crashing through the bush, but it was no dull grey hulk such as might be found in a naturist's textbook, or built of plaster of Paris in a museum display. This slate creature was splashed with red and ochre, as if the product of some demented creator-god who held sway over this impossible land.

The R.A.F. warrant officer had escaped the notice of that piebald behemoth, and so lived to fight for his survival another day. But he was no closer to his goal on this night than he had been back in that hellish day. For his companions were also abroad in the wild jungle that had no name, nor was found on any decent map.

Again came that feral scream. The warrant officer froze in his boots, eyes questing about, seeking the source of the awful tigerish roar.

Nothing seemed to move. The entire jungle was still, hushed by that terrible cry.

Pausing several long, interminable minutes, the aviator heard no further sound. Carefully, he crept forward, perspiration running from his brow, stinging his eyes with the salty fluid. Wiping at them, the man fought to pierce the dark, and in shifting his gaze about, spied a pair of eyes.

They reflected the steady moonlight with the chatoyant shimmer of a cat. Vertical slit irises suggested a feline of some species. The eyes belonged to no ordinary feline. For they were very large and loomed high on one tree. Their color was a shocking green.

Even more shocking still was the coloration of this perching predator. A tawny yellow, its coat was slashed by the black stripes of a tiger. The R.A.F. aviator's heart stopped in his chest and his lungs ceased functioning for several seconds, as if punched by paralysis.

For although striped like a tiger, the feline monster was immensely larger than even a Bengal tiger. Worse, its jaws sprang apart, disclosing great teeth the like of which had not gleamed since prehistoric days.

The thought no sooner crossed the stupefied warrant officer's mind that here crouched a species of saber-tooth tiger than with a sudden gathering and uncoiling of bunched muscles, the monster sprang downward.

Lifting his revolver, the astounded aviator commenced firing!

Chapter Twenty-Three

JATO

THE DISTINCT odor of a white man reached the sensitive nostrils of Tarzan of the Apes, caressing them—and just as quickly was gone.

The ape-lord stood up on the ridged back of Torn Ear, and instantly the pachyderm lurched to a halt. Tarzan partook of the night air, sniffing it curiously. The scent seemed to have evaporated. Strange.

Someone other than the Lord of the Jungle would have questioned his senses, but not Tarzan of the Apes. The odor belonged to a civilized man. It was predominantly sweat-smell, and mixed in with it was the musky scent of hair tonic and carbolic soap, as well as other aromas typically found in British military toiletry kits.

This told Tarzan that one of the surviving R.A.F. crew members was nearby. He sniffed the air again, waiting patiently. Sure enough, a vagrant night breeze brought the familiar scents wafting again in his direction. The breeze was coming from the southwest, so it was to the southwest that Tarzan would go.

Dropping off Torn Ear, the ape-man gave his elephant companion a reassuring shoulder pat and plunged into the leafy jungle.

He walked an eighth of a mile, every sense keyed up to its most sensitive pitch. Working through the tangle of greenery, Tarzan heard a sudden, savage snarl. He recognized the sound at once. The tigerish tones could only belong to the *jato*, the weird hybrid of tiger, lion and saber-tooth Smilodon that haunted the jungle lanes of the Land of Man.

The cry, which was soon repeated, came from the approximate direction from which the tantalizing odor of a civilized man continued to drift.

Leaping into the trees, Tarzan swung from branch to branch in the muscular manner of the great apes. He did this because it enabled him to make quicker progress, but also because the ape-man knew that tigers were arboreal and, if he were to face one, he would prefer to face it nose to nose rather than have one spring down out of the high branches to seize his pulsing throat in its powerful jaws.

Moving quickly, Tarzan leapt from limb to limb, flashing from one towering tree to another with a simian agility that was more than merely monkey-like.

With astonishing speed, the ape-man reached a spot where he could spy the *jato* crouching on a heavy, mossy tree limb, long tail twitching, its emerald eyes nearly crossing as it gazed down upon its prey.

Tarzan did not break his muscular stride as he pulled his father's hunting knife from its sheath, and charged in.

The jungle lord quickly discerned the object of the Smilodon's interest: a man, attired in an R.A.F. uniform similar to his own. Teeth bared to expose the gleaming ivory sabers to their full curving length, the tiger sprang for his meal.

A series of gunshots rattled out in close succession. But no amount of punishing lead could dissuade that plummeting form.

The aviator threw himself to one side; the tiger's extended claws swiped downward for his fragile flesh. Man and tiger tumbled together, forming a frantic ball—into which pitched Tarzan of the Apes, a low growl rising in his throat, his steel fang poised to strike.

Chapter Twenty-Four

THE BEAST-MAN

MU-BU-TAN heard the cry of the *jato* before he smelled the animal, but it was not long after the first warning snarl that the musky scent captured his attention.

Spear in hand, Mu-bu-tan rushed toward the sound, for he knew that *jatos* hunted many creatures for food, but above all other prey, they had an appetite for men.

Pitching madly through the jungle, spear hoisted high for a swift, lethal throw, Mu-bu-tan flung himself around obstructing trees until he burst upon a scene that brought him up short with shock and wonder.

A striped thunderbolt, the saber-tooth dropped out of the tree, landing upon a strange white-skinned man like a tawny vengeance. Jaw agape, its curved fangs were poised to sink into unprotected flesh.

The strange white man held a chunk of blunt metal in his fist. It began barking, spitting flashes of fire as if the wielder controlled some elemental magic.

These flashes illuminated the *jato*, but dissuaded him not.

The man flung himself to one side, but too late. On the ground there commenced a ferocious struggle, man against *jato*, with the outcome never in doubt.

Bringing his spear back over his left shoulder, Mu-bu-tan prepared to insert himself into the conflict when a new arrival flashed down out of the trees.

It was another white man—a pantherish giant, tailless, virtually hairless and smooth of skin, clad in but a scrap of white cloth about his loins, a long knife his only weapon.

Giving voice to a cry that was as blood-freezing as the *jato's* terrible snarl, this sun-bronzed individual landed on the back of the black-striped beast, thrust one muscular arm under the slavering jaws, and began plunging the knife into the tawny side of the creature, seeking its vitals.

So intent was the *jato* upon sinking its fangs into its prey that it utterly failed to see or sense this new attacker. So its foe's repeated thrusts went unanswered. But when the blade slipped around, catching under the saber-tooth's throat, the feline took notice.

Twisting its flexible spine, it released a ferocious roar, and suddenly the *jato* and the near-naked man were fully involved in a rolling struggle to the death.

The battle was like nothing Mu-bu-tan had ever before witnessed. Men did not fight *jatos* with mere knives. They employed spears, or they ran for their lives. Nothing else.

But this powerfully muscled figure fought the *jato* with a ferocity equal to the great cat itself, growling in a manner that was animalistic in the extreme. Time and again great claws ripped out and scored the naked man's bronzed flesh, yet each time the wild man evaded the worst of the blows, displaying a lithe grace that was tigerish in its own unique way.

Miraculously, they separated, the *jato* swiping out and attempting to hook the man's belly with its extended claws, trusting in them to eviscerate his opponent.

But the other was too swift, too nimble. Growling wrath, he leapt to one side, swept around, and once again threw himself upon the tiger's back with a reckless abandon that stole Mu-bu-tan's breath away.

Up and down plunged that sharp steel knife, now gleaming crimson in the moonlight. Once more the *jato* flung itself about, and succeeded in throwing the man onto the ground by rolling over him.

This seemed only to enervate the beast-man, who slashed out with his metal blade, which broke off the exposed tip of one of the hybrid tiger's saber teeth.

The creature screamed hoarsely at the insult, and the lithe man gave voice to a growling warning cry that was equally as intimidating.

Stepping about the thrashing battle, Mu-bu-tan tried to position himself to cast his spear, and settle the matter. But the determined battlers thrust about, making it impossible to strike one without risking harm to the other.

Just when it seemed as if the *jato* was gaining the upper hand, the naked giant grasped a fistful of growth and flung it into the tiger's eyes. Reversing the blade in his fist, this magnificent warrior employed the heavy hilt to smash the tiger's snapping teeth.

Another curving tooth broke; the tiger screamed anew.

Then, the naked man did an incredible thing. Dropping his blade, he reached under the *jato's* throat with both hands, simultaneously wrapping his muscular legs around the animal's midsection. Features fierce, he commenced twisting and wrenching, seemingly attempting to choke the animal, but in actuality doing something more audacious, if not impossible.

The sudden crack of the *jato's* neck bones snapping told that the half-naked one had succeeded in his mighty feat of strength.

The wild man let go, and the tiger rolled over, ripples of animation coursing along its striped sides. The great tail slapped the ground several times, then lay still.

The powerful one stood up, examined his limbs for lacerations, shook off trailing blood, but appeared satisfied that he was not seriously scored.

Then, setting one naked foot upon the vanquished *jato* and throwing back his head, he gave forth a hideous scream that tore the night asunder. It was a cry of triumph, unnerving in the extreme, which trailed off into a feral growling that soon subsided. The wildness seemed to go out of the beast-man's eyes. At once, he appeared more like a human being.

Mu-bu-tan strode forward, smiling in admiration, and announced himself.

"I am Mu-bu-tan of Bu-lur, and I have never beheld such a warrior as you. Who are you, fierce stranger?"

TARZAN OF THE APES looked up, and took notice of the new arrival for the first time. He saw the man's hairy, strapping physique, and his monkey-like tail. A thick coating of sable fur covered his entire form, closing in and framing the face so that only the prominent features were visible. The other's skin, where it was visible, was markedly pale, almost white, creating a dramatic contrast with the shaggy coating of hair.

The hirsute hands and bare feet displayed simian digits, having elongated big toes and thumbs, but the man-thing walked perfectly erect; moreover, he was ornamented with a belt and harness which gathered what few scraps of bright cloth passed for attire, principally a loincloth of spotted lion hide.

"Tarzan-jad-guru," the ape-man replied in the other's tongue.

"You are well named, Tarzan the Terrible," exclaimed Mu-bu-tan. "But I do not recognize from what tribe you hail, for while you are white like the Ho-don, you lack a proper tail."

"I am Tarzan of the Apes, of the tribe of Kerchak," clarified Tarzan. "I come from a land foreign to this one."

"Yet you speak the language of the Land-of-man."

Tarzan declared, "I have walked this land before. I count among my friends the Ho-don who dwell by the great lake and the Waz-don of the Gorge of Lions."

"I am neither Ho-don, nor Waz-don," the other said stiffly. "My tribe is the Waz-ho-don, who dwell in Moon City."

Tarzan nodded. "I have heard of the Waz-ho-don, but have never before met a member of your tribe."

Mu-bu-tan grinned at these words and showed teeth that were exceedingly bright, and rather sharp as to canines. The overall effect was strangely pleasant, if strikingly feral.

Turning his attention to the fallen white man who had been the object of the tiger's appetite, the ape-man moved to his side and saw that great damage had been done. The unfortunate one had been mauled to death. What remained of his shredded, gore-splattered R.A.F. uniform denoted him as a warrant officer.

Switching to English, Tarzan told him, "I am Flying Officer John Clayton. Can you speak?"

The warrant officer struggled, but no speech poured forth.

Finally, a single word escaped his lips. "Ilex...."

"Are you Ilex?" demanded Tarzan.

A slow hissing was the only response. It was a leakage coming from the man's dying lungs. He possessed no more strength to make words. Rolling his eyes up in his head, he expired quietly.

Seeing the way of it, Tarzan stood up and said hollowly, "I have come all this way for naught."

Hearing these strange words, Mu-bu-tan asked, "What language do you speak?"

Switching to the tongue of the Land of Man, Tarzan told him, "I speak whatever is required. I came here to find this man and return him to my people. In that, I appear to have fallen far short of my goal."

"I will help you bury him," said Mu-bu-tan.

"We will need appropriate tools," returned Tarzan.

"My spear will help turn the earth," offered Mu-bu-tan, shaking it so that moonlight glinted off its copper tip.

Tarzan nodded silently.

Mu-bu-tan remarked, "I have never heard of a man armed only with a knife who could defeat a *jato* in mortal combat."

Tarzan stated frankly, "Had that man not filled him with lead, it might have turned out another way."

Mu-bu-tan failed to understand the meaning of Tarzan's words, but pride forbade him from admitting so. Instead, he said, "Take my spear and commence the work. I will find another tool."

Silently, Tarzan accepted the weapon, and employed it to begin scoring the reddish loam, which turned easily.

Mu-bu-tan wandered off to the jungle, and Tarzan continued his toil.

A great deal of time passed and the hairy stranger did not return. Tarzan had by this time excavated a sizable grave hole and laid the fallen R.A.F. warrant officer into it.

Then, examining the state of the cotton drawers he wore in lieu of a loincloth, the ape-man cut a swatch of *jato* hide, skinned it into usable shape, scraped out the subcutaneous layer of fat, by this means fashioning for himself a suitable loincloth, which he tied firmly about his trim waist with a strip of twisted hide.

Once attired in the striped garment, John Clayton luxuriated in the feel of natural skin against his bronzed loins and felt himself to be fully Tarzan of the Apes once again.

Curious as to Mu-bu-tan's prolonged absence, the ape-man set off to discover what transpired. Following the Waz-ho-don's splay-toed footprints, Tarzan tracked them into the jungle, where they abruptly ceased.

The footprints simply stopped. There was no nearby tree into which he might have sprung, nor any sign of any other place that he might go. It was as if a great predatory bird had swooped down and lifted him off the earth with the ease of plucking up a helpless hare.

Tarzan looked up into the night sky, but saw no such bird—although he half-suspected the wild pteranodons of Pal-ul-don of making off with the tailed man. If so, they must have descended in uncanny silence and struck so swiftly that the Waz-ho-don warrior failed to utter any cry of warning.

Upon further consideration, the ape-man thought that unlikely, but no better explanation presented itself.

Having no other choice in the matter, Tarzan returned to complete the grim task of interring the British aviator. He finished up just as the sun was climbing over the eastern mountains.

Chapter Twenty-Five

CACHE

TARZAN OF THE APES toted the copper-tipped spear belonging to the Waz-ho-don warrior named Mu-bu-tan back to where he left Torn Ear, the elephant.

The magnificent reddish-brown pachyderm was patiently waiting, investigating a hole in a tree trunk with the curiosity of the bored cat.

"What have you found?" asked the ape-lord in the language that all Tantors knew.

Torn Ear declined to respond as he poked his prehensile trunk about in the dark hole. But a sprig of holly, which Tarzan was reasonably certain did not grow in Africa, much less Pal-ul-don, dropped to the ground, disturbed by the rummaging proboscis.

Presently, Torn Ear's dusty brown appendage emerged coiled around a singular object. Mumbling inarticulately, the pachyderm offered his find for inspection.

Stepping up, Tarzan regarded it with interest. He drove the tip of the spear into the ground and reached out bronzed hands in an attitude of willing acceptance.

The object presented to him was a boot. The ape-man took it in hand, and saw that it was well made, and obviously the product of civilization. Discovering manufacturer's markings on the thing, Tarzan read that it had been crafted in London—of all places.

Further consideration made it evident that this was a *woman's* boot!

If there was one boot, it was reasonable to assume there would be another. Tarzan directed Torn Ear to search the hole. The sinuous trunk returned to the hole, foraged briefly, and very quickly the second matching boot was produced.

The condition of both articles of footwear notched his high intelligent brow when the ape-man examined them closely. The boots did not possess a foul odor, nor any sign of decay, as would be the case had they been secreted there long ago. It was reasonable, therefore, to assume that they had been stuffed within this tree only in the last few days.

This led to an inescapable conclusion. Barring some other circumstance by which a member of civilization had stumbled into the Land of Man, these boots belonged to a passenger from the downed aircraft.

Why they had been hidden here could only be guessed at. But it began to turn in the ape-man's mind that he had been mistaken in assuming that the aviator who had been mauled by the *jato* was in fact the missing British Intelligence operative code-named Ilex. For Ilex is the Latin scientific term for holly! The green sprig had been hung on the tree as a sign to any knowledgable searcher.

The feminine connotations of the flower name decided Tarzan these boots belonged to the enigmatic Ilex, and that his quest had not in fact ended in tragedy, but was merely beginning anew.

Tarzan returned the boots to Torn Ear, and directed him to restore them to their hiding place. Marking the tree in his mind, the ape-man mounted his mighty steed, and pressed on with his search, knowing that he could return to this spot at any time.

As Torn Ear carried him into the jungle, Tarzan searched the ground for signs of bare feet which might indicate that the owner of the boots had gone in a certain direction. He found no such spoor, but here and there he spied heel prints showing that the owner of the footgear had come this way before divesting herself of the cached items.

Why an individual of recent civilization, and possessing the soft soles of a city dweller, would willingly part with her boots while traversing inhospitable terrain was puzzling. Tarzan gave it very little thought, however, for the night had been full of puzzles, and now it was the fullness of the day.

Thoughts of breakfast entered the ape-man's mind, and he directed Tantor to brush close to certain trees, so that he could reach up and pluck bread fruit from the low-hanging branches. Tarzan would have preferred meat, but that could come later. He ate well of the luscious fruits of Pal-ul-don.

The mystery of the disappearance of the missing Waz-ho-don warrior remained uppermost in his mind, so Tarzan guided the amiable elephant in the direction of the trail that had ended in inexplicable emptiness.

At this spot, Tarzan dismounted, the spear of the missing Mu-bu-tan gripped in his hand. Grey eyes sharpening, he examined the ground all around, plunging between ancient, primordial trees, searching for any signs of the Waz-ho-don warrior—or his ravaged body.

The ape-man realized that had a predator dropped down out of the treetops and somehow snatched up the missing one without leaving any trace, the remains of the meal would be found in high branches, if not on the ground below them.

No sign showed itself of any such consequence.

It was baffling. Tarzan's thoughts returned to the pteranodons which patrolled the skies over the mountainous reaches of the Land of Man. The ape-man had yet to spot any such creatures in the sky as the morning wore on. No doubt they dwelt in rookeries high in the mountain peaks, but there seemed to be few of them, for none so far had made an appearance.

Searching the forest, Tarzan happened on something that caused him to halt and freeze in his tracks.

It was a sandy clearing. In this clearing stood a towering baobab tree, around which, like satellites, reared up several lesser trees.

They had grown in a pattern that was identical to the great bottle tree in which he had been held captive briefly, and as Tarzan searched the branches, he spied hairy vines connecting the four smaller trees to the main giant in a pattern that was identical to the grove he had encountered before.

So similar was this grove to the other that for the briefest of moments the ape-man thought he had stumbled upon the first clearing, but his jungle senses told him that could not be. For so unerring was his sense of direction that Tarzan knew he was several miles from that other spot.

Here was a formation of baobab trees that was virtually identical to the other. It was unnatural. Yet the strange sight before him could not be denied.

Carefully, silently, Tarzan backed away from the grove as if it were a haunted thing. He was turning to leave this uncanny spot when a brief trumpeting from Torn Ear's uplifted trunk smote his ears.

Picking up his pace, Tarzan rushed toward the sound.

A sheltering tree stood between him and the place where the elephant had been left. As Tarzan broke out of the foliage, he came to this appointed spot only to find that the elephant was no longer there!

Looking about, the ape-man saw no sign of the great creature, but that could hardly be. Against the verdant foliage, the reddish-brown hulk should have stood out distinctly.

Yet there was no sign of him!

Kneeling at the spot where Torn Ear last loitered, Tarzan discovered many round elephant-pad prints that seemed to have trampled the underbrush, but otherwise went off in no direction at all.

As the ape-man examined this for any sign, a thrill as if he had been touched by the supernatural raced along his flexible bronze hide.

For, like the Waz-ho-don warrior whose spear Tarzan still toted, Torn Ear had been snatched away, as if by an invisible hand from the sky!

Chapter Twenty-Six

Mystery

TARZAN OF THE APES had encountered many peculiar things since the days long ago when he had been orphaned in the African jungle, to be raised up by the she-ape Kala as if he were her own little *balu*.

None of these things in this moment struck him as strange and uncanny as the disappearance of a full-grown elephant not very many yards from where he had recently stood.

Torn Ear had had sufficient time to trumpet out a single toot of complaint or warning. Of that, Tarzan was certain. Then he had vanished in a manner similar to that of the stage illusionist making an elephant disappear. Only this was no illusion, no trick of the magical arts.

Or was it?

Tarzan stepped around, feeling the undergrowth under his bare feet. The elephant leaves large tracks, and they can be very hot. It was still the cool of the early morning and, where the Tantor stepped, he would leave an impression not only due to his weight, but owing to the heat of his enormous body.

Walking in a circle around the mashed underbrush where the pachyderm had definitely stood but minutes before, Tarzan's naked feet detected no elephantine impressions by feel or by warmth.

He reasoned that no pteranodon grew so large that it could swoop down and pluck a full-grown elephant into the sky, and, even if such a fabulous creature might exist, it could not have accomplished such a feat without the ape-man having seen or smelled it.

If Torn Ear had not wandered off from this spot, nor somehow been translated up into the sky, it stood to reason that he was yet close by. For even at full gallop, an elephant cannot go very far in such a short time.

Tarzan sniffed the air carefully, and the odors that came to his nostrils mixed the familiar with the unfamiliar—the familiar being the juices of grasses that had been crushed by elephantine feet.

The unfamiliar odor brought to mind the scents that had clung to the baobab tree in which he had originally been imprisoned. Odors the ape-man associated with the pygmy-sized human spiders.

Carefully, borrowed spear firmly in hand, Tarzan walked away from the spot, as if completely baffled. He trotted some distance, working west and then north, as if seeking his missing companion.

But when he reached a spot that he deemed suitable, the ape-lord took to the trees, after first casting the spear up ahead of him so that it lodged firmly in a high crotch.

Finding a suitable branch upon which to stand, Tarzan reclaimed the spear and sat down with his powerful back to the trunk, his grey eyes staring in the direction of the spot from which Torn Ear had all but evaporated.

The ape-man waited patiently.

This patience was rewarded as the heat of the rising sun warmed the dense jungle. The day was now fully developed, and Tarzan heard a busy rustling that suggested men at work.

Hearing this, but unable to perceive anything, Tarzan began moving along the branches, stealthily and cautiously, taking his time, his alert ears honing in on the steady commotion of industry.

Thus it was that the ape-man arrived at the crown of a tree entirely unobserved by the creatures moving below.

They were the size of pygmies, and as pale as chalk dust, their round skulls entirely hairless, like oddly-formed eggs. In the light of day, additional features could be discerned. At every joint of their painfully thin arms and legs—shoulders, elbows, wrists, knees and ankles—black stripes had been tattooed. These gave the pygmies a coloration that reminded Tarzan of the tiger spider. But it also brought to mind the jointed construction of their bamboo blow pipes, so it was impossible to guess what effect the tribe strove to achieve.

These weird individuals were busily raking the underbrush aside, revealing a long rectangular spot that was covered in loose dirt. This was hastily brushed aside with broken branches jumbled with leaves.

Beneath the dirt, which had obviously been sprinkled there, was a woven section of rattan—or something resembling rattan.

Closer inspection showed that much of it was built of bamboo framing, and as he watched, Tarzan saw the cord-lashed construction being lifted like a door in the earth or, more properly, a great rectangular lid.

Sunlight filtering through the leaves illuminated the grave-like pit below.

In that pit lay Torn Ear, eyes closed, entirely immobile as if he had been interred in a fresh grave.

Swiftly, Tarzan comprehended what must have happened. The pygmy people had somehow ambushed the elephant, dropping on him so swiftly that Torn Ear had time only to offer a short, cut-off cry of complaint.

In some manner, the Tantor had been rendered helpless, and driven into the pit, which was hastily covered by bamboo, which was, in turn, concealed by a layer of dirt and broken branches to make it resemble jungle floor.

This ruse was an astonishing feat of legerdemain, but now that the ape-man saw the truth, it seemed merely clever, and no doubt well-rehearsed. His mind going back to the circumstances by which the Waz-ho-don warrior Mu-bu-tan had gone missing, Tarzan thought he understood how that must have been accomplished as well.

This brought to mind the ingenious sand spider, who likewise buried itself into virtual invisibility, and lay in wait, by which stratagem it would ambush unwary prey. The human spiders had learned well from the industrious arachnid.

No doubt they, too, had buried themselves.

Having excavated the pachyderm, the pygmy people now took up their blowguns which had been resting against trees, and removing long reed darts from antelope-hide quivers, began loading them into the elongated bamboo barrels. It was evidently their intention to finish off Torn Ear with these devilish darts.

Pulling back one mighty arm, Tarzan sent the war spear whistling downward, its decorative lion tail acting like the stabilizing tail of a kite. It struck the base of the tree with a loud *thunk*, which caused the spidery pygmies to freeze, then look up and around in abject alarm.

They were in the act of getting themselves organized when Tarzan gave vent to the victory cry of the bull ape.

The sound alone sent them scattering in all directions. They melted into the underbrush, leapt into trees, and one had the misfortune to attempt to ascend the very trunk harboring the watching ape-man.

Tarzan dropped down and, clinging to a stout bough with one hand, employed the other muscular limb to constrict the spindly neck.

The pygmy emitted whistling sounds of distress and attempted to reach for a dart in his quiver, his blowgun having fallen from his queer double-thumbed fingers.

With this, he meant to stab the ape-man with the poisoned tip.

But Tarzan read his intention, and simply dropped the man, who smashed to the jungle floor with a sharp sound which told that his thin neck had been broken. The ape-man fell to the ground, saw that the ghostly body was jittering in its death throes, and moved swiftly to the pit containing Torn Ear.

The elephant was still breathing, its visible flank expanding and contracting with the bellows-like action of his laboring lungs. Tarzan saw that a single dart had been embedded in the pendulous lower lip of the great creature. And understood at last how Torn Ear had been overcome.

The ape-man removed the offending object, driving it into the ground. Then he went to reclaim his spear.

Knowing that he could do nothing for his loyal companion until the poison wore off—if, in fact, it ever would—Tarzan turned to follow the pale pygmies, who had scattered in the direction of the strange sandy grove of bottle trees.

It was there, Tarzan knew, that he would find these ambushers. He firmly intended to mete out swift justice when he did catch up with them. The thin, reddening scar on his forehead, an artifact of a long-ago battle with the great ape named Terkoz, by whose defeat the young Tarmangani had cemented his status as the king of the apes, bespoke of his unvoiced intention.

Chapter Twenty-Seven

SNARED

THROUGH the forest ran Tarzan. Fleet like Wappi the antelope, he flashed between close-pressed trees, keen eyes alert, seeking a glimpse of the chalk-white spider pygmies.

Mindful of the silent blowguns that his foes carried, the ape-lord watched for any sign of pale, spindly limbs high in the trees, or the soft puff of air forced through one of the fat bamboo tubes. For he expected that the nimble spider people of the forest had taken to the high branches in emulation of the tiger spiders they so resembled.

In that surmise, Tarzan was in error.

He reached the clearing dominated by a central baobab tree and its lesser satellites, having neither spied nor encountered any of the diminutive force.

Tarzan snapped to a stop, halting and turning in place, grey eyes scanning the treetops all around. Not a limb rustled. Nor did any patch of pale white show anywhere.

The spider pygmies had vanished utterly.

Carefully, knowing that he stood exposed to a hail of deadly darts should his ghostly enemies be so inclined, the ape-man approached the central bottle tree, for it stood to reason that the fleeing ones had had time to reach it and, having done so, would have scrambled to the top, there to secrete themselves in its vast and doubtless hollow trunk.

Reaching the smooth bole, Tarzan crept around its impressive circumference, looking for a ladder of pegs, such as had been driven into the other tree, many miles distant.

To his surprise, the ape-man found none, nor any sign that any had ever existed. There was no way up the tremendous tree trunk.

With his spear, Tarzan tested the bark, seeking a weak spot. He soon found one. Out gushed a flow of water, hardly pure, but certainly drinkable. Catching some in the palm of his free hand, he sniffed it. No unpleasant odors struck his jungle-honed nostrils, so he bent down to drink his fill.

The flood of trapped water slowed, soon becoming a rill, then dwindled to a thin trickle before exhausting itself. Evidently, the ape-man had punctured a minor pocket that had collected rain water, not a reservoir as great as the trunk itself was tall.

The puncturing of the stupendous tree did not bring forth any of the spider people, as Tarzan hoped it would. But it did manage to stir something else.

Tarzan was walking around the prodigiously thick trunk when something landed with an unsettling *plop* behind him. Turning, his eyes fell upon a white spider, large enough to fill the palm of his hand. It began scuttling toward his naked feet.

With his spear, the ape-man fixed it to the ground, whereupon the arachnid beat its striped legs madly, and emitted a clacking sound that suggested mandibles working spasmodically.

The resemblance of the white spider to a zebra was marked. It also brought to mind the stark stripes of the spider people, who displayed similar transverse black markings at intervals along their arms and legs.

Stepping back, Tarzan looked upward into the tangle of root-like boughs that formed a green leafy crown at the top of the bottle tree. Had it dropped by chance? Or had it been flung down to sink its fangs into his naked skin? Tarzan saw no sign of the latter but, recalling the wind-borne webs embellished with tiny white arachnids that had sailed over the walls of the island fortress of the brutish turtle-men, he could not doubt the more sinister possibility.

The death struggles of the spider soon ebbed away and the ape-man withdrew his spear. Examining the copper tip, he discovered a noisome ichor that smelled of death.

The ape-man considered abandoning his spear for the moment. He was of a mind to try his luck ascending one of the lesser baobab trees, from its top to reach the central giant via one of the anchored vines that connected all five in the manner of a loose, ropey spider web.

Something that rustled caught his attention. Tarzan turned toward the sound. He spied the crowns of several trees shaking, and felt a morning breeze filtering through the air.

"Usha," he murmured. "Only Usha the wind."

Then something leprous white caught his attention. It was a hand—small, slim and wondrously long of fingers. It clutched a branch in the thick glory of an unfamiliar tree beyond the cleared grove, then hastily withdrew.

Racing to that spot on feet that made hardly any sound, Tarzan plunged back into the forest and prepared to take to the trees.

He managed only a few rods of hard running, when suddenly, all around him the ground sprang up and knots of muscular white forms swarmed up and enveloped him!

Chapter Twenty-Eight

TARZAN LEARNS RESPECT

THIN, bony fingers clutched at Tarzan of the Apes from all directions. They clamped with spidery intensity, having the dry, papery feel of sticks rather than human flesh.

These sensations impressed themselves upon the ape-lord in the first moments of the attack. But he had no time to pay them any heed, for long spiny arms enwrapped themselves around his muscular throat. Someone had leapt upon his back and, grasping his strong jaw, was attempting to force his head back, as if to break it.

Shrugging off the foe, Tarzan wheeled and found the other's throat. Bronze fingers made a vise and the creature began emitting strange chittering noises as the ape-man forcefully and inexorably constricted its fragile windpipe.

Six-fingered hands clawed at his face, attempting to rake his unprotected eyes. Others had seized his forearms. The feel of the double-thumbed hands suggested fleshless talons grasping and gripping.

Surrounded, Tarzan twisted his arms, and received the satisfying sound like a chicken neck snapping, followed by a throaty gurgle. He dropped his helpless foe, reached around and began prying off the clutching hands that tugged at him from every direction.

One foeman screamed as the ape-man broke the thin wrist behind the six-fingered hand.

The ape-man kicked him aside with disdain. He landed in a chalky heap, resembling a pile of bleached sticks.

Another, clutching his right leg, endeavored to climb Tarzan's towering physique, intent upon mischief. The ape-man found his throat with both terrible hands, took firm hold, and raised him over his head. Caught by surprise, the pale pygmy began yelling in a language unknown to Tarzan—if the screechy sounds it produced constituted a language.

Looking about, the ape-man spied other foes, lurking like leprous ghosts in the trees. One had produced a thin reed blowgun and was fitting a thorn dart into its mouth end.

Tarzan pitched his kicking captive in that direction, with the immediate result that he struck one spider-man with the other. Both fell ignominiously from the branches in such a way that they had become entwined.

A long-jointed hand suddenly grasped Tarzan by one ankle. He looked down. Before him lay a concealed pit, out of which had sprung the ambush, and from it came crawling more of the grasping, clutching enemy whose thin hands made one think of skeleton claws.

A swift kick upset this new attacker, and the creature tumbled back into his grave-like hole. Tarzan made certain he remained there by kicking back into place one of the bamboo-and-rattan shields that had covered the pit.

Stepping atop it, he ensured that those trapped below could not rise to challenge him anew. Nor did they. They merely pounded futile fists against the underside of the covering.

There were more foes to contend with, the ape-man saw. Two, seeing the power and ferocity of the great Tarmangani, had scampered high into nearby trees, and were struggling to bring their fat blowguns into line with the bronzed warrior.

Casting about, Tarzan saw a second bamboo lid lying nearby. He sprang for it and raised the awkward thing before him. Just in time, for the insistent ticking of tiny darts began making themselves heard.

Keeping the clumsy shield always before him, Tarzan started backing away. More darts came, piercing the air in their unerring flight.

One, aimed high, stirred his hair in passing, forcing the ape-man to hunker down in order to keep the top of his head safe from the silent missiles.

The necessity of defending himself at close quarters had forced Tarzan to drop his spear, and as he walked backward, he eyed the fallen shaft with regret. If he could but avail himself of it, the ape-man was certain he could settle accounts with the spidery snipers who sought to bring him down.

But there was no reaching the spear—not without risking being brought down by the poisonous darts which were fast accumulating on the far side of Tarzan's makeshift shield.

Another flashed for him, its white-tufted tail making it resemble a ghostly insect on the wing. Then another. Followed by a third. These were the long reed quills spat by fat bamboo blowpipes, which were only now being fielded. Every spider warrior appeared to be equipped with both types.

This quill, Tarzan saw, was fletched in scarlet. All of the others until this point had been white. Something about that scarlet streak made the ape-man ever more cautious.

Dropping to one knee, he set the clumsy shield on its edge and laid it against the trunks of two thin trees. So supported, the shield stood firm.

Crawling on his bare belly like Histah the snake, Tarzan of the Apes began working his way along the ground, protected by the thin barrier.

When he reached a thick tree, he ducked behind it and stood up. Looking upward, he discovered low-hanging branches. With a single bound, he caught one, levered himself up, and scaled the tree with the skill of a sailor climbing the rigging of a sailing ship.

Tarzan was soon lost in the high branches. He swung to an adjacent breadfruit tree, and then to another, circling around, keeping a wary eye peeled for chalk-white forms in the greenery.

He spotted none. They had appeared to melt away in a manner that smacked of the supernatural.

In barefoot silence, Tarzan worked his way around and reclaimed his copper-tipped spear. Then, returning to the safety of the trees, he made his way back to the shallow grave in which Torn Ear had been left, drugged and helpless.

THE BRICK-BROWN pachyderm was struggling to climb out of the pit into which he had fallen when Tarzan returned to his side.

The ape-man hissed a command for silence as Torn Ear spotted his dark-haired head coming into view. The elephant subsided. A light came into his eyes. It was a light of welcome.

Kneeling, Tarzan spoke softly.

"Can you stand, Torn Ear?"

The elephant waved its wrinkled trunk in a feeble gesture of half-helplessness.

"Then I will protect you until you are able," promised Tarzan.

Standing erect, the ape-man took up his spear and guarded the approach to the pit. If the spider pygmies dared to return, they would face the wrath of Tarzan of the Apes. If, on the other hand, they showed wisdom and retreated to their warrens, they would live.

Tarzan did not intend that they live very long, for they had insulted the Lord of the Jungle with their ceaseless attacks upon him. But neither did he intend to slay them unnecessarily.

That particular outcome would be up to the spider people.

As he waited, the ape-man remembered the tortoise shell shield that had been given him by the turtle-men. He leaped down into the pit, seeking it among the pack that Torn Ear had obediently borne before his ambush.

He found it, along with the bundle of clothing that contained his uniform, which had been fashioned out of parachute silk.

Feeling the weight of the latter, Tarzan remembered that his service revolver lay within.

It was not the way of Tarzan of the Apes to rely on a pistol, but he was Flying Officer John Clayton of the Royal Air Force now. And he would need every weapon at his command to fend off the spider pygmies and their devil-darts if he expected to complete his mission.

Untying the white bundle, Tarzan unearthed the heavy revolver and broke it open. The cylinder automatically ejected six shells, Tarzan caught them and returned each round to its chamber, then made the weapon again whole. Satisfied, he hunkered down to wait.

The sun was approaching high noon, and the heat of the day was becoming oppressive. But to Tarzan the sheen of perspiration on his naked flesh was more pleasing to him than his cotton uniform, which would be unpleasantly sticky had he still worn it.

Listening to the sounds of the forest, the ape-lord heard the rustling of animals in the brush, but these were not stealthy sounds, as would be made by the spider people. These were the noises made by honest animals seeking fresh water or the kill, as was their natural right.

Jungle-wise grey eyes tirelessly scanned the approach. Tarzan felt an unaccustomed thrill of fear. He was not afraid of Numa, the lion, nor Sheeta, the panther. These were foes he had battled before and overcome. These were enemies who fought openly and bravely. They gave no quarter, but neither did they practice the ways of treachery.

Neither the sharp native spear nor the civilized man's blunt bullets ever made the ape-man quail. He understood them. Either could kill him, but if Tarzan remained canny and alert, he could also avoid the swift death they dealt.

But the poison darts brandished by the sneaky spider pygmies were another matter entirely. They were virtually silent and, if one so much as pricked his skin, there was no resisting the creeping poison. No fighting back, no antidote, no second chance.

Tarzan resented the spider foe for that reason. And for that reason and more, he would show them no mercy if they attacked him again.

Chapter Twenty-Nine

"Nothing Is Ever Hopeless"

LONG into the humid afternoon Tarzan of the Apes stood watch over his faithful Tantor, Torn Ear.

As the day lengthened, with no signs of the spider pygmies manifesting, the ape-lord felt free to fetch water from a nearby stream. Employing his tortoise shell shield as a gourd, he scooped up a sufficient quantity of cool liquid to convey back to the elephant who lay on his side in the grave-like pit, regaining his strength.

When this cool smell of fresh water reached his nostrils, Torn Ear lifted his questing trunk, and dipped in the tapered tip. Snuffling out a yard of water into its flexible cavity, he first sprayed his dirt-coated side.

Then, Tarzan presented the receptacle brimming with water to the pachyderm's thirsty mouth. Torn Ear shifted in his earthen confines, and Tarzan poured the cool refreshment into the waiting mouth. Torn Ear drank greedily, and when he had his fill, the ape-man splashed the remainder along the pachyderm's dry and wrinkled flesh.

Next, Tarzan went in search of the kind of bark favored by elephants of this type, and, returning, hand-fed the roughage to him.

This luscious matter was devoured in methodical munching champs until all of it had disappeared down the pachyderm's great gullet. Seeing this, Tarzan next fetched back cane and shoots of green bamboo, which swiftly met the same gustatory fate.

Another hour passed, and the ape-man continued to stand guard as Torn Ear laboriously shifted his bulk about until he was kneeling contemplatively on all four knobby knees. He held that position for another hour. Then, strength returning, he lifted his brick-brown bulk until he was standing once more erect on padded feet, tail and trunk swishing about to chase off droning insects.

The pit was not terribly deep, but it was not sufficiently shallow for the elephant, in his current condition, to step out of it. So Tarzan employed his spear to excavate the earth at one end of the square hole. Then he gathered such rocks and flat stones as he could find, placing them there, thus creating a rough, stony ramp perfectly suitable for elephantine feet. Once the earth was prepared, Torn Ear swayed forward and, stepping gingerly, trod his way up onto higher ground.

Lifting its trunk, the pachyderm seemed on the verge of trumpeting, but Tarzan admonished him for quiet in the animal language that they both understood.

Gathering up his bundled clothes and other belongings, Tarzan again mounted his brown steed, and once he was firmly settled behind the massive head, he urged Torn Ear back onto the jungle path.

The elephant seemed to hesitate briefly, but Tarzan pointed out the way with his spear tip, and the brute obediently lumbered along, content to trust in the Lord of the Jungle.

It was Tarzan's intention to investigate the clearing in which the five baobab trees dominated. The spider people had all but vanished, and it was the ape-man's belief that they were nocturnal by nature, and must have retreated to some hidden warren that served as a spider hole.

The five towering trees, virtually identical to the other set he had encountered, suggested that it might be profitable to investigate them.

As Torn Ear ambled along the jungle lane, occasionally splintering a sapling that pressed too close, Tarzan scanned the treetops with his steel-grey eyes, seeking flashes of pale, chalky limbs.

Nothing appeared amid the trees that did not belong there, however.

Presently, they broke through the choking tangle of greenery and into the clearing composed of the type of sandy soil favored by bottle trees.

There, Tarzan took a comprehensive look around and, seeing nothing in the tops of the mighty trees, dismounted, taking only his knife and the lion-tailed spear of the missing Waz-ho-don warrior, Mu-bu-tan.

Feeling exposed, Tarzan moved quickly to the central bole, circling it, looking for any indications of a way up. He understood that this tree, like its mate some miles distant, was almost certainly hollow. Scanning the smooth bark, the ape-man again determined that no wooden pegs adorned the latter, nor was there sign that any such pegs had ever existed.

How, then, had the spider-men climbed its tremendous bole, he wondered?

Looking to the satellite trees, the ape-man saw that taut vines connected all five trees, and reasoned that it would be possible to climb one of the lesser trees and make the way across one long, hairy creeper to the greater tree in the center of the clearing.

Taking his spear, he drove it into the central tree, and was again rewarded by a flood of water, which looked clear enough to drink. He availed himself of this, capturing the water in both bronzed hands, and prepared to drink from the rude bowl thus created.

The water felt cool and refreshing, but a musty odor clung to it. Tarzan hesitated. Frowning, he released the liquid. It might not be poisoned, but the disagreeable odor was enough to instill caution in the ape-man. The spider warriors were masters in the cruel art of poison and the jungle lord would not become their victim.

Soon the flow slowed to a stream and then finally a trickle, until only a few dismal drops fell. This told the ape-men that he had struck another pocket where rainwater collected, but that the tree itself was not a great towering reservoir of rainwater. Some bottle trees, he knew, were almost entirely filled with water during the rainy season, hence their name.

Tarzan stared up at the Medusa-like mass of stunted root-like branches comprising the leafy crown but saw nothing of interest. He turned to go, when he heard a soft, dry sound directly beside him.

Wheeling about, the ape-man saw what had created the distinct sound. It was another spider—this one a large hairy brown specimen. But it did not move.

The ugly thing had landed on its back, but that was not what made Tarzan's grey eyes sharpen in concern.

Approaching, Tarzan probed the still form with his spear, and tipped it over, revealing what he had first only suspected. The fat arachnid had no legs!

It was a rain spider, he swiftly realized. The creature was unquestionably dead, and its eight legs had been pulled free at their roots. There were signs that the plump, hairy abdomen had been hollowed out.

While these signs suggested that the arachnid had been milked of its venom, the ape-man wondered if the spider had been devoured in part. But he knew of no natural predator who consumed spider limbs.

Again, Tarzan stared up into the tangle of root-like high branches. Had the eviscerated spider been dislodged by the wind ruffling the branches above? Was this the discarded remnant of a meal?

Tarzan did not know. Either possibility was equally probable. But his mind went back to the clouds of spider webs embellished by fat white spiders which had been sent across the lake waters to float over the walls of the fortress city of the turtle-men.

Striding over to one of the lesser trees, the ape-man set his spear against the trunk, and looked for a way up.

This tree, too, appeared to be unclimbable by ordinary methods, there being no lower branches to speak of. This did not dissuade the jungle lord from making the attempt, however.

Casting about in search of a suitable vine, Tarzan discovered one and with his hunting knife cut it down to an appropriate length for the task at hand. This he carried over to the trunk, and sweeping it around like a whip with one hand, he caught the snapping end of it with the other, when it returned to hand. This formed a loop encircling the bole, which he drew tight. Then, employing this tense noose for leverage, he applied the bare soles of his feet against the lower extremity of the trunk. Pulling on the loop with both powerful arms, the ape-man began to walk up the side of the baobab tree, in much the manner that some natives climb coconut palms, supported with loops of cloth.

The method of ascent was clumsy, but efficient. Tarzan shifted the vine upward every few steps, maintaining tension between the tree trunk and himself, propelling himself up by his bare feet.

In this fashion, Tarzan climbed the bottle tree as efficiently as a monkey might climb a ladder. This quickly brought him to the uppermost branches, where he could progress no further by this method, for the branches blocked any further upward shift of the liana loop.

Here, Tarzan faced his first difficulty. Holding himself steady with the braced line, he suddenly released one hand, snapping his strong bronzed fingers around a substantial branch above his head.

This transferred his mighty grip and left him dangling free of the tree trunk. Snapping the vine up and around, he snagged another branch, and so had two handholds to keep him suspended in space.

Showing agility far beyond that of a civilized man, Tarzan swung his great legs upward, thus clamping the branch to which he clung with his mighty thighs, and hanging upside down. Soon enough, the ape-man maneuvered into a seated position. Then he stood up, draping the useful vine around his neck after untangling it from a branch with a sharp snapping motion.

Tarzan walked the gnarled branch to the tree's summit, and came to a vine that was anchored cunningly at this end and draped awkwardly down from the grotesque crown of the central baobab tree.

He tested this hairy line, for he reasoned it was built for the pygmy spider people, not for a full-grown man—and certainly not for an individual possessing the towering stature of Tarzan of the Apes.

The jungle lord discovered that it would hold his weight, so he swung out and began ascending hand over hand upward, showing a physical strength that was not only splendid, but would have astonished an ordinary man had there been one to behold the feat of sinewy skill.

Climbing in this fashion, Tarzan soon found himself in the high branches of the great central baobab, and swung into those branches until he clambered atop the flat but slightly rounded top of the tree trunk.

Hunkering there, he examined it for any sign that the smooth hump formed a lid or a cork. He saw none, but drawing his knife, the ape-man carefully probed the wood, seeking any indication of a crack or seam. Tarzan soon found a spot that separated when his knife blade dug in. He pried upward. A long crack revealed itself, indicating that the top of the tree had in fact been excavated and fashioned into a lid. It was an exceedingly cunning artifice.

Lifting this weighty cork, the ape-man flung the lid aside, which went crashing down to the ground, bringing a startled tootle from Torn Ear, waiting patiently below.

Peering down into the interior, Tarzan attempted to discern what lay within. At first, his sharpening gaze perceived nothing, but, between the sinking sun and the patches of leprous white that marked the inner walls, he gradually began to discern that the tree trunk was hollow down to a great depth, just as he had suspected.

Listening, the ape-man also used his sensitive nostrils to sniff the odors emanating from below. Woody smells predominated but, mixed in with them was the definite scent of a man.

Something rustled below, but Tarzan saw nothing discernible.

"Who is down there?" demanded the ape-man.

He spoke English, and this question brought no reply. Switching to the language of the Land of Man, Tarzan repeated the inquiry.

A hollow voice called back, "Who speaks?"

"It is customary for the person who asks the first question to receive the requested answer," said Tarzan.

"I am Mu-bu-tan," said the voice, but by this time the ape-man had recognized the throaty tones of the Waz-ho-don warrior.

"Then you know me, for I am Tarzan-jad-guru."

"How did you find me, Tarzan-jad-guru?"

"I tracked the spider people to this spot, and since they had previously consigned me to the confines of a hollow tree very much like this, I reasoned that either they or possibly you might lie concealed within."

"That is sound reasoning," agreed Mu-bu-tan. "Now how do you propose to extract me from this predicament?"

"Are you free to climb?"

"No. I am fettered and helpless. Until now I thought I had been consigned to a deep pit in the earth."

Mu-bu-tan briefly told the tale of how he had gone in search of a spade with which to dig, only to find the ground opening up on either side of him and a swarm of ghost-faced spider-men dragging him down into the noisome earth. After which, he knew no more.

"No doubt they poisoned you with their devilish darts," said Tarzan.

"No doubt. For I woke in this dark place, entirely alone. But tell me, Tarzan-jad-guru, how do you hope to succor me?"

"I myself escaped from this identical confinement by virtue of hand- and foot-holds set inside the trunk but, if you are fettered, you cannot do that unless I come down to untie you."

Tarzan felt around the inner part of the trunk, seeking signs of notches by which he might climb down and rescue the Waz-ho-don warrior. Strangely, he found none.

The vine he carried around his shoulders was insufficient to lower him into the abyssal depths of the hollow, and the ape-man began to wonder if the spider pygmies had not lowered the prisoner by rope rather than climb down, bearing him with them. Without light, it was impossible to tell if there was any way down that could be employed safely.

Explaining the predicament to Mu-bu-tan, Tarzan said, "We will have to find another way to rescue you."

"From what you describe, the situation is hopeless," commented Mu-bu-tan.

"Nothing is ever hopeless," said Tarzan, and then he was gone.

Chapter Thirty

"Pele-Ul-Zali"

TARZAN made his way down the swaying vine that was strung onto the lesser baobab tree. He simply grasped the vine, which was stoutly anchored at both ends, and hooked his lower legs around the liana, using them for balance, went sliding down hand over hand in a manner much more rapid than his strenuous ascent.

Reaching the crown of the lesser tree, the ape-lord removed the vine around his neck and, by hanging upside down briefly, managed to flip it around the top part of the trunk, until he had hold of both ends, one in each hand.

Here again, descent was easier than ascent. Tarzan used his naked feet as brakes, as he increased and decreased the pressure on the vine liana, which allowed him to slide down the tree trunk in skidding stages.

Reaching the ground, he flung the liana away, picked up his spear and trotted back in the direction of Torn Ear.

Remounting the amiable brown brute, Tarzan commanded him to approach the great central tree. The elephant marched up to the smooth-skinned bole, and Tarzan dismounted again.

The ape-man had known from his previous investigation that the tree was rotted in spots, hence the ease with which his spear tip had twice penetrated the thick wood. Now he employed the spear to chip away at the trunk on the north side of the tree, where it was weakest. He spent the greater portion of an hour doing this, weakening the lower part of the tree.

As he methodically went about his work, Tarzan considered that this tree was very ancient, as were its satellites. The fact that they were planted in an arrangement identical to the five bottle trees in the other clearing inhabited by the spider people could only indicate that these strange pygmies were of an ancient race.

This told him little of their nature, but it was interesting to contemplate their ways. Tarzan had encountered nothing quite like them before.

When he had excavated a good portion of the north side of the tree trunk, Tarzan drove his spear into the ground and again climbed aboard Torn Ear.

Now the jungle lord commanded the elephant to press his great beetle-browed forehead against the tree trunk. The pachyderm did so. Tarzan impelled him to push with all his might.

Under other circumstances it would have been impossible for an elephant, no matter how large, to bring down a baobab tree of this magnitude. But this hoary specimen had been weakened by a combination of its extreme age, its severe hollowness, and the punky rot that had collected on one side of its base, which Tarzan had further eroded.

Torn Ear strained and strained, driving his mighty bulk forward, causing the towering tree to groan and lurch. Standing on the elephant's head, Tarzan lent his mighty strength to the effort, by pushing with his muscular brown shoulder.

In the fullness of time, the tree began to crack and shift. Suddenly, it was toppling, its vine web popping free of the green branches anchored to the satellite trees and producing a tremendous splintering groan.

Amid this thunderous uproar, the ancient tree crashed down upon its side, and became nothing more than a monstrous hollow log. Dust flew. Birds beyond this grove rose up in startled surprise, setting up a fluttering commotion that would have impressed a multitude of crows.

The stupendous bottle tree had landed so that its great crown cleared the sandy grove, but it did not strike any standing tree beyond the circumference of that clearing. The twisted branches that so resembled leafy roots had dashed themselves to pieces upon striking the ground, Tarzan saw.

Torn Ear trumpeted his victory, as if to proclaim that he was the mightiest elephant in Africa. No doubt he was among their most august number, for he was a veritable Goliath of his species.

Leaping off his massive head, Tarzan raced to the far end of the tree, and reached the open top amid the nest of splintered and broken upper branches.

Pushing these aside, the ape-man found the hollow end, and, cupping his hands over his mouth, called in.

"Are you well?"

"If you mean by well, astonished," replied Mu-bu-tan, "I am *very* well."

Tarzan laughed and entered the hollow, walking its entire length until he found the warrior, vaguely illuminated by ghostly lichen patches.

Discovering that Mu-bu-tan was bound in the same kind of fetters that had captivated him before, the ape-man employed his knife in the gloom to part the strands pinioning the man.

After his long confinement, the Waz-ho-don warrior was in no condition to walk to safety under his own power. Tarzan of the Apes gathered him up and bore him out the entire length of the tree, and into the fading light of day.

Setting him down upon the ground, Tarzan remarked, "You look no more the worse for wear."

Mu-bu-tan grunted, "I feel as if my arms and legs have died while the rest of me lives."

"That feeling will pass," smiled the ape-man. "When the blood returns to your limbs, we will be on our way."

"Where are you bound, Tarzan-jad-guru?" asked Mu-bu-tan, looking up.

"I seek the owner of a woman's boots."

Interest piqued the warrior's agreeable features. His long, sinuous tail snapped about. "By what name does this woman go by?"

"Ilex is the only name I know," said Tarzan.

"You have preserved me from the cruel webs of the spider-men, Tarzan-jad-guru," said Mu-bu-tan graciously. "So I will assist you in your quest. Even if your dramatic manner of rescue might have dashed out my brains in the accomplishing of it."

The jungle lord laughed again. "The sturdiness of the tribes of the Land-of man is well known to me, Mu-bu-tan. I did not fear for your survival. But had you been injured, know that Tarzan would have carried you safely back to your people."

Mu-bu-tan's white face looked nonplussed in the bristling black fringe framing his open face.

"And if I had perished?" he asked, standing up.

"Then I would have interred your corpse so deeply that neither *ja* nor *jato* nor *gryf* could have dined upon your cold flesh."

The Waz-ho-don warrior grinned. "You are wise in the customs of the Land-of-man, but I would have expected no less of you. Now let us be on our way."

"I will be happy for your company," returned Tarzan, and then went to fetch the warrior's spear, which the ape-man duly presented to its rightful owner upon his return.

Mu-bu-tan took it in his tail rather than his hands. Noticing the ugly blotch of viscous matter adhering to the copper tip, he inquired, "What is this foul stuff?"

"I speared a spider that happened to drop from this very tree."

"Was this spider white with the black stripes?"

"It was," confirmed the ape-man.

"Then you were very fortunate, for that specimen is exceedingly venomous and, had it sunk its fangs into your epidermis, you would have perished at once."

"I suspected as much," said Tarzan. "I also suspected that the spider pygmies dropped the creature from a great height for the purpose of assassinating me. Yet I discovered no sign of any lurking assassin."

Mu-bu-tan frowned. "My people know little of the spider-men, only that they, in some strange fashion, milk the black-striped spiders of their venom, into which they dip their devil-darts. For they range only in this northern jungle, and rarely venture out, except after sundown."

Tarzan asked, "Do they dwell exclusively in trees?"

The warrior shook his hairy head. "It is said that they hail from a cave beyond the great falls that empties into a deep crevice east of here, called by my people Pele-ul-zali, the Valley of Spiders. But that is only a story. No one knows if it is the truth, or not."

Tarzan considered. "I have seen with my own eyes that very waterfall. If necessary, we will investigate it. But first I must find the woman known to me as Ilex."

Mu-bu-tan glanced up at the reddening horizon and the handful of stars appearing in the cobalt sky overhead and commented, "Night comes. And with it, the spider-men will emerge from their dens."

Tarzan said simply, "They do so at their own peril. For I have a score to settle with them."

Chapter Thirty-One

ILEX

DURING all of Tarzan's perambulations through the jungles of Pal-ul-don, the object of his quest had been engaged in a struggle for survival.

Ilex was the name by which this British military intelligence operative was known to the ape-man, and Ilex is what we shall call her.

After the crash of the airplane, the aforementioned woman had a difficult time of it. Separated from the pilots, whose fate she did not know, Ilex blazed a trail north, toward what was fervently hoped to be civilization.

But after three days, no sign of civilization presented itself.

Trekking onward, the wanderer began to despair of locating a way out of the jungle, for the going was more than once blocked by deep cuts and even deeper canyons. So Ilex had secreted a pair of boots in the hollow of a tree, for reasons that will be disclosed later.

This was a calculated risk, inasmuch as jungles such as those that form the lowlands of Pal-ul-don were infested with all manner of reptiles, some of which were undoubtedly poisonous vipers. High-topped boots were as good a form of protection against such creeping reptiles as any—but again, the reasoning of Ilex remains obscure.

Therefore, the lost wanderer crept through the forest, and availed herself of whatever food and drink she encountered.

Fruits and berries constituted the greater portion of these found meals.

It was after three days that a hankering for meat devolved from a mere yearning to a desperate desire. Meat, of course, was plentiful in the Land of Man. The immediate problem was the obtaining of it. Ilex was armed in the conventional sense, possessing an Enfield revolver, but had expended half of her shells in driving off predators. She was loathe to waste any more, lest she render herself helpless in a life-or-death clinch.

That left only her nimble wits.

These wits began to focus upon the problem of obtaining meat in a land where there were no corner grocery stores or butcher shops, and the only available supply was determined not to relinquish itself for mere silver, or other redeemable promises.

Ilex was not without resources, however. She possessed a modern grasp of woodcraft, as well as other useful knowledge. Desperation also lent ingenuity to her gustatory yearnings.

Thus it was by the third evening of her exile from civilization that the resourceful woman prepared a snare by which to attain raw flesh for cooking.

This snare worked well, consisting of a flexible springy branch that was tied back until it was almost in the shape of a "U." A stake cut from sharpened wood was affixed to it by fibrous string.

A small furry animal walked into the snare, tripping the trigger, releasing the tension of the sapling, and driving the wooden stake into its side, piercing the beating heart. It perished instantly.

It was a relatively simple matter after that to cut out a generous portion of meat with a common clasp knife, and roast it over a fire ignited with a simple cigarette lighter.

The food thus roasted—nearly charred in fact—was nevertheless delicious. Stomach full, spirits replenished, Ilex resumed her quest through the Land of Man, whose name she did not know.

Nor did she suspect that Tarzan of the Apes was operating in the immediate vicinity, a fact that would have astounded the British Intelligence agent had she been aware of it.

Chapter Thirty-Two

Mu-Bu-Tan's Story

TARZAN OF THE APES was once more seated serenely atop his faithful elephant, Torn Ear, as they moved ponderously through the deepening dark of night.

Tarzan had not slept in a very long time, but so great was his physical conditioning that he showed no signs of tiring, nor did his energy flag.

Mu-bu-tan the Waz-ho-don warrior, on the other hand, had slept during part of his confinement, and was thus refreshed. He chose to walk the jungle floor, declining an offer to sit behind the bronzed giant, for he did not recognize Tarzan's elephant as among the creatures that ranged through the Land of Man. Although Torn Ear did not, except in the most general sense, resemble a *gryf*, it was nevertheless his general similarity to that carnivorous species of triceratops that made Mu-bu-tan chary of too close association.

Tarzan's bundle of clothing and other accoutrements rode tied by a grass rope directly behind the ape-man's naked brown back.

In spite of his simian feet, which appeared ideally suited for arboreal locomotion, Mu-bu-tan eschewed the treetops as well.

When Tarzan pointed out this fact, the long-tailed warrior acted injured, declaring that while the Ho-don and the Waz-don tribes did enjoy clambering among the upper forest lanes, the Waz-ho-don—a name which meant Black-white-men—did not, and had not in centuries.

"It is beneath us to prowl like monkeys," he said flatly, "when Jad-ben-Otho made us to walk upright on perfectly-formed feet. Also, to carry a hunting spear among the branches is not an efficient way to stalk game, or to fight enemies," he added, shifting his heavy spear from fist to tail and back to hand again.

Here, thought the Lord of the Jungle, was a specimen of manhood that would have delighted modern scientists—a hairy man who possessed the feet and supple tail of a monkey and who believed himself to be inherently superior to other tribes equally equipped!

As they trudged through the verdure, Torn Ear reached out with his trunk to toy with Mu-bu-tan's tail, which shifted about as he progressed. At first, Mu-bu-tan mistook the playful touches for insects buzzing him, and simply flicked away the imaginary pests.

But once, the pachyderm wrapped the flexible forepart of his proboscis around the warrior's ever-switching tail, and gave it a firm tug, causing Mu-bu-tan to whirl about, spear snapping into both hands, poised to defend himself.

Grumbling contentedly, Torn Ear seized the weapon, extracting it from the warrior's unprepared grasp and handed it to the ape-man for safe keeping.

Tarzan laughed good-naturedly, "Torn Ear is merely playing, for he has never before met a man possessing a tail," the ape-man explained, giving back the spear.

"And I," growled Mu-bu-tan, "have never before encountered a beast possessing two tails—one at the wrong end of his body."

"That is not a tail," smiled Tarzan, "but his nose."

The hairy man wrinkled his nose in vague disgust. "If that serpentine limb is a nose, then he must be related to the snakes that crawl through high grass."

"No snake," assured the ape-man. "Only a loyal friend. And a fierce foe to any who dare to challenge us."

The Waz-ho-don warrior accepted the testimony of the jungle lord, and they pressed on, Mu-bu-tan falling back so that his twitching tail remained out of Torn Ear's playful reach.

With the night closing in, the search evinced its futile component. So great was Tarzan's desire to locate the owner of the woman's cached boots that he insisted upon pressing on, even though the quest would be more difficult to prosecute after dark than it would have been by day.

Thus an entire day had been wasted with the events that had occurred since sunup. The ape-man was impatient to proceed with his search. Now he knew that the pilot and co-pilot of the British transport plane had both perished. Further, he also understood that the mysterious military operative known as Ilex was a woman and, no matter how skilled she might be, she was a civilized female alone amid the prehistoric terrors of Pal-ul-don. Tarzan would not permit another hour to be wasted while she blundered about the jungle, continually at risk.

As they passed through the thick, sheltering forest, Tarzan said, "Tell me of your people, Mu-bu-tan."

"We are a mighty race, combining as we do the best features and qualities of the Ho-don and the Waz-don, from whose loins we sprang."

"In the land whence I come," commented Tarzan, "some believe that the mixing of the blood produces lesser strains of men."

"Perhaps in the outside world, it does indeed," grunted Mu-bu-tan. "But when the tailed Ho-don and the Waz-don mate, great warriors are produced. Wonderful women, too. For we Waz-ho-don boast the pale skin of the Ho-don combined with the luxurious ebony hair coat of the Waz-don."

Tarzan said nothing. His mind went back to the time, long ago, when he first penetrated the gorges of Pal-ul-don. Therein, he encountered two dominant races, the hairless white-skinned Ho-don and the hairy black Waz-don, who appeared to be less developed, and each of whom believed that the Great God possessed or did not possess a tail according to their own religious dictates.

Apparently, the Waz-ho-don, being a mixture of both peoples, held different views.

Tarzan decided to test those views. "In some parts of the Land-of-man," he began, "it is believed that the Great God possesses a tail. In others, they hold firmly to the same Great God's absence of any tail. What opinion do the Waz-ho-don hold on that subject?"

Mu-bu-tan replied forthrightly, "According to our histories, the Waz-ho-don originally sprang from the tail of Jad-ben-Otho, the Great God. In olden times, our priests told us this story in solemn voices, and proclaimed that this made us superior to the Ho-don and Waz-don alike. They used to incite us to war against the other tribes. Generations ago, many bloody conflicts arose, but the only ones who profited were the priestly class. Over time, my people overthrew these unholy instigators and withdrew to our city at the bottom of the Land-of-man, never to trouble or be troubled by other tribes, who have graciously returned the favor for many generations."

A superior expression took hold of Mu-bu-tan's pale features.

"Consequently," he continued, "we modern Waz-ho-don do not subscribe to either belief. If neither the face nor the form of the Great God is known to us, we cannot presume or assume any attributes to this invisible Creator-of-all. If He should possess a tail, that is His right and privilege. Should it be that He possesses no such appendage, then that is entirely His business. We do not know, and we cannot know, therefore the people known as the Waz-ho-don harbor no firm opinion on that subject."

Tarzan nodded to himself. It was a sensible approach, and he wished that more men in the civilized world took a similar attitude. The notion of whether God in heaven possessed a tail, or not, was not a burning question among civilized theologians. Yet those selfsame theologians seemed oftentimes obsessed with their certain knowledge of God's celestial opinion of this or that, that it was often irksome and tiring. Thus the ape-man found the opinion of Mu-bu-tan refreshing.

"Where do your people live?" he asked.

Mu-bu-tan replied, "You are aware, no doubt, that the Land-of-man is cut by numerous deep gorges and shallow cuts?"

"I have explored several of them," replied Tarzan.

"Then know that we dwell in a lesser fissure, known as the Gorge of the Waz-ho-don, in the city of Bu-lur, at the south-ernmost tail of the Valley of Jad-ben-Otho. There we abide in our habitations in peace, having little to do with the ways of either the Ho-don or the Waz-don peoples, except on special occasions."

"Then how is it that the two tribes managed to meet and produce your people?" wondered Tarzan.

"That," said Mu-bu-tan, "is the sacred mystery of my people and, no offense to you, Tarzan-jad-guru, it is no more your business than it is ours as to whether the Great God possesses a tail or not."

Tarzan accepted that observation in silence. He saw in the Waz-ho-don warrior a frank-faced and forthright individual, and one not steeped in the muck of superstition, as were so many so-called primitive tribes of Pal-ul-don and elsewhere, who believed this or that improbability simply because a pack of priests had proclaimed that it was so. In short, despite his shaggy coat of hair and switching tail, Mu-bu-tan was, in Tarzan's estimation, thoroughly modern.

After considering all that, the ape-man offered this comment, "I have no quarrel with your views."

"And I have no quarrel with you, Tarzan-jad-guru."

THAT important point settled, Tarzan fell silent, his attention returning fully to the matter at hand. The remarkable pair trudged along, going in no particular direction since no direc-tion was any more promising than any other. But the ape-man continually sniffed the air, seeking any scent suggestive of a white woman from the outside world.

No such smell wafted to his sensitive nostrils, nor did his ears pick up any sound of a prowling woman. It was night, suggesting that the missing Ilex may have bedded down until the sunrise. At the same time, given the inherent dangers of the Land of Man, she may well have slept in some safe and secure place during the day, emerging only by moonlight when she was less likely to be seen by predators, with which Pal-ul-don manifestly teemed.

After a time, Mu-bu-tan spoke up. "Our quest is taking us to no certain conclusion."

Tarzan declared, "Quests conclude only when their objective is reached."

Mu-bu-tan nodded silently. The wisdom of the ape-lord was of a simple strain; nevertheless it was clearly wisdom. Tarzan had firmly asserted his quest would be over when he found the female for which he searched. It told the Waz-ho-don warrior more about the ape-man than a year's worth of comradeship would have gradually revealed.

After a time, Mu-bu-tan remarked, "Tarzan-jad-guru, you have not asked me what I am doing so far from my home of Bu-lur."

"I have considered that to be your business, and yours alone," replied the ape-man.

"Plainly spoken, and well spoken. So we will leave the matter where it lies."

And that terminated that branch of the conversation.

They had been ranging around in rough, incomplete circles, in an attempt to cover the greatest compass, but to no avail. No sign, no scent spoor of their elusive quarry manifested. Abruptly, Tarzan murmured words that brought Torn Ear to a plodding halt.

"Why do we stop?" inquired Mu-bu-tan.

"We stop," returned the ape-man, "because we are without direction, and there is no telling if we are moving closer to our objective, or farther away."

Mu-bu-tan looked up at Tarzan astride his great moving mountain of a steed. "Then what would you do, Tarzan-jad-guru?"

Tarzan reached into his bundle where his service revolver was nestled. Removing it, he stepped off Torn Ear, and walked several paces away, so as not to startle the pachyderm with his next action.

"What is that object?" wondered Mu-bu-tan as Tarzan passed him by.

"It is a weapon of the outside world."

"I assumed as much," remarked Mu-bu-tan, approaching. "If it is a war club, it has very little reach."

"On the contrary," said Tarzan. "In a sense, it is very much like a war club. But its reach is greater than any weapon a man could wield or throw at an enemy. In that wise, it resembles the blowpipes of the spider warriors."

"If we had an enemy at hand," stated Mu-bu-tan. "I would be very interested in seeing a demonstration of this magical club."

"An enemy is not necessary in order to demonstrate the efficiency of the pistol," declared Tarzan, aiming at a branch in a far tree.

Squeezing the trigger, the ape-man released a round that chopped the branch off the tree, precipitating it to the jungle floor below.

Mu-bu-tan flinched visibly from the unexpected report. The acrid stink of gunpowder was swept from the revolver muzzle, and drifted downwind, making him pinch his nostrils shut.

"It smells most foul, and is therefore powerful magic," remarked Mu-bu-tan. "But what do you hope to achieve by breaking the branch with your magical club?"

"My hope," replied Tarzan, "is that the woman named Ilex will recognize the familiar report of a pistol in operation and, knowing that it could only be wielded by one of her own kind, seek out the origin of the noise."

"I gather from that remark that we will make camp here for the night," Mu-bu-tan remarked.

Tarzan nodded. "This is as good a place as any. Do you not agree?"

"I could not disagree," returned Mu-bu-tan. "For any spot in this area of the forest where we make a camp is a spot in which the spider-men might discover us."

"They do so at their own peril," growled Tarzan of the Apes, firing a second round into the air, as if for emphasis.

Chapter Thirty-Three

GUNSHOTS

THE SHARP report of a gunshot split the night.

The British Military Intelligence officer code-named Ilex jerked to her feet at the unexpected man-made thunder. She did not know which—or if any—of her crew had survived the downing of the British transport airplane, but it was reasonable to assume that at least one had.

That gunshot would unquestionably be one of them discharging his service revolver.

Ilex waited for a second gunshot, which if properly spaced from the first, would signify that the timed reports constituted a signal. After a few minutes, it came. This enabled her to fix in a general way the location from which the noise originated.

She started in that direction. Unavoidably, Ilex could not walk in a straight line for very far, for the arrangement of trees in this part of the forest was not conducive to walking in straight lines. She had to wend her way around stands of cane and bamboo, and foliage-choked groves where trees had been growing wild for untold years, with no one to chop them down or otherwise clear them.

Accordingly, when a tree grew old and rotted, it became like the great red barns of the American Middle West, which are allowed to sag until their roofs and rafters begin caving in upon themselves. So it was that this portion of the forest was blocked here and there by lifeless trees, both greater and lesser, which had succumbed to death in one way or another, the rotting deadwood falling over and blocking the way, or becoming lodged amid the branches of other, hardier survivors.

It was necessary to duck under some of these half-toppled giants, crawl over others, or simply, where no other recourse presented itself, to walk around these natural obstacles of the unchecked primeval wilderness.

In this inefficient fashion did Ilex pick her way through the forest, feeling at times that she was on a dead reckoning toward the sound of the gunshots. In other, less certain, moments she became half-convinced that she had wandered severely off course.

Such was the weird terrain of primordial Pal-ul-don by night.

After a time, Ilex produced her own service revolver and was reminded that she was disappointingly low on shells. Nevertheless, this was an urgent emergency, so she expended one by firing it upward and at an angle, so the round, achieving its maximum height, did not fall back to earth and land on her head with possibly destructive results.

A few moments later, there came three evenly-spaced answering shots.

Ilex redirected her course toward that ugly noise, welcome as it was. She plodded along for approximately a kilometer, encountering no one or nothing of import when, while circling yet another fallen giant, she walked along grassy ground that felt unusually spongy.

This caused the barefoot woman to slow down in an excess of caution but, since it was the only path before her, she doggedly pressed on.

When the ground caved in under her feet, Ilex was caught entirely by surprise.

She landed in a heap, at the bottom of a sizable pit, and in the deeper dark, ghostly white forms moved with an insect-like nervousness. Surrounded, she brought her Enfield revolver to bear, and emptied the cylinder of its remaining shells in close succession.

The gun flashes revealed black bug eyes that made her fast-beating heart quail as nothing in her life before this moment ever had, for they looked utterly inhuman.

Chapter Thirty-Four

REVERSAL OF FORTUNE

WHEN, after Tarzan had released the shot that brought that answering report, Mu-bu-tan looked about and muttered, "The club thunder came from the east."

Tarzan nodded. "The east, in the direction of the north."

Mu-bu-tan jumped to his monkey-like feet and demanded, "Do we not hurry in that direction?"

The ape-lord shook his black shock of a head. "No," he said firmly. "Ilex has heard us, and she is on the move. Better we stay put, and let her find us, than to go rushing off—possibly in an oblique angle to her trajectory. You know better than either of us that these woods are difficult to traverse on foot. We will await Ilex here."

So saying, Tarzan fired three evenly-spaced shots to give a better indication of their location.

"As you say, Tarzan-jad-guru," intoned Mu-bu-tan. "But the thunder sounds will surely rouse the spider-men, too."

"If they prowl by dark," returned Tarzan grimly, "they are undoubtedly already abroad."

Mu-bu-tan nodded sagely. "The night belongs to them, and them alone."

The ape-man stated firmly, "The jungle belongs to Tarzan of the Apes, and him alone."

Mu-bu-tan's pale face frowned in its fringe of shaggy black hair. "Does the word apes denote the name of your homeland, or your tribe?" he inquired innocently.

"I was raised by the great apes of the tribe of Kerchak," supplied the jungle lord, as if that was all the explanation that was necessary.

"These great apes," prodded Mu-bu-tan, "do they all lack tails, as do you?"

"Both my human parents and the great apes who reared me are born without that superfluous appendage," supplied the ape-man.

The Waz-ho-don warrior accepted this incomplete and unsatisfactory explanation, for no apes of any kind dwelled in the Land of Man, only monkeys, which are not of the ape family. Thus, he had neither heard of nor encountered any such creatures.

A prolonged silence followed, during which their ears were busy seeking sounds of moving men. The forest was busy tonight, for things prowled and scavenged, but nothing untoward came in their direction.

And so they waited, eyes sharp and ears alert, looking continually to the north and the east so that they would miss nothing.

During the lull following the burst of gunshots, Torn Ear plodded closer, joining them, and becoming watchful. He was very quiet and his small eyes peered about with vague concern.

Presently, Tarzan climbed onto the elephant's broad back in order to see farther through the tangle of foliage. This point of vantage proved insufficient, and so he sprang from the knobby spine back into the trees, where he felt most at home, for it was his natural element.

Reaching the upper branches, the ape-man found a solid perch and there stood watch, like a sailor in the crow's nest of a great galleon.

Try as he might, Tarzan perceived no signs of a moving human form.

Time passed. Patiently, he waited.

Finally, it came. A succession of gunshots, coming very close together and mingled with it a feminine outcry, disturbingly brief and evidently cut short in mid-exclamation.

Tarzan of the Apes did not hesitate. Leaping from his perch, he flashed for another branch, and was soon swinging through the trees, hand over hand, with a power and ferocity a slack-jawed Mu-bu-tan had only once previously beheld.

The astounding sight of Tarzan-jad-guru plunging through the forest like a *jato* on the hunt caused the Waz-ho-don warrior to stand rooted for a few moments. Then he, too, charged off on foot, with Torn Ear the elephant lumbering along at a more decorous pace behind them.

MU-BU-TAN caught up with Tarzan of the Apes after a great struggle through the dense forest. He discovered the ape-man kneeling in the debris and rubble of one of the open snare pits of the pygmy spider people.

At the bottom of the pit sprawled one of the spider-men, mortally wounded.

Seen up close, the creature appeared otherworldly. From head to toe, he was covered in the chalky paste that made him resemble a pygmy ghost. His eyes were half open, and they were an obsidian black, appearing to be all pupil and no iris. For there was no line of demarcation between the intensely black pupil and the equally dark iris surrounding them.

Small, thin nostrils jerked in and out with the spider-man's spasmodic breathing. There was a hole almost in the center of his chest; this was the source of his mortal agony.

Tarzan immediately recognized it as a gunshot wound that was bubbling redly, for a bullet had struck a lobe of one lung. The little creature would not tarry long in this world.

Tarzan observed the spindly fingers with their extra joint, and the transverse black bands that marked the bare arms and legs. What passed for a garment was something akin to a loincloth, except it was not made of cloth, but some mixture of brambles and perhaps tree bark, forming a kind of paste or matrix that covered the creature's lower abdomen in a mass similar to the paper nest of a wasp. Coarse hair sprouted from this, giving it the aspect of an insect's abdomen.

Scattered about the creature were the bright brassy shells of expended cartridge casings. Thirty-eight caliber rounds, it was plain to see.

Tarzan was an expert at reading jungle sign, but it was hardly necessary in this case. It was clear that the person who had sent up the signal shot had stumbled upon one of the spider people's many snares, and been set upon by her would-be entrappers. Discharging her weapon, she had claimed the life of one of her assailants, and had endeavored to reload the weapon.

The others had apparently made off with her, for Tarzan, in searching the immediate vicinity, found small six-digit footprints similar to the deformed paws of monkeys, which went up to the rough bole of a large tree and then vanished.

Peering upward, Tarzan searched the surrounding trees, but nothing seemed to move amid their tangling branches, which were like a mad web filled with leaves.

Following him closely, Mu-bu-tan whispered, "The spider-men appear to have captured your friend."

Tarzan nodded. "They have taken her into the trees. I will follow."

"And I will follow you on foot," breathed the warrior, "for the trees are not my natural home, as it appears they are to you."

Tarzan said nothing in return, for he was soon up and moving vertically and then horizontally through the woody web-work that comprised the forests of the Land of Man.

It was not possible to follow the ape-man with any efficiency whatsoever, but Mu-bu-tan did his best and hoped for the most desirable possible outcome. In his heart of hearts, he doubted it very much. For while little was known of the spider people, it was rumored that those who fell into their six-fingered clutches were never seen again.

Mu-bu-tan hoped that such would not be the fate of Tarzan-jad-guru, whom he had known for but a day, but whose bravery, courage and consummate skill had impressed him as had no other fighting man in all Pal-ul-don. This, despite his distressing lack of a common tail.

Chapter Thirty-Five

Vengeance Vow

TARZAN OF THE APES made excellent time moving through the trees and, in their endless branches, he discovered signs of scent spoor mingled with the ordinary smells of *ja* and *jato* and other tree dwellers.

It was a rank stink that smacked of the spider pygmies. The ape-lord followed those where they took him, ignoring the other odors.

His quarry were very adept in their jungle craft, for they appeared to leave very few traces among the strangely-still leaves of the branches, but here and there, a freshly-fallen twig or a leaf crushed by a six-toed foot made a clear trail for him to follow.

Tarzan pushed hard along the arboreal lanes but to no avail. Ultimately, the spider people had the advantage of an earlier start than he; furthermore, they knew these treetops better than the ape-man, who was still learning them.

In the end, Tarzan lost the trail. The only sign of his frustration was the pale scar on his noble brow, which sprang into flaming life. His level grey eyes were chill in the moonlight as they scanned the surrounding jungle canopy, and gleamed harder than agate.

Frustration was smoldering in those same orbs when Tarzan reunited with Mu-bu-tan less than an hour later.

"You failed?" the warrior asked when the jungle lord dropped out of the trees.

"No," returned the ape-man. "The spider people succeeded."

"That amounts to the same thing," remarked Mu-bu-tan dryly.

"Tarzan does not fail. For long," the ape-man added quietly.

Again, the Waz-ho-don warrior was impressed by the fortitude of this strange tailless man from the outer world.

"Then we are no farther along in our quest than before," he murmured.

"No," countered Tarzan. "We now know that the one I seek has fallen into the hands of the spider people, which gives me a double reason to seek them out and exact proper vengeance."

"Then you had better be about it, Tarzan-jad-guru," pointed out Mu-bu-tan. "For among my people it is said that those who fall into the foul webs of the spider-men are never seen or heard of again."

"In this instance, we will create an exception," asserted Tarzan firmly.

It was at that point that a thin beam of spectral moonlight driving down from above managed to penetrate the thick forest roof over their heads. It illuminated something that caught Mu-bu-tan's alert attention.

"Did you say that you did not spy them at all?" he asked of the ape-man.

"Tarzan did not say. But it is the truth. They had too great a start on me."

"Evidently, they spied you." And reaching out, Mu-bu-tan plucked from Tarzan's black hair a feathery slim dart that had become lodged there, unfelt and unsuspected.

The ape-man snatched it out of the man's hands, half suspecting a trick, but when his sharp eyes fell upon the dart, he knew the truth.

"You are very fortunate, Tarzan-jad-guru," whispered Mu-bu-tan. "For this devil-dart must have flown in at a glancing angle and become entangled in your hair, instead of puncturing your skin. Had it done so, no doubt you would now be dead.

For the red feathers signify instant death, while the white feathers only inflict irresistible sleep."

Tarzan held the red-feathered missile in his hand a very long time without speaking. No doubt somber thoughts of how close he had come to an untimely demise were moving through his half-feral mind. For death to strike out at him so swiftly, entirely without warning, so that even after he had escaped it, it took another to point out this unpleasant fact, had temporarily given Tarzan of the Apes pause.

Wrapping the dart in a thick leaf, Tarzan inserted the deadly thing into the bottom of his knife sheath, where it would do no harm.

"Why would you carry that around with you?" wondered Mu-bu-tan. "It is very dangerous to do so."

"A fair question," returned Tarzan quietly. "But I intend to return this present to its rightful owner in a manner he will never forget."

"I understand," nodded Mu-bu-tan. "But how do you propose to accomplish that end? For the spider-men have vanished, along with their helpless captive. We are at a dead end."

"We are not at a dead end unless we are ourselves deceased," observed the stoic ape-man.

Mu-bu-tan's hairy brow bunched up in perplexity, his ebony tail switching behind his back like that of a frustrated feline. "I fail to understand you, Tarzan-jad-guru."

"Twice before, the spider pygmies have secreted their captives into the hollows of great bottle trees. This was done to me, as it was done to you. Let us seek out such a tree and see how much these human spiders are creatures of habit."

In the moonlight-shot darkness of the Pal-ul-don wilderness, Mu-bu-tan grinned. "Tarzan-jad-guru," he said, "I will follow you to the deepest, darkest lair in the crevice of the spider-men, if need be."

"In all likelihood," Tarzan returned, "It will come to that. For I will not leave off my search until I have accomplished my mission. And if the spider people harry my path, I will make of them flies trapped in their own wicked web."

Doubling back to collect the tardy Torn Ear, Tarzan of the Apes set about contemplating ways in which to make good on his vow of vengeance.

Chapter Thirty-Six

WEB-CAUGHT

ILEX—for that is the only name we will give to her at this point in our narrative—had emptied her pistol in the dank darkness of the spider pit and, all told, gave a credible accounting of herself, for a distressed grunt told her that at least one expended round had found lodgment in the flesh of a foe.

Her heart gave a leap of joy, but a small one, for her victory proved very short-lived indeed.

Hands, small and inhuman in their way, reached out and tore and grasped at her, ripping off the sleeves of her uniform blouse. Some, clutching at wrists and throat, felt odd and papery. Nor did the spindly fingers fail to alarm her, when moonlight disclosed them at intervals.

The fingers were long and sharp, like talons. They were also deformed, in what way she did not at first grasp. But when her eyes fell upon the one that seized her right wrist, she could clearly make out the extra joints that gave them their unnatural elongations. But it was the unexpected second thumb, mounted on the opposite side of the ivory-hued palm where the thumb is naturally found, that caused her to give out with a cry of deep, soul-searing horror.

A spidery hand attempted to clap over her mouth, endeavoring to silence her outcry. But the hand was too small.

From a leather pouch, a slim reed was produced. One end was fletched with white feathers, the other narrowed to a needle point. The tip gleamed wetly.

The dart found her exposed bicep and sank in like a cold, delicate fang.

In the smothering darkness, the line of demarcation between consciousness and oblivion was indeterminate. All that Ilex knew was that she struggled helplessly as something cold coursed through her veins, and after a bit, she struggled no longer.

The difference between the darkness of night and the oblivion of unconsciousness had ceased to be of any interest to her.

After she collapsed into the bottom of the freshly-dug pit, myriad hands took hold of her and even though she outweighed any of her individual assailants, they managed to lift her out and bear her off into the night, a struggling human fly at the mercy of semi-human spiders.

Chapter Thirty-Seven

THE DEAD GROVE

MIDNIGHT found Tarzan perched atop Torn Ear the elephant, who was pushing through the vine-choked forests of Pal-ul-don like a fleshy brown war tank mounted on remorseless legs rather than loam-chewing caterpillar tracks.

Tarzan straddled the pachyderm's sloping shoulders in his accustomed manner, but this time he carried before him the tortoise shell shield the turtle-men of the now-distant lake of the Land of Man had provided for his journey.

Mu-bu-tan strode along beside them, frequently stepping forward, as if to assert his personal bravery during their hunt for the spider people and their female captive. His long, sinuous tail switched and snapped so frequently that the ape-man half expected to hear at any moment a sound like the crack of a whip. Evidently, this was a mannerism peculiar to Mu-bu-tan when on the hunt.

Tarzan's eyes missed nothing on the ground nor in the tree-tops as they pushed ahead. Nor did he speak, despite several prompting remarks from the Waz-ho-don warrior. For the Lord of the Jungle was a man sparing with his speech.

Eyeing the shield, Mu-bu-tan commented, "You fear the spider-men."

Tarzan shook his head stubbornly. "I fear reporting failure to my superiors, who have entrusted me with an important mission. Otherwise, I fear nothing that moves in the forest, not even these cunning pygmies who behave like jungle spiders."

Mu-bu-tan hastened to say, "I was not casting aspersions upon your courage, Tarzan-jad-guru, but noting that until now you did not feel the need for that shield."

"I have learned a healthy respect for the darts of these spider people," returned Tarzan, "but in my zeal to pursue my quest I had neglected this shield, which was a gift to me from the people of Jad-brang-lul."

Mu-bu-tan frowned. "The people of the turtle lake? I do not know them."

"They are like the brutish Tor-o-don tribe who control the *gryfs*, except that they are masters of sea tortoises, and the hereditary enemies of the spider pygmies, for they never go about except when they are armored with the shells of turtles."

"I know them not," grunted Mu-bu-tan.

"Apparently, there are many different enclaves in Pal-ul-don, populated by different races, that do not have congress with one another," commented Tarzan.

"The Waz-ho-don do not treat with the tribe who ride *gryfs*," retorted Mu-bu-tan. "If these turtle-men are related to those, we do not mix blood with them, nor do we shed one another's blood. As I said before, we know them not. If the Great God, who may or may not possess a tail, wished us to have knowledge of these folk, he would not have placed us in our fissure and they upon their lake."

Tarzan remarked, "That is one way of looking at it."

Another silence followed, for their eyes were eager to sight their ghostly quarry amid the high, twisted root-like branches of a bottle tree, but there seemed to be none in the vicinity.

On they pressed, seemingly tireless, endlessly vigilant, and mortally certain of the righteousness of their quest.

Ere long, Tarzan sniffed something in the air that caused him to give Torn Ear a hard slap that steered the elephant to the east.

Mu-bu-tan hissed softly, "You smell spider-men, Tarzan-jad-guru?"

The ape-man shook his head firmly. "No. I smell bottle tree leaves."

At the sound of that, Mu-bu-tan fell back a few paces, until he was pacing alongside Torn Ear's great rolling mahogany rump, for the memory of his recent imprisonment in a tree of that type was fresh in his mind. It sank his spirits, although he did not care to admit as much.

In time, they came to a clearing and halted.

BEFORE them stood a familiar configuration. The central baobab tree, towering high enough to shake its twisted top roots at the waxing moon, surrounded by four smaller trees—although the modest adjective hardly fit these lesser monsters.

The four satellite trees were linked to the central trunk by carefully anchored creepers, as before. This was vaguely suggestive of a lofty web.

"Do we dare advance?" whispered Mu-bu-tan.

Tarzan nodded. "I dare." And giving Torn Ear a squeeze with both knees, he compelled the lumbering pachyderm to advance into the clearing that was otherwise devoid of growth but for the strange arrangement of bottle trees.

Mu-bu-tan heaved his spear atop his shoulder, as if to cast it at the first shadow that moved.

Tarzan raised his tortoise shell shield before him and unholstered his service pistol, an act that those who knew him best would consider out of character, but the ape-man was mindful of the advantage the spider people had if they were lurking in the branches ahead, long bamboo blowpipes pointing downward.

Tarzan listened for the first whisper and tick of flying darts slicing the night and striking obstacles.

At a stealthy pace, they advanced, but no darts came. The air was full of jungle odors, but not the unpleasant smells of the spider people, nor of any scent the ape-man associated with civilized females, for that matter.

Presently, they reached the central trunk and Tarzan dismounted, holding his knobby shield directly above his head, inviting Mu-bu-tan to stand beneath its hard shelter alongside him.

Cautiously, they circumnavigated the stupendous tree trunk, half expecting a downward hail of darts, but no such quasi-meteorological phenomenon materialized.

Tarzan carefully lowered his shield, which permitted him to look up into the branches. He did so, pointing his revolver skyward at the same time, fully prepared to loose a shot at the first sight of pasty white flesh.

Nothing of the sort transpired.

Nevertheless, Tarzan resolutely fired up into the high branches, to see what would result.

A few chopped-up leaves precipitated downward. That was all.

MEANWHILE, Mu-bu-tan was searching about the outlying trees, looking for signs of habitation—footprints or other traces of furtive movements.

When it seemed as if nothing would happen, blue lightning blazed across the sky, followed shortly by a reverberating peal of thunder.

With the startling abruptness of jungle weather, a downpour commenced.

Soon, the immediate jungle was drenched, and the tortoise shell shield was proving to possess a secondary use that the ape-man had not originally contemplated. For the spidery root-like branches above did not serve as very much of a natural umbrella.

Tarzan and Mu-bu-tan stood under the stout tortoise shell as the rain pittered and spattered around them, turning the surrounding greensward into a moist carpet. A pleasant smell resulted.

Not far distant, Torn Ear stood in the rain, and seemed to be enjoying himself. He threw his trunk about joyfully, as relentless rain pattered off his leathery brown skin, washing the trail dust from every wrinkle and crevice of that hide with each rolling wave of precipitation.

Mu-bu-tan laughed softly at the sight, but Tarzan of the Apes remained grim. He was no further along in his quest, and the abrupt downpour constituted a new impedance.

Then something strange happened.

Water began running down the sides of the great towering bottle tree as if it were erupting from a fountain. It cascaded all around them, turning the ground to mud.

With that, Tarzan of the Apes put distance between himself and the great tree, endeavoring to seek the source of the phenomenon.

No matter what vantage point he took, it was not clear, so the ape-man handed Mu-bu-tan the tortoise shell shield, and began scrambling up one of the lesser trees, employing a looped vine in the same manner that had served him so well before.

He did not get very far, nor did he need to. For not more than twenty-five feet up, he was able to satisfy his curiosity, after which he dropped down to the ground and padded over to Mu-bu-tan, his naked feet splashing with each step.

"What did you see, Tarzan-jad-guru?"

"The bottle tree was nearly full with water and now, with this new rain, it is overflowing."

Mu-bu-tan grunted. "That means no one could be hidden inside."

"That is exactly what it means," returned Tarzan of the Apes. "And having ascertained that important fact, we will be on our way, for this clearing has nothing to offer us, for good or for ill."

Remounting Torn Ear, Tarzan reached out and again took up the tortoise shell shield, which Mu-bu-tan handed to him, employing only his tail. The trio once more got underway.

They did not have a specific destination in mind, so they simply continued on, and after a while Tarzan asked of his companion, "Do you know the way to the waterfall that harbors the spider people from this spot?"

"I do," returned Mu-bu-tan.

"Then lead us there, for I do not wish to spend my days in a fruitless search for this pygmy band, when I can march on their stronghold and wrest from them the one I seek."

"Do you think this woman might have been taken there, Tarzan-jad-guru?"

"I do not know, Mu-bu-tan. But I believe in solving difficult problems in the most direct manner. I have seen this waterfall, so I know it is real. We will go there and penetrate its curtain, and woe to the spider people if they do not give up their secrets to me, Tarzan-jad-guru. Else I will teach them why I am so called in the Land-of-man."

It might have been the cool rain on his hairy skin, or it might have been the chill carried by the words of Tarzan of the Apes, but Mu-bu-tan momentarily shivered, not out of fear for himself, but in expectation of what Tarzan the Terrible would do to the spider-men when he laid his merciless hands upon them.

Chapter Thirty-Eight

THE VALLEY OF SPIDERS

PREDICTABLY, the way to the Valley of Spiders was reached by working along dense jungle trails until the path abruptly dropped out from under their feet at the edge of a declivity. Only Tarzan's superhuman visual acuity prevented the two searchers from being precipitated to their deaths, along with trusting Torn Ear, who backed up with nervous alacrity when the ape-lord bid him to halt his plodding gait.

By this time, night was in its final stretch. Dawn was still more than an hour away, so the only light was that of the distant lunar lamp, which was approaching full.

Tarzan dismounted from Torn Ear's trembling back when they reached the spot where the earth dropped away into one of the many chasms that slashed Pal-ul-don. But this was no vast gorge, like the Valley of Jad-ben-Otho which bisected the Land of Man diagonally across its great expanse. It was a painfully thin crack of a ravine, evidently opened up by earthquake and subsequently carved out by an ancient stream, now run dry.

Approaching the edge, the ape-man peered downward. The sides of the precipice were sufficiently rugged that a man could clamber down if he were nimble and adroit. But not an elephant, who is neither.

Mu-bu-tan remarked, "We will have to leave the brute behind."

Tarzan frowned. "I am loathe to do this."

Lifting his black tail, the warrior pointed the flicking tip in the direction of the nervous pachyderm. "There is no other way down of which I am aware, by which the creature could work his way to lower ground. And, if there were, the risk of a catastrophic stumble would still be great."

Tarzan nodded. Turning to the animal, he began speaking in the language that all Tantors knew.

Torn Ear listened peacefully, his thin tail switching back and forth. His trunk lifted, touched one of the ape-man's muscular brown shoulders, and a tear rolled down from one small eye.

Tarzan assured his four-legged friend that he would return with all due speed. "You are not being abandoned," he told the beast. "But you cannot follow safely."

A second tear leaked from Torn Ear's other eye.

Having no more words of reassurance, the ape-man turned and began to slip over the edge of the cliff.

Casting a farewell glance at the brick-brown beast, Mu-bu-tan followed suit, but first cast his lion-tailed spear down, so that the copper point embedded itself in the ground below. That way he did not have to carry the clumsy weapon down the cliff side, which might hamper progress and risk a nasty accident.

Mu-bu-tan showed that he was practiced in the art of scaling cliffs. But how could he not be, since he was a child of this gorge-scarred land? Furthermore, in addition to his simian feet with their extra-long toes, his monkey-fingered hands and prehensile tail served him well in grasping protrusions and rocky outcroppings wherever he could locate them.

Still, Tarzan proved the superior and more agile climber, showing an anthropoid dexterity that soon caused him to reach the midway point far ahead of the other. There, the jungle lord paused, holding onto a stony perch, looking up to observe his hirsute friend's progress, then searching the ground below with his perpetually observant eyes.

Nothing seemed to move down in the barren valley. The only sign of activity in the narrow crack in the earth was a steady rushing of falling water which smote their ears remorselessly and which, perforce, would mask any lesser noises.

The waterfall was not visible from this vantage point, which was one of the reasons Mu-bu-tan had chosen it. They could reach the ground out of sight of that spot, and work their way along the canyon floor, sneaking up on the forbidding place if they employed appropriate stealth.

Soon, Tarzan's naked feet touched ground. He knelt and searched all about with his sharp jungle-honed vision, while Mu-bu-tan completed his five-pointed descent.

After the hairy-tailed Waz-ho-don warrior smacked the earth with his callused, monkey-like feet, he padded silently to the place where his spear stood upright in the soft soil, and reclaimed it with a satisfied flourish that caused the lion tail depending from its nether end to flick and snap smartly.

He strolled back, evincing a smile like an echo of a tipped-over gibbous moon against his pale face. It was a smile both winning and slightly ferocious. For Mu-bu-tan's features, although pleasant in a wholly masculine way, were fringed in shaggy black hair and, furthermore, set atop a muscular body that was adorned with profusions of the same wild growth.

A thought crossed Tarzan's mind that Mu-bu-tan would not be a pleasant character to encounter in a dark declivity. But that was for the spider pygmies to beware. Tarzan trusted him. Moreover, the ape-man did not fear him, for he feared nothing that walked on two legs, or upon four.

Together, they walked along in silence, drawn by the sound of rushing water, every sense alert to the dangers that might rear up in the smothering darkness all around them.

NIGHT still held sway over Pal-ul-don as Tarzan and Mu-bu-tan worked their careful way around a tumble of great stones, which lay at the base of a cliff face that had collapsed for some unknown reason.

Tarzan studied the stones, and concluded that the cliffs in this part of the Land of Man were not as stable as others he had visited in times past. The paleness of the surface drew his attention. Walking up to one section, the ape-man inserted his strong fingers into one pale patch. It crumbled to the touch, and when he withdrew his hand, bronzed fingertips showed powdery white.

"Chalk," murmured the ape-man, and suddenly realized why the arboreal pygmies were so pale of skin. They coated their small bodies in chalk dust in emulation of the tiger spider.

Moving on, the two fighting men rounded the jumbled rocky disorder and there, surging in the moonlight, stood the tumbling waterfall Tarzan had earlier descried from a different vantage point.

The waterfall was a mighty phenomenon, a cascade that apparently fed off the great river beyond this weird ravine. A thick mist rose from it, looking spectral in the moonlight. It formed a low-hanging cloud that obscured the full majesty of the cascade.

At Tarzan's side, Mu-bu-tan whispered, "It is said that the spider people dwell behind that mighty curtain of water, which feeds off the River Id."

"Do they sleep?" wondered the ape-man.

"Some might. But the spider-men are known to forage by night and so presumably retire by day. But no warrior of my tribe has ever penetrated those waters, so all is conjecture."

Tarzan nodded quietly. "Then we do not know what we face?" he asked at last.

Mu-bu-tan replied in all sincerity, "We face the spider-men."

Tarzan had noted that among the tumble of stone and dirt were entangled uprooted shrubs, which were still green with recent life. Perched at the top of the cliff edge before it collapsed, they still clung to a fading existence, exposed rootlets nourished by infrequent rains.

Scavenging among the debris, the ape-man found one large enough that, with some pruning, it might serve as a kind of leafy camouflage.

Seeing this, Mu-bu-tan located a matching bit of brush, which required less trimming, since his coloring was exceedingly dark. His spear tip made short work of the excess greenery.

Tarzan had carried his shield slung awkwardly on his back thus far. Now he removed it and endeavored to tie the brush onto the face of the tortoise shell, so that when he held it before him, the combination resembled a bit of loose scenery.

So concealed, they padded their way forward, taking care to stop at intervals in order to study the unfamiliar terrain. Nothing living seemed to move. If there were predators lurking about, then they slept or were exceedingly stealthy.

The pair took their time approaching the steadily rushing water, reasoning that the spider people might post sentries. Yet no such pickets were encountered. Nor were their many places where they might hide. Brush did not grow in the shadow of the oppressive walls of the ravine. Even small animals were not seen.

Tarzan was reminded of the groves of bottle trees which even birds shunned.

The waterfall appeared to be entirely unprotected, although it stood to reason that the relentless cascade itself formed a curtain of protection for the cleft or cavern that presumably lay behind it. For, as they approached, Tarzan and Mu-bu-tan could see that the torrent's ceaseless power was sufficiently awesome that a man could not easily penetrate the thundering curtain.

As they drew nearer, a foaming pool could be discerned in the moonlight, partially obscured by the rising mists created by the cascade crashing upon turbulent water.

This was where the torrent deposited itself, and presumably drained away underground in some manner, for the pool, while large by the standards of natural pools, neither overflowed nor ran off into any visible river or stream. It was bound in natural granite, which kept the waters contained.

When they came to the pool's stony edge, Tarzan and Mu-bu-tan stood motionless for long minutes, watching, observing, and remaining still and silent in their hope not to be observed in return.

Finally, Tarzan murmured, "It may be that the surest way to enter the waterfall would be to swim unobserved through this pool."

"It may be the surest way, but is it the safest?" questioned Mu-bu-tan.

Tarzan did not know, and said so. Not in so many words.

"Do you know of another way?" he asked quietly.

"I do not," admitted the other.

"Then the pool remains our best avenue of entrance."

"Best, and hopefully wisest," muttered Mu-bu-tan, frowning.

Kneeling in the night behind their camouflage, they prepared themselves to dare the moonlit pool before the surging waterfall.

Tarzan removed the last vestiges of greenery from his tortoise shell shield, and strapped the cumbersome thing to his back. Mu-bu-tan divested himself of his own shrubbery, and took up again his supple spear, obviously reluctant to relinquish it.

"Can you swim with that in hand?" asked Tarzan.

"I do not know," confessed Mu-bu-tan. "What I do know is this: I would rather die with my ancestral weapon in my grip than otherwise."

Tarzan nodded. "Well spoken. So be it."

Without another word, he rushed forward and slipped into the foaming waters.

Mu-bu-tan hesitated only the briefest of seconds, pausing to mouth a silent prayer to the Jad-ben-Otho—the Great God. Then he slipped into the cool water feet first, wading out until, abruptly, only his shaggy head remained. Then it, too, slid from sight.

The water continued its violent foaming and churning.

Dawn still stirred beyond the mountains, expected but not as yet discernible.

Chapter Thirty-Nine

THE HATCHING

THE WATER was, as expected, exceedingly cold. It was also uncomfortably dark.

Moonlight failed to penetrate the bubbling surface of the pool. Further, the agitated water made swimming difficult, since no sooner had Tarzan and Mu-bu-tan immersed themselves than they were seized and flung wildly about by the churning eddies.

Tarzan adapted more readily to this, but not without difficulty. Unable to see clearly, the ape-lord swam in toward the spot where the water resurged. This was the terminus of the waterfall he sought to breach.

Mu-bu-tan had a more difficult time of it. He was tossed about, impeded by his flailing feet and long spear, which encountered stones in the water, throwing him further off-balance.

Finally, the hairy warrior got himself organized, but discovered he had no reliable sense of direction. Reluctantly, Mu-bu-tan struck out in the only direction that made sense: upward.

When his dark-haired head broke the surface, he looked about. There was no sign of Tarzan of the Apes. Breathing in a deep draught of air, he plunged back in, this time with a clear sense of where the waterfall rushed on.

Mu-bu-tan made no better account of himself than before. Again, his long spear made swimming difficult, navigating the tumbling torrent at times ridiculous.

Early on, the warrior had shifted his war spear from hairy hand to tight-clutching tail, thereby freeing up the former member. Trailing the spear by that prehensile appendage afforded Mu-bu-tan greater freedom and ease of movement as he swam in powerful strokes.

Suddenly, something took hold of the haft of the spear, and yanked it with impressive strength.

Mu-bu-tan fought to hold onto his cherished weapon, grabbing for it with both hands as well as his strong tail, and so was pulled along with it. He was prepared to fight for his life, when powerful hands seized him, and one, having taken him by the wrist, smacked his palm against something that was both hard and bony.

Suspecting that he had encountered some manner of underwater creature, the Waz-ho-don warrior fumbled to push the thing away, but quickly recognized an irregular surface. It was a shell of a turtle—the shield affixed to the back of Tarzan of the Apes.

Relaxing, Mu-bu-tan found the hard edges of the thing and took hold. A reassuring hand squeezed his forearm, and then Tarzan began swimming underwater.

Drawn along with him, Mu-bu-tan held on with one hand, gripping his spear with the other, attempting to keep it from catching on any obstruction. This was a task in itself. But he stubbornly declined to release the weapon.

Soon, the turbulence became overwhelming, and they were being thrown about like rag dolls. Only then did the pair realize that they were passing beneath the falls. Having no say in the matter, they surrendered to the tumult.

An eternity seemed to march back and forth as they were hurled about, their lungs straining for air. Breaking for the surface was now out of the question. They were at the mercy of watery forces direr than mere mortal flesh and blood.

A roaring sound began to lift in Mu-bu-tan's ears. Lungs ached with the strain. His vision wavered and blurred. Still the hirsute warrior refused to relinquish the shaft of his ancestral war weapon. It was unthinkable.

With that unbreakable intent in mind, the obdurate warrior lost consciousness....

WHEN he came to, Mu-bu-tan thought he had passed over into eternity. When his eyes popped open, the Waz-ho-don beheld not darkness, but light. His lungs no longer screamed for air, but breathed freely.

Treading water, he looked about. Not twelve feet away bobbed the magnificent head of Tarzan of the Apes. The ape-man was smiling in his grim way.

Mu-bu-tan blinked. "We live?"

"We are victorious. The waterfall did not devour us."

Mu-bu-tan looked about and realized that the roaring that filled his ears was still present. It was a different kind of uproar now, hollow and echoing. This was the rushing sound of the waterfall, now at their bobbing backs.

The light that made their eyes see again was the lurid glow of the rising sun, which was now streaming through the waterfall, transforming it into a surreal curtain. It seemed less composed of water than it suggested some ineffable, astral substance.

"Did you save my life?" asked Mu-bu-tan.

"I helped you to reach the surface," acknowledged Tarzan. "Your own will to live provided you succor."

Mu-bu-tan grinned. "Then we will share the credit, you and I."

They took stock of their surroundings. All around them wavered watery illumination. And beyond and above loomed the rocky grey walls of a vast cavern, whose sides were slick with perpetual moisture. Small things crawled along broken surfaces, slipping in and out of cracks. Spiders.

Above their heads, the ceiling was lost in dimness, but for its entire length appeared to be clogged by dirty grey cobwebs resembling a great, dead cloud. It made their skins crawl and the short hairs at their necks lift in anticipation of what monstrosities might descend on silent, silken threads.

Deeper within the cavern—only blackness. Impenetrable blackness. Not even the angelic sunlight could pierce it.

Tarzan began sniffing the air, and the way his rugged features contorted revealed that he did not care for what his nostrils received.

Mu-bu-tan did the same, and frowned distastefully.

"Well," he said, "that is the rank odor of the spider-men, magnified abominably."

Tarzan nodded. "Then that is where we must go."

Suddenly, a flicker of panic touched Mu-bu-tan's face, and he began splashing around, his tail emerging from the water like a startled snake.

"What is wrong?" demanded Tarzan.

"My spear! Where is it?"

Tarzan pointed past his shaggy shoulder. The ironwood shaft was floating on the surface, unbroken. In his last moments of consciousness, Mu-bu-tan's clutching fist had opened, releasing it into the waters.

The Waz-ho-don warrior swam over to fetch it, lifted it free with his prehensile tail and, employing both hands and eyes, examined every inch to be certain that it was whole and undamaged.

His sickle-moon smile revealed that it was. He shook it free of water, making the dangling lion tail dance.

"It is time then," breathed Tarzan.

Without another word, his head disappeared beneath the water's surface.

Mu-bu-tan took a deep breath, and followed suit.

MU-BU-TAN found himself in pellucid waters where scant light penetrated dimly. Visibility was not abundant, but it was acceptable. He spied Tarzan's kicking feet, churning the waters, and fell in behind them.

They swam deeper and deeper as the natural light dwindled, becoming thinner and thinner. Soon, an oppressive darkness overtook them. Yet even as it did, a strange visibility began to grow.

Here and there in the water were patches of a whitish-green substance. These were luminescent. The light they shed was weak and spectral, yet it was light to see by. So it sufficed.

Eyes sought those patches hungrily, and used the blotchy spots in the same way a ship employs buoys to navigate a channel of water.

On they swam, seemingly fearless, but in actuality determined to the bone.

The pale patches grew more plentiful, and the light they provided increased in proportion, but not in strength. Visibility still strained their optic nerves. Yet they could see, albeit dimly.

Up ahead, shapes resembling boulders began to appear on the floor of the watery channel. Some of these were splotchy with the luminescent patches. Thus they were able to avoid bumping into them.

Swimming over these dull humps, they noticed tiny air bubbles clinging to the surface of the submerged objects.

Mu-bu-tan thought this was odd, but no expression showed on the ape-man's bronzed features. He was too intent upon swimming so far as he could before he needed to resurface for air.

Suddenly, one of the luminescent boulders began to shake and warp fantastically.

Tarzan's eyes, attracted to this movement, went wide. A rush of air bubbles suddenly exploded from the boulder that was patently not a boulder after all.

The Waz-ho-don warrior had a momentary impression that made him think of a great egg hatching underwater, vomiting forth its embryonic inhabitant— along with a great spill of trapped air bubbles.

Then all around them, virtually every one of the weird eggs hatched, producing a similar erupting phenomenon.

Immediately, the waters around Tarzan and Mu-bu-tan came alive with pale man-things whose unblinking obsidian eyes fixed them with a cold, inhuman regard.

Taking up his war spear in both hands, Mu-bu-tan prepared to defend himself from these things, whatever they were. Almost immediately, he saw that his cause was hopeless. For he and the ape-man were not only surrounded, but they were entirely outnumbered.

Chapter Forty

THE FIGHT IN THE CHANNEL

IT CAME as no great surprise, the identity of their assailants. Puny and lean of limb and body, the warriors of the spider pygmies loomed within reach, their eyes like black buttons in their ghostly angular faces.

Mu-bu-tan feinted toward one with his spear and was countered by a long bamboo pole similar to the blowpipes of the spider-men. The wooden weapons clashed and banged against one another, making hollow sounds that carried underwater.

For all the muscular effort, no great damage was done to either party.

Then a questing hand reached out and took hold of the Waz-ho-don warrior's prehensile tail. Feeling the unfamiliar tug, Mu-bu-tan twisted about, bringing his spear point sweeping around.

This particular foe was holding onto his bamboo tube with a six-fingered grip, while the other talon had firm hold of Mu-bu-tan's tail. This put the spider-man at a distinct disadvantage. He could not wield the clumsy jointed barrel without using both hands.

Seeing this, Mu-bu-tan drove the copper spear tip into the center of his foe's unprotected chest, piercing the beating heart. After that, the attacker released his bamboo pole and simply floated, unmoving.

For his part, Tarzan of the Apes unsheathed his knife and, with one hand, enwrapped the spindly, banded wrist of his closest attacker. Drawing his attacker close, the ape-man inserted the steel tip of his blade into the other's pulsing jugular vein.

The results were immediate. Billows of red threads emerged from the sudden wound, which soon swelled, becoming a crimson cloud. Gurgling, the spider warrior clutched at his throat and swirled in the midst of gushing life's blood, thrashing about calamitously.

A swimming spider-man swept up behind Tarzan and attempted to brain him with his bamboo pole. But the resistance of the water softened the blow.

Tarzan shrugged it off. Twisting in the water, his blade sliced out, ripping open the creature's pale belly. Again, a mist of crimson erupted, followed by segment of entrail as the abdominal muscles, pierced, tore open, disgorging their unpleasant contents.

It was an excellent beginning to a foredoomed effort. The two comrades had drawn first blood, yet they were still outnumbered three to one.

Seeing the casualties mount, the spider warriors changed tactics. Each one was equipped with a bamboo pole and these they lifted above the waterline, taking the lower end into their mouths, sealing that end completely.

Cheeks puffed out. Then it appeared that the creatures, thus having cleared the hollow barrels of water by expelling their breaths, were drinking greedily of the fresh oxygen they were siphoning from above the water's surface.

Once their lungs were recharged, they swung the poles down, and resumed combat.

Tarzan and Mu-bu-tan possessed no such advantage. Their lungs were suffering, and every effort to move cost them precious energy.

Tarzan signaled with one hand, and began kicking his feet.

The two warriors swam on their backs, away from the descending spider-men, then changed direction to the vertical.

They broke the water's surface together, and inhaled reviving oxygen through open mouths and flaring nostrils.

"We can defeat them," Mu-bu-tan said fiercely.

"That remains to be seen," replied Tarzan frankly. "We are outnumbered."

Mu-bu-tan shook water off his copper spear tip and said, "This spear is a greater weapon than their blunt poles."

"Then make it count," said Tarzan, plunging back into the waters.

Taking a last greedy sip of air, Mu-bu-tan followed suit.

The two fighting men were quickly met by a squad of the spidery swimmers. Beneath them, rippling in the tumultuous waters, were the ruptured constructions that had resembled underwater boulders. Noting these, Tarzan swiftly understood that they were watertight shells, in which these guardians of the cavern of the spider people lurked, surviving off the oxygen sealed within, augmented by the bamboo tubes which they thrust up for additional air. The arrival of the two strangers had been detected by these guardians, who had torn free of their camouflaged lairs to bar their way.

All this comprehension occupied mere moments as Tarzan saw two swimmers arrowing in his direction, long poles thrust before them.

Here, the ape-man found himself at a distinct disadvantage. His blade of Sheffield steel was twelve inches long and, while his reach was greater than that of the spider warriors, their tubes were greater still.

As blunt ends drove in, Tarzan swept out his knife to fend them off. With the dull edge, he knocked one aside and, reversing, sliced a section from the other pole, severing it at the joint.

Only momentarily frustrated, the two attackers resumed their desperate prodding.

The ape-man was thankful that it was impossible to successfully expel darts through these tubes underwater, otherwise he and Mu-bu-tan would have been well-quilled and helpless by now.

Still, the situation was dire.

As the two bamboo rods swept in once more, the ape-man swiftly sheathed his blade and, reaching out with his bronzed arms, seized first one, and then the other, giving both barrels a tremendous twist, hoping to wrest them from their owners' grasps.

Alas, the six-fingered hands with their double thumbs seemed to possess the same adhesive power that a natural arachnid would in climbing a sheer wall. No matter how hard the ape-man pulled and wrenched, prodigious muscles knotting, the stubborn foe refused to surrender control of their weapons.

Recognizing this reality, Tarzan shifted tactics once more. This time he treaded water, and reached out with his mighty arms, separating the two enemies, then reversing course, bringing them back together.

Caught unaware, the two spider warriors collided, unwilling or unable to relinquish their bamboo. Their hairless skulls banged together which, had this same action taken place on dry land, would have resulted in a pair of satisfactory concussions. Water resistance prevented any such results. But the pair were nevertheless knocked for a loop.

Recovering his knife, Tarzan swept in, and cut the throat of the nearest man. His companion let go of his bamboo pole and swam away with alacrity, having no more appetite for combat.

Treading water, Tarzan turned in place, taking stock of his surroundings.

His eyes came to rest upon Mu-bu-tan, who was driving his spear deep into the soft belly of a helpless spider warrior.

Removing the spear point proved to be more difficult than inserting it. The stricken foe swiftly sagged, dragging Mu-bu-tan's spear along with him.

Having no choice in the matter, the Waz-ho-don warrior held onto the hardwood haft and, placing a monkey-like foot on the dying warrior's chest, attempted to extricate his copper tip.

This operation gave several of the spider warriors an opportunity to come up from behind and belabor Mu-bu-tan with their bamboo poles.

As if it possessed a mind of its own, the Waz-ho-don's long tail lashed out and found the throat of an enemy, wrapping around it. Constricting like a serpent, the appendage began choking the life out of a thrashing spider-man. He was soon floating limp, a pale, puny figure.

Tarzan swam in their direction in an effort to assist his comrade-in-arms.

The ape-man never reached his objective for, from all directions, came spidery white figures, intent upon cutting him off.

Setting himself, the ape-man prepared to hack and parry their bamboo shafts with his curved hunting knife.

It was only then that the bronzed giant saw that the questing tips of the bamboo had been capped in some fashion, and from these ends gleamed thin slivers of thorns that greatly resembled the devil-darts of the spider people.

Since these extensions were not fletched in white or red feathers, the ape-man realized that he had no way of knowing if the poison he suspected of coating these barbs was lethal, or otherwise. In one sense, it hardly mattered. The probable result of being scratched by any of them would lead to his ultimate destruction.

Tarzan should have retreated. A civilized man would certainly have done so. But the ape-lord was made from no such weak clay. Cold eyes fixed upon the nearest barb. He swam for it, employing his steel blade to hack it off before it could touch him.

Another rod of bamboo, churning bubbles, attempted to transfix him. Tarzan evaded this easily, then twisted convulsively, severing the bamboo rod in twain.

This gave him the opportunity to grasp the floating end. Suddenly, the tables were turned, for the ape-man now possessed the poisoned barbs.

This produced great consternation among the spider warriors immediately facing him. There commenced a weird underwater duel in which the jungle lord, wielding a shaft only half as long as his black-banded antagonists', attempted to beat off their poisoned rods and inflict paralyzing damage upon his foemen.

All told, Tarzan gave a good account of himself. But he was still outnumbered, and wielding an unfamiliar weapon.

The barbed bamboo was very clumsy in the handling and, although he managed to scratch the long, lean forearm of one attacker, which sent that worthy into immediate convulsions, Tarzan of the Apes could not avoid every thrust or stab inasmuch as he was accumulating attackers faster than he could dispatch them.

His familiar blade back in its scabbard, Tarzan fought mightily and well, but in the end it was sheer numbers which prevailed.

As the ape-man fended off an enemy to his front, a cruel barb raked his naked back, leaving a long red scratch. Turning, Tarzan took hold of the offending pole, and gave it a powerful twist, throwing his tormentor off-balance.

All this commotion occurred in near silence, broken only by the exhaling of bubbles and the roiling disturbance of water churned by frantic limbs.

Another barb drove in, piercing Tarzan's left shoulder. This one stung deeply, drawing blood. Rapidly losing his strength, the ape-man released his unwieldy pole, and began reaching for the horn haft of his sheathed knife. Tarzan never succeeded in withdrawing it.

A crimson mist passed before his eyes and the last thing the ape-man saw was Mu-bu-tan, his tailed spear finally wrenched free of an enemy's ribcage, being subjected on all sides to the fusillade of poisonous injections.

The dimness of the underwater channel shaded to a disconcerting greyness, upon which was wrung down a heavy curtain of utter blackness.

In that irredeemable darkness, the Lord of the Jungle knew no more....

Chapter Forty-One

PRISONERS WITHOUT EYES

TARZAN OF THE APES awoke in Stygian darkness.
His eyes snapped open, and he became aware of his
surroundings. Said surroundings were as dark as the pit of
Erebus of legend. The ape-man moved his curious eyes about,
but failed to perceive anything other than the absolute lightless-
ness that surrounded him.

Deprived of his vision for the moment, the jungle lord listened
intently.

At first, he heard no sounds. The silence was as utter and
complete as the surrounding blackness that prevented his eyes
from perceiving even the tiniest shreds of illumination.

There was a moment in which Tarzan wondered if he had
not perished, and had been translated into some version of the
afterlife. The ape-man had no particular preconceived notion
of what an afterlife might be, but this absence of anything
perceptible began to present itself as a possible alternative to
the Heavenly Gates and angelic choirs so blithely promised by
civilized clergymen.

Having no other recourse, Tarzan felt his immediate environment. It was apparent that he lay upon a hard surface, and taking
hold of his muscular arms, he discovered himself to be perfectly dry. Even the fresh scars created by the poisoned barbs
of the spider people no longer bled. They merely ached.

The ill-fitting tortoise shell shield he had been wearing when
consciousness and liberty had been taken away from him no

longer reposed on his broad back. No doubt it had been torn loose during his ordeal in the channel.

This led to the inescapable conclusion that the ape-man had been without consciousness for many hours, since the last thing that he distinctly recalled was being immersed in the channel water of the grotto of the spider people.

The ground under his feet felt flinty and hard. Otherwise it was very clean.

Sitting up, Tarzan began to feel the area around him, ascertaining that he apparently sat on a surface consistent with granite. This made him think that he was somewhere within the cavern that he and Mu-bu-tan had penetrated.

Listening intently, Tarzan heard very little that was significant. There were faint sounds, but he could not place them. They were difficult to discern, apparently owing to the acoustics of the chamber in which he lay—assuming that this black space was, in fact, a chamber which contained him.

Tarzan commenced crawling in the handiest direction and soon came upon a rough wall that, when he explored it with his fingers, brought mental images of a granite outcropping. He began following it, not standing but more or less walking on his knees, for the natural caution of the jungle made him feel as if any abrupt movement might have repercussions that could prove to be unfortunate.

The granite outcropping turned and turned again, until the ape-man came to an apparent opening in the irredeemable blackness.

Again, caution took hold of the bronzed giant. Instead of plunging through, he crawled on hands and knees to blindly grope his way forward.

It was well that he did so, for Tarzan quickly discovered that the rock chamber floor dropped off sharply where the granite ceased to wall him in.

Experimentally, he backed away and moved in a different direction, finding the opposite wall, and feeling along that in both directions until he was satisfied to a certainty that there was but one opening.

Further exploration brought the ape-man into contact with a pile of thin bones in the center of the chamber. These had been stripped of all flesh and sinew and were entirely disarticulated. Picking them up and running his fingers along their porous lengths to measure them with his mind, Tarzan soon concluded that here lay the skeleton of a long-deceased spider pygmy. The bones of a six-fingered hand cemented that conclusion in the jungle lord's canny mind.

Was this the midden of a predator who preyed upon the spider warriors?

It seemed unlikely, for any such creature would have dragged back more than one victim to devour at its leisure. Nor were there any signs of droppings. No, this was not a lair, but something else.

Retreating well back of that bone pile, Tarzan sat down and pondered his predicament. Absent any light, the ape-man dared not exit the chamber.

He cast his thoughts back to the time when he had first come to Pal-ul-don, many years ago now, and recalled the living quarters of the people who inhabited the Land of Man. Many dwelt in caves cut into the sides of the great rock cliffs of the Valley of Jad-ben-Otho. There, they were safe from the various predators of Pal-ul-don, as well as from rival tribes. It was a Spartan existence, but it allowed the tailed humans to survive.

Those chambers had been furnished after a fashion, but here Tarzan found nothing—not even a heap of grass upon which to sleep—in his cold confines. Thus, he reasoned, this was not a dwelling place, but some form of confinement.

Those cliffside dwellings, Tarzan recalled, could be reached by crude ladders—pegs hammered into the stone of the sheer cliff face. Perhaps the same arrangement might hold true here. Tarzan crept forward very carefully and, reaching the edge of the stone floor, dropped his muscular arms over the lip, and groped about for any such means of escape.

His questing fingers found none.

Once that was ascertained, the ape-man backed away and tried the only thing left for him to do, which was to stand up to his full height.

Unfortunately, the interior of the rock chamber was evidently designed for persons much smaller than the Lord of the Jungle, for he soon banged his head against a rocky roof.

This roof was curved and apparently only five feet above the floor, which forced Tarzan to once again be seated. There would be no standing during his lightless confinement. Touching his short mane of hair, he discovered it to be matted with some sticky substance that he assumed was cobwebs. He brushed this gauzy matter away.

Tarzan sat in silence a great while, listening carefully. He attempted to make sense of the sounds reaching his ears, but they were too faint and intermittent. Placing them proved to be impossible. Contemplating his remaining options, the ape-man decided to see how alone he might be.

Pursing his lips, he began to whistle, very low at first, but with increasing volume. His whistling was random and unmusical, simply an attempt to evoke a response.

Eventually, one came. A like whistle, somewhat distorted by the weird acoustics, reached his eager ears. It, too, was not melodious.

So Tarzan evinced a few bars of a popular song. There came a response which made his crafty eyes gleam in the darkness.

The whistling was a fragment of the traditional air, "God Save the King."

The ape-man knew immediately that this was not the work of Mu-bu-tan the Waz-ho-don warrior, for he would be ignorant of such an anthem. Therefore, it could only be the product of the missing British Military Intelligence operative code-named Ilex.

Tarzan gave for a reply the following few bars of "God Save the King." A sharp exclamation, entirely without words, rewarded this effort.

Searching his memory, Tarzan recalled the recognition sign he had been given by Flight Commander Armstrong.

Raising his voice, he said aloud, "The sun is boiling."

Back came a feminine voice in reply, "And the moon is in the soup."

"You are obviously Ilex," stated Tarzan.

"Evidently I am," returned the feminine voice.

"I have been sent here to rescue you."

The other voice did not lift in excitement or anticipation. Instead it inquired, "And who might you be?"

"Flying Officer John Clayton, Royal Air Force," supplied Tarzan.

"I am pleased to make your acquaintance, Flying Officer Clayton, even though it is not possible at this time to shake your hand."

"That will come soon enough," promised Tarzan. "First tell me, how long have you been a captive here?"

"Less than a day."

"Then I have not been a captive for very long?"

"No, you have not."

"I came upon your aircraft, which appeared to have been shot down, presumably by Germans."

"No," corrected Ilex. "By Nazis, who could not capture the spy they knew only as Mildred Schoener, and so attempted to destroy her. Obviously, they failed miserably." Her voice shook off its irked tone and became eager. "Tell me, did you locate my crew?"

"I regret to inform you that you are the only survivor," related Tarzan.

A SUITABLY prolonged silence attended this revelation. No

words passed between the two prisoners for some moments. Although he detected no sounds of grief, the salty scent of freshly shed tears reached the ape-lord's sensitive nostrils.

Finally, Tarzan asked, "Does the sun ever shine here?"

"I have seen no such phenomenon," returned Ilex. "But I have not been in this wretched hole long enough to be certain, for I have slept a great deal."

Tarzan said, "I take it that you are confined to a rock chamber similar to mine."

"That is correct, Clayton. I can neither stand upright, nor escape. My predicament appears to be hopeless since, in the event, I cannot see a particle."

"My situation is similar to yours," assured Tarzan, "but I do not consider it to be hopeless. Quite the contrary, for I can remember being in worse predicaments."

"You must have had a remarkable military career up to this point," remarked Ilex with a trace of dryness.

Instead of responding, the ape-man changed the subject. "I was taken prisoner with another. Do you know of him?"

Ilex replied, "From noises I have heard from time to time, there are two new prisoners, of which you are one."

"How many prisoners in total?"

"That, I fear, I do not know, for the strange pygmy people who took me prisoner also use these chambers, of which I understand there are many, to imprison their own criminals. Thus the limited compass of these caves."

Tarzan absorbed this in silence, and his sharp ears caught once more the low sounds.

"Why is it so quiet?" he inquired.

"These pygmies apparently do not have speech. Instead, they sign with their long fingers, augmented by the cracking of their knuckles and associated cartilage, to communicate with one another."

"I have never heard of such a thing," remarked Tarzan, "and I have traveled far and wide, encountering many unusual people."

Then, the ape-man noticed something that had been present continually, but had not registered upon his consciousness. It was a faint steady sound rather resembling radio static, but not static.

Listening carefully, Tarzan decided that the ceaseless noise was the distant roar of the waterfall that concealed the grotto of the spider people. This told him that he was very, very deep into the cavern—far from any natural light source.

Presently, the ape-man felt about his person, and discovered that his loincloth was intact, as was his scabbard. The hunting knife of his father, however, was missing. He was not greatly surprised. But Tarzan made a silent vow to himself to recover the blade at his earliest opportunity.

Such was the confidence of the Lord of the Jungle that, finding himself in this place, as dire as it seemed, was not disheartening to him in any way. Even mindful of the uncanny darkness and the probability that he was marooned high up on some granite cliff all but stark naked, Tarzan of the Apes was determined to escape at his earliest opportunity, carrying away the object of his quest, the British woman known to him as Ilex.

As a gesture in that direction, Tarzan shifted to the open mouth of the cliff cave nearest the source of the woman's voice. He leaned out.

Previously, he had explored the rock's face in a downward direction; now he felt to the side. His fingertips brushed more rock, but nothing else.

Tarzan spoke up. "I have stationed myself at the mouth of my cave cell, and I am endeavoring to see how close toward your cell I can reach. Why do you not do the same?"

"Very well," returned the woman coolly. "We shall see if our fingertips might brush one another. Although I fail to see how that would conceivably benefit us."

A short scuffling followed, and the woman evidently did as she promised, for it was not very long before Tarzan's questing fingertips brushed those of another's.

"Our chambers are quite close together," observed the ape-man.

"I fail to see to what possible use that information might be applied," returned Ilex dispiritedly.

Tarzan instructed, "Please retreat to the deepest recesses of your cell. I intend to join you presently."

An inward-drawn breath of surprise came, followed by more scuffling.

"I am ready when you are ready," reported Ilex.

Tarzan felt the rock face that separated the two chambers and found it was sufficiently irregular that there existed usable hand- and foot-holds—although not very trustworthy ones. Finding one, this gave him confidence. The ape-man began to emerge from the chamber, and made an effort to find firm ridges upon which his strong toes might rest.

After a great deal of feeling about, he found one short ledge. Only someone with Tarzan's steely muscular development might attempt such a mad maneuver, but almost immediately the ape-man then placed himself in the precarious position of clinging to the rock by one set of fingers and one group of toes.

It was too difficult and dangerous to seek another foothold, so Tarzan used his free hand alone to seek something he could grasp firmly.

His efforts were not immediately rewarded, and the strain on his iron thews almost caused the ape-man to retreat back to the safety of his own cell. Had there been any light, the proposition might not have been so desperate and daring but, in this weird blackness, Tarzan could trust nothing except what his fingers and toes told him.

His free fingers brushed something, but it was not hard. Something dangled from above. Tarzan reached out, constrained from doing so with anything other than simple caution.

His clutching hands found, to his astonishment, something that felt like a vine or a rope. He gave it a tug, and it proved to be solidly anchored.

Suddenly, Tarzan began to conceive of the other prisoners who might be deposited into these cuts in the sheer rock face. They had been hoisted to their stark prison cells by anchored rope.

The stress on his fingers and toes proving to be almost unendurable, Tarzan took a mighty chance. Seizing the rope with corded fingers, he pulled it closer and suddenly grasped it with the other hand.

Immediately, he found himself dangling in sheer space, and began rocking back and forth. This maneuver proved to be particularly easy to achieve, and so the ape-man increased his rocking motion, forcing himself to scrape across the sheer rock face, for his naked brown skin was soon abraded by the rough surface texture of the cliff.

By experimentation, he discovered the other opening, and hoping it was sufficiently wide, flung himself within.

The velocity with which Tarzan of the Apes entered the other cave was so great that he went skating all the way to the back wall, as Ilex cowered in the utmost rear.

She gave a surprised gasp when his great body collided with hers, and reaching out with her hands, Ilex took hold of his mighty arms, saying, "My goodness, you did it!"

Almost as soon as the words were out of her mouth, the startled woman hastily withdrew her cool fingers and reproached him firmly.

"Flying Officer Clayton, it appears that you are out of uniform."

Chapter Forty-Two

REUNITED

A STRAINED silence followed Ilex's awkward observation of the ape-man's state of undress.

After careful consideration, Tarzan decided that the simplest thing to say was, "I was forced by circumstances to abandon my uniform."

"You must be very uncomfortable then," commented the woman.

"I would be much more comfortable if I were not confined in this small space," he admitted.

Another silence followed. Then, Ilex remarked casually, "Your voice strikes a familiar chord in my memory."

Preoccupied with their predicament, Tarzan stated, "It is unlikely that we would have met, since I only recently concluded my flight training."

"I see," said Ilex. "Well, Flying Officer Clayton, how do you propose that we escape this horrible captivity of ours?"

"Quietly," replied Tarzan. "For no doubt our captors are sleeping."

"What makes you say that?" questioned Ilex.

"The very silence of this place suggests a lack of activity."

"You may well be right, Clayton, but I still fail to see a way out of our present predicament."

Tarzan attempted to stand up and discovered that the roof of this particular cell was no higher than his own. So he was forced to be seated again, once again to brush dirty cobwebs from his hair.

Squatting on his haunches, he stated, "I came here with a comrade. I am wondering where he might be."

Ilex considered that comment and said, "Having had no more illumination than what you see around us, I would naturally have no idea."

"I understand," said Tarzan.

"But I have heard noises, furthermore, that suggest prisoners dwelling directly above our heads. If they represent the criminal elements of these horrid pygmies, then of course they would make no speech, uttered language being unknown to these beastly beings."

Tarzan groped around the chamber, looking for something solid, such as a stone. He found nothing of the sort.

"Have you anything on your person that you do not need?" he asked Ilex.

"Such as?"

"Such as could be dropped from this cell, and would give me an indication of how high above the ground we are situated."

"I believe I have a few bob in change."

"Give them here," requested Tarzan.

A handful of round metallic coins were pressed into the ape-man's hand and he crawled to the mouth of the cell and dropped what felt like a shilling downward.

Listening carefully, Tarzan heard the clink of it landing. He dropped another. The second coin was larger and the clink of impact was subsequently louder.

Tarzan held onto the third coin and crawled back to the waiting woman.

"I would judge," he said, "that we are situated approximately one hundred feet above ground."

"Assuming that is so," corrected Ilex, "was it ground the coins struck? Or possibly a projection you cannot discern."

"That is true," admitted Tarzan. "They may have struck a ledge or something similar."

Turning to the mouth of the cave, the ape-man pitched the third coin straight out the farthest as he could, and awaited the sound of it landing.

It was more difficult to tell, but Tarzan concluded the flat surface below extended quite a distance, suggesting a floor of some sort.

"I am satisfied that a solid floor exists some one hundred feet below," he told Ilex. "Before we leave," Tarzan added, "I must locate my missing friend."

"What is this fellow's rank?" wondered Ilex.

"He has no ranking that I am aware," replied Tarzan. "For he is a native of this land, but we have become fast friends, for he is very brave."

"Oh. I am unaware that there are any natives to this land. For in my travels I have only counted wild beasts. Frightful monsters such as existed at the dawn of time."

"You are fortunate to have survived to this point," remarked Tarzan.

"I prefer to think that I am resourceful and determined," returned Ilex with a trace of flint in her voice. "For I was given a mission, and I remain determined to bring back to my superior officers the fruits of said mission."

"In that," said Tarzan simply, "you and I are of one mind. For you are my mission, and I must return you to my superiors."

"We will see who returns what to whom," said Ilex tartly.

Tarzan laughed roughly; he was beginning to appreciate the spark of this mysterious woman.

"What are you bringing back to your superiors that is so important?" he wondered.

"That," she replied sharply, "is between me and those above me."

Tarzan offered, "I discovered your boots in the hollow of the tree marked by a spring of holly."

Ilex's voice came sharply, "And I trust that you returned them to their proper hiding place?"

"I did," assented Tarzan. "But why did you leave them behind?"

"So that I could recover them if I survived and, if I did not, there might remain some scant chance they would survive to be discovered by any rescuers who came this way. For I had every expectation of being devoured by a prehistoric predator, which might be expected to consume my leather boots, along with my living flesh."

Tarzan considered this reply. "From what you say, I deduce that something important is secreted in one or both of those boots?"

"I will decline to answer that prompting, except to say that it is imperative to convey those boots to our superior officers," Ilex said firmly. "The future outcome of the entire war may depend upon it."

In the darkness, Tarzan nodded silently.

"If it can be done," he added, "it will be done. I promise you this."

"Very good," answered Ilex crisply. "But we still have to find our way to daylight, much less civilization."

"There is a vine rope hanging between this cave and my former cell," Tarzan said. "I do not know how far down it goes, but I have reason to believe it is used to climb this cliff, for I think we have been imprisoned in shallow cuts along the cliff face."

"Yes?"

"What I propose is to climb down that vine and determine if it will serve to bear our weight to the ground below."

"While I consider myself to be very brave," admitted Ilex after a long pause, "I am not certain that I am sufficiently courageous—or perhaps I should venture to say sufficiently foolhardy—to slide down an uncertain rope in this impossible darkness."

"That is why I intend to go first," said Tarzan simply. "Await me here."

And with that, the ape-man returned to the cave's dark, unseen mouth, and stuck out as much of his torso and upper body as he dared, feeling in the Stygian murk for the vine he knew to be adjacent.

When he located it, Tarzan pulled the vine close, and felt along its length, finding that it was composed of some fibrous woven matter not unlike a hempen rope, and quite possibly as stout.

"I shall return," said Tarzan, launching himself into space, his formidable fingers embedded in the fiber.

The swinging rope held, as the ape-man knew it would. It had already borne his weight once before. Now Tarzan used the strength of his upper body to slip down the rope, clutching and releasing the heavy thing with his powerful grip, until at last his naked feet encountered solid stone.

Releasing the vine, he turned about and realized his immediate situation was not greatly improved. In this complete darkness, it was impossible to tell if there were pits or crevices he might stumble into once he set off.

Creeping cautiously, the ape-lord reconnoitered, taking his time with it.

The absence of any illumination whatsoever was beginning to wear on his nerves. The Lord of the Jungle was a creature of the outdoors. He loved the sunlight of day, enjoyed the cool lunar illumination of night, but this utter lack of any light whatsoever was oppressive to his feral spirit.

This, in part, explained why, after a cautious perambulation, Tarzan padded back toward the spot where he had released the strong woven vine. Without light there was nothing to be accomplished alone, and if he was going to dare the deeper depths, he would have to have the woman he sought to rescue with him, as dangerous as that might be.

It took some time to relocate the rope, but when he did, Tarzan began climbing upward. He had a canny sense of height, and so climbed until he thought he had reached the spot where he had left Ilex.

Pausing, he called out softly.

"I have returned," he said.

The voice that answered was not feminine in any way, but rather hoarse. It said with a trace of bafflement, "Is that you, Tarzan-jad-guru?"

Fortunately for the ape-man, surprise was not a thing that affected his nerves, otherwise he might have released the rope in his astonishment.

"Mu-bu-tan?"

"The very same," replied the Waz-ho-don warrior.

Tarzan could tell that the voice was coming somewhat above his head, so he clambered higher than he thought he should, and said, "I am here. Are you in a cave?"

"I am, Tarzan. Where are you? I can see nothing!"

"I am hanging from a vine rope to your left. If you will reach out, you will be able to feel this rope."

"Why? I do not think that is a wise thing to do in this darkness," counseled Mu-bu-tan.

"Is there any wisdom in remaining a captive?" countered Tarzan.

"None that I can think of contemplating," admitted the warrior.

"Then reach out and take hold of the rope, for we are in the act of escaping."

There was a long silence in which Mu-bu-tan apparently contemplated his options, few that they were. Evidently, he decided to go along with the ape-man's advice, for Tarzan felt the rope above his head jerk and tremble as an unseen hand presumably grasped it.

"Tarzan, I do not think I can transfer to the rope, for I have captured it with my tail, but it remains out of reach of my fingers."

"Wait," said Tarzan, and began swinging on the vine, which swung closer and then further away from the hairy hands he could not perceive straining out for purchase.

Finally, feeling the rhythm, Mu-bu-tan leaped out into the void, and successfully took hold with monkey-like fingers that nature might have designed for exactly such a maneuver. His long tail slapped Tarzan across the top of his head and the ape-man took this as the signal to start his descent.

They reached the ground in short order and Tarzan stepped aside to allow Mu-bu-tan to alight comfortably.

In the darkness, they clasped hands. Tarzan said, "I have located my missing countrywoman and I must convey her down safely. Wait here for me."

Harboring a reasonable doubt that he had climbed the wrong vine in the first place, Tarzan felt his way along the cliff's forbidding face until he came to another rope vine. This he ascended, using only the tremendous muscular prowess of his thews.

This time, the ape-man reached the estimated height, whereupon he hissed a single word: "Ilex!"

"Here," called the woman. "I was afraid you had gotten lost."

"I have found my friend, so it is time to go."

Ilex asked, "How am I to grope around in the darkness and reach the ground safely?"

It was an excellent question, but Tarzan had already given it consideration.

Holding on with both hands, the ape-man used his bare feet to find a ledge on which to rest his naked toes. Once safely perched, he sought hand-holds and discovered one.

This gave him a three-point anchorage, so with his free hand he released the rope.

Tarzan instructed, "Remove whatever article of clothing is most suitable and use it to grasp the rope that I am going to push in your direction. Use both hands. If you are sufficiently strong, you may slide down the rope without friction burning your hands."

"Oh, that does not sound like a very sound plan in the darkness," Ilex commented.

"Since I am holding on rather precariously, I do not think this a proper time to argue the point," retorted the ape-man. "In any event, the vine is coming your way."

It took four tries before Ilex was able to catch the rope with her garment, and another long minute before she felt she had mustered up the nerve to drop from a seated position into unguessable space.

The sound of her cry of fear combined with the whizzing of the rope in her cloth-covered hands made it seem to Tarzan that Ilex might have plunged to her death.

When she struck ground, it was with a perceptibly dull thud.

Chapter Forty-Three

THE ARACHNID

CAPTURING the swaying vine in one hand, Tarzan transferred to the rope and went down, dropping hand over hand, as before, not at all intimidated by the dangerous drop to the hard cavern floor below.

He was soon firmly on the ground, and bending over Ilex, who was sprawled there. The ape-lord knelt and felt about, finding such limbs as he encountered in the darkness to be unbroken.

"Are you all right?" he demanded.

"I appear to be," said Ilex, rather breathlessly.

Tarzan reached down, found her wrists, and felt of her palms. They were very hot. Pressing firmly with strong thumbs, he asked, "Does this hurt?"

"It does not," responded the woman.

"Then you appear not to have suffered any rope burns," decided Tarzan. "The initial portion of our escape is therefore successful."

Hovering nearby, Mu-bu-tan demanded, "What language are you speaking? And who are you speaking to?"

Helping Ilex to her feet, Tarzan told the warrior, "This is my countrywoman of whom I have spoken. And her tongue is not one you know."

"I understand," nodded Mu-bu-tan.

"Then understand this: henceforth please call me Clayton, for I do not want this woman to know me by my other name."

"Very well, Clayton-jad-guru."

"Clayton is sufficient," corrected Tarzan.

To Ilex, Tarzan said, "I cannot properly introduce you to my friend, Mu-bu-tan, inasmuch as he does not speak English. Nor does he understand it. But we can trust him."

"Thank him for me, Flying Officer Clayton."

A moment later, Ilex expressed consternation. In the darkness, she shifted suddenly.

"What is wrong?" asked Tarzan.

Her voice was an unsettled hiss. "Something appears to be grazing the backs of my legs. It feels like a snake, except that it is rather bristly."

"One moment while I investigate," said Tarzan, pulling her aside and bending down until his groping fingers encountered something long and hairy, which jumped aside at his touch.

"I have discovered the source of your discomfort," he informed her. "It is Mu-bu-tan's tail. I will instruct him to keep it close to his person at all times."

"Your friend has a—*tail?*" wondered Ilex.

"Many of the men of the tribes of this land possess prehensile tails. It is just something to which one becomes accustomed after a while."

"But I do not think I will ever become accustomed to that idea but, so long as it remains dark I do not think it will bother me very much."

Tarzan said, "Very well. Let us be on our way."

The notion of getting on their way was an appealing one. However, they had no more inkling of the correct direction that would lead toward freedom than before. Nevertheless, at Tarzan's urging, they linked hands and the ape-man took the lead.

Ilex was in the middle of the human chain and perforce grasped Mu-bu-tan's hirsute digits. The sensations associated with holding the Waz-ho-don warrior's simian fingers were disconcerting to say the least.

To Tarzan, she remarked, "The hand of your friend appears to be uncommonly hairy."

"By the standards of civilization," admitted Tarzan, "Mubu-tan is altogether too hirsute for common company."

"I feel as if I am holding onto a monkey's paw," she added, low-voiced.

Tarzan said nothing, intent upon feeling the way ahead, using nothing more than his bare feet to reassure himself of sound footing, and his acute nostrils to detect anything untoward that might be coming in their direction.

The trek was long, and they encountered no obstacles for a time.

After a while, a dim sense of illumination was received by their brains. Tarzan was the first to notice this, and his sight-starved eyes reacted as if they were not certain of the reality of what they perceived. He was forced to shut his eyes periodically, before his vision adjusted to new conditions.

"There appears to be illumination before us," he whispered.

Straining eyes searched for the source of that vague light, and all three escapees began to fix upon it as they crept along.

They did not realize that they were turning a corner until suddenly their eyes were struck by a great expanse of greenish-white phosphorescence which, although not strong, struck the optic nerve with the force of direct sunlight.

This was not the thing that wrenched stunned gasps from their throats; it was what hung before the greenish glow.

It was an incredible thing, a stupefying thing, a thing that their brains refused to accept at first.

A spider hung before and above them. Huge, titanic, resting in the center of an orb web that was as large across as the wingspan of a British bomber plane.

Arrayed around the great eight-legged monster were fuzzy white shapes that brought to mind the unhatched eggs of terrestrial spiders, but of comparatively monstrous size.

That they were, in fact, eggs was brought forcibly to their attention when these oval forms began to tremble and in some spots break apart, disgorging small bodies possessing long, pipestem legs.

There was no other way to interpret the horrific sight. The eggs of the gigantic arachnid were hatching spiderlings!

Chapter Forty-Four

Devil-Darts

THERE are moments that seem to stretch into a timeless eternity.

For Tarzan of the Apes and his two companions, this was one such slice of time. Their stunned eyes were drinking in the sight of the stupendous spider web with its central occupant, great bristled legs sprawled to the inner edges of the weave. Then, the whitish eggs started disgorging their hatchlings, and the cold sense of dread that had seized them turned into a sensation of impending alarm.

The great arachnid did not move, except insofar as the spiderlings clambering down its web caused the strands to react like plucked violin strings. The vibrations shook the entire web, and consequently the great spider's body shook in sympathy.

But it did not otherwise stir.

As the first spiderling dropped to the hard stone floor, Tarzan heard behind him the voice of Ilex climb in horror. A scream was torn from her throat. She released Tarzan's hand.

The ape-man turned. His grey eyes fell upon her head twisting away as she recoiled in horror. Then, blundering into Mu-bu-tan, Ilex received her first good look at the Waz-ho-don warrior, with his marvelously hairy body and unusual physiognomy.

A greater cry was wrenched from her lungs. Shrinking from Mu-bu-tan's momentarily dumbstruck expression, Ilex stumbled backward, almost colliding with the ape-man, who came rushing to her defense.

A great deal was happening all at once. To Tarzan's reckoning, Ilex had simply stumbled over a stone, for no sooner had she lost her footing than she pitched forward, landing face down, her head turned to one side, her features obscured.

Bending as he ran, with the intention of scooping her up in his great bronzed arms, the ape-man was oblivious to the abbreviated whispers that were cutting through the cool cavern air. He had almost reached the woman's side when suddenly Mu-bu-tan emitted a yipping sound that was unlike anything the ape-man had ever before heard emerge from his bearded lips—if the shaggy mass of hair that ringed his pallid face could be rightfully called a beard.

Gaze veering sharply in the warrior's direction, Tarzan saw that Mu-bu-tan's chest was seemingly sprouting short white feathers. But it was not that at all, he quickly realized.

Darts! The warrior was being quilled by darts!

Eyes rolling up in his head, Mu-bu-tan collapsed where he stood, his wiry form so filled with poison that he could not summon up a gesture toward escape.

As Tarzan's eyes whipped back to the prone form of Ilex, he saw that she, too, had acquired a feathering of darts. Only then did the keen eyes of the Lord of the Jungle detect the whispers that traced through the still cavern air like passing needles of sound.

Perhaps it was mere luck. Possibly it was a minor miracle, but Tarzan had not yet been struck. As greatly as his heart yearned to succor his fallen friends, the ape-man understood that he was but seconds away from succumbing to a similar fate.

In that moment, instinct took over. The right of self-preservation is an absolute one. It was no less so with the mighty jungle lord.

Tarzan threw himself flat, the better to present a less tempting target. He paused, listening. But only one dart struck stone nearby, rebounding harmlessly to land with a faint click.

Not wishing to risk more missiles, the ape-man swiftly rolled, clambered to his bare feet, and went shooting for a bulky rock that offered a modicum of shelter. From this spot, he sought greater refuge. Grey eyes soon found it. An outcropping, almost the size of a boulder.

Flashing for this, Tarzan flung himself behind its impenetrable shelter. Soft sounds came to him. Bare feet slapping cold stone.

Looking around him, Tarzan spied some loose stones. He gathered up three, cradled them in his left arm while he sought to climb the great rocky barrier.

It was awkward, but he succeeded.

From its rounded summit, the ape-lord looked down.

The pale spiderlings were filtering through this arm of the cavern. Tarzan could see them clearly now. These creepers were not hatchlings, in the accepted sense of being infant offspring, but young examples of the spider people. Why they had hatched from eggs was beyond Tarzan's ken at the moment, but it was an insignificant matter against the enormity of the peril he faced.

The spider-men were actively hunting him, dark eyes gleaming.

Kneeling, Tarzan set the dornicks at his feet, took one in hand and waited, listening. Soft padding of bare feet drew closer. He stood up, and let fly in a manner that would have impressed an American baseball pitcher.

The stone flew true. Whistling, it collided with the chalky skull of one of the approaching spiderlings. He went down, the sharp sound of rock striking hairless pate suggesting that the skull bone had been broken. The creature did not rise after that.

This commotion caused the others to turn, their narrow eyes turning to slits of jet.

By that time, Tarzan had sent a second stone en route. It beaned another spiderling, who was knocked off his feet. The sound of his head colliding with the cavern floor was not pleasant to hear. At least, not to his fellows, for they began lifting their hands and manipulating the long-jointed fingers and paired thumbs, apparently communicating in some silent mode of semaphore speech.

The knuckles seemed to pop and crackle, adding to the effort.

Tarzan had only one stone left, so he chose his next victim carefully. He selected a straggler far from the knot of others. Aiming for the chest this time, he struck the shoulder, sending the small figure into a half-spin that caused his blowpipe to go flying away.

It was that weapon that the ape-man desired. Leaping from his perch, Tarzan smacked the stone floor with his feet and sprinted for the fallen weapon.

He reached it with a speed that rivaled that of Ara the lightning. For the ape-man knew that his life hung in the balance. Falling upon the tube of bamboo, he scooped it up and veered for the fallen spider pygmy who lay dazed on the stone floor. Stepping on his chest with one foot, Tarzan reached down and snatched up his quiver of darts. Six-fingered hands groped for his ankles. The ape-man settled that with a hard slam of his bare heel against the creature's thin jaw. All efforts became feeble, then ceased.

Wheeling, Tarzan extracted a dart, inserted it into the mouth of the tube, then brought it to his lips. The spiderling needed both hands to hold the fat tube in balance; the ape-man required but one. He blew out a sharp breath, which emptied the hollow shaft.

His first dart missed, owing to his unfamiliarity with the clumsy weapon.

But it had a satisfactory effect. For the spider people, apparently possessing keen eyesight resulting from a lifetime of dwelling in cave conditions, traced the white feather fletching and their faces expressed shock and surprise that the dart had come so close.

Tarzan took from that the idea that his larger lungs gave him an advantage the pygmy spider warriors could not match. But that advantage was of no value if he could not place a dart into a foe's pale skin.

Loading another needle, Tarzan tried again. He inhaled sharply, then expelled the contents of his lungs. This time, the dart struck a crouching figure, and the spiderling gave a cry that trailed off into a thin wail. Keeling over, the pale foeman succumbed to the poison's cold bite.

This brought a small flurry of devil-darts in the ape-man's direction. He returned the favor, striking a patch of white skin in almost the exact center of the forehead.

This, incidentally, was a fluke. Tarzan had been aiming at the general shape, not at his enemy's brow.

But when the spider foe flopped backward, then collapsed on his naked back, the eyes of his long-limbed comrades saw clearly that the dart had bisected his brow.

This engendered a general retreat—a retreat in which whispering darts were hurled back as if they were contemptuous insults.

Tarzan evaded them all, noticing that the feathering was invariably white. He remembered that white feathers promised sleep, not death.

Not wishing to wait around while the spider people regrouped and returned with more lethal ammunition, Tarzan faded back behind another buttress of stone, and attempted to ascertain the totality of his situation.

It was bleak. All around were rock walls. Going back the way he had come would be to plunge again into impenetrable darkness and its attendant dangers. To go forward would be to pass under the gargantuan spider web and its enormous inhabitant. Not to mention its guardian spiderlings.

If there existed another way out, Tarzan would have to locate it. And the sooner the better. He did not possess the luxury of leisure. Nor did the ape-man have the possibility of bearing his unconscious friends out of the cavern. Not if he wished to evade skin-seeking darts. Without clothing, and bereft of any armor, he represented a vulnerable target once the enemy got themselves organized.

Since there was not the opportunity for reflection, or making plans, Tarzan would have to act rapidly if he was to preserve his life. For the ape-man knew that if he did not, the lives of his helpless friends were surely forfeit, there being no other hope of rescue than himself.

Having absorbed that grim reality, Tarzan emerged from his shelter and began sprinting toward the spider web and its awful owner, running without fear but also harboring the certain knowledge that he was charging blindly into unknown peril.

Chapter Forty-Five

Ignominious Escape

T HE SPIDER PEOPLE had retreated to their great orb web whose longitudinal strands were anchored high into the dimness of the cavern walls and roof, which were dappled with patches of phosphorescence which lent a somber light into the stony chamber.

They were clambering up the transverse cross strands, seeking positions of advantage, no doubt with the intention of turning and unleashing a few salvos, if not a biting cloud of poison darts, upon their enemy, Tarzan of the Apes.

For his part, the ape-man was sprinting toward their immense refuge, which was constructed over a thin trickle of a stream that wound through a rocky defile which permitted the pale pygmies to clamber up and gain the lowermost edges of the vast spider web which stood stark against the lichen patches glowing ghostly around it.

Casting his gaze upward, he saw the web once again twitching and vibrating, the spider sprawled in its precise center jerking slightly, its eight legs also twitching, as if stirring into slow life.

In his career of adventure, Tarzan had beheld his share of monsters. But nothing like this gargantuan arachnid had ever loomed before him.

Although it hung in its web with the patient stillness habitual to spiders who wait for unwary flies to wander into their sticky domain, this creature made no moves. It might have been asleep, and the twitching merely the product of its own mindless nightmares.

But Tarzan well understood that if it roused to life, despite its size the frightful thing could clamp his head in its poisoned fangs in a trice.

The ape-man had no intention of permitting it that opportunity. As his swift feet carried him closer and closer to the web, Tarzan naturally ducked, seeking to avoid contact with the ropy strands of the web.

It was well that he did so, for one of the spiderlings chanced to turn his head about, and saw the ape-man sprinting closer.

One hand clutching a web strand, the other lifted and began making the hand signs that were attended by joint and knuckle popping that appeared to be the language of the spider people. To add to the alarm, he slapped one of the longitudinal strands hard, causing the entire webwork to quiver like a struck bell.

These actions alerted his fellows. Two of the more nimble of the spiderlings dropped to the ground, intending to block the ape-man's rush. Six-fingered claws clutching, their ebon eyes were alien orbs resembling nothing human.

Tarzan still clutched his blowpipe, but whether by aversion to its use, or sheer necessity, he declined to load it. Instead, taking it by both hands as a batter would a baseball bat, the ape-man employed this flimsy weapon to pummel the first spider-man who leapt into his path.

Tarzan managed to splinter the pipe while battering the other's skull, but the result was what was required. The spiderling fell, bloodied, his brains turned to pudding by the jungle lord's punishing might.

Releasing his now-useless tube, Tarzan appropriated that of his fallen foe. Wheeling, he fell upon the other spider warrior.

That one had the presence of mind to load his weapon, and was in the act of exhaling, when Tarzan's pilfered tube came crashing down, knocking it out of the enemy's hands and violently extracting several front teeth in the process.

The ape-man's brown fist made short work of the squirming pygmy. Still clutching his tube, Tarzan flung himself under the web, and raced to the far side, following the sound of rushing water—the noise of the mighty cataract that barred the entrance to this dim den of noisome creatures.

That he was leaving behind a trusted comrade, as well as the object of his search, and his mission, pained Tarzan greatly. But for all his feral wildness, the Lord of the Jungle was a logical man. He knew that if he fell in battle, it was unlikely that another opportunity for escape would ever come.

So he ran for the water, as whispers of death again filled the dank air, knowing that only by escape could he regroup and storm this cavern on another day.

His racing feet took him around a right-hand turn, and then one that shot left. The relentless waterfall sounds grew ever louder. The clean scent of fresh water filled his pulsing nostrils.

Rounding a rocky corner, Tarzan came upon the stony channel, but instead of plunging in, he stopped, whirled, dropped to one knee and loaded his blowpipe.

Silently, he waited. The sound of bare feet disturbing loose cave detritus told the ape-man that his enemy was approaching.

Tentatively, a bald head stuck out. It was larger than the others he had seen. On the forehead glowed in the gloom six pale green spots over two dark eyes. This arrangement seemed to constitute some resemblance to the customary eight orbs of the eight-legged arachnid. Tarzan took this to mean that here was a spider pygmy of high ranking, for others of his kind had sported fewer such eye spots, or none at all.

The searching dark eyes fell upon the ape-man finally.

And Tarzan released his pent-up breath.

This time, his loose dart struck the exact center of the forehead on purpose, for Tarzan well appreciated the psychological effect this would create.

Eyes rolling upward, the owner of the head sank into a pile resembling a clutter of pale sticks. One hand retained the strength to lift a weird double-thumbed hand, and briefly they worked in a way that was reminiscent of a spider spinning its web.

Once again, the ape-man had the impression that this is what passed for language and speech among the otherwise-silent white pygmies.

Recharging his blowpipe, Tarzan waited several minutes. But no new foe poked his ghostly features around the corner. Instead, the unconscious body was dragged from view by unseen hands.

Someone released a warning dart, which ticked off a rock wall.

That was enough. Tarzan began walking backward, not taking his eyes off the spot where his victim had been lying and, without a word, slipped into the water.

Still retaining the blowpipe, Tarzan swam beneath the surface, pausing every so often to stop and push the bamboo up, blowing out whatever water clogged it, and using the hollow tube to breathe through his mouth.

In this way, he did not have to surface, and expose himself to any hunting darts.

It was during one of these pauses for rest and replenishing oxygen that the ape-man discovered his tortoise shell shield lying on the channel bottom. Dropping the blowpipe, he picked it up, saw that it was intact, and strapped it to his back, securing it with the bone buckles. Recovering the blowpipe, Tarzan resumed swimming, this time on the surface.

To anyone who might be watching in the somber gloom of the grotto, it looked as if a half-submerged turtle was swimming along.

Tarzan listened for the ticking of hunting darts striking the nodular carapace, but nothing of the sort took place. Only then did the ape-man become confident that his spidery foes were declining pursuit, and all that the Lord of the Jungle needed to do was breast the cataract in order to reach the outside world of Pal-ul-don.

In his beating heart, he felt a pang of regret over the unknown fate of Mu-bu-tan and the woman named Ilex, whose face he still had not clearly seen.

Chapter Forty-Six

Torn Ear Wanders

TORN EAR the elephant grazed patiently near the precipice where Tarzan had left him.

The chocolate-brown pachyderm did not stray far from the designated spot. In his mind, he expected his master to return to this very place. His great heart ached with loneliness. He did not want to miss the return of the one who had saved his life only days before in the saurian-infested swamp.

Yet, loyal as he was, Torn Ear was also subject to the urges and instincts of survival. In this wild land which was unfamiliar to the elephant, blundering unknown things moved through the well-trammeled jungle paths.

A distant grunting, coupled with a musky odor being carried upon the wind, told the grazing beast that something massive was muttering along as he rooted through the forest.

Confident in his raw power and sharp tusks, Torn Ear nevertheless had no appetite to engage another such specimen as the horned *gryf* he had earlier bested. So in order to avoid an unnecessary conflict, in which no food or territory were at stake—inasmuch as the elephant was an herbivore in unfamiliar country—Torn Ear lumbered away from the tangled brush that marked the spot where he had been temporarily abandoned.

Wandering about, the pachyderm drifted farther and farther away from a nettled bush that was firmly imprinted upon his elephantine memory for future reference. In his aimless perambulations, he heard other crashing sounds that suggested an altogether different *gryf*. Scents reached his twitching and sniffing trunk that made him leery of any unexpected encounter.

Retreating, Torn Ear attempted to avoid the problem by going in yet another direction, this one toward the long jagged rift in the earth beside which he had foraged for green shoots of delicious bamboo.

Hours of this evasive dodging brought him to a section of cliff precipice that was savagely eroded. This portion constituted a chalk cliff, and whether by relentless action of the elements or, as a result of being excavated by the spider people to make the pale paste that whitened their bodies, something had caused the face to collapse, creating a kind of rough ramp.

Looking down the incline of jumbled rock, dirt and chunks of chalk, Torn Ear was tempted to brave it, thinking it would bring him to the rift floor where Tarzan presumably hunted. For what other business would his friend be about, but hunting for game? So went the animal's simple reasoning.

But the great beast had been enjoined to remain at the other place, beside the nettled bush. Perhaps it would be better to return to that spot, lest the ape-man have already returned.

Such were the ruminations of Torn Ear the elephant, who did not know the ways of man, much less the ways of the Lord of the Jungle, who had earned his undying loyalty.

As his small eyes studied the tempting terrain, Torn Ear patiently flapped his good ear, stirring what remained of his bad ear. He did not hear the *gryf* until it began charging, head lowered, blowing and grunting like a bull rhinoceros.

Wheeling with uncanny grace for one so large, the elephant turned to face the oncoming brute, whose blue-ringed eyes glowered in its beaked yellow face. Lifting his trunk, Torn Ear gave out a piercing scream the like of which perhaps had never before echoed through the fissures and crevices of the Land of Man.

Now the battle cry of an elephant is not like its trumpeting, which can be loud and carry far. No, the terrifying scream is a kind of thunder that pummels eardrums and causes the surrounding trees to shake their delicate leaves.

This particular bull triceratops had never before encountered an elephant, but, having spied its brown haunches, saw the irresistible sight of tempting meat.

Only when Torn Ear turned about did the *gryf* become aware of the formidable ivory tusks. By this time, the carnivorous triceratops was fully committed to the attack.

That is, until the elephant lifted its trunk to permit its mouth to open at its widest. From that pendulous orifice emerged the most unearthly animal cry the *gryf* had ever heard.

This, combined with the great curved tusks of gleaming ivory, was sufficient to change its brutish mind. The triceratops, not wishing to display cowardice in the face of a foe, did not balk its own charge. Instead, it simply veered to the left, clawed feet tearing up ground, blowing angrily, and went plunging onward.

Plunging onward—and over. For the *gryf*, perhaps miscalculating, or more likely simply panicked, continued its thundering gallop even after the ground shaking under his earth-gouging claws unexpectedly gave out.

The bellowing creature landed with an indescribable thud, combined with the snapping of its neck bones and bony head carapace.

The wheezing of its lungs was short-lived. Very quickly, it became inert—undone by its own reckless hunger for food.

Nonplussed, Torn Ear drifted back to the cliff rim, and peered downward. He saw that the great tri-horned creature was without animation, and decided forthwith that he had nothing more to fear.

Returning to the sloping incline of powdery chalk and rock, the patient pachyderm carefully set his forefeet down, tested the solidity of footing and, finding sufficient purchase, commenced to pick his laborious way down to the ravine floor.

In his loyal heart was the high hope that he would sooner rather than later encounter Tarzan of the Apes.

Chapter Forty-Seven

AGAINST THE TORRENT

THE SWIM toward the wavering, watery light whose rushing thunder signified freedom for Tarzan of the Apes was not a difficult one. Even with the cumbersome tortoise shell carapace strapped to his back, he managed it handily.

It was only when Tarzan emerged into the brilliant sunlight that warned of the necessity of breaching the raging cataract that matters began assuming daunting proportions.

Charging his lungs with oxygen, the ape-man sank underwater in order to avoid being battered by the rushing torrent. While sparing him the worst of it, Tarzan was nevertheless tossed about helplessly as the remorseless fall of river water caused the waters at the cavern's mouth to surge and roil endlessly.

The difficulty lay, the ape-man quickly discovered, in avoiding being so overwhelmed that he failed to reach a source of oxygen.

Tarzan was ultimately forced to drop his blowpipe, which was useless in the water, and doff his shield, which hampered him more than it had during his initial foray through the cataract. Thus disencumbered, the ape-man was able to fight his way to the surface, a few yards beyond the surging curtain, in the outer reaches of the ever-active pool.

When he popped to the surface, he greedily imbibed oxygen through his open mouth.

Once fully revived, Tarzan swam about, seeking his tortoise shell shield, but to no avail. It was lost in the tumult of the falls.

The bamboo blowpipe, however, surfaced in the sudsy foam, and having no other weapon, he reclaimed it.

Once back on dry land, Tarzan cast a farewell glance at the raging cataract, and began making his way back to the cliff side where he had left Torn Ear the elephant behind, and where the ape-lord fully expected the loyal pachyderm to be waiting for him.

Chapter Forty-Eight

UNARMED

TARZAN OF THE APES soon reached the tumble of rock and stone that had been his entrance into the deep ravine of the spider people without incident.

Looking upward, he spied no sign of Torn Ear the elephant. This did not concern him at first. So the ape-man began his careful climb to the lip of the precipice.

More than halfway up, failing to scent the creature, he paused to give voice to a cry the elephant would recognize.

Nothing came back in response.

Resuming his climb, Tarzan reached the top and stood on high ground. He looked about carefully. There was no sign or scent of Torn Ear. A grim frown troubled the ape-lord's brow.

Amid the profuse greenery that marked the jungles of Pal-ul-don, a reddish-brown pachyderm should stand out strikingly. But one did not.

Searching the ground, Tarzan found the heavy pad prints that indicated the elephant had wandered about in search of forage. Eventually, it seemed to have struck out in a southerly direction.

The ape-man followed the spoor. In due course, he came to the spot where the chalky cliff face had eroded into an incline. Tarzan picked out the disordered tracks of pachyderm and *gryf* in close proximity, and deduced that the two brutes had clashed not long before.

Peering down into the declivity, he saw the results. A dead *gryf*, its slate sides unmoving, its red carapace badly broken. And pressed into the powdery incline, clear signs that Torn Ear had picked his way down to the valley floor below.

Following suit, Tarzan came to the corpse of the vanquished triceratops.

Feeling its tough skin, the ape-man wished he still carried his hunting knife. With its keen cutting edge, he might have carved out a sufficient patch of hide to fashion some form of protection against the devil-darts of the spider pygmies.

The tempered blade was now property of the spider people, and that fact alone would compel the ape-man's return to their preserves, had he possessed no higher or more compelling motivation.

Following the wayward tracks of Torn Ear, Tarzan of the Apes continued on, recognizing that the pachyderm was plodding resolutely in the direction of the waterfall of the spider people.

The ape-man was without his blade, or any other weapon worth carrying.

He did not hold that the bamboo blowpipe and its handful of spider-venom darts were worthy tools for Tarzan of the Apes.

Despite these unsettling facts, Tarzan walked confident and unafraid. For although he was bereft of his customary weapons, he was yet Lord of the Jungle. Moreover, he was a flying officer of the R.A.F., and he had a mission to perform.

Any vengeance he might extract from the spider-pygmies would be incidental to the successful execution of that mission.

Chapter Forty-Nine

AWAKE TO HORROR

MU-BU-TAN was the first to awaken.

The Waz-ho-don warrior came to consciousness slowly, as one does when he has suffered the after-effects of a pernicious poison. His dark eyes fluttered open as his sluggish brain struggled with the return to self-awareness. Light striking his dilating irises was weak, and for a time Mu-bu-tan did not fully comprehend his surroundings.

The air in his nostrils was dank and musty, tinged with odors he found far from agreeable. His head throbbed in such a way that he could feel the blood pulsing through the veins of his shaggy forehead and throat.

That he lived, slowly became evident. Nothing else was as yet clear to him. His last recollection was of the horror-stricken face of the woman whose hand he had held as an aid to guiding one another out of the cavern of dread darkness. It had been the first glimpse of her features Mu-bu-tan had enjoyed.

Even twisted in terror, it had been a handsome face. The woman had been no mere youth, but a fully mature woman. Her dark hair was rather short for a woman's natural tresses, but pleasingly composed for all that.

Then, she had fallen, and in short order, so did Mu-bu-tan. Of the fate of Tarzan-jad-guru, the Waz-ho-don warrior had no inkling.

The throbbing of his awakening brain fast became a steady pounding, and Mu-bu-tan became alarmed that he had been injured on the head when he lost consciousness. Squeezing his eyes shut, he reopened them, hoping to clear the last of the fog that appeared to have hazed his vision.

When his sight returned to clarity, Mu-bu-tan beheld why his head pounded so. He was hanging upside down!

Below lay rock flooring, smooth in a way that suggested generations of bare feet had whetted the stony ground into evenness. A pulsing flicker of light suggested a dark vein of a creek or stream cutting through the ground. Tumbled stones stood on either side of that expanse of stone.

Mu-bu-tan lifted his head laboriously. On either side, he caught glimpses of a near wall—the natural arch of the cavernous grotto. But what caused the moisture of his mouth to suddenly dry up and his heart to freeze in mid-beat was that which was arrayed all around him.

A great orb web, whose strands were as thick as woven rope!

Attempting to move, Mu-bu-tan quickly became apprised of his true predicament. He was trapped in this foul weaving. Wrists and ankles, he quickly saw, were lashed to the coarsely hairy strands. He attempted to pull one arm free, but no amount of straining succeeded.

The great skein to which he was attached shook under his exertions. Attempting to draw up one leg by bending it at the knee produced no more useful a result. Even less, for the web only shook some more, but the knee barely bent.

Flexing every hirsute limb in turn, Mu-bu-tan learned that his warrior's strength was unequal to the task of tearing free of the great ropey web. This was not the sticky substance that comprises spider silk, but some matter as thick and tough as jungle creepers. Nor could he reach those hateful bonds with his sharp, pointed teeth.

Only his tail hung free and loose. He could feel it trailing down over his left shoulder, the tip dangling.

Mu-bu-tan attempted to impel it to life, but the useful and always-obedient appendage refused to obey the commands of his brain. No doubt its lowermost extremities were pinned to the skein, for the warrior was affixed to the web so that his spine pressed against it.

Thus helpless, he hung for some moments in utter frustration, feeling thoroughly trapped. A sinking cold feeling settled into the pit of his stomach, yet his warrior's heart did not quail at contemplation of his situation.

After a time, Mu-bu-tan craned his head around in order to see more clearly his predicament, for his still-rousing brain began to remember what it had mercifully attempted to forget.

Searching eyes tracked the strands of the heavy skein until they discovered another form. It was the white-skinned woman, whom Tarzan had called Ilex.

She, too, was bound to the enormous web, head also hanging downward, lolling on her columnar neck as if it had been broken. Her pale features were still, composed as if in death, although her mouth hung open.

Mu-bu-tan was again struck by her ethereal beauty. She rivaled the women of his own village, although she was distressingly bereft of a coat of body hair, which marred her perfect form only slightly in the warrior's appreciative eyes. For his people had mated with the white-skinned hairless Ho-don tribe as often as they took as mates the hairy black-skinned Waz-don.

But that spiritual sensation quickly passed, for Mu-bu-tan's wandering gaze soon fell upon dark blobs interspersed about the web—the gauzy white eggs of the spider.

That was when Mu-bu-tan glimpsed a great still arachnid leg, hairy in the extreme. Off to his right it lay, resting on the great orb web as if affixed to its strands.

The Waz-ho-don warrior turned and wrenched his head in order to follow the hideous member back to its innermost root, but when he did so, Mu-bu-tan had to fight a suffocating urge to shut his eyes and invoke the death prayer to the Great God, for he feared that his life was nearing its conclusion.

Directly above him hung the monster arachnid, head downward, eight gleaming eyes regarding him steadily, unblinkingly, the way a common spider stares at the ordinary fly that has wandered into its den.

The fangs of the thing were distended. But Mu-bu-tan had no eyes for them. It was those eight bright eyes, arrayed about the blunt black visage of the monster, luminous as if with a dull intelligence, that froze his hairy warrior's body as if its poisonous fangs had already injected him with cold, creeping death.

Chapter Fifty

DEVIL WITH WINGS

SEEKING his elephant companion, Tarzan of the Apes took notice of the position of the sun.

Before, it had not mattered to him how much time had passed during his period of captivity among the spider pygmies, but now he noticed the dimming of the day, and realized that nightfall was again approaching.

Following Torn Ear's trail, the ape-man was determined to locate his elephantine ally before the sun set and conditions deteriorated. He also became aware of his hunger, for he had not eaten in over a day. This was an important matter, for in order to rescue his friends, Tarzan would require a full stomach and all that it contained in the way of nourishment.

Obtaining food was not normally a challenge for the jungle lord, but he was without his customary weapons, toting only the odious blowpipe of his enemies and a small pouch of poison darts.

Taking stock of the latter, he discovered that it contained several white-fletched darts and three whose feathers were scarlet. These latter, he knew, were lethal.

Moving stealthily, his flexible brown skin rippling with the play of his panther-like muscles, the ape-man conned the cliffs on either side of him, searching for enemies.

Ahead, the rushing of the endless cataract told that he was again approaching the den of the spider people. Although this was his ultimate goal, Tarzan had other business to settle before he penetrated that noisome grotto once more.

A familiar scent reached his keen nostrils not long after.

Bara the deer! Tarzan's heart leapt in anticipation. Here was good, succulent food for the taking.

Moving cautiously, the ape-man underwent a striking transformation, becoming a feral hunter, searching the ground for tracks, while following the sweet scent wafting on the canyon breeze.

Before long, Tarzan had the spoor and, shifting into a moving crouch, began to stalk his prey.

Bara was stealthy, too. But not so stealthy as the Lord of the Jungle. For Bara possessed hooves which clicked as they struck stony ground and made distinct sounds, whereas the toenails of Tarzan of the Apes were cut short and the thick pads of his bare feet produced no warning sounds.

Soon, the ape-man spied the deer wandering along, nibbling at such shoots as it chanced upon.

Fortunately for Tarzan, the wind in the ravine was almost non-existent, the breezes blowing across the top, and not down into the narrow crevice. So Bara had no warning.

Unfortunately, the jungle lord was not the only hunter on the prowl as the day settled into dusk. For above the heads of the hunter and his unsuspecting prey, something glided along air currents, making no sound, and peered downward with avid, unwinking almond-shaped orbs.

Only a shadow, great and unsettling, warned the ape-man that he had a rival.

For something spiraled out of the sky and beat him to his goal.

Tarzan sensed danger before his other senses apprised him of the approaching menace. A flat shadow fell upon him, and with the instinct of one who had been in his own turn prey to others, the ape-man suddenly shifted off to one side, seeking a cluster of rocks in which to secrete himself.

His eyes sought the shadow's source. It was a pteranodon, some twenty feet from wingtip to wingtip. Flinging up its bat-like pinions, it reached down with a clutching foot adorned with monstrous talons, and these folded over the hapless deer.

Bara screamed, but to no avail. Its kicking hooves left the ground.

As Tarzan watched, the pteranodon strained maroon wings and attempted to vault back into the sky, taking Tarzan's struggling meal along with it.

The suddenness of the creature's attack had caught the ape-man off guard. But this lapse was momentary.

Reaching into his pouch, he drew forth one of the deadly red-fletched darts and leapt out into the open. Steadying the tube charged with the thinly vicious messenger of death, Tarzan pressed it to his lips and expelled a mighty breath.

The dart was driven upward, and Tarzan drew the second red dart. This, too, leaped from the other end of the tube, to seek lodgment in the fleeing winged terror.

For a long minute, Tarzan thought he had failed to strike true. The pteranodon was clawing into the sky, its meal squirming in its fearful claws, its snaky, barbed tail snapping in its wake.

Then, abruptly, the angular wings began jittering and convulsing, and a weird scream was emitted by the long hatchet-blade beak.

Flapping and faltering and jerking its narrow skull about, the pteranodon seemed uncertain what had befallen it. Its black orbs took on a stricken light. Then, one bony wing simply folded. It beat empty air as if maimed. Falling off the other wing, the awful creature keened out a death cry that terminated in a startled squawk, and released the deer.

The deer landed first. Landed hard.

The pteranodon swung about, still struggling, its devil's tail whipping about madly. But the poison coursing through its thin veins evidently worked swiftly. For the reptilian brain ceased to operate normally.

Perhaps thinking it was closer to the ground than it truly was, the pteranodon stretched its quadruped talons downward, seeking to alight.

Instead, it crashed, bony beak first, making a sound like dry brush snapping into kindling. No utterance emerged after it fell, stretched-skin-and-bone wings folded awkwardly, a pitiful wreck of a thing. Its toothless jaws chattered briefly. That barbed tail twitched feebly, then fell still.

Tarzan raced to the deer and discovered that it had broken its neck in the fall.

This was a relief, for the ape-man did not wish to use his remaining red-feathered dart to finish off Bara, which might render the sweet meat inedible and, besides that, he was loathe to employ the unclean weapon of the spider pygmies against a beautiful creature such as this deer.

There remained only the conundrum of how to extract a haunch of flesh without the proper tools.

Chapter Fifty-One

THE WEIRD SHIELD

A N HOUR later, Tarzan of the Apes stood up from the remains of the deer.

His handsome features were encrimsoned, and his fingers sticky with fresh blood. Having no sharp tool with which to pierce the deer's hide, the ape-lord had employed his strong teeth. It had been a messy job of work, but in the end Tarzan enjoyed all the warm satisfactions of a full belly.

Padding over to the wreckage of the pteranodon, the ape-man studied it intently.

The monster was unquestionably dead, but it was not idle curiosity that prompted Tarzan's inspection. During a previous journey, he encountered similar creatures in the prehistoric land deep in the center of the earth called Pellucidar. Those particular pterosaurs, although similarly formed, were markedly different in coloration, and were known to the inhabitants of that underground domain as *Thipdars.*[*]

Having noted the differences between this creature and those others, Tarzan's active mind seized upon an idea.

The pteranodon had some qualities of a living kite, its great leathery wings consisting of a tough skin stretched membrane-like between the thin hollow arm bones which gave them shape and structure. This construction made the ape-man wonder if a dart-resistant shield might not be fashioned out of these bony remains.

---

* *Tarzan at the Earth's Core*

277

It would take a certain amount of labor, not to mention a good strong blade to attempt the job. At his home plantation far east of Pal-ul-don, Tarzan had been shown how to construct an antelope-hide shield by his friends, the Waziri. What they had taught him might be applied to salvaging the makings of a similar shield from this fallen monster.

With that thought in mind, Tarzan resumed his search for Torn Ear the elephant. If the pachyderm had not lost the pack tied to his back, his military uniform and sidearm would still be available to him. With the revolver, he would have a means to reenter the grotto of the spider people and reclaim his father's hunting knife. It would be far better to have the shield before that, of course, but first things, perforce, must come first.

The trail that Torn Ear had left in his lumbering wake was plain to follow. Knowing that he would soon lose the light, the ape-man set out at a rapid pace, moving with the easy grace of a tawny jungle lion.

Matters might be hastened by calling out to his companion, but Tarzan knew that any sound he made would echo along the cliff-walled crack in the ground and reach the ears of the spider pygmies, who were certain to come out of their dens once the light of day was quenched.

Luck was with the ape-man, for rounding a turn in the ravine, he came upon Torn Ear, who was spraying himself with water which he sucked up from a small pool of rainwater.

Quickening his pace, Tarzan stole up upon the pachyderm from behind, taking care to make only small noises, which would alert the watchful beast, but no other creature.

Hearing these approaching sounds, the elephant flapped his good ear, and commenced turning around ponderously. Spying Tarzan with one curious eye, he lifted his quivering trunk and the ape-man leaped forward, seizing him by that member and squeezing it, enjoining the elephant to keep silent.

Tiny burbling sounds of pleasure escaped the brown brute's mouth, but these subsided quickly. His small eyes shone with a worshipful light.

Leaping atop Torn Ear's broad back, Tarzan took his customary spot, knees tucked behind those great, rippling ears, and turning around, reclaimed his pack.

Very quickly the ape-man removed his gun belt and sidearm, buckling these on. Doing so, he remembered that the metal tongue of the belt buckle might be sharpened and used as an awl. It would not be up to the demands he required, but it would be better than nothing.

Tarzan considered his best course of action—to push on to the cavern of the spider people, or retreat to the vanquished pteranodon and see what might be accomplished with its corpse. He had a thought that Torn Ear could be persuaded to bring his mighty feet down upon those angular wings and break them off in such a way that the toil could be started.

The ape-man considered. Since the fate of his friends remained unknown, he did not have time on his side. Whichever course of action he decided upon, the result must include the rescue of Ilex and Mu-bu-tan. Otherwise, all his strenuous efforts would have been for naught.

Giving the brown flank a hearty slap, Tarzan compelled Torn Ear to continue in the direction of the sheltering waterfall. The animal quickly fell into a steady stride that caused his passenger to roll with his rocking, swaying gait.

Very soon, the light almost completely failed, owing to the high cliffs intercepting the dying rays of day. Tarzan searched the way ahead with increasing inefficiency of vision.

Still, the ape-man was accustomed to jungle travel by night, and although the moon had yet to rise above the sheer cliffs on either side to fill the grim crack of a ravine with silvery light, Tarzan's sharp hearing and finely honed sense of smell were also at work.

Perhaps some instinct, as primal as that of the first hunter at the dawn of time, was also operating. For as they trundled along, man and elephant, the rider happened to glance up and his grey eyes narrowed at what he beheld.

They did not move, so at first the silhouetted shapes might have been mistaken for smooth, egg-shaped stones ringing the rugged cliff rim. But no stones ever gleamed with cunning eyes. Nor did they sport semi-luminous eyespots that brought to mind the unnerving pattern of myriad arachnid orbs.

Pretending not to notice, Tarzan nevertheless took stock. He counted seven heads, all off to the right. Slowly, so as not to draw attention to the act, he extracted his Enfield revolver from its holster, and surreptitiously cocked the pistol.

Carrying it loosely at his side, out of view of the watchers who did not move, the ape-man continued piloting his trundling steed along.

Then one of the unmoving heads suddenly came erect, a long tube jutting from its lower portion.

Tarzan brought his weapon up and around, and split that skull with a single well-placed bullet.

Screaming, the spider warrior pitched forward—and what remained of his brains dashed out against a fallen chunk of ledge stone at the bottom of the cliff.

The remaining spider-pygmies leaped to their feet, and Tarzan judiciously dropped off Torn Ear, landing on his opposite flank.

Calling for the pachyderm to come to a halt, Tarzan hunkered down in the shelter of the great animal, whose thick, wrinkled hide was proof against the deadliest spider-venom darts.

Unfortunately, it was not possible to conveniently aim a revolver from this sheltered position without exposing head and gun hand. Tarzan holstered his weapon, and considered his options. He still had the blowpipe and its remaining darts. But the same consideration applied. He could remain in shelter, or he could fire back. Shelter seemed the most rational choice for, once exposed, the ape-man was likely to be fixed by any of a number of whispering devil-darts.

Seeing the way of it, Tarzan reached out and grabbed a loose flap of Torn Ear's shoulder, compelling him to back up by the simple expedient of tugging firmly.

Walking backward himself, the ape-man kept the elephant's far flank always between him and the spider warriors, whose blowpipes started puffing again and again.

None struck the Lord of the Jungle.

WHEN the sinister intermittent whispering ceased, Tarzan called for Torn Ear to halt completely. By now there was no light, and whether the fusillade ended for that reason, or due to a lack of ammunition, was impossible to say with certainty.

With firm gestures, Tarzan compelled Torn Ear to turn around so that they could retreat more rapidly. For, now that they had been ambushed, continuing on to the waterfall was no longer practical.

Exposing the opposite flank, Tarzan, by using his hands, discovered numerous quills lodged in the rugged reddish-brown hide, which he extracted and placed in his pouch, not wishing the poison barbs to lie about, lest he step on them on another occasion. For the ape-man fully intended to come back this way when it was prudent to do so.

No further attacks were launched as they retreated. The egg-shaped heads again hunkered down, dark eyes watchful. But they did not follow.

When at last they came to the pteranodon's broken husk, Torn Ear made sounds of low distress deep in his great body. Tarzan quieted him with a few gentle words and, by a combination of whispers and pantomiming, attempted to make clear what he wished of the great brown beast.

Taking a wing in hand, Tarzan unfolded it, stretching the hideous member out to its full length. The ape-man pointed toward it. With palpable hesitation, Torn Ear brought his mighty forefeet down on the root of the framework of skin, producing a great crunching and snapping as the wing and its thin supporting bones snapped under his prodigious weight.

The rest was tough, muscular work as Tarzan ripped the wing free of its anchorage, then fell to examining the severed fragment of skin and narrow bone.

It resembled a great bow of stretched skin, held together by the arm and finger bones of the creature's strange hand—for each wing was nothing less than a splayed digital extension. The forefinger phalanx formed the upper framework on which the skin wing hung. The fact that it folded in the center made what the ape-man contemplated distinctly possible.

As it was constructed, the wing was too large and cumbersome for the purpose Tarzan had in mind. But folded along its natural joint, the grisly thing was more manageable.

Torn Ear had backed away from the corpse, not out of a modicum of respect, but an abundance of trepidation. So Tarzan dragged the weird wing over and flung it up so that it draped across the elephant's sloping shoulders.

Climbing up, the jungle lord lifted the ungainly appliance, and took his customary throne of elephantine flesh and bone. Once firmly seated, Tarzan lifted the wing, and arranged it awkwardly before him, in the manner of a bat-like mainsail.

It was very light for its size, but difficult even for the ape-man's fabulous strength to hold steady over a prolonged period of time.

Ready at last, Tarzan urged Torn Ear to retrace his steps. He fell to lumbering back in the direction of the watery cascade they could not see and only faintly hear.

It was a dangerous thing to press ahead, Tarzan knew. He had no certain knowledge that the pteranodon wing would protect him. Only that it seemed as if its taut skin was sufficiently strong to perform the job.

Whether or not that tightly-stretched hide was up to the task at hand, Tarzan of the Apes was determined to reclaim all that was due him—including a measure of retribution.

Chapter Fifty-Two

AGONY

THE BRITISH MILITARY INTELLIGENCE officer thus far known in this account as Ilex was slower to awaken than was Mu-bu-tan, the Waz-ho-don warrior. But awaken she did.

Ilex was being held in much the same surroundings as was her fellow prisoner, and her reaction was much the same, with the exception of her typically English stiff upper lip. The woman was entirely stoic.

When Ilex became aware that she was ensnared in the sprawling orb web dominating the grotto of the spider people, her trapped limbs trembled for some minutes. Like the Waz-ho-don warrior before her, Ilex's thoughts immediately careened in the direction of the great arachnid that inhabited this dismal skein.

At first, she was loathe to cast her gaze about and ascertain where she stood in the web in relation to the loathsome spider. But necessity demanded that the British operative not hang helpless and ignorant for very long.

There was also the fact that the mighty web was shaking in a manner that was surprisingly active.

Ilex struggled to move her head about and saw, to her shocked horror, the black-haired native whom Flying Officer Clayton had called Mu-bu-tan.

He hung in the web, head downward, entirely helpless. At first, she mistook him for a large ape of some kind, perhaps a long-armed gibbon or a baboon. The manner in which his rangy

283

body was coated in sable hair evoked that mental comparison. Indeed, it also brought to mind a wire-haired terrier in human form. The black-haired hands and feet with their pale thumbs and large toes jutting out at right angles to the rest smacked of the simian, not the canine. And then there was the hint of a long, sinuous tail.

Around his hirsute body, crouching specimens of the spider pygmies were arrayed. In their hands, they held tiny thorn darts, with which they were attempting to prick him.

The hairy one yelled his defiance, but he had no other recourse. He was firmly caught in the thick-stranded weave.

Moving about the web with their six-digited hands and feet, the spider-men skittered in and out, inserting their vicious thorn needles into his hairy arms and legs, which shook in anger.

Before long, the black-haired one lost all animation. He appeared as one who had died. In this queer half-light and at such a distance, it was not possible to see whether the darts were fletched with white or red feathers. Ilex feared the worst.

Worse, however, was yet to come.

Moving in, the spiderlings began unfastening their victim from the vast skein. A rope of some kind was tied under the man's arms, so that when he fell free of the web, Mu-bu-tan was caught up by this loop.

There he dangled, swinging to and fro, until his momentum ceased.

Three of the spider-men took hold of the rope at its topmost point, and began hauling upward in the manner of stevedores hoisting cargo onto a ship's deck. Others, scrambling along the transverse strands of the web, got beneath the long-tailed individual, and helped hoist him upward.

The body was obviously too much for any single spider-man. Even working all together, the seven of them had their difficulties.

But by means of both pulling and pushing, the spiderlings inexorably moved the helpless one in the direction they wished. Up. Straight up. Directly into the waiting fangs of the tremendous arachnid whose eight gleaming eyes mirrored the symmetry of its eight twitching legs.

When the immediate objective of their efforts became apparent, Ilex bit at her lips to suppress a scream, closed her eyes, and turned her strained face from the horrible spectacle.

For it seemed that the spider people were in the act of feeding their victim to their great progenitor!

It was at that point that the black-haired monkey man showed that he had not been utterly senseless, but only drugged into helplessness. He began protesting in a growling voice that was filled with animal rage. But there was nothing he could do, for his limbs were paralyzed by spider venom.

The brave woman struggled with the mix of pity for the poor unfortunate man, and horror for her own future. For Ilex had no doubt in her heart of hearts that, once the monster feasted, she would be next....

Chapter Fifty-Three

Tarzan Rides Into Danger

WHEN the moon rose, it was near to full.
Tarzan of the Apes waited until the lunar orb transited sufficiently high to illuminate the entirety of the jagged and forbidding ravine of the spider people.

It was a calculated risk he was taking. To proceed in darkness carried with it the blanket protection of near invisibility. But in order to storm the cavern of the spider pygmies, the ape-man needed to be able to see. Otherwise, he was at risk of being cut down by the whispering, nearly-invisible darts whose touch brought instant sleep—or certain death.

Carrying the pteranodon wing vertically, wearing only his loincloth of *jato* skin, his Enfield revolver strapped to his hip, empty knife scabbard dangling from the opposite side, Tarzan resembled some savage knight of the jungle astride the rolling mahogany hulk that was Torn Ear, the barbaric standard of his cause held high before him.

Now and then, a wayward breeze cut through the fissure, threatening to tear the crude skin sail from the ape-man's hand. Tarzan gripped the leathery wing by the dead fingers protruding from its main spar of bone. He had balanced the thing at the base of Torn Ear's skull, where it found lodgment nestled between two of the pachyderm's nodular vertebrae.

Carrying it aloft thus, the ape-man was in a position to swing the formidable wing in whatever direction danger threatened.

286

Moving ponderously, tail swaying, trunk lifted, Torn Ear conveyed the Lord of the Jungle to his destination. They might have been out for a moonlit promenade, except the light in Tarzan's eyes glinted hard as agate as his magnificent head swiveled continually about, seeking signs of danger.

Soon, the noise of the rushing torrent swelled louder and they rounded a turn, bringing it into clear view.

In the lunar light, the waterfall resembled a curtain of liquid silver and diamonds dashing itself into a pool that was spectral with shivering moonglade. Seen unexpectedly, the cascade presented a spectral and otherworldly appearance.

Tarzan gave it no more regard than necessary. His grey gaze was fixed on the cliff-rim precipices overhead and on the way forward, for trouble, he suspected, would come from those vantages.

When it arrived, however, danger came from an unexpected direction.

The ape-man's eyes were scanning the limited horizon of the surrounding cliffs and only veered to the waterfall as necessary. He did not at first see the things shooting over the falls to plop into the spreading pool. Only when these odd objects began accumulating in the turbulent waters was his attention drawn irresistibly.

First, it appeared as if large stones were floating in the pool, but of course Tarzan knew that boulders do not float. They would sink.

Then, another of the oval objects arrived. Carried by the river above, it came plunging down in the cataract to briefly submerge and then pop to the surface, to be pushed away from the thundering torrent of water by its constant roiling.

Eyes falling upon this new arrival, Tarzan saw it burst open—and he recognized the thing for what it was. It was another of the rock-like constructions that he had previously encountered navigating the channel beyond the waterfall.

Those objects had served as submerged guard stations; these evidently were some form of water transportation, rather like an enclosed coracle. They appeared to have been partly formed of wood and sealed with some organic matter the ape-man did not immediately recognize.

With growing alarm, Tarzan did recognize that more of the greyish eggs were arriving, and those that had already splashed into the pool were being rent asunder from within by long, bony limbs whose ghost-pale talons possessed six digits, two of which were matched thumbs!

Knowing that blowpipes and reed darts would manifest next, the ape-man lifted one arm, and took hold of the leading edge of the towering wing, sweeping it downward so that it served as a flexible shield.

The first spider darts were not long in arriving. They began penetrating the membranous hide stretched between the thin pterosaur bones. The needle points caught there, unable to punch through entirely. A few bounced off, showing that the shield was stronger in some places and weaker in others.

So far, the contrivance admirably served the purpose for which it was intended.

Even as the ape-man became cognizant of the efficacy of his makeshift shield, more eggs tumbled down, some to break apart from the force of the fall, others torn open from within by long, spidery fingers.

The ceaseless turbulence of the pool pushed the first of these arrivals toward shore, and onto dry land padded the pale pygmy spider warriors, their ebon eyes weirdly gleaming, their hairless skulls shimmering with moonlight.

Now, they began expelling their devil-darts in earnest. Some wielded the long bamboo blowpipes that sent long reed darts zipping through the air, while others fielded short blowguns which peppered the ape-man and his elephant with fletched barbs of thorn and other short but sharp missiles.

Tarzan knew he was very vulnerable, for his wing-shield did not protect his lower extremities, nor was it perfect in its contours, leaving his head at times exposed. Attempting to hold the shield steady with one bronzed fist, the ape-man lifted his service revolver from its holster and, aiming carefully, began exacting a grimly determined toll.

The pygmy warriors evidently had no previous truck with firearms. Because when the first of their number jumped backward, driven by a bullet slamming into his breastbone, the others started scrambling madly for cover.

Tarzan took his time, picking his shots. He had limited ammunition. The revolver jumped again and again, the night air filling with gun smoke, and not once did he miss.

Soon, the cylinder ran empty, and to break it open and replenish the ammunition—of which there was a meager supply—would have meant dropping the shield. This, Tarzan dared not do.

Holstering his pistol, Tarzan slipped off Torn Ear's back, which enabled him to swing up the wing vertically, the better to cover the entirety of his splendidly symmetrical physique, and advanced. Tucked into his gun belt was the blowpipe the ape-man had captured earlier, alongside the provision of darts remaining. It was of no use to him under present circumstances, but that condition might change at any moment.

Holding high the vertical sail, Tarzan braved the pool where more spider warriors were bursting from their egg-shaped vessels as rapidly as they arrived.

Peering around the wing's edges, the ape-man caught glimpses of his alien-faced foes. He dared not linger in his scrutiny, for even to expose one observant eye was to risk catching a dart in the face. But by stealing quick glimpses, Tarzan perceived that the enemy was becoming frustrated by their inability to bring down a lone antagonist.

Fists raised, they made the weird finger-and-thumb gestures that passed for speech among their brethren. Evidently, they were discussing strategy.

Since Tarzan did not understand the finger language, he could only guess at what was transpiring. But he knew it foretold an imminent change in tactics.

VERY quickly, it came.

The spider warriors who had stumbled onto land began picking up loose stones, banging them together until they broke into sharp shards. These simple weapons were swiftly pegged in the ape-man's direction.

What had been a solid defense against poison darts suddenly proved to be deficient as the jagged stones began punching holes in the tightly-stretched skin. Where numerous darts had already perforated it, the membrane was correspondingly weakened, and in those spots the hide was rent and torn.

A fusillade of stony missiles struck again and again, battering the wing into shapelessness. A section of bone snapped. Another. The shield fast became unmanageable.

Seeing that his cause was growing hopeless, Tarzan dropped to his stomach in order to present less of a target. His broken shield-wing fell in front of him, affording limited protection.

Breaking open his Enfield revolver, the ape-man inserted the last of his remaining shells, and quietly and methodically picked off three more spider foes.

This caused the others to break off the attack and retreat.

Tarzan looked up, perceived no more of the egg-shaped coracles tumbling over the waterfall, and assumed that all the spider warriors who were going to arrive had already splashed into the pool.

In that wise, he was mistaken. But the ape-man had as yet no inkling of that unhappy truth. His barking revolver discharged its last shell. Tarzan returned the weapon to its holster and brought up the blowpipe, first inserting a long reed dart.

Blowing through the bamboo tube, the ape-man began paying his enemy back in their own coin. The jungle lord was not as practiced in the art of the blowgun as he was with the modern revolver, and so he missed a time or two.

Nevertheless, most of his darts sped true. In short order, Tarzan accounted for five more spider enemy. The survivors, seeing that their fellows were succumbing to their own poison-dipped barbs, became extremely agitated, as if the idea of falling victim to their own artifices was some form of personal insult.

The effect was greatly desirable, for the surviving pygmies simply dived back into the water and disappeared beyond the cataract, presumably to retreat back to the grotto that promised them the safety of their own kind.

Seeing this satisfactory result, Tarzan stood up. Tossing the blowpipe to the ground with a contemptuous gesture suggesting that it was galling to the touch, the ape-lord looked resolutely about, his features as grim as if carved from living granite.

Behind him, Torn Ear was staggering about, and the look in his eyes was watery and weak.

Rushing to his comrade's side, Tarzan examined the creature. The ape-man could see that the elephant was trembling and in distress. Its broad beetle-browed forehead had accumulated a feathering of darts, of which the greatest number were white. But here and there scarlet darts trembled in the breeze.

Communicating his desire, Tarzan compelled Torn Ear to lower his trunk so that the pachyderm could be mounted. The ape-man stepped onto the plump proboscis, and thus was conveyed up to a height which allowed him to pluck the offending barbs from the animal's blunt crown.

Removing them one by one, the ape-man determined that none had drawn blood, which made him wonder what was producing the intermittent trembling that ran from trunk to tail of his staggering friend.

Searching about, Tarzan soon discovered the terrible truth.

One of the devil-darts had found a home in Torn Ear's intact ear. This had done very little damage, but on the opposite appendage, at the ragged edge that was still raw from having been ripped by the giant crocodile of the morass, a single red-tailed dart had penetrated.

Tarzan withdrew the hateful thing and examined it carefully. It was tipped with crimson, showing that its virulent poison had mingled with Torn Ear's healthy life fluid.

Dropping to the ground, Tarzan took hold of that livid edge with both hands, and applied his mouth to the wound. He sucked it, spit out the vile-tasting blood, and repeated the process four times.

Then, he stepped back, saying, "Do not fear. Tarzan will not permit you to perish."

Torn Ear lifted his trunk, and gave a weak tootle. Then, like a strange tree, he began to topple over to one side, trunk swaying aimlessly and tiny eyes slowly closing.

As he beheld his friend roll over onto his heavily-heaving flank, the ancient red scar on the brow of Tarzan of the Apes sprang into full fury under the silver moonlight. Kneeling, he placed one hand over Torn Ear's heart, and felt its steady pounding. The organ felt strong, but it was beating faster than normal, like a drum under frantic palms.

More than ever, the ape-man wished that he had his father's hunting knife, for with it he could have hacked away at the remnants of the pachyderm's damaged ear, and prevented the passage of poison from that extremity to the mighty heart.

But that desperate desire was quickly extinguished by the next event that came to pass.

While Tarzan was ministering to the elephant, chalky skulls lifted up from the pool of the waterfall and regarded him, malign contempt in their jet-black orbs.

Some instinct caused Tarzan to turn his head, and he beheld the pale forms rising from the water like the ghosts of the drowned.

It had been Tarzan's plan to ride Torn Ear boldly into the cataract, and penetrate deep into the cavern of the spider people to rescue his friends. But that plan was now in tatters.

For as the pale pygmy people lifted out of the water like specters from another world, one of their number—Tarzan recognized him as the eight-eyed individual he had previously vanquished—let out a shrill screech of a sound.

It might have been pure emotion given voice. It might not have been anything like speech. But the intended meaning was self-evident.

This man-like creature was calling on his soldiers to attack.

Chapter Fifty-Four

TARZAN STALKS HIS ENEMIES

TARZAN OF THE APES was no coward, either by temperament or reputation. Running from a fight was not part of his jungle code. Yet once again, for the second time since his return to Pal-ul-don, the Lord of the Jungle found himself in an untenable position, one from which retreat was the only possible—indeed, only sensible—stratagem.

Loathe as the ape-lord was to abandon his last remaining comrade, Torn Ear the elephant was incapacitated, and likely mortally wounded. But even at the peak of his health, the great beast could not flee this canyon of whispering death with the necessary dart-defying speed of which only Tarzan of the Apes was capable.

Tarzan had two possible routes of escape. To charge the spider pygmies and plunge into the foaming pool where their devil-darts were next to useless was very tempting, since the pool bubbled but yards away. The only other recourse was to retreat.

But to charge the enemy was to dash headlong into a storm of poisonous missiles, his naked skin unprotected. Death would certainly be the ape-man's reward.

Reluctantly, Tarzan flashed backward ahead of the first whizzing darts and, as much as it galled him, the ape-man took refuge behind the prone form of Torn Ear. The recumbent elephant's hide began collecting barbs, but there was nothing that could be done about that under present circumstances. For the ape-man to complete his mission, he must survive; otherwise, the lives of his friends were forfeit.

Collecting such stones as were at hand, the ape-man started hurling these crude weapons in the direction of his assailants. He had better luck than he had with the spider-men's blowpipe darts. With the stones, Tarzan did not miss once.

Rocks collided with skulls, shoulders and bellies. Those spider warriors who were not knocked off their feet were driven back, a few dropping their blowguns. Many began bleeding profusely.

When the ape-man exhausted his store of stones, he made a break for it.

With a final reassuring pat on Torn Ear's trembling shoulder, he whispered, "Tarzan will return for you, loyal friend."

Then the ape-man ran as he had never run before, a magnificent specimen of masculinity combining the fleetness of the gazelle with the tawny muscularity of a lion. Every fiber of his being, from mighty thews to snapping sinews, worked in unison.

Tarzan zig-zagged wildly, in the manner of a football player attempting to avoid being tackled, but in this instance the danger lay behind, not ahead of him. So swiftly did the ape-man race that the sounds of any pursuing darts were lost upon him, for the wind of his own rushing whistled in his ears.

Whether it was due to his ferocious counterattack or the speed with which he crossed the gorge's floor will never be known, but Tarzan managed to clear the turn in the ravine that put stony shelter at his naked back, and afforded momentary protection from the flying fangs of his enemies.

The ape-man did not slacken his pace, for he knew that, once the spider warriors got themselves organized, they would be in rapid pursuit. On and on he ran, not looking back, not daring to pause. The will to live, the surging desire to survive, the burning fierceness to live another day to exact revenge for his losses, caused the scar upon Tarzan's forehead to burn more brightly still.

That crimson brand was still flaming when Tarzan of the Apes at last came to the tumbled incline of earth down which he and Torn Ear had earlier passed on separate occasions.

The naked dirt and stone of this stark cleft in the earth did not appeal to the the ape-man. He was a creature of the jungle, a master of woodcraft. Racing up the dirt incline, he reached the top of the cliff ledge, and plunged into the thick jungle, where he had first known life, the green abode in which he had grown to manhood, and the leafy domain of which he was absolute master.

Let the spider-men pursue him here. They may know this dense wilderness better than he, but Tarzan was Lord of the Jungle, and always would be.

The moon painted his bronzed hide as he leapt with quick-silver skill from open trail into the interlacing canopy of branches that was like home to him and worked deeper into the thick foliage of the treetops.

Tarzan knew that the spider people were not confined to the gorge but roamed the forest by night, hiding among the con-cealing leaves and the twisting branches and within the great bottle trees which they had established as outposts on the fringe of the jungle. Among the same leaves and branches there was shelter, a kind of protection, and the type of woodsy travel lanes that the ape-man could navigate with a skill equal to that of the crafty spider people.

Now Tarzan was more defenseless than previously. Carrying only his empty revolver in its holster and no remaining darts in the pouch—which he swiftly discarded as a useless impedi-ment—he lacked anything of defensive value.

There remained only the empty scabbard, but it no longer held the knife that had helped him win many a dark day in years gone by. More than the bullets for his revolver, the ape-man missed this most of all. The keen blade was now the personal property of one of the spider pygmies, and would have to be reclaimed by force.

Tarzan found a heavy branch in which to lie down and recoup his energy, breathing heavily at first and then more normally, and finally in a relaxed way that signified that the ape-man was attempting to husband his amazing vitality for the struggle ahead. He did not rest in the sense of going into a deep sleep. There would be time for sleep later. Sleep or eternal rest, depending upon events yet to be....

BUT Tarzan did indeed rest. Although that rest was destined not to last for very long. For even as he settled into the comfortable lull of temporary respite, a breath like a passing insect whizzed by one ear.

That sound was one the jungle lord had come to know very well. As was the soft tick of a spider-dart striking home. In this case, the barb had struck the shaggy bole of the butterfly tree behind which Tarzan's head rested.

Snapping into action, he spied the tiny sprinkle of feathery white which told that a spider pygmy had attempted to bring him low.

Leaping from his perch, the ape-man spied a lower branch, landed upon it on all fours, and used it to swing to another bough, departing this leafy abode of shelter entirely.

Moving like a long-armed simian, swinging from branch to branch until he was six trees to the south, Tarzan then paused, crouching in an ape-like posture, eyes sharpening, seeking the source of danger.

Gaze alert for creeping shadows in the moonlight, the ape-man detected nothing. His keen ears heard only the rustle of the wind as it stirred leaves and luxuriant blossoms. Yet he knew, despite the evidence of his senses, that a six-fingered pygmy—if not many of them—was lurking in the interconnected tree branches like venomous spiders inhabiting their own webs.

In his youth, Tarzan had learned to live among the great apes despite his inferior human strength, which nevertheless had grown to be greater than that of an above-average human being.

One trick he had devised had served him well as a stripling. Looking about the trees, the ape-man sought a creeper or liana that might be turned to good use, as it had been when he was a mere apeling.

Crawling carefully, Tarzan picked his way through the forest branches, more like Histah the snake than a great ape. But stealth was an absolute necessity, for it was impossible to spy a devil-dart before it arrived to do its dirty work.

The ape-man came across several good specimens, but none that he could make use of, lacking a blade with which to hack off an appropriate length of vine. He moved on, keeping always to the most heavily-leafed boughs, for he knew that flying needles striking waxy leaves would make warning sounds in passing, and might also be knocked off true course, sparing him.

Finally, Tarzan found what he needed—a fat vine that was severed at one end and rotted at the other. Taking hold of this, he snapped it free of its natural anchorage, and gathered up the creeper.

One end was weak, but beyond that the vine was strong. Given time, he might have woven something even stronger. But, as it was, the ape-man fashioned a lariat suitable for his purposes.

This was soon done. Tarzan climbed to the crown of the breadfruit tree in which he had landed, and moved into the highest branches to an adjoining trunk, grey eyes seeking signs of furtive movement, any subtle shadow of a crawling enemy.

For a great long time the ape-man rested, almost immobile, only his eyes switching back and forth, searching for any sly movement that would signal an opportunity to strike back.

Eventually, something did show. It was so faint that at first it was difficult to discern whether it was moonlight reflecting off a knob of wood high in a tree, or possibly some pendulous breadfruit.

But the pale round object shifted slightly and then moved again. Then, Tarzan caught a glimpse of luminous eyespots, three in number, which he had previously decided were probably significant of rank.

Seeing what looked like moon-silvered branches shaking, Tarzan grew confident that he had pinpointed the location of his phantom stalker.

There was fruit in this tree, of a type the ape-man did not recognize. But he was not intent upon a meal. Pulling one drupe free, Tarzan threw it so that it whistled through the trees, snapping off twigs, and landing with a pulpy thud.

As a strategy, it was crude, but evidently the pygmies were not accustomed to such decoys. With an animated celerity, a spider-man came skittering down his tree, passed to a neighboring branch, and then another, seeking the spot where the thrown thing had landed.

Tarzan espied him clearly then, and marveled at the adroit way he moved through the web of wood, employing only one long-fingered hand and both prehensile feet, keeping always his blowpipe in the other hand.

Dropping to the ground, this spider creature began rustling about, seemingly puzzled and confused. While he was thus engaged, Tarzan moved with the greatest stealth at his command until he had reached the tree above the hunter's hairless skull.

Positioning himself above the pale pygmy, the ape-man dropped his lasso over the creature's painfully thin neck, and holding the other end of the vine in one strong hand, dropped down to a lower branch.

The center of the makeshift rope caught on the branch just vacated, creating tension. The noose—for that is what it was—drew closed, and the vine hoisted upward, with the stout branch acting as a fulcrum.

Gagging, the spider warrior suddenly danced in mid-air, six-fingered hands grasping at its throat, unable to break the taut strands that were inexorably cutting off its air.

Crouching at a lower bough, Tarzan hauled the vine downward, which caused the noose to rise even more, making the hapless figure perform his jittering dance of death ever higher off the ground. Strangling noises came horribly, then subsided.

Only then, with a contemptuous gesture, did the ape-man release the makeshift rope, which sent the helpless creature plunging to earth.

Climbing down, Tarzan found him asprawl, shuddering in his death throes.

Picking up the fallen blowpipe, the ape-man considered appropriating it as a weapon, but was filled with disgust at the hollow barrel.

The blowpipe and darts, he felt with conviction, was not a worthy weapon for a man, but less Tarzan of the Apes. Discarding the bamboo, the ape-man strode away in search of another vine—one stronger than the strand with which he had so successfully strangled his unwary foe.

Chapter Fifty-Five

THE SCARLET DART

TARZAN did not sleep that night. Nor did he rest. Instead, he prowled the jungle lanes in search of more spider-men. Knowing from past experience that the pale pygmy tribe took to the trees by moonlight, the ape-man well understood that he was not safe so long as they were abroad.

Taking up a position in any tree, no matter how lofty and sheltering, was simply an invitation to be discovered and attacked. The fate of the unfortunate R.A.F. pilot who had become entangled in his own shroud lines came to mind.

Tarzan was by nature and upbringing a hunter. The role of the hunted was not something he relished. It offended his jungle-dwelling, ape-reared spirit.

So, rather than seek sleep, the jungle lord took the initiative.

Wound around one shoulder was a fresh lariat, its noose contrived to be large enough to drop over one of the chalk-white skulls, and just as quickly snapped tight around thin enemy necks wherever he found them.

In the hours leading up to midnight, Tarzan moved with great skill, every sense alert to fix a spider-man before it spotted him. The pygmy people tended to travel in packs, so the ape-man gave his greatest attention to the solitary scouts, whom he knew without question were seeking him out.

Three spider-men perished before the moon was at its zenith in the night sky. Each one had been warily hunting, but none of them suspected a silent stalker lurking higher in the treetops until their thin throats felt a sudden constriction, after which they were hoisted skyward, choking and helpless.

Tarzan was not a cruel man. He did not allow any of his enemies to strangle unnecessarily. Each time he yanked one of them off his feet, he allowed the unfortunate one to drop to hard ground shortly thereafter, invariably breaking thin neck vertebrae. It was a quicker and more merciful death than they perhaps deserved, but the noble Tarmangani had no appetite for torture.

Had he possessed common speech with the enemy, Tarzan would have captured one alive and wrung from him whatever necessary information that would permit him to learn the fate of his friends, Mu-bu-tan and the British Military Intelligence officer, Ilex.

But the barrier of language was insurmountable. There was no fathoming the popping finger signals that allowed the spider people to communicate with one another, and, even if Tarzan could emulate their gestures, he did not possess the grotesque extra thumb—which would have been the same as lacking key vowels in any spoken language. Or so the ape-man supposed.

During his nocturnal prowling Tarzan discovered the occasional white-fletched dart embedded in a still branch that signified he was still being stalked.

Always they missed him, for as crafty as the spider-men were, the ape-lord was sly in a way that they were not.

As the night wore on, more and more of these weird whisperings came to his ears. As it was virtually impossible to see through the jungle tangle very far, Tarzan could not ascertain whence these pointed teeth of peril hailed.

Once, he vaulted from one great tree to another, only to discover an immobile spider warrior clinging to the branches beneath him.

Alarmed, the spider-man brought his short reed blowgun into play. Fortunately, it had not been charged with a devil-dart.

This necessitated extra moments while the six-fingered hands performed that hasty operation.

The necessary delay enabled Tarzan to drop straight down and, having no other weapon at hand, he employed the barrel of his Enfield revolver to knock the hollow reed from clutching fingers.

Those same fingers sought his opponent's throat but, grasping the thin, black-banded wrists, Tarzan removed them by muscular force, and then pitched the hapless one headfirst to the ground.

The ape-man did not bother to ascertain the results of his effort, for the sound of neck bones crunching told the tale more eloquently than any visual examination would have.

On into the night, Tarzan worked his way through the supporting branches of myriad trees, bare feet never once touching the jungle floor, where he would be most vulnerable to his arboreal enemies.

To this point, the ape-man had been more than holding his own. Then the tone of the hunt changed.

Pausing to rest in the crotch of a tall elephant tree, Tarzan absently felt for the handle of his revolver, which was at risk of dropping out of its holster, the protective leather flap having worked loose during his strenuous perambulations.

As he did so, the ape-man discovered something that made his blood run cold in his veins. A spider dart had struck the holster, embedding itself in the leather. But that fact alone was not sufficient to chill the heart of the Lord of the Jungle. It was the color of the feather fletching that made his pulse pound.

For it was the scarlet of fresh blood.

Examining the wet tip, Tarzan was reminded of loyal Torn Ear, whose fate was as yet unknown. Most likely, the ape-man imagined, the brave brute was dead. Anger caused the scar on his forehead to become like the searing mark of a brand. The veins in his temples pulsed in frustration.

Splintering the tip against tree bark, Tarzan discarded the hateful object. Then, he resumed his course, and his quest. Tarzan the hunter, who was also the hunted....

Chapter Fifty-Six

ONE YET LIVED

ONE thing could be said for the hairy-bodied warrior, thought Ilex.

Tail notwithstanding, he was a man. And he died a man.

The British operative was forced to turn away in order to spare herself the horrid sight of the poor victim being fed into the fangs of the great arachnid of the grotto of human spiders.

Lashed as she was, Ilex could not press her palms to her ears and shut out his death cries. But it proved unnecessary.

It was not that the black-haired man did not protest his imminent fate, but his cries were ones of rage and not fear. Ilex could tell this even though his speech was impenetrable to her.

Soon enough, those cries of protest died. They seemed to have been swallowed in stages, until exhausted. The suggestion of consumption was horrible to contemplate.

A silence followed, one in which the cool air of the cavern seemed uncannily still.

The web began to shake like a carelessly plucked harp. Ilex imagined the many-legged monster rocking its web as it consumed its morsel of living meat.

The shaking reverberated silently for a very long time as well. It seemed interminable.

Dimly, Ilex could hear soft clicking and snapping noises, which she knew were the sounds of the phalanges and knuckles of the spider people as they manipulated their weirdly-jointed fingers in otherwise-silent communication.

Eventually, those ghoulish noises also faded away. The wavering web became still.

Remembering that an ordinary spider often ceased all movement for days after eating, Ilex began to consider that it might be some time before her turn came.

She resisted the urge to look up at the monster arachnid, but some perverse need to know finally caused her to open her eyes and lift her downward-hanging head. Wide-eyed, she gazed upward.

A dizzying height above hung that horrible monstrosity that should not exist. It was still, its eight eyes softly shining.

There was no sign of the tailed Mu-bu-tan. Not around the sharp fangs. Nor were his bones to be discovered clinging to the vast web.

Dropping her head, Ilex shuddered for over a minute. The other had been consumed whole. Once more, his bravery impressed her. He had not uttered a single scream as he went to his awful doom.

A fate that awaited Ilex some unguessable period in the near future.

Chapter Fifty-Seven

MIDNIGHT SIEGE

DEEP into the longest night of Tarzan's adventurous career, the ape-man sighted a bottle tree looming over a portion of the jungle that was otherwise a cluster of lofty but lesser boles.

This was not one of the towering trunks that formed the outpost of the orderly bottle tree groves of the spider pygmies, but one that grew apart and on its own. Nor was it as tall as the others he had earlier climbed.

Spying it, the Lord of the Jungle saw in its tangled crown of root-like branches potential refuge. Refuge is what he most needed now, refuge and respite.

Tarzan swung from tree to tree, moving sometimes with great speed, but at other times creeping with uncanny stealth.

The spider people were filtering all through the great wooden web of the jungle, blowguns and blowpipes at the ready. They were abroad in full force.

Their unpleasant personal scent impinged upon the ape-lord's sensitive nostrils.

Often, a devil-dart had winged its deadly way toward the ape-man. Each time, virtually naked and without protection, Tarzan had eluded every threat. But as the post-midnight hours passed, the darts showed more and more bright red feathers. Very few were white. After a time, Tarzan became certain that the spider warriors, coming across their own fallen dead, had decided among themselves that they no longer wished to take the ape-man alive. They only wanted him dead.

Knowing that the stakes had been raised from undesirable capture to ignominious death, Tarzan sought some place where he could climb above the jungle canopy, which was crawling with long-limbed pygmies stealing their silent way along.

This solitary bottle tree was exactly what he wanted.

Swinging from branch to branch, his grip certain, his superb balance verging on the superhuman, Tarzan worked his way as close to the towering tree as he could.

Fortunately, a nearby breadfruit tree also lifted very high.

Picking through that woody basket of a crown, Tarzan found a creeper of wonderful length, and harvesting it, fashioned a simple lariat at one end.

He cast it again and again until he snared a lower branch of the bottle tree, many yards above his head.

Once it felt secure, Tarzan threw himself into space, and the line swung him into the side of the smooth-barked giant. Bracing himself against the shock of hitting the broad bole with his springy feet, the ape-man paused, holding on by dint of his unbreakable two-handed grip.

Bare toes touching the bole, he steadied himself, began hauling himself up, hand over hand, his fabulous muscles panther-like in their rhythmically methodical action.

With the greatest alacrity, Tarzan gained the crown and disappeared among the sheltering tangle of branches, where he plucked one of the fruits, and quietly consumed it.

His hunger momentarily satisfied, the ape-man examined the top of the tree, endeavoring to see if it might be another hollow fort of the spider people. He found no evidence of such, and thus was able to relax to a degree.

Cool moonlight bathed his scarred brown skin as the jungle lord considered the present situation. Tarzan pondered the fates of Mu-bu-tan and the British woman known to him only as

Ilex as captives of the spider pygmies. Did they still live? If they did, could he succor them?

His thoughts ranged back to the plantation he had left at the start of the war and his dear wife, Jane, whose face he had not seen in countless months, nor lips kissed. He wondered how the plantation fared in his absence. Had his son, Jack, gone off to war, despite Tarzan's enjoining him to remain home to guard their jungle savannah home?

Many years before, when the ape-man was previously abroad in Pal-ul-don, the son of Tarzan had tracked him down. Korak the Killer could not know that his father was once again marooned in the Land of Man. This was a secret mission. If Flying Officer John Clayton failed to return, his family would be apprised of that stark fact, but no more than that. His death would be a mystery of wartime.

Returning to the issues at hand, Tarzan wished only for one thing: his hunting knife, with which he could better defend himself.

Time passed, and the surrounding trees below his lofty aerie shook in the cool night breezes—but also rustled under the weight of crawling creatures, some of which the ape-man doubtless believed to be spider warriors searching tirelessly for him.

From time to time, Tarzan shifted position, changing branches, peering out and down from every compass point, alert to danger.

Despite their ghostly paleness, the spider pygmies managed to keep themselves out of view. So, too, did Tarzan hope to remain out of their fields of vision.

THE NIGHT was well along when something caught his eye, and Tarzan realized he had been spotted.

A cottony cloud lifted into view, carried along with the southerly breeze in his direction. Had it not been for his experience among the turtle folk, Tarzan would not know what to make of the approaching matter. But he understood full well that this mass was a detached web containing venomous spiders which, if it landed anywhere in his tangled perch, would soon fill the branches with scuttling death.

Twisting a handy branch loose, Tarzan lifted up and flung it at the innocent-appearing cloudlet. The bough caught the thing squarely, and carried it to the jungle floor below. The startled white spiders immediately disgorged and dispersed themselves.

It was not long before another patch of gossamer fluff lifted up, and Tarzan was forced to expose himself once more.

This time, soft puffing sounds not far distant told of blowpipes coming into action. Hastily, Tarzan flung a fresh branch, but missed. Taking more careful aim, he tried again, for while the spiders were an imminent threat, the darts lifting in his direction were undoubtedly fatal. Of the two, he would rather contend with the creeping spiders.

Dropping into the shelter of the gnarled branches, the ape-man let the darts whiz by. Peering through the leaves, he discerned the occasional flash of blood red, confirming his suspicion that all efforts against him were now to the death.

Never before had Tarzan felt so vulnerable. In all of his life dwelling in the jungle, animal-skin loincloth had always sufficed. Now with these tiny needles seeking him out, he felt truly naked and unprepared to defend himself.

A volley of darts passed by. Most fell short. There was a pause, another succession of puffing sounds, and a fresh volley clipped through the air. Few reached so far as the spreading bottle-tree branches, for the sheltering spider-men were forced to fire upward, there being no nearby trees as high as Tarzan's.

The ape-man did not notice the arrival of the second diaphanous cloud until it plopped only a few yards away from his left shoulder.

Turning, he saw the gauzy thing quiver where it had caught the twisting branch, and its quivering was not the quivering of a breeze-tossed web. It was the awful animation of clotted spider silk giving up its loathsome cargo.

The spiders were very small, but they immediately began working their way along the anchoring branch. As soon as they came to the root, the eight-legged creatures started dispersing, seeking other avenues of attack.

Without anything in the way of weapons, Tarzan knew he could not pass the remainder of the night harassed by these arachnids, whose number was prodigious.

Plucking one of the pendulous fruits, the ape-man flung it at the branch supporting the quivering web of horror. It made a mushy splash as it burst upon impact—and carried a greater portion of the webby mass and its trapped inhabitants to the ground.

While this helped, it was hardly enough. There were not enough fruits within reach, and to harvest the outlying specimens would be to risk exposure and instant death by venomous barb.

It was the swiftness by which the spider-poison worked that caused Tarzan of the Apes to feel cold in the core of his being. A man with a knife or a spear or even a pistol could defeat a mortal foe in open combat. He had done so many times. In truth, the ape-man had conquered well-armed attackers with only the terrible strength of his bare hands and bared teeth.

But one scratch of a flying needle, and Tarzan knew he was mere minutes, if not vanishing seconds, away from an ignominious death by poison. His magnificent brown hide bore marks and scars of many past battles, but every one of those wounds had soon healed, leaving the ape-man stronger and wiser for the encounter.

In a sense, they were gifts—whether inflicted by the fangs of enemy apes, or the spear points of human foes. Each one had taught Tarzan how better to survive.

What the devil-darts of the spider people had taught him, Tarzan reflected bitterly, was fear.

On his forehead, the old thin knife scar again flamed into life, for a rage was burning in the breast of Tarzan of the Apes—a rage that was driving out the coldness in his heart and the dread of helplessness from his magnificent being.

Suddenly, a wildness came into the ape-lord's eyes, a feral strangeness that went back to his savage youth in the jungles of Africa, where the only family he had was the great apes of the tribe of Kerchak.

Leaping erect, Tarzan cupped his hands over his mouth and from deep within his chest came a weird, bloodcurdling scream—the defiant battle cry of the great apes.

That terrible sound carried to the surrounding jungle, making birds fly up from their night roosts, and causing other animals to jerk about, seeking the sound of that blood-freezing outburst with anxious orbs.

By all rights, a fusillade of death-darts should have peppered Tarzan's chest, but the sound carried such a weight of fury and promise of retribution that the surrounding trees became alive with the panicked reaction of spider warriors, scampering in retreat—for the reverberating cry had brought terror to their craven hearts. This was their forest, their domain, but here was a sound new to them. They comprehended not what it portended.

Grey eyes scanning his surroundings, Tarzan saw flashes of light, fleeting glimpses of moonlight reflecting off hairless skulls, and the occasional dropped bamboo barrel where unnerved spider-men fled for their lives.

When he realized what he had done, Tarzan calmly walked over to the branch from which his vine rope hung, and slid down it. The creeper was sufficiently long that it permitted him to reach almost to the ground, after which he dropped off, his powerful leg muscles cushioning his hard landing.

Flinty gaze going to a certain tree, Tarzan began walking in that direction with the graceful stride of a conquering lion.

Among the fleeing figures the ape-man had spied one who wore about his neck a woven cord. And to this cord was attached something that flashed and danced in the moonlight.

It was the hunting knife of his father. One of the spider-men was wearing it as a trophy, the weapon being too large and heavy to be carried any other way.

It was the absolute determination of Tarzan of the Apes to hunt down that diminutive individual and wrest from him, by any means, the one weapon that would permit the Lord of the Jungle to seize control of the night of Pal-ul-don.

Chapter Fifty-Eight

A FLASH OF STEEL

BLACK-BANDED limbs scurrying, the chalky pygmies continued their retreat through boughs whose leaves hardly shook at all in response to their artful maneuvers.

There was no doubt but that the spider warriors did not expect to be pursued so brazenly. While they were in full retreat, it was their clear intention to regroup and consider how best to bring down their seemingly dart-proof enemy.

Tarzan crept along the jungle floor, level grey eyes constantly searching the thick canopy overhead, knowing that the arboreal spider-men would be found in the greatest numbers amid the interlacing branches of the treetops.

Tarzan stole along silently, only the soft slapping of his empty knife scabbard against his churning thigh accompanying his march.

Search as he might, the ape-man perceived no ghostly limbs amid the upper reaches of the close-packed trees. The coal-black bands that marked their arms and legs served as a kind of crude camouflage, breaking up the spindly limbs into segments so that their angular lengths could not be perceived for what they truly were.

Tarzan walked with the supreme confidence that befitted his undisputed position as Lord of the Jungle, which had been his right and his heritage since he first came to manhood in Africa. Something in the way the crafty spider people scurried into abject retreat gave him renewed heart.

The danger was undiminished, but Tarzan of the Apes was weary of feeling vulnerable, subject to being the prey of an alien tribe that he considered to be vastly inferior to himself. For despite their cunning and their skill, the ape-man perceived the spider people with their six fingers and their insect-like ways as distinctly subhuman. They were not so-called civilized men like the whites he had known, nor noble and natural like the blacks comprising the Waziri tribe who held sway over the jungles and savannah surrounding his plantation estate.

The double-thumbed, narrow-faced pygmy creatures appeared to be some perverted offshoot of evolution, more kin to arachnids than to humans, a cave-dwelling tribe of man-spiders that did not belong in the Twentieth Century. They deserved to be stamped out.

Emboldened by their craven reactions, Tarzan, now and then pausing in the shelter of a creeper-entangled tree trunk, and exercising reasonable caution, advanced steadily.

During one pause in his reconnoiter, a sudden strong odor told the ape-man that something sinister was lurking close by, with the immediate consequence that a bony bundle landed softly behind his back, and fell upon him.

Hastily, Tarzan flung the thing off before long-jointed talons could clutch at his exposed throat.

The brazen spider-man landed on its back, the breath knocked from its scrawny chest. Tarzan knelt down, drove his fist into the center of the stunned face, collapsing the nose into a bloody ruin, thereby robbing his assailant of consciousness. Then, he seized the spindly neck with fingers the hue and hardness of bronze, breaking that neck with a shrug that produced a snapping sound of finality. Finally, the ape-man flung the limp corpse away as he would so much rubbish.

Straightening up, Tarzan peered upward, detected no further attackers. He moved on.

It was impossible to track the spider people in the trees, the way the ape-man would stalk prey along the ground. They left no visible spoor. Their musty scent, a product of cave dwelling, told Tarzan much, however.

Moving from tree to tree, taking shelter often, Tarzan scanned treetops, which seemed to be filled with shining silver webs. Those scattered moonbeams, he knew, would pick out any pale form that moved into them.

The ape-man was less interested in the stalking pygmy creatures than he was in the last one he had sighted—the individual who wore a hunting knife on his bare chest. His penetrating vision sought that treasured object, and that alone.

At last, something flashed that was not pale like bleached flesh, but looked strikingly like naked steel caught in moonlight.

Tarzan did not hesitate one instant. Jumping up into the nearest nest of branches, the ape-man gained the middle branches, and leapt into the adjoining tree; grey eyes questing about, fixed unerringly upon his prey.

For Tarzan was no longer the hunted, but once again the hunter.

Chapter Fifty-Nine

AMBUSH

CONFIDENCE is a strong trait to possess, and marks the man of action. But it can sometimes become overconfidence.

So it was with Tarzan of the Apes as he tracked the solitary spider-man around whose throat dangled his all-important knife. But the ape-lord did not once take his sharp eyes off the dancing reflection that told of its ever-shifting location.

The creeping, climbing man-spider did not leave the upper jungle lanes, nor did he seem to suspect the determined pursuer crouched at his feet. He crept along at a steady pace, taking care, whenever he took hold of a branch, not to disturb it so that no leaves shook in betrayal of his presence.

Stepping from tree to tree, dropping back to the hard ground where it suited him, the Lord of the Jungle stalked his quarry with the canny, silent stealth of Sheeta the panther, entirely unobserved by all but the droning insects of Pal-ul-don.

Wise in the ways of the jungle, Tarzan knew that serpents often lie coiled amid dry leaves and brush during the night when it was cooler. But the ape-man relied on his keen sense of smell and acute hearing to apprise him of reptilian danger. Too, he took pains not to step where a den might lie hidden.

These precautions proved not to be sufficient.

Treading carefully, inhaling the surrounding scents of the jungle, narrowed eyes cast ever upward, Tarzan did not perceive his danger until it had sprung up to meet him.

On either side of the jungle trail, and directly before him, the ground was suddenly forced upward, creating choking clouds of dust and dirt. Half-buried rattan mats were flung aside, exposing dark holes.

Three spider pits—and out of each one erupted a hissing foe!

They had been lying in wait while the quarry with the knife had been slyly leading the ape-man into this clever trap. Too late for self-recriminations now. Three blowpipes pointed in his direction, and three sets of pale, gaunt cheeks sucked inward, preparatory to spitting forth silent death.

Tarzan dropped flat. It was pure instinct, of course. No time to think, nor was there any other logical maneuver to be executed. Landing on his belly, the ape-man had only one thought in mind. It was to take as many of the spider warriors with him as practical. For he had no doubt that he would be transfixed by the deadly darts expelled in his direction.

Lunging for a black-banded ankle, Tarzan yanked its owner off his feet, and struck again and again with his bronzed fists, pulping his foe's pale face.

Thinking that he had but moments to live, the ape-man scooped up a handful of the disturbed dirt, and flung it into the face of the spider warrior who had sprung up directly in his path.

That one had been in the act of recharging his blowpipe, but Tarzan's unexpected move presented him with a face full of dirt, which momentarily blinded him. A weirdly-configured hand pawed at his fast-blinking eyes as he stumbled backward.

One ambusher yet remained. Tarzan whirled upon this one. He, too, was in the act of recharging his long bamboo tube.

Reaching out a long arm, Tarzan seized the far end of the blowpipe and pulled it from the six-fingered hand that stubbornly refused to relinquish it.

This brought the enemy to within reach of Tarzan's terrible hands, and he grasped the man-spider by his scrawny neck, and dug his steely fingers into the fellow's larynx.

Gurgling deep in his throat, the spider warrior fought for his life. But he was no match for the powerful thews of the mighty ape-man, who steadily throttled him into unconsciousness, and then tossed him contemptuously aside as if he were less than a rag doll.

That left only the one who had been blinded. Turning, Tarzan was advancing on this pygmy when a fresh foe dropped down from the trees.

This one landed atop the ape-man, knocking him to the ground. Tarzan quickly scrambled to his feet, however, and found himself confronting a single antagonist whose hairless head barely reached his own powerful chest.

Moreover, the spider warrior before him brandished the much-sought-for hunting knife, gripping it in both six-fingered hands, for the blade was too large and heavy for one of its bony talons.

Yet this foeman seemed to understand what to do with the blade, albeit in a crude way. Hissing like a snake, the pale pygmy stepped in, dark eyes narrowing, apparently intent upon a disemboweling stroke.

Tarzan had great respect for his own blade, and knew that, even in these unskilled hands, it could be wielded to deadly effect. Too, he was nearly certain that at least one of the deadly darts had found him, and was even now leaking its poison into his bloodstream. Had he the time, the ape-man might have examined his person and plucked out the offending barb.

But the knife wielder came rushing on, and Tarzan was determined that if he must die, he would perish with his father's hunting knife in hand; or, at worst, lose his life fighting to possess it one last time.

Chapter Sixty

VANQUISHED FOES

ONE of the peculiarities of the anatomy of the spider pygmies was that their arms were exceedingly long, rather along the lines of a baboon's elongated forearms, but without the unruly hair or phenomenal muscular strength.

Thus, this creature had a superior advantage in reach, while Tarzan of the Apes possessed a different advantage in that he towered over his murderous foes.

Holding his vicious blade double-handed, the man-spider feinted and sliced with a wildness that made up in ferocity for what it lacked in art and skill.

Tarzan was forced to leap aside, all the while in the back of his brain loomed the cold dread of creeping, poisonous death.

The steel blade sliced the air and, on the back swing, the curved tip almost scored the ape-man's abdominal muscles. Tarzan shifted about, seeking a fresh line of attack. He weighed more than twice what this human spider did, but this provided him with little benefit. And for his intended purpose, the pygmy stood at the perfect height to rip out the ape-man's entrails once he inserted the sharp steel fang into unprotected muscle and hooked it out again.

Another savage sweep, and Tarzan felt the blade slice into a reaching forearm. Withdrawing, the jungle lord saw that the mark was not deep, although it commenced bleeding copiously. There was no time to attend to the wound now, for the spider pygmy was weaving the blade around two-handedly, as if invoking his doubtless dark gods with his new-found talisman.

Mindful that his life might even now be ebbing away, Tarzan swung a fist, and knocked the double-handed clasp aside.

The blow would ordinarily have struck the blade from any enemy's hand, but the twelve fingers formed an interlocking basket of bones that was all but unbreakable. All that Tarzan accomplished was to splatter some of his own blood across the chest of his enemy.

Above and around him, amid terraces of overhanging branches, man-spiders were creeping closer, their blowpipes held loosely in their bony claws, cold-eyed fascination written upon their angular features. All were interested to see the outcome of the personal combat below, much like soldiers in any army the world over, throughout history.

The spider-men may not have been true men in the sense that Tarzan knew, but evidently they had their own code of chivalry, or something like it. For although the ape-man was entirely vulnerable to their darts, no blowgun was raised to any pale lip, nor would one be employed until the outcome was determined.

The knife-wielding spider warrior may or may not have been aware of this, so fixated was he upon Tarzan's rippling stomach muscles, and so focused on slicing them open.

Gripping the blade lower, he charged again, this time aiming for the groin, where important arteries and tendons could be swiftly severed.

Tarzan had previously sidestepped the weapon, but tiring of that stance, he instead charged. Whipping his wounded forearm about, he splashed crimson into the enemy's narrowing eyes, which momentarily stung.

Hissing violently, the spider warrior flung one hand before his eyes in an effort to paw clear the salty fluid. That left the heavy knife held in but a single pale fist.

With breathless speed, Tarzan swept in and plucked the blade of his father from the wicked six-fingered claw. Four fingers and two thumbs were not sufficient to balk him. It was his once more.

The knife flashed up once, expertly, severing the unprotected jugular vein, after which Tarzan kicked the bewildered man-spider to the dusty jungle floor. Stepping on the quivering corpse, the ape-lord raised his knife skyward, and once again gave vent to the resounding victory cry of the bull ape.

This terrible sound caused the spider pygmies to shrink back and retreat into higher branches, their hearts quailing in their thin, chalky chests.

Going silent, Tarzan saw that he was for the moment alone. Sheathing his blade, he sent careful fingers running along his lithe arms and legs and torso, searching for any sign of spider-dart or puncture wound.

Miraculously, Tarzan found none. Dropping to the ground before that first attack, he had evidently managed to avoid being peppered. His jungle-honed reflexes were astounding, but even the ape-man had not believed that he had acted in time to preserve his own life.

Looking about, Tarzan found one red-feathered barb lying on the ground where he had nearly stepped on it. Another jutted from a time-pitted tree trunk. He collected the third, and only then was the ape-man absolutely certain that death had spared him this night.

Liberated from the concern of imminent demise, he melted into the jungle, knowing that dawn was not far off and that the spider people did not prowl by daylight.

Now that he had reclaimed his cherished weapon, Tarzan knew what he would do, and how he would go about it. During the longest night of his life, a plan had formed in his brain, a campaign that had seemed far-fetched, if not impossible. But now thanks to the blade in its leather scabbard slapping against his lean thigh, it was now not only possible, but the ape-man was bound and determined to make it a reality.

Chapter Sixty-One

REUNION

FLIES were buzzing lazily about the carcass of the dead deer when Tarzan of the Apes strode down into the rift of the spider pygmies, a freshly-woven grass rope looped around one broad shoulder, his hand filled with thin wooden sticks and a flexible stave he had cut from green saplings.

No other predator had seized the carcass which had not yet spoiled in the night. Shooing the flies away, the ape-man knelt at the haunch opposite the one upon which he had previously feasted, and cut out a good warm steak, which he consumed with relish.

His hunger satisfied, the ape-man began working at the carcass, opening up the legs, and severing the tendons, for which he had especial use.

Finally, Tarzan skinned out the makings of a fresh loincloth, which he donned forthwith. For the old one of *jato*-hide had become tattered from hard traveling.

Leaving the dead thing behind, he next went to the crumpled carcass of the pteranodon, which looked forlorn in the growing light of dawn. Its drooping hatchet head, one eye closed and the other blindly open, made it appear as if it were simply sleeping. But the severed wing destroyed that casual impression.

Flies swarmed about this cadaver, too, but fewer of them. Tarzan went to the surviving wing and, employing his blade again, removed the bony member whole.

Then, the ape-man sat down and began working. Long ago, he had learned the art of shield-making from his Waziri brothers-in-arms, but their shields were constructed of antelope hide, which required days of curing. There was no time for such niceties now. There was work to be done.

The skin of the pteranodon wing was sufficiently tough that it needed no curing for this intended purpose. Tarzan bisected the wing at the finger joint, and once again held up something akin to a triangular sail.

Now he trimmed this at its pointed end until he had something more manageable, if irregularly shaped. As a shield, it was far from perfect. But if wielded adroitly, the ape-man could shift it about his body and fend off such spider-darts as came his way. Provided, of course, that he could see the enemy expelling them, or he was not surrounded on all sides.

Stripping the skin from the long bony bow of the discarded portion of the wing, Tarzan had a nearly matching frame.

Cutting the tendons, Tarzan created a catgut-like thread. This he used to tie to the opposite ends of the wooden stave, forming a simple longbow, but one requiring tremendous pull to fully draw. Taking up one of the sticks he had brought with him, the ape-man showed that they were simple arrows, their tips ground to a point against a flat stone and hardened with fire. They were not fletched, but after fitting one into the bowstring, Tarzan shot the crude bolt into the pterosaur's skull, splitting it with a loud crack.

What the arrows lacked in sophistication, Tarzan would more than compensate for with his great animal strength.

The ape-man harvested more sinew and tendons. All that he needed now was to find a way to attach the loose bone to the open edge of the wing, thereby completing the shield's framework. For that, a sewing needle would be required. He had none on his person, but a small military sewing kit rested within the kit in his pack of possessions.

This was Tarzan's next destination.

Carrying the awkward but light makings, the ape-man padded steadily along the dirt floor of the fissure of the spider people, enjoying the feeling of the rising sun as it touched his tousled black hair, and warmed his sun-bronzed features.

Tarzan walked with the measured pace of a determined tiger, covering distance rapidly, but not wasting energy, for the campaign ahead would require great effort. The play of muscles under his flexible skin was something to behold.

At last, the ape-man rounded the rocky headland, where his pack lay alongside the fallen friend, Torn Ear.

Tarzan was surprised to discover that the elephant had dragged himself to the edge of the foaming pool into which the great River Id emptied noisily—a name he recalled meant "silver" in the tongue of the tribes of Pal-ul-don.

Morning mist made the approach hazy and the air moist in his mouth. All that the ape-man could see of his fallen companion was the inert, wrinkled rump. Evidently, in its death agonies, the pachyderm had managed to drag itself to the pool and steal a final taste of water.

Tarzan's heart was heavy to see how such a magnificent beast had been laid low, and by such a tiny weapon, too.

The pack was lying some distance away, where it had fallen off the elephant's back. Tarzan went to it. He was in the act of digging through his possessions for his sewing kit, when out of the corner of his eye, something flickered.

Turning, the ape-man saw that Torn Ear's twitching tail was making the motion.

Rushing to the pachyderm's fallen form, Tarzan spoke low words.

"Torn Ear...."

The mahogany beast did not lift his head, but the heavy trunk waved feebly, then dipped into the water momentarily. When it arose again, a dribbling of water emerged from the fleshy tip.

Reaching the elephant's side, Tarzan touched the broad brow. Torn Ear responded with a low muttering that could not be analyzed.

Cupping his hands in the water, Tarzan took a sip of cool refreshment, then splashed the remainder on the elephant's head, although what good that might do was beyond his understanding.

Moving about the wrinkled brown bulk, the ape-man discovered no more darts, indicating that the creature had been left alone to perish at his own pace.

Torn Ear had not perished. Whether by some miracle, or perhaps the stout constitution of the Herculean pachyderm was sufficient to stave off death, the Tantor was nevertheless in deep distress.

Tarzan cupped more water and splashed a quantity into the parched mouth. The dry tongue stirred to life and began lapping and questing about. More water was provided. This disappeared down a greedy gullet.

Temporarily abandoning his makeshift shield and other possessions, Tarzan departed the ravine of the spider people with great speed, but was not gone long.

When the ape-man returned to the elephant's side, his mighty arms were filled with roughage, ranging from grass to freshly peeled tree bark.

This delicious matter he carefully fed to Torn Ear. The elephant's first nibbles were tentative, then he began consuming what was fed to him with increasing relish.

The morning passed with Tarzan dividing his time between a makeshift sewing operation and patiently giving Torn Ear servings of water and greenery, interspersed with the plum-like fruit plucked from the elephant tree—so named because the gentle giants were especially fond of the fruit, often shaking these trees in order to dislodge the high-growing delicacies.

The blazing sun was high overhead when the reddish-brown brute began showing signs of renewed activity. Rolling over, he ponderously found a way to kneel on bent legs and dusty belly. There, he rested, eyes both dazed and grateful.

Dripping his trunk into the surging pool, Torn Ear snuffled up quantities of water, and lashed it back over his head, squirting his broad back, cutting the dust it had accumulated. Then he inhaled more, squirting it into his waiting mouth.

Another few hours went by before the elephant felt up to climbing to his feet. He stumbled twice, but Tarzan let him be. Either Torn Ear possessed the strength to stand on his own four pads, or he did not. Nothing the ape-man could do would change or alter that circumstance.

But finally, Torn Ear stood fully erect. Stepping about, he tested his legs, and seemed to do a ponderous little dance that shook the ground nevertheless. Then, lifting his mighty trunk, the pachyderm trumpeted his victory over the foul poison of the spider pygmies.

Tarzan smiled to see the formidable beast restored to vitality. His companionship would make the task ahead that much more enjoyable. He returned to his toil.

When at last he was satisfied that the pteranodon wing-shield was structurally sound, the ape-man placed it on Torn Ear's broad back, and leapt atop the beast's spine.

Again, the elephant lifted his trunk, but Tarzan admonished him for silence. Instead, the flexible appendage waved about with barely restrained joy.

Bending low, the ape-lord whispered in the Tantor's good ear murmurings that only one of his species could understand.

Torn Ear seemed to hesitate, but then Tarzan squeezed the animal's broad shoulders with his own knees, and the pachyderm lurched forward and began walking into the pool whose thundering filled their ears.

Together, they pressed toward the raging torrent, bold and unafraid. Without hesitation, they passed into it, a determined warrior and his indomitable steed, resolute in their combined will to complete their mission.

Chapter Sixty-Two

Fearful Fate

WHEN her turn came, it was sooner than the British Military Intelligence operative called Ilex expected.

She had been thinking in terms of a respite of several days, if not longer. This was based upon her knowledge that spiders did not eat for days after a meal. Of course, Ilex was thinking of the garden variety of arachnid, not some atavistic monster of a primeval past of which history did not contain any record.

A full-sized man such as the monkey-tailed Mu-bu-tan seemed to be the equivalent to a fly, but evidently the spider's appetite had reawakened after barely a day.

Possessing no wristwatch, Ilex could not be certain that a day had, in fact, transpired. Nor did she have any other method of reckoning time since in the grotto of the spider people a perpetual gloom enlivened only by vague phosphorescent patches smeared on the cavern walls was all that passed for day or night. She had fallen asleep several times, a result of nervous exhaustion and simply to turn off her brain from contemplating her inevitable fate.

The twitching of the great web to which she was affixed roused Ilex out of sleep. Lifting her upside-down head painfully, she peered about, and saw a trio of spiderlings clustering about her, two above and one below.

They began to unfasten the seemingly unbreakable strands that held her fast to the transverse strands of the skein. They did this not with their six spidery fingers, but with their sharp teeth, for the lashings were not composed of knots, but some kind of sticky strands.

When one hand came free, Ilex formed a fist, and let an unwary spider-man have it on the point of his angular chin.

Caught off-guard, the chalky creature scrambled to retain his awkward perch, but only succeeded in becoming confused. He tumbled off the web without ceremony.

A sharp hissing came from the two others, and they carefully withdrew.

Patiently they waited, clinging to the web, coldly regarding her with jet eyes that seldom blinked. They seemed oddly inhuman, despite their human-like anatomy—an impression that was reinforced when a winged cave insect resembling a dragonfly wandered by and one of the creatures snapped it up in one splayed hand, which it swiftly brought to his mouth.

Chewing motions were briefly observed.

Other insects came into range, and met similar fates. Evidently, these horrid creatures subsisted upon members of the insect kingdom, much in the way certain native tribes consumed ants and grasshoppers.

Some time passed, and another spiderling lifted a six-fingered hand from the web and made gestures that were brief and emphatic. Evidently, this was a signal.

Crawling close, they began working at Ilex's ankles, undoing the lashings with their teeth. This procedure smacked of being nibbled upon so much that Ilex could barely stand it. Closing her fear-dulled eyes, she wished herself back in England.

Chapter Sixty-Three

INTO THE GROTTO

AS BEFORE, the light shaded into gloom before Tarzan of the Apes, astride Torn Ear the elephant, had progressed many paces into the grotto of the spider people.

Sufficient sunlight followed them to permit an acceptable acuity of vision, however. The water of the channel slapped and sloshed about Torn Ear's leathery shoulders and haunches. As his thick legs churned and propelled them forward, he kept his serpentine trunk lifted, as if pointing the way ahead.

Tarzan held his shield in one hand, his freshly-devised longbow grasped in the other. A simple belt of twisted deer hide sufficed to hold the fire-blackened arrows about his waist, there having been no time to sew together a suitable quiver or pouch.

Back in the jungle, Tarzan had considered fashioning a spear along the same rough lines as his supply of arrows but, while practical to create, such a hindrance would prove impossible to tote along with his shield and bow. So he had abandoned that idea.

As it was, carrying the shield and bow would quickly become cumbersome once he fell under the life-seeking whispers of spider-darts. It was the ape-man's hope that he could loose his arrows before the human spiders could attack him, the range of the bolts being greater than the breath-propelled poisoned needles.

Wavelets slapped the arching sides of the channel, which Tarzan noticed for the first time were composed of limestone. Here and there, a bat hung silently. They reminded the ape-man of the great devil-winged pteranodons in miniature.

Sweeping his gaze about, the giant of the jungle conned the way ahead. From his vantage point on the back of the rolling and rocking pachyderm, the push was a very different prospect this time. For one thing, it was possible to discern that the channel bent gradually to the left. Previously, Tarzan and Mubu-tan had been overcome by pygmy darts before they had penetrated very deeply into the cool preserves of the spider foe.

Above his head, dirty grey cobwebs stretched ahead like a long thundercloud that had become trapped in the rock chamber. Vague things crawled along its meandering length. One spidery form slipped down, eight hairy legs splaying.

Torn Ear lifted his trunk and seized it. The arachnid was promptly dunked in the channel to drown. When the trunk lifted free of the water, it was empty.

A fang-like projection of rock close to the water warned the ape-man that he was approaching the zone where once before he had encountered the rock-like artificial eggs at the bottom of the cavern river, which marked the outpost of the spider pygmies.

He did not know whether fresh guards had been secreted in those watertight confines and were now lying in wait, but sweeping the waters ahead and around him, the ape-man assumed that some had.

Torn Ear picked his sure-footed way ahead, unaware. Tarzan tapped the center of his blunt skull as a warning that they neared danger.

The elephant snorted once, and continued on.

Not long after, the great beast stumbled. Tarzan squeezed the rough-skinned shoulders with his muscular thighs, as he held firm to his weapons. The elephant pressed on, but all around them the dark waters took on the hue of blood. And so, Tarzan knew that one of the lurking pickets had been crushed under plodding feet that were like striding tree trunks.

The ape-man set himself for a reaction. He was not disappointed. It soon manifested.

An uprush of bubbles disturbed the water beneath the pachyderm's brown belly.

Then a hairless dome popped up, followed by a narrow face. Dark eyes fell upon him, squeezed into knife-edge narrowness.

Up came a dripping blowpipe. Tarzan lay his bow across his legs, bringing his shield sweeping before him.

A puff, followed by a soft impact that jarred his arm, and the ape-man knew that his shield was tough enough to ward off enemy missiles.

Taking up his longbow, Tarzan whipped out an arrow, and fitted it into the bowstring, drawing back the latter with a muscular strength an ordinary man could never equal.

The man-spider was attempting to recharge his weapon when the ape-man let fly. The bolt struck the enemy square in the throat, splitting its Adam's apple, causing a great flow of life fluid that added to the crimsoning of the waters.

The hapless enemy sank in a frantic splashing of alien hands.

Another foe emerged, but Tarzan had already nocked his bow again. The loosed arrow slid into a left eye as it registered the mounted invader's presence. Again, the consternation of the injured one was brief, but noisy. The figure sank, an upwelling of violently expelled bubbles marking the spot.

Peering around, Tarzan sought any others. He was looking left when a man-spider popped up to his immediate right and seized his ankle with one of its cold, clutching claws.

Twisting on his perch, the ape-man spied the expected blowpipe coming up, not yet brought to bear upon his virtually naked physique.

The attacker attempted to expel a dart, but the bamboo barrel proved to be waterlogged, and all that emerged from the near end was a squirt of foul water.

Reaching down, Tarzan twisted the jointed tube from his foe's clutch, then brought it down sharply on his bald head. Hissing, the man-spider released the ape-man's ankle, attempting to grab hold of the blowpipe. Tarzan permitted this.

Gleeful that he had regained his prize, the spider warrior had not cleared his weapon when Tarzan quickly restored his longbow across his knees and reached down with one powerful hand.

He found the painfully thin neck, lifted the enemy bodily from the water, and severed its jugular vein with a steel blade that eagerly leaped from its scabbard.

Flinging the unclean thing back into the water, the ape-lord looked about and was soon satisfied that he had vanquished the last outpost guard of the spider people.

Tarzan dismounted his steed so that he could recover one of the arrows, which had popped back to the surface, sticking out of one eye of a floating spider corpse. He had only a dozen missiles, and each one was precious, for there would be no opportunity to fashion more in this barren cavern. And Tarzan of the Apes fully intended to send every one of them into a spider pygmy before he was finished.

He urged Torn Ear onward. The elephant lurched ahead. On and on they marched, pushing the channel water before them, creating dark ripples that spread outward, ever outward, like gathering waves of impending doom.

Chapter Sixty-Four

CRY OF VICTORY

ILEX felt her wrists and ankles come free, one by one, as alien hands seized her at every joint.

Free of the ghastly web, she struggled mightily. One bare foot kicked out and knocked a spiderling away. Again, it leapt upon her leg, taking firm hold just below her knee.

Kicking to shrug it off, Ilex held tightly to such strands as she could wrap her bruised fingers around. Small teeth, uncommonly sharp, bit down on her leg, and the unexpectedness more than the pain caused her to shriek aloud once.

They swarmed about her, and began pulling her upward, ever upward.

Still clutching the web, she refused to let go. For Ilex had learned from the abhorrent fate of Mu-bu-tan, the queer native man cursed with a hairy body and a prehensile tail.

Unable to budge her hands, the spider-men instead lifted Ilex up by legs and ankles, fully intending to drag her feet first to the waiting jaws above.

But try as they might, the pale pygmies could not overcome her stubborn resistance, which verged on the ferocious. The woman's fingers might have been fleshy clamps, for they refused to relinquish their desperate hold.

In her fury at her cruel captors, Ilex cried out a wordless rebuke. This stunned the voiceless creatures momentarily. Pausing, several of them communicated with one another through digital manipulations that only they understood. Their dark eyes were unreadable opals.

Looking downward, Ilex stared at the rocky boulders below and began to contemplate the possibility of letting go, in the fatalistic hope that her weight would drag herself and her tormentors down to a smashing, final conclusion.

Before she could make up her mind, the struggling woman was startled by a strange sound.

It was an echoing trumpet of a noise. It sounded for all the world like the strident call of an elephant, reverberating along the rocky cavern confines.

Of course, there would be no elephants in this hideous grotto.

Then came a swishing sound, followed by another, accompanied by explosive grunting.

One, and then another, spider-man dropped from the web, hissing as they fell, mortally wounded, wooden shafts protruding from their bare chests, to dash their spindly bodies on the cruel rocks below.

Then came a thrilling sound that Ilex recognized at once, although she had not heard it uttered in untold years.

It was the victory cry of the great apes!

Chapter Sixty-Five

AGAINST THE SPIDERLINGS

STRIDING through the watery channel, Tarzan prepared to round the bend that he knew would bring him within sight of the great orb web of the pygmy spider people.

An eager anxiousness filled his breast. He had no great and abiding desire to face the man-spiders again in mortal combat, yet the ape-man yearned to pay them back in full measure for their misdeeds against him and his friends. For they had harried him the length and breadth of upper Pal-ul-don relentlessly. It was high time that they paid the price for their temerity.

The Lord of the Jungle did not kill for sport, or for the joy of it. True, he enjoyed the hunt. Stalking game for the feral pleasure of consuming warm meat full of the red juice of life was to the ape-man a thrill unsurpassed in life. But killing for its own sake was not one of his imperatives, as it can be with some so-called civilized men.

But in this case, Tarzan was eager to be about the grim business of avenging all the wrongs that had been done to him by these foul human spiders.

Moreover, the ape-man was eager to be done with this task, and return to his military duty. His time in Pal-ul-don had not been a pleasant sojourn, despite the relief and break it had given him from the confining strictures of military life. But John Clayton, Lord Greystoke, had not joined the R.A.F. as a diversion. He had left his wife Jane at his estate, along with all of his friends and retainers, in order to defend his native land, and he was anxious to be about that business, for as soon as this war was successfully prosecuted, Tarzan of the Apes could return to the private plantation life he knew and loved so well.

So Tarzan rounded the rocky turn, mighty loins girded for battle, determination pounding in his mighty heart.

It was during that steady navigation that Torn Ear again stumbled.

This time the great mahogany beast had not stepped on a hapless spider warrior; apparently, he got his left forepaw stuck in something else. For Torn Ear was moving it around clumsily, as if attempting to free the heavy-nailed pad.

Assuming that it was a stony cleft or other natural obstruction, Tarzan set his longbow and wing-shield carefully atop the pachyderm's broad skull, and slipped off into the water to help his friend.

It was very dark below, and so the ape-man was forced to take hold of Torn Ear's thick foreleg, and feel his way down. When he reached bottom, Tarzan discovered the elephant had stopped with its foot resting in the hollow of some thing that was not naturally found on the channel bed.

Feeling around, the jungle lord discovered hard edges, and a nodular surface on the convex side that felt familiar to the touch.

Tarzan's agile brain suddenly realized what the obstruction was. Torn Ear had unwittingly stepped into the concave inner surface of the very tortoise shell shield the ape-man had lost more than a day before!

Taking hold of the elephant's ankle with both hands, Tarzan guided it upward, and the pachyderm obediently complied. His foot came free. Groping for the shell, the ape-man brought it to the surface and examined it more with his hands than his eyes, for the light in this extremity of the grotto was deceptively dim.

Although it had been cracked, the horny carapace had not split. Therefore the protective shield presented to him by the turtle-men was still serviceable.

The makeshift straps were still intact, as well. So Tarzan inserted his arms into the loops, and made it fast across his broad bronzed back. It fit him poorly, but for all that the shield offered a measure of defense from the lethal devil-darts that was not to be despised. This safeguard, along with the pteranodon-wing arm shield, would afford the bronzed giant even greater protection as he went into battle.

Firmly seated once again behind Torn Ear's neck, Tarzan of the Apes impelled his patient steed forward, steering him around the rocky outcropping that marked the bend in the channel leading to the dim den of the spider people.

Here, the light shifted from the faint illumination of sunlight filtering through the restless waterfall far behind his back, dwindling in the limestone grotto whose sides were speckled and spotted with patches of luminous lichen. This wan half-glow was not much better; in fact, it was deceptively indistinct.

There were no shelves on either side of the channel at this juncture, and so the water slopped and splashed unobstructed against the cavern walls as Torn Ear methodically moved along.

Tarzan's narrowed eyes remained alert, as his optical nerves adjusted to the wavery luminescent greenish light.

Here and there, one of those patches seemed to wink, or black out; the ape-man knew that silent human spiders were crawling unseen before them.

Eventually, they reached a spot where the clog of spider webs above their heads were not old and grey, but shimmered with silken life.

A sound came. A kind of chittering. A signal, Tarzan perceived.

From the clustered webs above, arachnids descended like deformed and disembodied puppet hands. They hung in the gloom like living symbols, silken strings faintly visible, silently pantomiming a spectral warning to venture no further.

Growling, Torn Ear fell to slashing at them with his flexible appendage, tossing them aside, precipitating the unclean things into the dark water. He made short work of a number of them as he barged ahead.

Tarzan used his long wing-shield to batter aside those the determined pachyderm failed to find. One spider dropped atop Torn Ear's skull and made for the ape-man, mandibles clicking together.

Withdrawing an arrow, Tarzan impaled it, fitted the shaft into his bowstring and sent the injured arachnid flying into the gloom where human spiders lurked half-seen, watching all.

The point struck a faint form, and wrenched from it a death shriek that echoed resoundingly. A pale body dropped into the water, and writhed there until it sank from view.

Whether death had eventuated from the piercing shaft or the introduction of spider venom did not much matter to the ape-man. But in his heart of hearts, he rather hoped it was the latter.

Nothing moved in the stony shadows after that. This last line of defense vanquished, Torn Ear plodded onward.

Finally, Tarzan began to discern the great woven web of the arachnid god of the spider people, which hung over tumbles of piled rock, between which a thin stream of water trickled like a dark vein dimly perceived. The monster still hung in its lair, not moving, seemingly brooding as it had for eternities uncounted.

Once again, the ape-man felt an impressive sense that he had blundered into a realm that was more ancient than human imagination. Who the spider people were, what constituted their evolutionary lineage, baffled him completely. Had they existed before the earliest men of dawn? Were they some atavistic offshoot—a vestige of a forgotten era where enormous insects and arachnids ruled? Were they even human by Twentieth Century standards?

Tarzan did not know. And he shrugged off these unanswerable questions, for now it was time to settle accounts.

As if sensing his thoughts, Torn Ear gave voice in a trumpeting roar.

Up ahead, the ape-man detected movements in the great spider web. Things scuttled there, then came a piercing shriek— brutally short, as if cut off. A woman's inarticulate cry!

NOCKING an arrow, Tarzan attempted to fix a target with one grey eye. Owing to the greenish half-light, this was no easy task.

He imagined rather than saw Ilex trapped somewhere in that stupendous weave, and had no heart to impale her by accident. So the ape-man was more careful than he might otherwise have been. He assumed, also, that Mu-bu-tan might be ensnared somewhere in that dimly-perceived skein.

Then, spotting a pale blob with spindly black-banded limbs, Tarzan let fly.

A hissing wail was his reward. The ape-man had already lined up a second shot. Once released, this flew true, and another exclamation of shock echoed back.

The sound of two puny bodies striking blunt stone, one after another, told more eloquently than any vision might that two spider pygmies would fight no more. He only wished that the hardened arrow points had been smeared with spider venom.

Knowing the psychological effect this would have on the enemy, Tarzan opened his mouth, threw back his lordly head, and screamed forth the terrifying victory cry of the bull ape.

The narrow walls of the grotto caught that shudder-producing challenge, making it rebound and re-echo the length and breadth of the cavern. This evoked great alarm among the inhabitants of the web. There came a frantic scuttling commotion, followed by a still and eerie silence.

Some instinct warned Tarzan of the Apes to raise his wing-shield.

Thin reed blowguns began hissing, but the spider-darts they expelled fell short. The longer, stouter bamboo blowpipes were brought into play next, and one fletched quill whizzed by, while another impaled itself upon the upraised shield.

Again, the cry of a woman resounded up ahead. Lifting his voice, Tarzan cried out, "Ilex! Are you safe?"

A strained voice echoed back. "I daresay that I am not! For I am hanging on for dear life."

"Keep up your courage! I am coming."

And Tarzan urged Torn Ear to charge. Roaring, the great elephant blundered forward. Tarzan nocked another arrow; this one he sent into the great abdomen of the prehistoric monster arachnid.

The great web quivered noticeably in the dim light. But the eight monster limbs remained still. It was as if the creature was oblivious to it.

Frowning, Tarzan loosed another bolt, sending this one into the area of its myriad eyes. Again, the web quivered and shook, but the monster did not react.

What manner of creature was this that could absorb sharp arrows and not cry out or recoil? As he drew closer and closer, Tarzan of the Apes began to suspect the answer.

Switching targets, he let fly with another arrow—and another man-spider fell scrambling from the web.

Scuttling pale figures were climbing for the great eggs that adorned the web on all sides of the shaking monster, plunged inward, and reemerged with long blowpipes clutched in their weird long-fingered fists.

Tarzan remained beyond range of only the most far-traveling dart. Picking his targets carefully, adjusting himself to the rolling stride of Torn Ear, who trumpeted a curt warning, Tarzan felled victim after victim until he was entirely out of missiles.

Throwing the now-useless bow aside, the ape-man brought his shield before him, methodically removing his steel knife from its scabbard.

Lifting his voice again, Tarzan inquired, "Where is Mu-bu-tan?"

The answer was slow in coming. Finally, a female voice, thick with emotion, flung back, "I fear that the horrid monster has consumed him."

Hearing this, Tarzan called out in a voice that rang with inner steel, "Then I will make the abomination pay."

Slipping off the elephant, Tarzan dropped into the water, which sloshed shallowly at this point. The ape-man hung back, allowing Torn Ear to precede him, then brought up the rear, crouching off to one side, peering over the triangular pteranodon-wing shield, so that he could bring the thing to bear in self-protection when he perceived devil-darts arriving.

A startled grunt came from Torn Ear, indicating that the first thorn needles had lodged in his forehead and shoulders. The elephant had folded back his bad ear protectively, knowing that it was his most vulnerable point. Lowering his massive head like a war elephant about to batter down enemy walls with his formidable skull, he closed his eyes to protect them as well.

The channel floor began to slope upward, and when Tarzan saw that he was emerging from the water with each step, the ape-man picked up his pace and raced on ahead of his trudging companion.

Tarzan leapt up on dry land, and charged forward, mindful that every moment counted. Torn Ear continued plodding in his wake, momentarily stymied by the increasingly difficult way as the channel petered out, and anxious to avoid rocky traps.

Darts started peppering the fleet ape-man. Yet his shield, despite its narrowness, was sufficient to catch them. He felt something riffle his hair, but charged on, knowing that if he were struck, he had but seconds left in which to inflict whatever vengeance he could before succumbing.

Veering to the right, the ape-man sought one side of the grotto. In the weird half-light, he sped to one of the lower anchor strands where it was affixed to a stony outcropping by some means Tarzan could not discern.

His blade flashed, biting into the heavy anchor strand. Sawing swiftly, he severed the coarse thing. A great trembling and shaking disturbed the web. More importantly it caused startled spiderlings to scramble and clutch at their resting perches.

That accomplished, the ape-lord leapt into the skein, and commenced climbing it the way a sailor mounts coarse netting thrown over the side of a ship. His pteranodon-skin shield was gripped in one hand, but its triangular shape was starting to get in his way. Having no other choice, the ape-man let it drop, freeing up that hand for close combat.

Climbing with great rapidity, Tarzan reached the dim form of the woman who was hanging by both hands, one heel hooked into a strand, offering her some measure of shaky support.

Finding a coign of vantage beside her, Tarzan instructed, "Quickly clasp your arms around my neck, and I will carry you down."

"Tarzan!" the woman cried. "It *is* you!"

"Hurry!" urged the ape-man.

Balanced on both feet, Tarzan took Ilex by the waist, lifted her up. The woman's deathly-cool hands wrapped around his sinewy neck. He shifted her around until Ilex was draped awkwardly across the tortoise shell shield upon his back. Then the ape-man started to lower himself, using only his strong hands. Soon, he was within reasonable distance of the stone floor below, over a spot that lay relatively smooth between heaps of tumbled rock, through which the shrinking channel coursed like a wavering vein of inky-black water.

Dropping the last few yards, Tarzan managed to land on his bare feet, bending his knees so as not to lose his balance.

Ilex was forced to release her grip, but it no longer mattered.

"Run for the shelter of the elephant!" directed the ape-man, pointing toward a looming hulk. "Get behind him. Their darts cannot pierce his hide."

The British agent needed no more encouragement. She raced for the channel, up which was striding Torn Ear, a light of battle in his small eyes, for in his eagerness to confront his master's foes, he could not keep them closed.

Knowing that the woman would be fully exposed to enemy darts during her sprint, Tarzan raced to the opposite wall, found the anchoring guy-wire strand there, and sawed at it until it, too, broke loose.

Although the great orb web shook and trembled anew, it remained firmly situated. Teeth set, the ape-man sprang back up into its lower reaches, his knife clenched in his jaws, hands and feet climbing higher, ever higher, until he reached a quadrant not far beneath great arachnid legs, which splayed over his head.

Taking his knife again in hand, Tarzan cut into several longitudinal strands, not severing them, but cutting them so deeply they began to unravel under the strain of holding the entire skein together. In their thickness and rough texture, they reminded the ape-man of the creeper webs found in the bottle-tree groves.

Perhaps this skein was not spun after all....

The entirety of the web shook as spiderlings reacted with animated alarm. Their stealthy silence had not changed, but their movements were those of blind panic and consternation.

Popping sounds were heard. Strands parted. Others sagged.

So rapidly did the web deteriorate that the spiderlings gave no thought to their blowguns and blowpipes. Indeed, several of the bamboo tubes began falling free, for in their panic, the spider pygmies—as beings do the world over—turned their immediate attention from self-defense to self-preservation.

Tarzan moved up, and continued his cutting. He was very methodical about it, never severing where he could weaken, moving from strand to ropey strand in an effort to wreak as much damage as possible without jeopardizing his precarious position.

Shifting over to the other side of the circular net, the ape-man repeated his actions. The heavy skein began to sag alarmingly.

It was then and only then did the repellent monster arachnid finally bother to stir....

Chapter Sixty-Six

TARZAN THE AVENGER

AT FIRST, Tarzan of the Apes thought that the monster's movements were simply a reaction to the web strands straining and commencing to pop. For snapping sounds here and there bespoke eloquently that the colossal weave was starting to unravel.

But the great abdomen shook and shook and shook, as if the monster was about to give birth.

Then, it apparently did!

From out of the rear of the bloated abdomen, where the spinnerets with which arachnids spin their webs protrude, something pale and grotesque emerged.

First, it was a head, but not a bald head such as the spider pygmies possessed. No, this head was round and plump, and wreathed in a long black pelt of hair that might have been a kind of matted hair. The features were pallid and greasy, twisted in a mad fury that hissed venomously from its puckered mouth. The skin of the thing was not the flat white of chalk, but rather the sickly pallor of an albino.

Angry pink eyes quested about and came to rest on Tarzan's naked form. The rubbery mouth opened, and a horrible spitting issued forth.

Wriggling, the rest of the creature emerged. The ape-man took in the horrid webwork of blue veins visible under the translucent, dead-looking hide. The entire form shook with uncontained rage. Here was a creature of the underground, a being which had never beheld sunlight. That was not the most disgusting thing. Far from it.

Tarzan saw to his great astonishment that this plump form was distinctly female. Pendulous breasts swayed as it fought its way out into open air.

But that revelation was not the thing that caused the ape-man's eyes to widen. Although human in much the way that the man-spiders seemed to be human, this female of the species possessed two sets of arms, so that while she did not own the eight limbs of a true spider, she was not formed of four limbs such as were typical specimens of the human race.

For his part, Tarzan had no interest in fighting this female, imagining as he did that she was some kind of arachnid equivalent to a queen bee. But then his eyes fell upon her throat, around which was a familiar object, which gleamed golden in the dim cavern light.

It was his mother's locket, which Tarzan had worn during his flight south. Seeing such a revered object hanging around such an unclean neck, unbounded fury consumed Tarzan of the Apes. He left off his severing of the web strands, and began climbing.

The ape-man's object was nothing less than to rip the locket off the neck of the six-limbed monstrosity.

From out of the different eggs—which Tarzan realized were some form of woven huts, and not true eggs—emerged more spiderlings, blowpipes in hand.

Climbing faster, the ape-man sought the grotesquely bloated thing that had now completely emerged from the abdomen of the arachnid monster. One bronze-skinned arm reached up as if to snare the locket, but never achieved its goal. For more devilish darts were beginning to fly.

Abruptly, the ape-man swung about, presenting his tortoise shell back to the spiderlings above. Breath-expelled darts began arriving, and their sound against his nodular shield was like a nervous ticking.

Tarzan understood that his head, arms and legs were unprotected. He sought to keep his back arched upward, but this made it difficult to hold onto the web, especially as an intermittent popping warned of guy-wire strands, stretched beyond endurance, that were fast coming apart.

Fortunately, the bamboo tubes had to be reloaded after each expenditure of flying death. But in those pauses, the six-limbed female began to grope and crawl toward him, hissing violently. Her hands possessed the same double-thumbs as the males of her sinister species, but the nails were exceedingly long and black in a way that did not appear natural.

The hackles on the back of the ape-man's neck began to lift, and it dawned upon him that those nails might be coated with the same spider-poison as the devil-darts that so avidly sought his life.

Tarzan harbored no great desire to slay a female, but this creature smacked of utter foulness. In some manner he did not fully comprehend, this spider-queen was the mother of all these hissing spiderlings arrayed about the web. This meant that she was the ultimate author of their depredations.

The she-monster crawled closer, four hands and matching feet grasping and releasing the jittering web strands as she came. Tarzan prepared to plunge his steel fang into her unlovely form. The ape-man knew, however, that to get close enough to accomplish that act, he would unavoidably bring his bare skin into range of those ebony talons and the death they portended.

Then, a flash of memory intruded. He remembered something he had all but forgotten. Deep in the bottom of his knife sheath nested a red-fletched spider-dart, which he had secreted there after finding it caught in his hair days before.

Clamping the blade in his teeth, the ape-man shook the dart from his scabbard—all while clinging to the huge web by hooking his free arm around a fat strand. Its leafy envelope fell free.

Sheathing the knife again, Tarzan took the deadly dart between his teeth, clamping it by its bright red feathers, an exceedingly difficult maneuver, as the bloated monstrosity crawled inexorably toward him, hissing intermittently.

The ape-man swung about, changing his position. Then, he commenced climbing up to meet his foe, spider-dart still in his mouth.

Hissing, the spider-queen reached out with her black talons.

Lunging upward, Tarzan grasped the devil-dart, and struck like Hondo the hornet, piercing the grasping spidery hand along one of its thumbs. That hand recoiled. The queen saw the sprig of scarlet sticking out of her own flesh, and a low wailing wound tortuously out of her panic-stricken mouth.

The ape-man saw his opportunity then. The spider-queen was hanging upside down, and the precious gold locket was depending from her plump neck, almost within reach.

Whipping out his knife, Tarzan sprang to one side and scampered up, keeping well away from the four arms that clutched and waved frantically in turn as the female struggled to retain her balance while the poison seeped into her pulsing, hideously visible veins.

With the tip of his blade, the ape-man reached in and severed the gold chain, hooking it free. It dropped to the rocky ground far below.

What would have happened next was never recorded.

Once more the ape-lord gave out the ringing cry that chilled the blood of man and beast alike. The cry he had learned as a youth among the great apes of the tribe of Kerchak.

For not far below him, a muffled voice called out.

"Tarzan-jad-guru, is that you?"

The ape-man hesitated. "Mu-bu-tan! Where are you?"

"I think I am inside the monster, Tarzan," Mu-bu-tan said without great alarm.

Slipping down several strands, Tarzan sought the voice and said, "Speak your name again."

"You know my name, Tarzan-jad-guru."

"I merely wanted to hear your voice, to better fix your position in my mind," returned the ape-man and, employing his blade, began cutting into the rough, papery skin of the great arachnid.

The flesh was dry and easily opened up. Tarzan cut and cut again, until he had excavated a ragged hole.

A shaggy hand shot out of that hole. It began pulling and pushing at the aperture until it was enlarged greatly, aided by a second hand. The head and shoulders of Mu-bu-tan were the next to emerge. Tarzan reached down to pull him out.

Mu-bu-tan beamed. "Your timing is very sound, Tarzan-jad-guru. For I think that bloated she-thing was intending to devour me."

"Our timing may not be as sound as you think, Mu-bu-tan," rejoined the ape-man. "For this web is fast coming apart."

The Waz-ho-don warrior did not need any more warning than that. With Tarzan's help, he pulled himself free and together they began climbing down the web as fast as their hands and feet could find purchase and release.

It was not fast enough, unfortunately. With a succession of popping sounds, the web started to come apart.

Looking down, Tarzan saw why.

Torn Ear, no doubt observing the ape-man battling the four-armed spider-queen, had rushed in and, wrapping his python-like trunk about the great ropey strands, was methodically pulling at the entire weave.

Already weakened by Tarzan's earlier efforts with his steel blade, the web began surrendering to the tugging pressure of the powerful pachyderm.

This had been Tarzan's plan all along—to bring down the home web of the spider people. But he had not yet given that order.

Seeing the ape-man's peril, the enraged elephant had taken matters into his own hand—or trunk, in this case. Stepping from strand to strand, Torn Ear was methodically uprooting the anchoring cables.

There was no stopping the beast, Tarzan knew. There remained only time to escape the imminent collapse. Having scrambled as far down as they could, Tarzan and Mu-bu-tan leapt free, and fell hard to the stone floor below.

Mu-bu-tan appeared stunned, but Tarzan jumped quickly to his feet and scooped up the golden locket of his mother. Then, the ape-man took up the Waz-ho-don warrior. Holding his burden before him, he began racing for the water.

Over his shoulder, Tarzan called, "Torn Ear! Follow!"

The elephant did not immediately respond. Stubbornly, he plucked at another bit of web, set his great feet and, backing up, wrenched it free.

"Kreegah!" called Tarzan in the language of the great apes. "Beware!"

The brown brute, seeing that he had wrought great damage, wheeled about and charged after the ape-man. Together, they splashed into the channel where Ilex stood watching with shocked features.

Behind them came a horrible sound or, to put it bluntly, a cacophony of sounds. The web ripped free of its anchorage, collapsing to the ground, taking hissing spiderlings, their grotesque queen, and the great monster arachnid within which they abided, crashing to the ground below.

A great upwelling of dirt, dust and other cave debris rose up, and Tarzan and Mu-bu-tan dived into the water to avoid its smothering pall.

Unable to submerge his mighty bulk, Torn Ear emitted a scream more fearful than fearsome and presented one rugged flank to the gusty commotion, protecting his friends with the immobile wall of his great bulk.

Behind him, Ilex closed her eyes and clapped pale hands over her ears to keep out the awful sounds that could not be described.

A silence, still and terrible, eventually settled over the grotto of the human spiders.

It was not broken for a long time....

Chapter Sixty-Seven

The Proposal

FIRST, Tarzan broke the surface of the waters of the cavern channel, soon followed by Mu-bu-tan's hairy features.

The Waz-ho-don warrior wore a grateful smile, his strong, pointed teeth almost incandescent.

"Once again, I owe you my life, Tarzan-jad-guru."

"I am pleased that you still possess your life," remarked the ape-man dryly, "having been consumed by a giant arachnid as you were."

Mu-bu-tan laughed. "It was not alive, Tarzan-jad-guru. It was but a dried husk of a mummy, a thing that lived and died ages ago, in whose hollow thorax its worshipers dwelled."

Tarzan's eyes flashed. "I suspected as much when it did not react to my arrows."

Turning their attention back to the grotto, they saw that the great orb web had collapsed into a dirty, disordered heap in which the broken and dried monster arachnid limbs stuck out at odd and frightening angles. Intermingled with these artifacts were spindly pale limbs whose lifeless hands displayed weirdly long fingers and matching thumbs.

Mu-bu-tan remarked, "Some of them may yet live…."

"If they do," commented Tarzan, "let them have their wretched lives. I am done with this unclean place. Henceforth, I seek only fresh sunlight and reviving air."

"Then let us be on our way," suggested Mu-bu-tan.

Turning, they waded over to Torn Ear. Tarzan found Ilex sheltered behind the elephant's great rump. Her hair was wet, greatly in disarray, pale features indistinct in the dim light.

"We are done here," announced Tarzan. "We will be on our way."

"You have expressed my sentiments exactly," Ilex said sincerely.

Giving her a boost onto the back of the elephant, Tarzan climbed behind the woman, while Mu-bu-tan waded in their wake, his eyes searching the water's surface.

"There is room for a third passenger," suggested Tarzan.

Mu-bu-tan returned, "Somewhere in these waters floats the spear of my ancestors. I wish to reclaim this shaft if I can find it."

They waded along for a time, but Mu-bu-tan was forced by the increasing depth of the channel to resort to swimming, which gave him the opportunity to search the murky waters below.

When the warrior found his spear, which he did in short order, his hirsute head broke the surface and Mu-bu-tan raised the copper point aloft and gave out a cry that could not be translated into any language, for it was an expression of pure, unbridled joy.

"I have my spear," he exulted.

"And I, my father's knife and my mother's locket," smiled Tarzan.

To which Ilex added, "And all that I require is to recover my boots, with which I am sure you will assist me, Tarzan."

The jungle lord smiled. "It is the last duty that remains for us to accomplish in Pal-ul-don. After which, we will ride together on the back of this elephant through the morass and into the thorny boundaries where we will find our way back to civilization."

That decided, they trudged along until they made the turn that brought the relentless sound of the waterfall and the wavering sunlight filtered by the torrent to their senses, which lifted the party's spirits tremendously.

Mu-bu-tan broke a long silence when he remarked, "Tarzan-jad-guru, do you recall that I once told you that I was abroad in this part of the Land-of-man for a reason?"

"I do."

"Before, I intimated that it was my business, and mine alone. But I think it is time that I reveal to you that reason."

"I am listening," encouraged the ape-man.

"I was sent out by my father, Ko-bu-tan, who is *gund* of Bu-lur, to investigate a great metal bird that had fallen from the sky, from which had been seen people floating beneath perfectly round white clouds, that appeared to bear them safely to earth."

Tarzan nodded. "The great bird that you saw conveyed this woman and the two white men who later died to the Land-of-man. There is nothing more to investigate."

Mu-bu-tan spoke sincerely. "It is custom among my people when a man reaches a certain age to set out on his own to capture a mate from among one of the other tribes. This is how the Waz-ho-don people perpetuate their splendid race. For as you know, my tribe is neither Waz-don nor Ho-don, but a mingling of both strains. My father urged me, while seeking the strange bird which fell from the heavens, to locate a worthy mate, if I encountered one on my wanderings. For I am now of age to take on this responsibility."

Tarzan nodded. "Then I take it you will be about that earnest business once we part company."

Mu-bu-tan was silent for a time. Then, he spoke again. "I have been through much at your side, Tarzan-jad-guru," he said deliberately. "And even more beside this woman of your tribe, whose language I do not speak. I am wondering if you could convey to her in your speech my interest in making her my mate."

Tarzan chuckled.

"Why do you laugh, Tarzan-jad-guru?" he asked with a trace of ire in his deep warrior's voice.

"This woman is not free to marry, for she is a warrior of my people and, as such, owes her allegiance to our King. Even if she wished to marry you—which I strongly doubt—she would have to be released from her vows of fealty to do so."

"How would one go about arranging for that release?" wondered Mu-bu-tan.

"You would have to come with us to the outer world," explained Tarzan, "and plead your case among my people. But first, I will have to discuss the matter with her."

Mu-bu-tan nodded somberly. "I trust that you will make my case as well as you are able, for I am determined to take this comely beauty back to my tribe as a worthy mate, whose bravery as well as beauty inspire me to acquire her."

"Count on that," promised Tarzan.

By then, they were coming up to the great torrent, and the moist mists began to bead their features as the welcome light increased.

Tarzan said in English, "It would be best if we dismounted at this point and swam the rest of the way, the force of the waterfall being punishing—for I endured its pounding on the way in."

"Yes, of course," responded Ilex.

Signaling for Torn Ear to halt, Tarzan dismounted, and floating in the water, lifted up his arms to receive the woman.

It was then, in the pellucid light, that the ape-man saw clearly the face of Ilex for the first time. A look of surprise bordering on shock warped his bronzed features, and so astounded was Tarzan that he nearly missed catching her when she slipped down.

Seeing this, Mu-bu-tan demanded, "What is wrong?"

The ape-man found his voice.

"I know this woman."

"Of course you do. You just rescued her."

Tarzan shook his head. "No," he explained, "I know her from years gone by. Her name is Patricia Canby."

Chapter Sixty-Eight

HOMEWARD BOUND

SHAKING off his astonishment, Tarzan led them under the waterfall, first shucking off the clumsy shield of the turtle-men, which had once again preserved him from the darts of the spider pygmies.

As they swam into the turbulent pool, Torn Ear smashing through the torrent like a muscular elephant of war, trunk waving about as if he enjoyed the pounding of water against his back, Tarzan's mind flashed back to the last World War, some twenty-five years before. That was when he had first encountered the British agent, then a young woman known to him as Bertha Kircher, which had been her alias during a period when she had been a double agent, pretending to serve the Kaiser.*

The years had been kind to her, and although Patricia Canby was more womanly than girlish now, she was still beautiful—and it looked as though she would remain so for years yet to come.

Tarzan had encountered her at a time when he thought that his wife, Jane, had been savagely murdered by German soldiers during the previous global conflict. That proved not to have been the case. When the ape-man had later tracked Jane Clayton to this very enclave of Pal-ul-don, he had rescued his lost wife from a last German holdout, a cruel man named Lieutenant Erich Obergatz.

---

* *Tarzan the Untamed*

Those events were very long ago now. During the intervening years, the ape-man, together with his family, had ingested a witch doctor's magic pills, which promised to prolong their lives almost to the point of immortality. Thus far, the brew seemed to be achieving the desired results.*

Tarzan fully expected to die someday, but the decades had weighed less heavily upon him than conceivably possible. On the outside, the ape-lord had barely aged, though in place of natural wrinkles, he had acquired many more battle scars. Perhaps he had traded one mark of advancing years for another.

When they reached the stony shore, they scrambled onto dry land and sat in the hot blaze of day, allowing the solar rays to dry them off.

"I had not known that was you until I heard your familiar cry as you advanced," remarked Patricia Canby, formerly Ilex of the British Military Intelligence Service. "It is a sound never to be forgotten."

Tarzan nodded. "When we first met one another, we had no opportunity to see each other's faces in anything but darkness, or in the worst possible light. Despite its vague, unplaceable familiarity, I had not recognized your voice, not having heard it in so many years."

"Nor I, yours, Tarzan. Or should I say, John Clayton?"

"Since we belong to the same military organization," said the ape-man, "I suppose you should address me as Flying Officer Clayton."

"Well, in that case, Flying Officer Clayton," the woman said tartly, "I suggest that you are still out of uniform, and should remedy that forthwith."

Tarzan's firm lips curved in a half smile. He got to his feet and padded over to the pack of clothing he had left behind. In short order, he had donned his military uniform and boots, but retained the well-worn scabbard with his father's hunting knife firmly in place. When he was restored to the state of dress

---

*   *Tarzan's Quest*

appropriate to his rank, his noble visage wore a disappointed expression.

Patricia Canby laughed. "You look rather uncomfortable, Flying Officer Clayton."

Tarzan frowned. "I will have to get used to this cotton uniform all over again. For my sojourn in Pal-ul-don has caused me to revert to my old ways."

A sudden flicker crossed his features.

"Is something amiss?" asked the woman.

Tarzan shook his head. "When I was given this assignment, I was told that I would find you readily, despite a lack of description. Now I understand why. Military Intelligence no doubt knew that we were acquainted."

"I see. No question now that their judgment was entirely correct."

Listening to this exchange without understanding any of it, Mu-bu-tan reminded Tarzan, "Are you making my appeal?"

The ape-man's face lightened. "I was just about to."

Turning to Patricia Canby, Tarzan—or should we say Flying Officer John Clayton, Lord Greystoke, of the R.A.F.?—stated, "My comrade has come to admire you greatly."

"He is very brave. Even if he is rather hideous."

"Mu-bu-tan tells me that he is seeking a mate, and finds you most appealing," added Tarzan.

Patricia Canby's blue eyes startled. "Surely, he cannot be serious?" she burst out.

Tarzan went on in a sober tone. "He is willing to accompany us to civilization and make his case to your superiors."

"If that is the case," said Ilex, "please inform the gentleman with the tail that I have been happily married for the past twenty-odd years. For I am no longer Patricia Canby, but Mrs. Harold Percy Smith-Oldwick."

"I will tell him that," promised Tarzan. He walked over to Mu-bu-tan and spoke to him quietly and earnestly for nearly a dozen minutes, his mien serious.

The Waz-ho-don warrior took it well, and expressed very little disappointment beyond an agitated snapping of his tail. The look on his fur-fringed features was one of profound discouragement.

"You are not greatly disappointed?" inquired Tarzan.

"No, for now that we are all together in clear light, it has dawned on me that your female friend has certain deficiencies."

"She is not as young as when I first knew her," admitted the ape-man. "But for all that, she would make anyone a suitable mate, being strong of heart, mind and body."

"I do not doubt your words, Tarzan-jad-guru," said Mu-bu-tan. "But as I study her under sunlight, I detect no sign of any tail."

"That is because she has none," remarked the ape-man.

"In that case," sighed the Waz-ho-don warrior sadly, "I withdraw my offer of marriage. My father, Ko-bu-tan, would never permit the mate of the future *gund* of Bu-lur to go about unashamedly tailless. It would be a scandal."

Tarzan made his expression more serious than he felt, so as not to laugh in the face of his disappointed comrade-in-arms.

"That is perfectly understandable," he imparted.

"I must be on my way, then," Mu-bu-tan said firmly. "For I have trekked a great distance and enjoyed many intriguing perils, but I have yet to find my mate."

Tarzan smiled appreciatively. "We will accompany one another out of this wretched ravine."

As Torn Ear climbed out of the pool reluctantly, and shook his great body like a dog flinging off a good soaking, the ape-man added, "South of here lies the Ho-don city of A-lur, below the Kor-ul-gryf and on the shores of Jad-ben-lul, the big lake. Many years ago A-lur was ruled by a good friend of mine, a *gund* named Ja-don. If you are brave enough to go to the City of Light and present yourself, announcing that you are a friend of Tarzan-jad-guru, I am certain that Chief Ja-don will introduce you to a suitable mate in due course."

Mu-bu-tan brightened. "Surely? You do not jest?"

A mischievous twinkle in his eyes, the ape-man said gravely, "Tarzan-jad-guru does not jest, ever."

Mu-bu-tan cocked his shaggy head quizzically. "Ever?"

"Hardly ever, but not in this case. For finding a mate is the most important task of all."

"Well spoken," said the Waz-ho-don warrior, taking his spear into his coiling tail.

Walking together, they returned to Patricia's side.

The ape-man addressed the woman, saying with a grave face, "The matter is settled. The two of you will be wed in a village not far from here tonight. A witch doctor of good reputation will officiate."

A look of profound shock came over Patricia Smith-Oldwick's drawn face. She was entirely speechless for a full minute.

"It turns out that the people of Mu-bu-tan's tribe are amazingly liberal in these matters," added Tarzan. "That you already possess a husband is of no consequence to him."

"This—this is outrageous! You cannot mean what you are saying!"

Tarzan laughed, unable to maintain his serious demeanor any longer. "I was merely joking, for while Tarzan of the Apes seldom jests, sometimes a good joke is well-deserved after a difficult ordeal. The truth of the matter is that you are married and, more unfortunately, possess a greater deficiency that disqualifies you from becoming the mate of Mu-bu-tan."

The woman looked blank. "I fail to understand."

The ape-man explained, "You lack a proper tail, without which you would scandalize his tribe."

This did not mollify the former Patricia Canby. "In that case," she snapped, "I will thank you to lead me to my boots, and we will be on our way."

"Tarzan will be happy to do that."

"Thank Tarzan for me, *Flying Officer* Clayton," she retorted stiffly.

After Ilex had been restored to her perch atop Torn Ear, they worked their way along the narrow rift of the spider people, who by all accounts were now extinct, or virtually so. Before long, Tarzan asked the ruffled woman a question.

"I have been curious as to what is contained in those boots that is so important."

"Flying Officer Clayton, we have been through this once before. I am on a secret mission, and as a military man, you should know that I am both unable and unwilling to divulge any details of my mission."

"You are correct," said Tarzan. "Please accept my apologies for overstepping my bounds."

"But since you saved my life and we are not yet out of danger, I will tell you this. Each boot heel contains one half of a map, without which the other half is useless. Once I surrender both halves to my superiors, they will have the location of a highly important German secret that may affect the future course of the present war."

Tarzan nodded. "More than that I do not need to know."

"If anything dire should befall me," she added, "it will be your bounden duty to convey both portions to your highest superior officer."

"Count on me to prevent that eventuality from coming to pass," promised Clayton.

In time, they put the gloomy rift behind them and passed on into the highland forest where they reclaimed the boots that still reposed safely in the hollow of a tree.

Once this was accomplished, they bid a final farewell to Mu-bu-tan, who intended to strike south toward the city of A-lur, and the bright prospect of a mate.

Laying a hand on Mu-bu-tan's hairy shoulder, Tarzan added, "Go in peace, my friend, and find your happiness where you will."

Placing a hairy hand on the Tarmangani's opposite shoulder, the Waz-ho-don warrior said sincerely, "I will never forget you, Tarzan-jad-guru."

"Nor I, you."

Then, the bronzed giant's face grew strange.

"What is wrong?" asked Mu-bu-tan.

"In the lake of the turtle folk who gave me the shield that enabled me to wrest this victory from the spider pygmies, they called me by another name."

"What name?"

"Tarzan-jad-ojo. I have long wondered what it meant."

"If the speech of the turtle-men is equivalent to the speech of my people, then they were calling you Tarzan the Brave."

The Lord of the Jungle chuckled good-naturedly. "That is a relief to hear. For I was half certain that they were calling me Tarzan the Mad."

A commotion caused the two to look to the north.

There, Torn Ear was butting an elephant tree with his heavy skull, which caused its fruit to drop heavily to the ground. The elephant picked up one specimen in his trunk and conveyed it to his waiting mouth. His mouth moved patiently.

Mu-bu-tan mused, "My father will never believe me when I tell him I encountered people without tails and a beast possessing two tails, one on either end."

"Then do not tell him," suggested Tarzan.

"That is excellent counsel. You are very wise. Goodbye."

So saying, Mu-bu-tan walked over to Torn Ear and picked up a fruit with his sinuous tail and ate it, never once touching the food with his hands.

When he was done, his tail and Torn Ear's trunk touched and coiled in farewell. Then the hairy warrior vanished into the bush.

FROM there, the trek out of the Land of Man was a march of two days, during which they skirted two blowing *gryfs* without incident, ate an assortment of delicious fruits and nuts, broken by a stomach-satisfying feast on an antelope Tarzan slew, until at last they reached the awful morass that bounded Pal-ul-don.

Coming upon the swampy ring, Torn Ear was hesitant to step into the water. His memory clearly lived up to the reputation of his kind.

Tarzan was obliged to go in first and swim about, making a great splashing and commotion to show the elephant that the path was clear and unobstructed by voracious reptiles.

Thus reassured, the trembling pachyderm stepped into the water and began churning his way across with the former Ilex seated comfortably on his back.

Tarzan of the Apes remained in the water, knowing that if a saurian reared its ugly head, it would be his job to settle the monster.

Fortunately, they had no reptilian encounters.

Finally stepping out into the great thorny brush, the party stopped by the wreckage of the downed transport plane that had conveyed the former Patricia Canby to this wild land, and Tarzan, his military uniform again restored to his muscular frame, carried out the aircraft radio, which was powered by batteries.

Ilex warmed up the set, tuned it to a secret frequency, and, after identifying herself, used it to summon a rescue plane. When she received reassurance that one would be sent forthwith, Tarzan turned to the woman he had not seen in over twenty years and asked, "Was it the truth you told me when you said you were married?"

"Under the circumstances, I would hold you to tell that unusual creature anything to escape his unwelcome intentions, however sincere they might be."

"But you did not answer my question," reminded Tarzan.

"I am aware of that, Flying Officer Clayton. And for the time being, that will have to serve as my reply."

"Are you still angry with me over my little joke?"

Her stiff face softened slightly. "I am grateful to you for all that you have done, but after what I suffered through, I would like to forget this little adventure of ours ever happened."

"You might," suggested Tarzan, "leave out a great deal when you write your official report."

"Our reports will have to match in all particulars, you know."

Tarzan considered this. "In that case, you might not want to mention the inconvenient fact that your would-be suitor possessed a tail."

"That is very good advice, Flying Officer Clayton. I believe I shall take it."

That was the last they spoke of the awkward matter of Mubu-tan and his ardent desire to take for a mate a British Military Intelligence agent.

There still remained the necessity of breaking through the great thorn barrier, which Torn Ear happily blazed for them, absorbing or shattering all the thorns and nettles that would have otherwise harried and hampered them, until at last they happened upon open savannah.

They strolled along for a time, enjoying the freedom of unobstructed grassland, stopping only when they came upon an expanse of bare ground that would serve as a rude but serviceable landing zone.

Hours later, a Vickers Wellington bomber, escorted by a pair of Gloster Gladiator fighters which remained circling protectively overhead, dropped down onto the sun-baked ground, Hercules motors howling.

Tarzan turned to Torn Ear, and a single tear rolled down the pachyderm's right eye when he realized that he would see the ape-man no more.

"Go in peace, faithful friend," said Tarzan in a gentle voice.

The elephant made snuffling sounds as he touched Tarzan's form at various points as if to inhale the ape-man's scent for the final time.

The Honorable Patricia Smith-Oldwick had already boarded the transport plane and Tarzan turned to go. When he was at the cabin door, Torn Ear lifted his trunk and trumpeted out a final salutation.

Turning, Tarzan gave vent one last time to the victory cry of the bull ape, and the two sounds blended and rose above the idling plane motors.

Then, Tarzan disappeared inside the cabin, the door banged shut, whereupon the plane turned into the wind and launched itself into the brilliant blue sky.

On the ground, Torn Ear pushed his wrinkled brown bulk in the direction of the disappearing plane, as if to follow the wing-thing to its distant destination. But that could not be.

Tarzan, Lord of the Jungle, was returning to his civilized life as Flying Officer John Clayton, R.A.F.—perhaps never to come this way again.

About the Author

WILL MURRAY

WILL MURRAY has been writing about popular culture since 1973, principally on the subjects of comic books, the pulp magazine era and its authors and heroes, and film. His monumental survey of the Western fiction magazine, *Wordslingers: An Epitaph for the Western*, is considered definitive. As a fiction writer, Murray is the author of over 60 novels featuring characters as diverse as Nick Fury and Remo Williams, the Destroyer. With Steve Ditko, he created  Squirrel Girl for Marvel Comics. Murray has also written numerous short stories, many on Lovecraftian themes.

Murray discovered Edgar Rice Burroughs when he purchased a Ballantine Books edition of *The Gods of Mars,* and soon became a fan of all things Burroughs, quickly exhausting the Mars novels and moving on to Tarzan and the others. Twice in the past, his name has come up as a possible Tarzan writer, but not until the 21st Century did that cherished dream become a reality.

"Having been an Edgar Rice Burroughs fan since 1968," says Murray, "the opportunity to bring this iconic character back to life means a great deal to me. I've pulled out all the stops to faithfully replicate the storytelling style of the great Edgar Rice Burroughs and recreate the original era of Tarzan of the Apes."

Currently, Murray writes the Wild Adventures of Doc Savage for Altus Press and produces the Will Murray Pulp Classics series of audio and ebooks for Radio Archives. His acclaimed Doc Savage novel, *Skull Island*, pits the pioneer superhero against the legendary King Kong, and was written with a Burroughsian sensibility. Murray wonders if, somewhere back in the 20th Century, Edgar Rice Burroughs' mighty ape-lord ever encountered the beast-god of Skull Island and, if so, will that awesome tale ever be told....

About the Artist

Joe DeVito

JOE DeVITO was born on March 16, 1957, in New York City. He graduated with honors from Parsons School of Design in 1981, studied at the Art Students League in New York City. Joe's art often displays a decided emphasis on Action Adventure, SF and Fantasy, and dinosaurs. Over a professional career spanning more than 30 years he has also periodically lectured and taught university illustration courses on painting and sculpting.

DeVito has painted and sculpted many of the most recognizable Pop Culture and Pulp icons. These include King Kong, Tarzan, Doc Savage, Superman, Batman, Wonder Woman, Spider-Man, *MAD* magazine's Alfred E. Neuman and various other characters. He has illustrated hundreds of book and magazine covers, painted several notable posters and numerous trading cards for the major comic book and gaming houses, and created concept and character design for the film and television industries. In 3D, DeVito sculpted the official 100th Anniversary statue of *Tarzan of the Apes* for the Edgar Rice Burroughs Estate, *The Cooper Kong* for the Merian C. Cooper Estate, Superman, Wonder Woman and Batman for Chronicle Books' Masterpiece Editions, and several other notable Pop and Pulp characters, including Doc Savage.

Having illustrated all of Will Murray's Wild Adventures of Doc Savage novels, Joe again joins Will to illustrate *Tarzan: Return to Pal-ul-don*.

"It is always a treat painting covers for Doc Savage adventure yarns," DeVito says. "And now comes Tarzan, the granddaddy of all the great action-adventure characters. After sculpting the Centennial Tarzan statue for ERB, Inc., in 2012, I was hoping to get a crack at a Tarzan cover painting as well. Will's book provided an opportunity to combine them both!"

www.jdevito.com
www.kongskullisland.com
FB: Joe DeVito-DeVito Artworks

About the Patron

Gary A. Buckingham

T HE FIRST time I read an Edgar Rice Burroughs tale was when my parents, Lynn and Allen, picked up 1967's Whitman children's edition of *The Return of Tarzan*. My collection had begun.

Over time, I noticed a limited number of new stories authorized by ERB, Inc., for his characters. To my knowledge, the last of these featuring Tarzan that did not drastically revise the canon was the completion and publication of a 83-page Burroughs manuscript twenty years ago.

When collaborating (in a small way) with Will Murray and Joe DeVito for The Wild Adventures of Doc Savage *Skull Island* volume, I decided to mention an idea. I had vaguely mused during my engineering career about becoming a published writer in fiction. So I suggested to Joe and Will that we team up for a Tarzan book, Will to write a novel and I a short story, topped with the wonderful art of Joe in a hardcover wraparound dust jacket and interior illustrations. It has been in development for two years; the first version of my narrative was completed August 6, 2013. My profoundest appreciation is expressed for the encouragement of Will and Joe and all their gracious assistance in getting my part of this project done.

"Tarzan and the Secret of Katanga" will be a sequel to Will's adventure, with a key part of his saga being the *raison d'être* for the exploit described in my novelette. Although you won't find it in this softcover from Altus Press, my story and additional art from Joe DeVito will be in the forthcoming hardcover edition of *Tarzan: Return to Pal-ul-don*. As to the cover on this paperback, I recalled reading that Burroughs tried repeatedly to get the Tarzan newspaper strip artists to include Lady Greystoke's golden locket, with little success. I am glad to convey that this is the final item added to Joe's painting.

About Edgar Rice Burroughs, Inc.

FOUNDED in 1923 by Edgar Rice Burroughs, as one of the first authors to
incorporate himself, Edgar Rice Burroughs,
Inc., holds numerous trademarks and the
rights to all literary works of the author still
protected by copyright, including stories of
Tarzan of the Apes and John Carter of Mars.
The company has overseen every adaptation
of his literary works in film, television, radio,
publishing, theatrical stage productions, li-
censing and merchandising. The company is
still a very active enterprise and manages and licenses the vast
archive of Mr. Burroughs' literary works, fictional characters
and corresponding artworks that have grown for over a century.
The company continues to be owned by the Burroughs family
and remains headquartered in Tarzana, California, the town
named after the Tarzana Ranch Mr. Burroughs purchased there
in 1918 which led to the town's future development.

www.edgarriceburroughs.com
www.tarzan.com

THE ARGOSY LIBRARY ™

SERIES 1 INCLUDES:

* DENT * KETCHUM * KLINE *
* MacISAAC * ROSCOE *
* ROUSSEAU *
* SELTZER *
* TUTTLE *
* WIRT *
WORTS

THE BEST FICTION
FROM THE FRANK
A. MUNSEY LINE

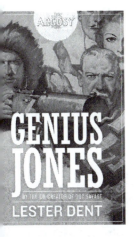

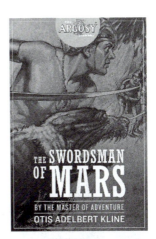

GENIUS JONES
BY THE CO-CREATOR OF DOC SAVAGE
LESTER DENT

WHEN TIGERS ARE HUNTING
THE COMPLETE ADVENTURES OF CORDIE, SOLDIER OF FORTUNE, VOLUME 1
W. WIRT

THE SWORDSMAN OF MARS
BY THE MASTER OF ADVENTURE
OTIS ADELBERT KLINE

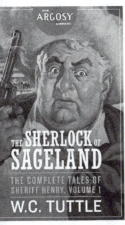
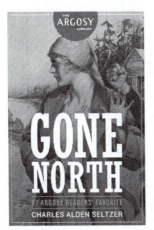

THE SHERLOCK OF SAGELAND
THE COMPLETE TALES OF SHERIFF HENRY, VOLUME 1
W.C. TUTTLE

GONE NORTH
BY ARGOSY READERS' FAVORITE
CHARLES ALDEN SELTZER

THE MASKED MASTER MIND
BY THE AUTHOR OF PETER THE BRAZEN
GEORGE F. WORTS

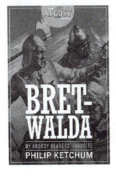
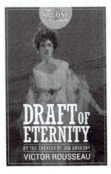

BALATA
BY THE AUTHOR OF THE RAMBLER
FRED MacISAAC

BRET-WALDA
BY ARGOSY READERS' FAVORITE
PHILIP KETCHUM

DRAFT OF ETERNITY
BY THE CREATOR OF JIM ANTHONY
VICTOR ROUSSEAU

FOUR CORNERS
VOLUME 1 • BY ARGOSY LEGEND
THEODORE ROSCOE

The Martian Legion: In Quest of Xonthron

- *An Epic Adventure Novel in the Grandest ERB Tradition!*
  - *The Finest ERB Collectible Ever Produced!*

Written in spirit by Edgar Rice Burroughs with an assist from Jake Saunders.

- A quarter million words of high adventure! Like getting four ERB novels in one!
- Tarzan, John Carter, The Shadow, and Doc Savage battle the Holy Therns!
- First 100 copies signed by Saunders, Grindberg, Hoffman, Mullins, DeVito, Cabarga, and Cochran.
- Featuring 24 full color painting and illustrations, plus 106 spot illustrations by Tom Grindberg, Michael C. Hoffman, and Craig Mullins, including....
- Leather bound, full color, 11-1/4-in. x 12-1/4-in. x 1-1/2in., 423 pages.

Now available at <u>TheMartianLegion.com!</u>

THE ALL-NEW *WILD* ADVENTURES OF

DOC SAVAGE

Doc Savage:
The Desert Demons

Doc Savage:
Horror in Gold

Doc Savage:
The Infernal Buddha

Doc Savage:
The Forgotten Realm

Doc Savage:
Death's Dark Domain

Doc Savage:
Skull Island

39924693R00218

Made in the USA
San Bernardino, CA
07 October 2016